THE UNDERCURRENT

ALSO BY PAULA WESTON

The Rephaim:
Shadows
Haze
Shimmer
Burn

Paula Weston is the author of the widely acclaimed and much-loved Rephaim series. She worked as a print journalist for many years before becoming a government media and communication specialist. She grew up in regional South Australia and now lives in Brisbane with her husband.

paula-weston.com
facebook.com/PaulaWestonAuthor
@PaulaWeston

THE
UNDERCURRENT
PAULA WESTON

TEXT PUBLISHING MELBOURNE AUSTRALIA

textpublishing.com.au

The Text Publishing Company
Swann House
22 William Street
Melbourne Victoria 3000 Australia

First published in 2017 by The Text Publishing Company

Typeset in Sabon 11.5/16 by J&M Typesetting
Book design by Imogen Stubbs
Cover images from iStock and Shutterstock

Printed in Australia by Griffin Press, an Accredited ISO AS/NZS 14001:2004 Environmental Management System printer.

National Library of Australia Cataloguing-in-Publication entry
Author: Weston, Paula, author.
Title: The Undercurrent / by Paula Weston.
ISBN: 9781925498233 (paperback)
ISBN: 9781925410433 (ebook)

For Dad, who would have enjoyed this one the most—
and the conversations we would have had!
Miss you every day.

For Mum, who has always been my biggest fan
and still gives the best hugs.

Prologue

It's on every channel.

The gutted science lab, smouldering classrooms and water-soaked textbooks. The quadrangle dusted in ash. Students with oxygen tanks and angry parents. It's the same on each news update: accusation and speculation.

And Jules' name is everywhere.

By the window, Angie De Marchi tightens her grip on the TV remote and checks her daughter. Jules is curled up on their worn couch, finally asleep, her school uniform stinking of smoke. Her face flickers in the light of the TV, cheeks streaked black.

The newscasters talk about grief and teenage rebellion. The legacy of a lost father, a war hero killed in his prime. They can't help themselves: they show a photo of Mike. It's the one they always use, him in his dress uniform, chestful of medals. Not smiling. He'd hate them using it—using *him*—to paint Jules as an overwrought sixteen-year-old.

> His widow, journalist and activist Angela De Marchi, was arrested six weeks ago in yet another Agitators protest outside Paxton Federation, and has already been linked—

Angie stabs the remote at the TV, killing the power before she sees her own face again. How can she protect Jules now? Grief claws at her, tight and familiar. What would Mike do? But she already knows the answer: he'd do whatever it took to keep their daughter safe.

It's dusk outside but Angie doesn't turn on the lamp. The local cops are still on the street and that means the cameras are too. The vultures want to interview Jules—better yet, film her being dragged from the house in cuffs. Nadira Khan, the federal agent who brought Jules home an hour ago, promised neither would happen, at least not tonight. But Angie knows all too well how easily reporters can pressure decision-making. She's built a career wielding that sort of power. Right now, though, all the influence is out on the street.

Khan is in the kitchen making another pot of herbal tea. She's not going anywhere until the circus packs up.

Angie's phone vibrates on the coffee table. She waits a few seconds—Jules doesn't stir—and reaches for it.

It's over.

Angie's chest tightens. Really? They want to come at her *now*?

She's pissed a lot of people off over the years but these messages warning her away from the Agitators—always from an unlisted number—have become more frequent over the last fourteen months. Since Mike died.

She doesn't respond.

With the TV off, she can hear snatches of fuzzy chatter on the police radio outside. The last time Angie peered through the blinds a crowd had gathered across the street. None of the faces are local. She can't bring herself to count the parasites out there taking selfies in front of the house.

On the couch, Jules whimpers in her sleep and Angie almost reaches for her. What could she have done differently today? Jules was fine when she left for school this morning. There was no sign she was on the edge, no sign this would be the day that undid them. Something must have happened at school. Something Jules doesn't want to talk about in front of Khan.

The phone buzzes again. Angie glances at the kitchen door, hears the kettle boiling and china clinking as Khan rinses their cups.

Cut contact with the Agitators.

That's *it*. She jabs at the screen, her fingers furious.

Or what?

A pause. Another message arrives. Angie reads it and her heart stumbles.

Or I'll show the world how that explosion today really happened.

Two years later

Jules hears the shouting as soon as she reaches the street. Her mouth was already dry, the skin between her fingers tacky, but now there's a stab of panic. She steps from Central Station into the steamy morning, her heart thudding.

Even from two blocks away the sense of the mob reaches her. It feels *huge*. She needs a second, but there are too many people surging out from the station to get to work or coffee or whatever they're late for. A pinstriped suit bumps past Jules, swearing. A woman—fitted lilac dress, oversize sunglasses—steadies her by the elbow before pushing past. Jules is carried along in the throng down to the street. Nervous energy crackles under her skin and dread snakes through her. She clenches herself tight. The last thing she can deal with right now is a *moment*.

Jules reaches the traffic lights and draws in the tension, tries to settle herself. People crush closer, fidgeting, impatient for the lights to change. She forces herself to focus on the *tock*, *tock* of the pedestrian signal. Sweat gathers in her armpits: thankfully she's wearing a white shirt. But what was she thinking? Pantyhose in this weather?

Jules takes a shaky breath and straightens her skirt. At least her shoes survived the train ride. Nobody spat or stomped on them, she even managed to avoid the usual funk on the carriage floor. Designer heels are an improbable luxury for her, an aberration. Even during the argument with her mum about coming in here today, Angie didn't say a word about the shoes. When else was she going to get a chance to wear them?

Her heart skitters at the thought of her mother sitting on the edge of their couch watching the protest on TV, picking away at the stitching on the big yellow cushion and swearing at the newscasters.

Jules can make out the chants now, louder than the traffic. Reverberating against steel, glass and concrete.

Pax Fed. Global dread.

On the street, she feels eyes on her: a guy about her age in a black singlet with a skateboard tucked under one pale, skinny arm. Staring, recognition dawning. He takes a step back, glances up at the lights.

Another head turns. The energy shifts, ripples. Traffic stops.

The pedestrian signal flips over—*whirrup*—and all attention snaps to the flashing green man on the opposite side of the road. People flood the crossing. Jules falls into step with the cotton and polyester herd, dodging oncoming walkers and avoiding eye contact. Wobbling a little on her four-inch heels. She reaches the other side of the road and heads down into the belly of the city.

She's not late, anyway. Not yet.

It's been five months since school finished. Twenty-six job applications and only one offer of interview: the one locked in for this morning. Paxton Federation is the last place on earth she wants to work. The agency only told her yesterday it was Pax Fed who'd shortlisted her and by that point she was too desperate to back out. What's that old saying? Beggars can't be choosers. She and her mum aren't beggars yet, but if this job doesn't come off...A swell of anxiety pushes the air from her lungs. She takes three quick breaths, straightens her handbag strap. She has to keep it together and convince these people she's not a liability. The Pax Fed recruiters know who she is, her history. Who her mother is. So they're not interviewing her to amuse themselves. Right?

Pax Fed. Global greed.

What do we want? Pax Fed to bleed.

Today, at any rate, they have more pressing concerns than her.

Her handbag bumps lightly against her hip as she makes her way down Edward Street. She passes a hole-in-the-wall espresso bar, smells coffee and brioche. There's enough cash in her wallet to grab something on the way back if her nerves have settled.

The crowd mostly deserts Jules at the next intersection. The protest is a block away, around the corner out of sight, and nobody wants to get any closer than they have to.

Jules has to.

Rain clouds are suspended over the breathless city, drawing down the sky. Steel and glass crowd in. She feels the static on her skin a split second before the distant roll of thunder. *Please, not now.*

Jules is twenty metres from Queen Street. It's blocked to traffic by two marked cop cars parked nose to nose. The chanting drowns out the usual hum of the city. A lime-green hatchback with a peeling stick-figure family slows as it reaches the inter-section, blinker flashing as if the driver plans to turn. Two cops step into view and wave it on. Across the street at the edge of the mall, a mob huddles with bucket-size disposable lattes, straining to see over the cop cars. Obviously tourists—locals are far too cool to be caught gawking. It's not like these protests are new.

Jules is conspicuously alone on her side of the street. She turns her face from the traffic and the dark-haired girl keeping pace with her, window by window, is stiff and nervous-looking. She's spent the past two years trying to avoid this sort of atten-tion but here she is: Brisbane CBD in peak hour, heading for an Agitators protest outside Pax Fed headquarters.

She braces for a reaction from the mall crowd but nobody calls out or even notices her. They're too busy watching what-ever is happening further up Queen Street. Jules almost makes it to the corner before the older of the two cops spots her and cuts her off, one hand on the butt of his gun, the other out in front of him.

'Road's closed. You need to cross over.'

She can't tell if he recognises her because his eyes are shuttered behind police-issue sunnies. Jules stops, blows out a nervous breath. 'I've got an interview at Paxton Federation.'

'Not today you don't. Nobody's going in or out of that building until this street is cleared.'

There's no way for Jules to know if the interview has been cancelled. Every network in the city went down twenty-four hours ago when the federal police caught wind of the protest. Standard procedure under the new *Commonwealth Civil Order Act 2028*. Which means everyone except cops, security authorities and professional hackers are offline and off-air. No voice service. No data network.

Jules tries to ignore her reflection in the cop's sunnies. 'I can't *not* show up if there's a chance they're expecting me.'

The cop measures her for a good five seconds. She checks out the sergeant's stripes on his shoulder and wonders if he knows anyone from her neighbourhood. Those guys would recognise her from fifty metres.

'Come here.' The sergeant gestures for her to follow him to the corner and points up the street. 'Look.'

As soon as Jules steps out from the protection of the building, a wall of energy hits her, forceful and frenetic. It's like being shoved in the chest by a scrum of front-rowers.

Protesters—hundreds of them—are packed behind six-foot mesh barricades less than twenty metres away. They press against the metal, chanting at the line of cops guarding the revolving door into Pax Fed Tower.

Pax Federation, strangling our nation.

Placards sprout up like weeds. Almost all feature the Pax Fed logo, but instead of the trademark colours, the buff head of wheat and bright yellow sun, the awn is painted toxic black and the sun is bleeding. Other signs are more literal:

SAY NO TO GMO.

WE WON'T EAT MUTANT MEAT.

Someone lights up a placard and tosses it over the barricade. A cop breaks from the line to stamp it out, the crowd cheers. Jules tries to swallow. Thank God her mum didn't come. This rabble would have recognised Angie De Marchi in a heart-beat and dragged her into the throng—probably carried her on their shoulders. Jules searches instinctively for the news crews and finds them at the other end of the barricades interviewing protesters through the fence. A wave of nausea bubbles up.

'You really want to go up there?' the cop asks.

She really doesn't.

But when has life ever been about what she wanted? For a heartbeat she imagines herself rushing back to Central Station and catching the first southbound train home. Curling up on her bed and blocking out the world again. But then that other fear kicks in—the one where she and her mum can't pay the rent or the electricity bill due next week or put food in the fridge. That fear takes charge again.

Jules gestures to the two-way radio tucked against the sergeant's shoulder. 'Is there someone you can talk to at Pax Fed? Can you find out if my interview is on?'

The sergeant looks her up and down, lingers on her shoes. Sighs. 'What's your name?'

Oh.

In any other situation she'd consider lying, but that's not going to get her inside Pax Fed Tower. 'Julianne De Marchi.'

His fingers stall. 'Is that meant to be a joke?'

'Please.' Her skin tingles. 'Ask if I still have an appointment.'

He slides his sunglasses down, peers at her from under his cap. A bead of sweat slides from his hairline and down his sun-reddened neck. He depresses the handset and turns away to speak. Between the chanting and the traffic, all Jules catches is: '...you sure you want her in the building today?'

When he turns back, his eyes are shaded again and she can't read them. 'You stay by my side and do exactly what I tell you to do.' He's all business now, checking the clip on his gun holster, jamming his cap down tighter. 'You pull any kind of stunt, I *will* arrest you. Understand?'

She nods. What does he think she's going to do in four-inch heels and a pencil skirt?

'I don't want the reporters to see me.'

'Then don't draw attention to yourself.'

He leads her to the footpath on the Pax Fed side of Queen Street. The cops—in uniform, not riot gear—have moved further back from the barricade out of range of burning placards. They don't seem overly concerned by the rabble; they're acting like it's a peaceful protest. It doesn't feel peaceful to Jules. The air sizzles, lifting the fine hairs on her forearms and setting a tremble to her fingers. She walks quicker but the entrance isn't getting closer fast enough.

The sergeant is back on his radio; a hulking cop from the police line waves them through and they draw level with the barricades. The sergeant uses his body to shield Jules and she turns her head, tries to hide her face. Her heart is anxious against her ribs. A quick glance and she can see the tower entrance less than ten metres away, the front door slowly revolving.

Five metres. They're going to make it without being noticed—

'De Marchi? *De Marchi*!'

Jules ignores the shouts, puts one foot in front of the other.

A chant starts up. *De-mark-ie. De-mark-ie.*

'Julianne!'

Jules looks up, realising too late that nobody she cares about would be in that crowd. Faces are mashed against the steel, trying to get a better look at her.

'You know what to do, girl!'

One of the news crews has broken away from the barricade: a leggy woman gripping a microphone and a guy balancing a camera on his shoulder, both calling out for Jules to wait.

The sergeant grabs Jules' wrist, jerks her towards the door. Jules has a fair idea what's coming next and there's nothing she can do to stop it. A new chant starts up as the revolving door propels them inside.

Burn it down!
Burn it down!

Ryan is caught between the barricades and the crush of protesters. He needs to get out. Now.

But first he needs to finish setting his placard on fire. Maybe one more after that.

He shouldn't be enjoying this as much as he is. All the shouting and rattling steel, banging shoulders with strangers... it's a relief to scream at the world, channel a bit of anger and get paid for it.

It's hard not to be pissed off when he's surrounded by reminders of why he's here.

SAY NO TO GMO.

His old man said no and look where that got him. For a second, Ryan imagines what might be happening two thousand kilometres away, wishes he was back on the farm despite everything. He thinks about training under a cloudless sky on an oval as dry as crepe paper. Running on dirt roads, swallowing flies and recovering in the shade of the old ghost gum, caked in sweat and wheat dust.

Ryan's been wondering since yesterday whether this was a legit assignment or another test. Right now, he doesn't care. He pushes back against the press of overheated bodies, holds up the placard—a photo of Tom Paxton, chairman of the Pax Fed board—and sets the lighter flame to the corner.

'Fuck *you*, Tom,' he shouts, and lifts the blazing corflute.

Flames lick at the old man's soft chin. Adrenaline surges and for a few seconds he feels powerful. Free. The crowd shrinks back and Ryan lobs the placard over the barricade. Like the others, it lands harmlessly in front of the cops, scorching the bitumen and prompting a rush of foot-stomping to put it out. The mob cheers.

Ryan turns from the fence, the moment pulsing through him. He elbows aside protesters ripe with sweat and sees Waylo deep in conversation. The bloke he's talking to is shorter, nuggety and old-fashioned-looking: covered in ink, hair slicked back in a retro man bun. Ryan's heart gives a hard thump. It's the guy they're here for.

Waylo glances Ryan's way, his black skin shining. They ignore each other as they're supposed to, but there's something about his roommate—an uncharacteristic tightness in Waylo's shoulders—that grabs Ryan's attention. Reminds him why they're here. Has Waylo been approached or is something else going on? Adrenaline spikes again, this time with anticipation. Ryan takes more notice of the protesters around him. It's a hard crowd to read, hard to know which direction the threat could come from.

They call themselves the Agitators. It used to be left-wing soccer mums and hipsters who turned up to these protests with their professionally printed signs, pithy slogans and organic snacks. Now it's this lot. Mostly blokes, and mostly under twenty-five like him, venting their rage at the world. This week it's Pax Fed. Next week they'll be back in George Street hurling burning effigies at Parliament House, now tucked behind permanent barricades since last year's riot. But there's a rumour they're mixed up in something bigger and deadlier, something stirring to life in South Australia.

Ryan always thought the Agitators were just a bunch of dickheads but it turns out their protests are a talent pool of dissent, attracting criminals with more violent agendas. That's why Waylo's here: to be recruited for the trip south. Apparently being black 'heightens his likelihood for disaffection'. Waylo says that's bullshit—everyone with a pulse is disaffected these days—but to Ryan it suggests homegrown terrorists are as bigoted as anyone else.

The two of them are here to blend in, make some noise and keep their eyes open. Ryan's only managed two out of three so far. He let himself get distracted by the fact today's job involved Paxton Federation. He got caught up in the moment—*incited*—when the protesters swarmed towards Queen Street. He resists the urge to fight his way back to Waylo and find out what's going on. That's not his job today. His job just arrived.

More pushing and shoving and Ryan clears the crowd. He keeps walking, pulling a sweat-stained cap low over his eyes and keeping his head down. His heart rate's up but it's all business now. His new knee feels good. Strong.

He ducks into a convenience store and heads for the back. The tiny shop smells of Chiko Rolls, hot chips and raspberry slurpee. He passes a chiller packed with shiny red apples so big you'd need two hands—even his hands—to eat one. Happy Growers stickers on all of them—part of the Pax Fed empire. *That's* what the Agitators should be throwing at the building: Pax Fed's own mutant apples. Guaranteed crisp and sweet. Guaranteed to break toughened glass.

As expected, the back door is unlocked. Ryan slips into a narrow laneway and jogs around a delivery truck. He hears voices inside the neighbouring Vietnamese restaurant and picks up his pace before the driver comes out.

An unmarked white van is waiting on the corner, engine running. Ryan opens the side door and a cool blast of air hits him. The back of the van has been gutted except for a bench seat down one side. Clean trousers, a pressed shirt and a tie are waiting, along with a bag of toiletries, fake ID and a suede satchel. He peels off his T-shirt, freshens up his neck, chest and armpits with wet wipes, kicks off his runners and drops his cargo shorts. A blast of deodorant, a quick slather of product through his hair to slick it down, and he struggles into the clean clothes. The tie is already knotted. All he has to do is slip it on and tighten it. He hasn't worn a shirt and tie since the best and fairest back home over a year ago, and this getup feels as stiff and unnatural as it did then. At least his boots are practical: heavy-soled and sturdy.

The van starts forward. He's not ready. Ryan drops to the seat and drags on cotton socks that stick on his tacky feet. He leans to one side as the van rounds the corner. When it stops a block later, his boots are on and a short blade is tucked against his ankle. He bangs on the glass separating him and the driver.

The screen slides open.

'Ready?'

Ryan blinks. He knows that growl and it doesn't belong in this van. Ryan leans forward to prove himself wrong, but there he is: the Major, wearing a black T-shirt, grey cap and mirrored sunnies. Ryan's never seen him in civvies. In over a year, the boss has never sat in on an assignment, let alone sat behind the wheel. Ryan's eyes drop unconsciously to the Major's mangled ear and the shrapnel scars that disappear beneath his beard.

'Sir...?' His voice is raw from shouting.

'Are you set?' the Major asks, impatient. He's alone in the front. That's also odd.

'Yes, sir.'

The Major nods at the ID around Ryan's neck. 'That won't stand up under scrutiny so don't draw attention to yourself. Do your job and get out. I'll meet you at the rendezvous point. And Walsh?' A pause. 'Keep your wits about you. The option autho-rised for this job is a contingency only. It's only to be exercised in the event of an immediate and deadly threat. Understand?'

'Yes, sir.'

'And don't lose that satchel.'

The Major pulls away as soon as Ryan clears the van. Leaves him standing on the footpath, his cotton shirt already sticking to his back. A street away, the protesters keep chanting. He sets off towards Pax Fed Tower, tapping out a quick beat on his thighs as he walks. He's jittery, like before a big game. But this is more than nerves. He's spooked.

And he has no idea why.

Jules is on the forty-fifth floor wedged into a weird-shaped chair, her feet barely touching the polished marble floor. She tucks her fingers under her legs to stop them trembling. She's trying to keep still because every time she changes position the armchair makes a farting noise, and whenever it does the receptionist's head comes up to check on her.

It's been ten minutes since the sergeant relinquished his grip on Jules in the lobby downstairs. It took two security guards and a phone call from Pax Fed's human resources director to convince him he could let her take the lift—and only then after he'd rifled through her handbag. Twice.

Now she's stuck in a chair so deep it's like sitting in a giant baseball glove. Her neck is clammy, even in the artificially cool waiting area, and her skin buzzes. The air in here has been scrubbed clean and feels too thin, but if she can steady her breathing she'll be fine. On the wall, a large screen has footage of golden wheat fields and fat sheep grazing in a lush paddock. A siren sounds from the street below, loud enough to cut through the folksy soundtrack.

'I hope the police arrest the lot of them.' The receptionist is watching Jules, her face half-hidden behind a vase stacked with red and white pebbles. Wispy chestnut hair frames green eyes and fuchsia lips. 'It'd be nice to come to work without worrying about being spat on.'

Jules nods but doesn't answer, busy tamping down the anxiety. The receptionist waits a beat and then resumes tapping at her keyboard.

The phone rings and Jules flinches.

'This is Sheridan. Yes, she's here.' Jules holds her breath. 'I'll let her know.' Sheridan hangs up. 'They're almost ready for you. Would you like a glass of water before you go in?'

Jules swallows, nods. 'Thank you.'

Sheridan stands and straightens her skirt. She's two or three years older than Jules and moves with casual grace. Jules watches her disappear behind frosted-glass doors. What would it be like to be so comfortable in your own skin? To be so effortlessly contained?

Jules struggles out of the chair as soon as the door closes. It's a good thing she's alone because even with a knee-length skirt on she's managed to flash the room. She checks her hair hasn't escaped its bun and carefully applies another coat of lip gloss with a shaky touch. The sky tugs at her. She moves to the window, walking on her toes so her heels don't click on the marble tiles.

The clouds are heavier now and lower...no, she's higher. Jules presses her palm against the cool glass, feels the tower thrum. If there's something gathering in the sky she can't sense it from in here. She takes back her hand and watches the ghost of her fingertips linger on the pane.

'Hello, I'm Tom Paxton.'

Jules whips around, heart in her throat.

The chairman of the Pax Fed board isn't in the room: he's onscreen, smiling out from under an Akubra. He's sitting on the back of a ute in a freshly ploughed paddock. Jules' heart gives another startled skip and then settles. Of course he's not here. Tom Paxton rarely leaves his penthouse; certainly not to introduce himself to eighteen-year-old convicted arsonists. The image onscreen cuts to giant trucks unloading grain; scientists in gleaming labs. Finally old Tom is back, this time with his son Bradford. Talking about resource demand, population growth and a hungry world, and reassuring Jules that Paxton Federation (nobody here calls it Pax Fed) is part of the solution. Thank God her mother isn't here to listen to this.

They're still talking when Sheridan returns with the water.

'I *love* your shoes.' Sheridan hands over the glass, wiping condensation from her fingers onto her own skirt. 'Gucci?'

Jules nods and takes a careful sip. 'Boxing Day sales, year before last.'

They'd been celebrating. Her mum had been paid for a free-lance job she'd picked up from one of the two editors who still talked to her. It was the most money they'd seen in months— since Angie De Marchi cut ties with the Agitators. The fridge was restocked and the bills paid, and her mum wanted to splurge. Even hugely discounted, the heels were beyond their budget but they'd both assumed there would be more work. More regular paydays.

Sheridan smiles. 'Killer taste.' Her teeth are flawless.

Tangled in nerves and memories, it takes Jules a second to recognise what just happened: Sheridan isn't seeing her as Julianne De Marchi, Arsonist and Threat to the Community. All she's seeing is another girl with great shoes.

They're the same.

The realisation untethers something in Jules, sets her adrift in open waters. The phone rings again and Sheridan hurries to answer it, leaving Jules drowning in a longing she can barely name.

'Right, Julianne.' The smile lingers. 'I can take you through now.'

Jules follows her down a wide hallway, desperately trying to anchor herself. She needs to remember who she is, not who she wants to be. This isn't the time to drop her guard, not when her life is about to be raked over and picked apart. Too much is riding on the next few minutes.

The interview room is windowless, the walls bare. A large boardroom table takes up most of the available space. Sheridan ushers Jules in and retreats without speaking to either of the two people waiting on the other side of the table: a woman with short ginger hair and dangling hoop earrings, and a guy with a weirdly long neck—

Jules falters.

What is *he* doing here?

It's Bradford Paxton, co-vice chair of the Pax Fed board and number two on Angie De Marchi's shit list (Tom Paxton has top spot). He glances at Jules before going back to the tablet in front of him, barely acknowledging her.

Jules has never seen him in the flesh before. He's a younger, leaner version of his father, and smaller than she would have expected. *Less.* His energy ripples across the table, cold and forceful.

A touch on her elbow makes her flinch.

'Julianne.' It's the redhead. She's moved around the room without Jules noticing. 'I'm Ruby.' Jules forces a smile and gathers herself. They shake hands. Ruby's palm is cool, her skin softly wrinkled. There's no clamminess, no spike in her energy. 'Thanks for coming.'

Jules sits down and balances her handbag on her lap, her fingers again nervous. *Is it normal for Bradford Paxton to interview for an internship?* She takes out her resumé, notebook and pencil and sets them equal distance apart on the table. The polished surface catches the lights overhead and momentarily blinds her.

'Usually our interns are second- or third-year students,' Ruby says, back on her side of the table and acting like it's no big deal Bradford's in the room.

Jules' vision hasn't quite cleared but she attempts eye contact. Nods. Maybe if she ignores Bradford like he's ignoring her everything will be fine.

'We were impressed by your application, Julianne. Your Year 12 results are exceptional and I see you've been accepted into Behavioural Science at QUT. Is there any reason you've opted not to move straight into study?'

Jules flattens the crease in her resumé, glances at the notes she's scribbled in the margins. Bradford Paxton and Ruby must know she can't afford to go to university, not since the government halved the student loans scheme and her mother stopped getting work.

'I'm hoping for real-world experience,' she says, sounding more confident than she feels.

'Why Paxton Federation?'

A tight smile. 'You offered me an interview.'

Ruby's lips soften, acknowledging the honesty. 'And how did the Agitators react when they saw you downstairs?'

Jules holds Ruby's gaze but feels another set of eyes on her.

'They think I'm here for them.'

'Are you?' Ruby asks. Not an accusation *exactly*.

'No.'

Ruby glances down at her paperwork as if needing to confirm her next question.

'I see there's been no further trouble since the incident two years ago.'

It's not a question so Jules doesn't respond. But she doesn't look away either, even when her cheeks flush. If they're serious about giving her a job they can't pretend she didn't plead guilty to burning down a classroom block and science lab. Or, more precisely, destroying the wing Pax Fed donated to her school.

'Do you feel that part of your life is behind you now?' Ruby asks.

'Yes.' Jules says it without hesitation even though she knows she can't make that promise. She *wants* it to be behind her. 'The federal police can confirm that. So can my local station.'

'What about your mother?'

21

The question is from Bradford. He's watching her, his long fingers splayed on the table in front of him. Nails trimmed short. His head looks tiny at the end of that long neck, like a bearded turtle.

'She can vouch for me too.'

'That's not what I meant.'

Ruby clears her throat, smiles. She gestures to the piece of paper in front of him. 'Let's start with our formal questions, shall we?'

Bradford pushes the page aside. 'What does your mother think about you being here today?'

'Is that relevant?' Jules keeps her tone pleasant but unease snakes up into her chest.

'If you were to have regular access to this building, would she have expectations of you?'

'I don't think…What sort of expectations?'

'You know full well what I'm talking about.'

'I really don't.'

He presses his lips together as if she's being uncooperative. 'Your mother's obsessed with vilifying our company.'

'My mother hasn't been a journalist for two years.'

'She hasn't had a full-time job in two years. Angela De Marchi will always be a journalist. Why would you set foot in this building if not on her behalf?'

Ruby shifts position in her chair. She glances at Bradford and there's no doubt who's in charge.

'I'm here because I need a job.'

Bradford laughs. 'And you thought *we* would give you one?'

It takes a beat before the humiliation hits, hot and sickening. Bradford blurs into a smudge of grey across the table.

'Before your mother quit the Agitators she led a defamatory campaign against Paxton Federation, and *you* destroyed a building funded through our schools program.'

'Mr Paxton, can we—'

'No, Ruby. She's not a child.'

Jules drops her gaze to the notebook, tries to focus on questions she'll never get to ask. She'd convinced herself that all the hard work, all the effort over the past two years had earnt her a fresh start. Even maybe with Pax Fed.

But Angie was right: Jules was naive.

'I need a job because my mother can't get one,' she says, measuring her words. 'And that's because you've threatened to pull advertising from anyone who publishes her work.'

'Ah, I see paranoia runs in the family.'

Anger flares and she forces it down. She's good at it: she's had plenty of practice.

'Why persecute her? Angie left the Agitators—'

'If your mother had her way, the world would stay hungry forever. She wants to feed the starving but only if we keep using the same methods that have failed us for a century.'

'I think you'll find my mother's issues with your company run a little deeper than forcing farmers to use genetically modified grain and breed mutant sheep.'

Bradford leans forward, everything about him sharpening. 'So she's still blaming us for your father's death?'

He says it so easily. It's not easy to hear. Beneath her skin, the charge surges and stings and Jules has to get out of this room right now. She folds her resumé with a violent swipe and stands on shaking legs.

'I know what people think of me and my mother, but if this had been a legitimate opportunity and you'd given me a job—'

'Julianne.' Ruby stands up, earrings jangling. 'As far as I'm concerned this was a legitimate opportunity for you.'

'You know nothing about my mother,' Jules says to Bradford. 'She would never ask me to do anything that compromised my values, no matter how much she hates this company and all it stands for.'

'Please, Julianne—'

'Thanks for your time, Ruby.' It comes out splintered. Jules crushes the resumé back into her handbag.

Stupid, stupid girl.

Bradford sits back in his chair, loosens his tie and exhales as if the confrontation has been taxing on *him*. Jules forces herself to walk, not run, from the room, each step stilted. Face burning. The reception is empty—thank goodness—and she rounds the corner to the bank of lifts, stabs the button three times.

The lift nearest her pings almost immediately and a second later the doors open. There's a guy inside with a satchel slung across his chest. Tall, all shoulders, shaggy blond hair past his collar. Wearing a striped shirt and tie that looks a little too tight. He moves forward as if he's getting out and then his eyes meet hers. He freezes.

Of course he knows her. Doesn't everyone?

She steps inside and plants herself in front of the doors. On a better day, she'd move out of the way so he could get around her. On a better day she'd feel bad about freaking out a guy fit enough to run down forty-five flights of stairs if he wanted to. Not today. If he doesn't have the guts to ask her to move or to step around her, he'll have to ride back down to the ground floor.

She turns her back on him, jabs the console and closes the doors.

Ryan stares at the back of Julianne De Marchi's head. What is she doing heading downstairs already?

He wasn't expecting her, not yet. She's supposed to be in an interview and *he's* supposed to be in the waiting area. Just in case. He got in a quick sniff before the lift doors shut. He couldn't smell smoke—and nobody was shouting—so maybe there was no drama.

De Marchi lets out her breath in a huff. A strand of dark hair has escaped, disappearing beneath the collar of her white shirt. She scoops it up with quick fingers and wraps it around the bun. He watches her reflection in the mirrored wall as they pick up speed. She's already somewhere else, not bothering with the second glance he gets from most girls. Ryan keeps staring, thrown by her sudden proximity. And then the lights go out and the lift jerks to a stop.

The blackness is absolute. It presses against him, crushes his chest. He hears De Marchi suck in a breath but she doesn't make any other sound. She's fumbling about, orientating herself. He takes a step, then falters. Blood rushes in his ears and his breaths come short and sharp. The panic hits in waves, draining his legs of feeling. He needs to stay still for a second and keep his head. Remember the assignment. A bell rings once, too loud in this tiny space. De Marchi's found the alarm.

'You got a lighter?' His words are strung tight.

'No.'

The darkness is suffocating. 'Matches?'

She's silent for a second and then: 'Don't be a smartarse.'

He barely registers the insult. He's too busy remembering how to breathe.

She exhales. 'No, I don't have matches, or a lighter—'

Pale blue light flickers in the lift and relief floods through him: the emergency generator has kicked in. Julianne De Marchi is right in front of him, one hand on the mirror to steady herself, the other out in front protectively, almost touching his chest. Their eyes lock and she looks as startled as Ryan to find him so near. She steps away first.

The console is dead. Ryan hits a dozen buttons anyway. There's enough backup power for the bulb in the corner but not enough for anything else. He drops to one knee and prises open the door to an old-fashioned emergency phone. His unease is settling now, spooling around his feet. He's annoyed he let that dusty old fear get a grip again after all these years.

'Does it work?'

Ryan looks up, the handset to his ear. 'Nah, just for show.' He jams it back in the console. De Marchi moves to the far side of the lift to widen the space between them. They watch each other for a moment, bathed in the eerie light. It's probably a routine blackout—not unusual this time of year—but Ryan is thinking about Waylo's expression downstairs. He scans the ceiling and locates the hatch in case the lights go again. It's not confined spaces that mess with him, it's darkness and lack of air. The inside of the old fridge down the creek back home—

A muffled *bang* in the elevator shaft snaps him back to the lift a split second before it jolts sideways. *What the fuck?* He stumbles and heat blasts through the tiny car. Ryan pulls De Marchi away from the lift doors and puts himself between her and the metal surface.

'You okay?'

Her back is flat against the mirrored wall. She's breathing hard. The lift sways a little. 'How far down was that?' she asks.

'Dunno.' He checks the ceiling again. 'We can't stay in here.' Ryan dumps the satchel on the floor and springs up the wall, his boots finding purchase on the handrail. He swings his weight around so his spine is pressed into the corner; when he trusts his balance he reaches for the ceiling hatch. A firm push is enough to dislodge it. It lands with a thud somewhere on the roof as Ryan feels around beyond the opening until he finds something solid to grab. The metal rail is warm from the blast.

'What are you doing?'

He glances down at De Marchi. He's sweating and wishing he'd taken off the stupid tie. 'Finding a way out. We shouldn't be too far from an access panel.'

Ryan hoists himself up one-handed until he can get a better grip. His biceps burn with the effort but he gets his head and shoulders clear of the elevator car. The shaft is muggy and stinks of smoke and scorched concrete. Emergency lighting stains the darkness, enough for him to find what he's looking for. He drops back inside.

'A short climb and we're out.'

De Marchi is standing where he left her, gripping her elbows. 'You know who I am, right?' she asks.

'So?'

'You shouldn't be in here with me.'

He's only half-tuned in, sizing up the hatch and running through what he needs to do to get her out. It's only when he looks down that he sees the tightness around her eyes, the hard line of her mouth. 'What's going on?'

'The blackout, the explosion...' A pause. 'It could be about me.'

Ryan thinks about why he's in the building. Clearly there's more going on than he's been told, but it can't be about her. She might be a pyro, but her old man's a freaking war hero.

'Did you miss the protesters on your way in?' he says. 'My money's on them causing whatever's going on downstairs and there's no way they're after you.'

'Agitators don't use explosives.'

'Maybe they do now.' Ryan wipes his hands on his pants. He's figuring out how he's going to get De Marchi out of the lift in that outfit she's wearing when she speaks again.

'You go.'

He blinks. 'What?'

'I'll wait here. You go get help.'

'You're not staying here.'

'It's safer—'

'No, it's not.'

'—for you.'

He opens his mouth, closes it again. She's trying to protect him.

'This isn't the first time something like this has happened, okay?' She's getting impatient. 'The last time—'

Whoop-whoop-whoop.

The emergency alarm drowns her out. Pax Fed Tower is under evacuation. And no easing into it with the 'stay-calm-and-prepare-to-leave-your-workstation' signal either—it's gone straight to 'get-the-fuck-out-of-here-right-now'. It must be pretty hairy downstairs.

Ryan points to her and then to the ceiling. 'Out,' he shouts. The alarm is so loud he can't hear himself. She wets her lips and shifts her weight again. He points at her and the ceiling hatch again, emphatic. Maybe whatever's happening is about her, maybe it's not, but he's not letting her hang around on her own to find out. He does another round of pointing. '*Now,*' he mouths at her.

She waits another beat and then shakes out her arms like she's limbering up. Ryan points to her high heels, signals for her to take them off. She shakes her head.

Is she serious? They're fucking *shoes.* He rips off his tie and fake ID and flings them aside, staring her down. How is he going to make this work? He undoes the top buttons on his shirt and rolls up his sleeves. His eyes fall on the satchel—

Another blast sends them both sprawling sideways. Scorching heat rolls over the car. He snatches up the bag and empties it out. Sheets of meaningless paper hit the floor and fan out in all directions. Ryan holds out the satchel towards De Marchi. Points for her to put in her shoes. This time she doesn't argue. She steps out of the heels and slips them in the suede bag.

'And those,' he mouths, gesturing to her stockings. He scoops up his tie and ID and jams them in with her shoes. De Marchi hesitates a second before bunching up her skirt. Ryan positions the satchel strap across his chest, watches her push down the nylons, one leg, then the other.

The car shudders. Cables creak.

He kneels down, links his fingers and cups his palms and nods to her.

De Marchi readjusts her handbag and comes closer. She touches his shoulder to steady herself, but her skirt's too tight and she can't keep her balance long enough to step into his hands. Their eyes meet. De Marchi blows out her breath, shakier now. She hesitates, and then wrestles the fabric of her skirt up and over her knees, tries again. Her instep is warm against his palm, soft as velvet. Ryan should keep his eyes on her face but her bare thigh is centimetres away, pale and firm. Close enough for him to see a smattering of freckles above her kneecap even in the murky light. For a full three seconds Ryan forgets what he's supposed to be doing.

Fingertips dig into his collarbone.

Focus, dickhead.

Ryan boosts De Marchi and guides her through the hatch. This time he keeps his eyes to himself. When he looks up she's disappeared.

He waits for her to give him a signal she's okay. She doesn't.

Ryan's heart gives a hard thump. He doesn't bother using the walls: he jumps from a standing start and hauls himself up through the hole. De Marchi is frozen against the cable rig—exactly where she shouldn't be—knees drawn tight against her chest. Thighs again covered.

'I hate heights.' She doesn't have to shout. The evacuation alarm is nowhere near as loud in the shaft.

Ryan goes to the edge of the car and peers over. Definitely a shit-your-pants kind of drop. Far below, orange light flickers in the shadows. The stench of smoke is stronger now but there's space out here and he can finally haul in a lungful of air.

De Marchi scans the shaft above them. 'Where are the doors?'

'We're riding the express. No doors for the first twenty-five floors, but there's another way out.' He points to the access panel three storeys up. 'That's how we get to it.'

De Marchi's gaze shifts to the steel ladder bolted to the concrete shaft. 'You're joking, right? How high are we?'

He shrugs. They're up at least twenty storeys, probably more, but Ryan can't see how knowing that will help her. He holds out his hand but she doesn't budge.

'Move, or I'm throwing your shoes over the side.' He lifts the satchel strap like he's seriously thinking about it.

She glares at him but lets him help her to her feet. Her skin is hotter now, clammy. 'You weren't so tough when the lights went out,' she mutters and grabs his shirtsleeve to keep her balance.

Ryan hides his surprise—was it that obvious?—and realises that if she can take the piss she's doing okay. 'Come on.' He leads her to the edge of the elevator car. The good news is that the ladder is right there, an arm's length away. The bad news is that De Marchi has to step out over the chasm to get to it. He positions himself behind her, ready to guide her onto the nearest rung. 'I'm right here.'

She pushes back against him. 'Give me a sec.'

30

His fingers find her hips and hold her in place. 'We don't have a sec. These lifts have safety brakes but they're not inde-structible. We get a big enough blast—'

'Just *wait*.' He can hear the anxiety now, feel her shaking. 'What's your name?'

'Ryan.' *Shit*. He should have given her the name on the ID. 'Can we go now?'

She takes a deep breath and reaches for the ladder.

'Keep your eyes up.' He doesn't let go until she's bearing her own weight, and then he climbs onto the rung below, shielding her body with his. 'You can't fall unless I do and I'm not going anywhere.'

She climbs a rung, stops. He does the same.

'Ryan.'

'Yeah?'

Even in the shadows he can see her knuckles are white. 'Those shoes are the most expensive things I own.'

'Okay.'

'In case something happens to me, I don't want you to think—'

'Nothing's going to happen to you,' he says.

But he feels a prick of guilt because he's the last person who can make that promise to her today.

Jules is trying not to panic—and only just succeeding.

She's scared she's going to totally freak out. That she'll hurt Ryan and they'll both plummet down the shaft.

The flaking ladder is rough against her skin and hard to grip. Worse than that, it's metal. Five minutes into the climb and the current under her skin is almost unbearable. It's always like this when she's under pressure: harder to contain, like holding back a sneeze. She was doing okay today, even with the nerves and Bradford Paxton, but this is something else entirely.

'Keep climbing, De Marchi. We're nearly there.'

They're not, and that's the problem. Her fingers are slick and she keeps stopping to wipe her palms on her skirt. Ryan is right with her. She pauses again, feels his heartbeat against her shoulderblade. Steady and controlled. She wonders what a guy like Ryan does at Pax Fed—a guy who wears heavy-soled boots and knows about access panels in elevator shafts; who's quick to throw off his tie and is comfortable hanging from a wall twenty storeys up. It doesn't quite fit and she doesn't quite care: she's too grateful having him between her and that head-spinning drop.

When the lights went out she convinced herself it was a coincidence—blackouts happen, even at Pax Fed. But then the explosion came and she knew: he was here.

Him.

The one who knows the truth about her, who knows exactly

what happened at the school two years ago because he caused it and filmed it. The man blackmailing her mother. He must have known she was coming here today. Does he want to hurt her? Set her up again?

Either way she's in trouble: trapped inside a Pax Fed building after an explosion. Bradford Paxton's going to have a field day with this.

'Keep going,' Ryan says.

She should warn Ryan, tell him what happens when she can't control the current. But how can she explain it? And it's not like he can get off the ladder in a hurry. She wipes her palm on her skirt again—it's filthy now—and they resume climbing. Jules focuses on the concrete blocks, on drawing her energy back into herself and slowing her pulse; all the things she used to practise with her dad.

The alarm stops so abruptly the silence hurts her ears.

'You okay?'

She doesn't answer.

'De Marchi—'

A flare of irritation. 'I have a first name.'

'Are you okay, *Julianne*?' His words warm her neck.

'I'm concentrating.'

'On what?'

'Not falling.'

'Look left.'

She does as he says and the relief almost buckles her. They're level with the access panel. But when she gets a good look at it her relief evaporates. It might be a flimsy piece of plywood but it's fixed tight against the concrete.

'How are we getting through that?' And why didn't she ask that question before they left the elevator car?

'I'll show you.'

She looks over her shoulder and finds Ryan *right there*. Catches a waft of deodorant and sweat.

33

'You're carrying a screwdriver?' she asks, sceptical.

'Something like that.' He nods up at the ladder. 'I need you higher. Only for a minute.'

She climbs three more rungs, feels exposed without him behind her. When she looks down, Ryan is hanging on to the ladder with one hand and reaching down to his boot. Her pulse stutters when she sees the blade. It's short and deadly looking and there's no mistaking it for anything other than a weapon. He leans out from the ladder and goes to work on the first screw, using the tip of the knife like a screwdriver. He doesn't look up, doesn't give an explanation.

The first three screws are gone in under a minute. Ryan gets the blade under the wood and uses it to lever the other screw loose. His leg is hooked through the ladder and his ankle tucked under a rung to hold him in place. He's sweating hard, his shirt clinging to his back and shoulders. The satchel with her shoes dangles over the chasm.

The wood bends and groans as Ryan forces it outwards but he can't get enough muscle behind it to finish the job. Jules grips the ladder harder, holding her breath. Holding the charge.

'Screw it,' Ryan mutters. He shifts his weight to the ladder and regroups. Glances up at her and away. The knife goes back into his boot. He climbs up another rung. 'Nearly there.'

The panel is warped, now bellying out from the wall. Ryan stretches out his leg to get his boot in behind it. He rests his forehead against Jules' spine, kicks backwards, and the panel flies free. It sails out into the shaft, clipping the lift on the way down before it melts into flickering shadow. Ryan swings back and leans into her as he catches his breath. 'Internal panel next and we're outta here.'

This time when he leans out, he flattens his face against the concrete and swings his fist into the access space. Jules hears something give inside.

'Right. I'll climb in, pull you after me.'

Jules closes her eyes, trying not to think about the plummeting shaft beneath them. If something goes wrong while she's hanging there over the void…

Ryan tosses the satchel into the building ahead of him. 'Ready?'

Not even close. The charge is pulsing so strongly she's surprised he can't feel it through the ladder. He's behind her again, radiating heat from exertion. He takes a moment to gather himself and then swings both legs up and into the opening like it's the easiest thing in the world. A second later he lets go of the rung and wriggles backwards until more of him is inside the building than out.

'Sit tight while I make sure we're clear,' Ryan says, and disappears.

Sit tight?

Jules wipes her hands again—carefully, one at a time—and waits. The seconds stretch out. The yawning shaft pulls at her, pulls the strength from her legs. She strains to hear sounds inside: voices, footsteps on carpet, anything to reassure her Ryan hasn't changed his mind and left her behind. The buzzing under her skin is almost unbearable—and then a new sound shatters the silence close by.

Gunfire.

Jules can't tell if it's in the shaft or the building, but it's too much.

She releases the charge.

Ryan smells it as soon as he sticks his head back into the lift well: burnt metal. Falling sparks light up the shaft further down.

'What was that?'

De Marchi is clinging to the ladder, eyes wide. 'Gunfire,' she says.

'Not that. Did the power come back on in here?'

She shakes her head but he knows something's happened. She's totally spooked. It's his own fault: he shouldn't have taken so long but he needed to get a fix on the shooters. They're on this floor as far as he can tell, but on the far side of the building. To be this high, they've either come in through the roof or they were already in the building before the power went.

Ryan positions himself so his hips and legs anchor him inside the building. They don't have long. 'Grip my arms.' He slaps each bicep and reaches for her.

More gunfire. Definitely semiautomatic and definitely not part of the plan.

'Ryan, I don't—'

'Grab me!'

She jerks free of the ladder and clamps her hands onto his bare skin. He flinches—her palms are *hot*—but he keeps his grip. Her weight leaves the ladder and she lets out a panicked gasp. Desperate fingers claw at him.

His nostrils burn with the stink of charred paint and a smell that reminds him of an electrical storm. He holds her tight, his pulse jackhammering. She's heavier than she looks. 'I've got you.' Everything in him strains as he hauls her up, and then she plants her feet on the concrete and takes back some of her own weight to help him. Ryan drags her through the opening and they land side by side. Her fingers stay locked around his arms and her breath is hot on his face, sour with fear. Another volley of gunfire. Who are they shooting at? Ryan hauls De Marchi to her feet and heads for the stairwell.

'We have to move.'

Her breath hitches and he sees it: she honestly believes the shooters are coming for her. He grabs the satchel—*those bloody shoes*—and pulls her after him. She doesn't resist. Ryan cracks the door to the stairs and listens for a second, feels the erratic pulse in her wrist. The stairwell is bathed in murky blue light and echoes with harried footsteps and urgent voices.

Another explosion and the stairs shudder. People scream. Ryan can't tell if the detonations are intended to bring the place down or are just a diversion. He doesn't have enough experience with explosives to know the difference.

'Stick to the wall.' They're on the nineteenth floor. On his own, he'd take the stairs two at a time but there are a lot of floors between here and the way out and he has no idea of De Marchi's fitness. Her file wasn't that detailed. She's a step behind, one hand on the cinderblock for balance. After two flights, Ryan stops glancing over his shoulder and listens for her instead. His new knee aches, but he knows it well enough to push through the pain. He's found his rhythm, even with the satchel bumping his hip.

If this is the work of Agitators, they've had some serious outside help. But if it's not, if there's something else going on and it's about De Marchi, then she must have done more than burn down a school building.

'Ryan.'

De Marchi has pulled up on the landing above him, sucking in deep breaths, her palm up in a wordless plea. Her face is flushed and her hair loose, long strands sticking to her throat. The gunfire has stopped.

'Nearly there,' Ryan manages, and De Marchi straightens and nods. Willing herself to get moving again.

Ten more flights—slower—and he signals for her to stop at a door marked 2. 'This way.'

De Marchi glances down the next flight—the way everyone else is leaving the building—but doesn't argue. Ryan opens the door a few centimetres and strains to hear movement. The air conditioning hasn't been off long and already the place smells stale. He leads De Marchi inside, hoping he memorised the floor plan correctly. Daylight filters through thick glass beyond the row of cubicles. There are new sirens outside: fire and ambulance. Ryan picks up his pace. Another blast shakes the floor and dust floats down from the ceiling, settles in his hair. He cuts a zigzag path, dodging spilt paperwork and a toppled photo of a laughing toddler. When they reach the exit in the far corner, Ryan pauses long enough to make sure De Marchi is with him before he releases the latch. He squints against the glare outside, tries not to think about what he's going to do with her when they make it to the street.

One thing at a time.

The emergency exit opens onto the adjoining rooftop. It's clear. They sprint past overturned chairs and abandoned coffee mugs, an overflowing ashtray. They're on the far side of Pax Fed Tower but the shouting and sirens carry from Queen Street. It takes an adrenaline-charged few seconds to find the fire escape, slightly to the left of where Ryan was expecting it. The steel stairs take them down into the laneway and—

Relief swamps him.

The van is idling at the Eagle Street end. He grabs De Marchi by the wrist and pulls her after him, running hard. They're less than ten metres away when the Major steps from the cab and slides open the van door.

De Marchi baulks and tries to wrench herself free. 'No—'

'It's all right,' Ryan pants and hopes he's not lying. He doesn't let go, even when he sees how frightened she is. She struggles against him, bringing her fist down hard on his forearm, trying to break his grip.

'Stop it.' He keeps dragging her. They're almost to the Major. He can't change his mind now.

'Let go!' She clamps her fingers around Ryan's wrist and—

Stinging pain explodes up his arm and he lands on his backside so hard that he bites his tongue and tastes blood. *What the fuck?* His wrist tingles and aches where she had hold of him. De Marchi is already halfway back up the alley, skirt bunched and arms pumping, blackened feet kicking up behind her.

'Go,' the Major orders, jumping into the van.

Ryan sprints after her, his calves burning from the stairs and his arm weirdly numb. The Major guns the engine, passes Ryan and swerves to cut off De Marchi. He doesn't clip her, but she has to prop and change direction, and it's enough for Ryan to close the distance. He grabs her in a bear hug from behind, pinning her arms. She kicks and thrashes, no air left to accuse or abuse him.

'Sorry,' he manages as the two of them tumble into the back of the van and the door slams shut.

Jules scrambles away from Ryan and wedges herself between the bench seat and the cab, ready to kick out if he comes any closer, her blood thundering. The van accelerates out of the laneway and rocks her to one side. Her hip and elbow throb. It's dim in here, tinted glass front and back filtering the daylight. She should get up, get past Ryan. Get out. But fear pins her to the floor.

The charge is building again—too soon—but even that feels disconnected, like music from another room.

She trusted Ryan.

Right up until she saw the other one step out of the van and she understood they were there for her.

Ryan sits on his heels in front of the sliding door, hanging on to the latch as the van takes another corner. His free hand is outstretched, a pointless attempt at reassurance.

'Calm down, it's fine.'

Fine? Then why did he tackle her and throw her in here? And why doesn't he sound like he believes it?

She tries to think through the crushing fear. Who will care that she's missing? Who'll even know?

Angie.

Another stab of panic, sharper. The news crews were right there and the attack will be all over the TV. Jules has to get to Angie before her mum does something stupid. She has to get out of this van.

'Where are we going?' Her mouth is so dry she can barely form the question.

Ryan doesn't answer. He glances at the window between them and the driver.

He doesn't know.

'What does Pax Fed want?'

Still no response, and now he can't look her in the eye. An uneasy thought creeps in. 'Do you even work there?'

His gaze cuts back to her and he doesn't have to respond: she can see the answer for herself. The walls of the van crowd in and her head swims. She swallows once, twice, but the panic stays lodged in her throat. Cool air from the vent washes over her, chills her clammy skin.

'Was that you, then?' Barely a whisper.

It takes a second for him to catch on. 'The explosions? No.' He's crouched in front of her, steadying himself against the sliding door. He undoes the rest of his shirt buttons and peels the fabric from damp skin to let it hang open. 'De Marchi, are you okay?'

She doesn't respond because the answer should be obvious: of course she's not.

The van brakes, gently. The driver's keeping calm, taking his time. Jules cranes her neck to get a better look out the back window. She could lunge for it, bang on the glass to attract attention while they're stuck in traffic. But then what? The news crews saw her go into Pax Fed Tower. Her old mug shot has probably been all over TV since the explosions. Who in a city of panicked people is going to be happy to see her, let alone help her?

'Did I hurt you?' Ryan presses.

He says it as if he accidentally bumped her with his elbow. He *threw* her in the back of a van. He hasn't tried to touch her again—hasn't made any move to come near her—but that doesn't make up for the fact that he did.

'What do you want?' The question is thin, breathless. For once in her life she wishes she could maintain a rage like her mother, but that's never been her gift. Suppression's more her thing.

This time Ryan holds her gaze. 'No idea.'

'I don't believe you.'

The window to the cab slides open.

'Julianne.'

Of course the driver knows who she is—why else grab her?—but it's a shock to hear him say her name. He's older than Ryan, gruff. They're stopped at lights and he's speaking over his shoulder. All she can see is the peak of a cap, mirrored sunglasses, a trimmed salt and pepper beard...and an ear that doesn't look quite right. He waits for her to acknowledge him. She doesn't.

'There are better places to sit.'

Jules tries to work out what advantage it will give them if she's on the bench seat instead of the floor.

'Don't make your life more difficult than it needs to be.' The driver pauses for a reaction. Doesn't get one. 'Or you can stay down there until we get you home. Up to you.'

The screen slides shut and the van rolls forward.

Home.

Does he mean that? Why doesn't Ryan know about it? The rush of hope and fear makes her dizzy. When the sensation subsides, her anxiety swerves back to Angie. How long's it been since that first explosion? Twenty minutes? Long enough for her mother to go on the warpath. For once Jules is glad they can't afford a car. At least Angie's offline and stuck in Woodridge, assuming the trains have stopped running.

Ryan gestures to the seat. Jules resists, but she's sore from the stairs and needs to stretch.

'You want a hand?'

She ignores Ryan and climbs onto the seat, positioning

herself so she can keep an eye on him and see into the cab. Ryan settles to the floor and straightens his legs, rubs his right knee. He takes up a lot of space. It's only now she notices what else is in the van: a scrunched-up T-shirt and cargo shorts, battered tennis shoes. A sports bag with a can of deodorant poking out through the top and two empty wire hangers jangling as they turn another corner. The sirens are further away but the van is still in the city, moving at a crawl.

'How do you know where I live?'

'I don't.' Ryan nods at the cab.

'Who is he?'

'Can't say.' There's no hesitation, no apology. Ryan relaxes back against the door and a patch of tinted daylight paints his face. His blond hair is wilder now, messier than when she first saw him in the lift. He was always too scruffy to be an office worker, and with his tie gone and shirt undone, he looks even less the part. He and the driver can't be Agitators, surely—could they get access to a Pax Fed ID if they were? So who are they?

Ryan watches her watching him, his fingers tapping a beat on the metal floor. Jules feels it from where she's sitting: the coiled energy radiating from him, even now.

'What did you do to me back there?' He keeps his voice low as if he doesn't want the driver to hear.

Jules remembers the sensation of the charge surging from her fingertips and onto his skin. The fleeting triumph when his grip was gone.

'Nothing.'

'I didn't fall on my arse cause I'm clumsy. What did you use?'

She positions her handbag on her knees and fiddles with the strap. He thinks she had a weapon. 'Can't say.' She gives him back his own words, sharpened, and he tips his head to acknowledge the shutdown.

They ride in silence.

It takes forever to clear the CBD. Jules tracks the journey

through the cab window, finds familiar buildings, the on-ramp to the freeway. If the police are putting up roadblocks the driver's managed to evade them. They pick up speed on the freeway and she sees enough to know they're heading south. It's the right direction but her heart stays lodged in her throat. She's aching and sweaty and clinging to the hope the driver's not a liar, scared to consider what it means if he is.

Could she release another dose of current if she had to? She's never been able to summon it on demand. The energy builds on its own, feeding on stress and fear. It's an effort to trap the charge beneath her ribs until it's safe to let go, like holding back a squirming terrier: the second her grip eases, it's gone, ripping along her nerves and grounding out through her fingertips. The backyard she grew up in was scarred with scorched grass and blackened trees from years of practising with her dad, trying to hold the power in her hands—and failing. Her dad didn't understand why the current existed but he always believed she'd master it one day. She's yet to prove him right.

Jules measures the distance between her and Ryan, catches him checking out her legs. His gaze cuts up and away. Jules keeps him in her peripheral vision while she finds landmarks through the windscreen: the Enviro-Nuclear Science Centre at Dutton Park...the Princess Alexandra Research and Repatriation Hospital...the forest of privately funded housing commission towers along the train line.

The need for answers eventually burns through her anxiety.

'You were at Pax Fed Tower because of me. Why?'

The tapping stops as he weighs the question. 'You make people nervous.'

'Who? Pax Fed?'

He shrugs and a deeper, darker fear stirs.

'Were you there to hurt me?'

'Only if you were a threat.' He means starting a fire but he thinks she needs matches to do it.

44

'Why didn't you leave me behind?'

'It wasn't safe.'

'And *this* is?' Her voice breaks a little.

Ryan glances at the cab. 'If the—' he stops. 'If he says he's taking you home, he is.'

'And then what?'

'Dunno.'

Silence returns. Jules keeps track of every exit they pass. When hers is next, her pulse shifts up a gear. The van changes lanes and hope and fear go to war under her ribs.

Hang on, Angie.

They're on the service road and turning right at the lights. She counts off every intersection, each one taking her closer to home. Every turn shortens her breath.

Come on, come on.

The van finally stops. They're not at her house, they're in the next street. She can see the old paperbark tree listing over the footpath from the last storm, and the rusting Impreza on blocks in the Tamatoas' yard on the corner.

'This it?'

Jules nods, not looking at Ryan. She slides to the edge of the seat, her fingers digging into the fabric and her breath trapped in her chest. The driver gets out and Ryan repositions himself in a crouch, blocking her exit. 'Wait,' he warns.

The door rumbles open and overcast light floods in. The driver is there, filling the space. He's about the same height as Ryan but at least two decades older. The street pulls at her.

Ryan reaches for the satchel. 'Her shoes,' he says.

The older man looks from the bag to Ryan and nods, steps aside. Ryan swings out onto the street.

'De Marchi. Go.'

Jules scrambles out of the van, snatches the bag and takes off before they change their minds. Her legs protest but she pushes herself to a sprint, bare feet stinging on the bitumen. With every stride she expects to hear Ryan's boots behind her. She takes the corner at full pelt, not looking back.

Mrs Tamatoa is on her front verandah, drinking tea and playing solitaire like she always is at this time of day.

'Julianne, you okay girl?'

Jules doesn't answer because she's only four doors from home and can't spare the breath. She grips the satchel in one hand—it's bouncing against her thigh—and fixes her eyes on the only house that matters.

The front door of the weatherboard bangs open and Angie De Marchi is rushing down the steps—*she stayed home!*—wearing the same grey trackpants and T-shirt she had on at breakfast, dark hair piled on top of her head. She reaches the footpath and keeps coming.

'What happened? Are you—'

She stops, her attention shifting to the road, and Jules risks a look. It's the van, crawling towards them.

'Mum, get inside.' Jules says, reaching her. She grabs Angie by the arm and pulls her towards the gate. 'They're coming.'

'Who?'

'The guys who brought me home—'

Angie jerks to a stop. 'Cops? Feds?'

'I don't think so.'

Angie breaks free and gets between her and the road. The van keeps coming, slow and purposeful.

'Let me see.'

The van is almost level with them. There's nobody else around except Mrs T, sitting forward on her camping chair, cards laid aside. Jules grips Angie's forearm, braced for...she doesn't know what.

Ryan's in the passenger seat, eyes hidden behind aviator sunnies. Glare on the windscreen hides the driver. Jules braces for her mother to react—to swear, thump the van, anything to rattle these guys as they pass.

46

But the drivers side window comes down and Angie falters.

'Angela Margaret.'

The bearded driver nods at her as he rolls past.

Jules' mum is still standing there speechless when he guns the engine and speeds away.

'Can you turn that off while I'm here?'

Federal agent Nadira Khan sits across the kitchen table from Jules, a mug of green tea untouched in front of her. The investigator taps her pen against a notepad, distracted. Jules wraps her fingers around her own cup, wishing she'd had time for a shower before Khan arrived but the agent turned up barely minutes after they came inside.

On the TV, the Pax Fed building is still burning—the 'Pax Attack', as it's been dubbed.

...among those likely to be questioned is Angela De Marchi, renowned activist and long-time critic of Paxton Federation. De Marchi blames the global giant for the death in Pakistan of her husband, war veteran Lieutenant Michael De Marchi. Lieutenant De Marchi was among those killed when insurgents bombed a desalination plant co-funded by Paxton Federation at the Karachi Port. Angela De Marchi inexplicably withdrew from the public eye two years ago and sources within Paxton Federation have long suspected she has continued to work covertly with the Agitators. Peta Paxton, co-vice chair of Paxton Federation board and daughter of magnate Tom, has so far refused to comment on that speculation, or to link the attack with the Priority Agricultural Practices Bill drafted by her brother Bradford, due to be debated in the Senate in coming weeks.

Jules' eyes flick to the screen—to shaky footage of her running into the Pax Fed building, hiding her face—and then to her mother at the sink. Angie sets the kettle back on its base, offers Khan a tight smile. 'Jules has a right to know what they're saying about us. She needs to see for herself that there's no evidence to support this witch hunt.'

The agent twists around to face Angie, shoulder holster whispering against her starched shirt. She's wearing a fitted jacket despite the warmth, shirtsleeves buttoned to her wrists as usual, and her long black hair trapped in a sleek bun. 'Let's not get ahead of ourselves.'

'Oh come on, Khan. Do you think I'd let Jules anywhere near that building if I knew someone was going to drive a truck into it?' Angie wrings out a teabag with her fingers and dumps it in the sink. 'I haven't been in contact with anyone from the Agitators in two years, as you well know.'

'Perhaps you're better at subterfuge these days.'

'Better than your surveillance capabilities?' A bitter laugh.

Jules finds the chip in her cup handle, rubs her thumb back and forwards over the rough edge. This antagonism between her mother and Agent Khan is nothing new: it shouldn't make her feel this anxious.

Angie measures the agent. 'Is Jules a suspect?'

'We can't rule anyone out.'

'Drop the crap, Khan. Do *you* believe Jules or I had anything to do with that attack?'

Khan holds Angie's gaze but a small sigh escapes her. Kohl-rimmed eyes soften for a moment. 'I'd like to think you're smarter than that.'

Jules allows herself a flicker of hope that the last two years haven't been for nothing after all.

'Then shouldn't you be more worried about those guys?' Her mother gestures to blurry footage of two masked figures sprinting across a rooftop littered with plastic chairs. They're using the same escape route as Ryan and even in low res it's obvious they're armed with rifles. The coverage cuts back to the Pax Fed headquarters, its first three storeys crumbling as if a bite's been taken out of it. Burning papers flutter to a road strewn with rubble. Jules looks away so she doesn't have to see the bodies covered in blue tarps.

'The Agitators have lifted their game,' Khan says.

'You can't seriously suspect they did *that*?'

Khan gives Angie a strange look. 'They're not the group you walked away from, Angela. I doubt you'd recognise them, or their methods.'

...The attack started when a delivery truck smashed through the police blockade in Queen Street and rammed into the Paxton Federation Tower foyer. The first explosion came a minute later. As you can see from footage captured by our crew on the scene, the blast came from the basement. This has led to speculation the truck was a diversion, drawing police into the building and enabling a second attacker to enter the basement car park and tamper with gas lines. During the building evacuation, two heavily armed individuals broke into the tower via the roof, terrorising evacuating staff on the upper floors and destroying mainframe servers.

It's been the same story on repeat for the past two hours. Eight people are dead—three protesters, two Pax Fed security guards and three cops. Another thirty-eight people are seriously injured, including the sergeant who walked Jules into the building. The sergeant wouldn't have been near the tower if she'd walked away when he told her to. And he's been hurt for what? So Bradford Paxton could humiliate her in that boardroom? She feels sick over it.

Jules can't accept the Agitators are responsible for people dying. In her mum's days, the group was always about nonviolent, non-criminal resistance. But the school explosion two years ago and its collateral damage made a mockery of that: made it easier for people to believe the group is responsible for the blood and destruction now featuring on every channel.

'Julianne,' Khan says, 'tell me again about these two men and the van.'

Jules turns her cup around twice, takes a slow sip of luke-warm green tea. She wishes Khan knew *more*—she's never felt comfortable lying to her, not since the agent's become a regular in their home—but it's too late for that. So she repeats the parts of her story she can tell.

'And you didn't recognise the guy in the elevator or the older driver?'

'No.'

'What about you, Angela? Did you get a good look at either of them?'

Angie shakes her head, keeps her expression neutral.

Jules knows it's not the truth. Not only because the driver acted like he knew her mother, or even that he used her middle name (only ever uttered in court appearances, and even then under sufferance). It's how her mother reacted. Or, rather, how she didn't.

Angie's phone vibrates and she ignores it. Khan arches neatly manicured brows until Angie huffs and turns the device to her. Jules recognises the name, a reporter who used to hang out at their house when her dad was alive. Now he only calls when there's a story.

'You know your journo mates believe you were paid to shut up, right?'

'Yeah, and you can see what I did with all that hush money.' Angie gestures to the cramped kitchen. There's barely enough space to fit the kettle and microwave on the bench, and if Jules pushes her chair back from the table too far, the fridge won't open. The place is older than Angie and even more brittle. It's stifling in summer, bone-cold in winter and invaded by mould every time it rains—which is half the year. When they moved in after her dad died the walls were yellowed with age and the floors scarred with cigarette burns. Angie and Jules pulled up the lino and rotting carpet and polished the boards themselves. They bought cheap paint and spent every weekend for a month working their way through the house. The owner agreed the place looked better and tried to put up the rent—until the property manager explained it wouldn't be worth the aggravation to take on Angela De Marchi.

Jules gets up and rinses her cup in the sink.

'Julianne, why are your feet black?' Khan asks. 'What happened to your shoes?'

'I took them off to climb the elevator shaft. Ryan carried them.'

Khan's eyebrows shoot up again. 'He carried your shoes?'

Jules points to the satchel resting by the front door where she left it. 'In that.' She walks over to show the agent.

'Don't touch it!' The agent's sharpness stops her short. Khan is up from the table, eyes fixed on the bag. 'This guy—Ryan—tells you he's at Paxton Federation to keep an eye on you. When everything goes bad he helps you get out and kidnaps you, only to deliver you home. And then he hands you a bag to bring into your house?'

'With my shoes in it.' Even as Jules says it, her heart skitters.

'Outside.' Agent Khan crosses to the front door, unclipping the mobile from her belt. 'Now.'

The agent makes them wait down the street by the corner, out the front of Mrs T's place. Grey clouds crouch overhead, pensive. A gust of warm wind stirs leaves in the gutter.

Jules should have grabbed her thongs from the front deck because the bitumen hurts the soles of her feet. Worse, it's shifting beneath her like a commuter train—except it's not the road that's moving. She grips with her toes, tries to anchor herself.

There's nothing in the satchel but her designer heels, there can't be. She wraps her arms around herself and stares hard at their house, willing it to stay intact. The gutter sags over the entrance and the timber cladding is flaking from too many years of sun and storms. The water-stained blinds in her room are pulled up and her window's wedged open to let in the breeze. The place is beaten and tired and it's seen better days but it's home.

'It's just a house,' Angie says. She's standing close enough that Jules can imagine her touch.

'Mum, everything we own is inside.'

'It's only stuff.'

'It's *Dad's* stuff.' His tattered novels, his vintage T-shirts, the superhero comics he bought for her...'Oh God,' she whispers, leaning forward to absorb the grief. 'I'm so sorry. All I was worried about was those stupid shoes—'

'Stop it.' Angie says. 'I didn't think twice about bringing that bag inside and I should have.' A sideways glance. 'Are you okay?'

Jules knows she's not talking about her emotional state. 'It's not back yet. I'm fine.'

The charge that was building again in the van is gone; she released it in the yard about thirty seconds before Khan knocked on the front door. All Jules feels now is the faint undercurrent— and dread swirling low in her stomach.

Khan is speaking into a two-way radio, one arm resting on the open drivers side door of the unmarked sedan. Her flexiphone is on the car roof, useless. Whatever's going on in the city, it's prompted authorities to take all digital communication offline, even the networks that are meant to be secure.

There's action on Mrs T's deck. She's shuffling to the railing, listing from side to side as her arthritic ankles warm up. Silver hair is pulled back, and her floral dress ripples in the breeze. 'You girls got trouble?' she calls out.

'Not sure yet,' Angie says.

Mrs T catches Jules' eye. 'The boys aren't far away if you need them.'

Jules nods, but she's not sure how the four Tamatoa lads are going to help if her house explodes. Still, the brothers were handy in the days after the school fire. It was the boys—not the cops— who pushed the news vans back to the next street. Literally. She remembers the spotlights, the cameras, the frantic activity any time she cracked the blinds to see outside. The thought of going through all that again...

Jules crosses to the far side of the street and sits in the gutter. She tucks the grimy skirt under her legs, hooks her arms around her knees and watches her mum stare down their house, daring it to defy her. Angie's agitated, shifting her weight from foot to foot, wiping her palms on her trackpants.

Jules bites the inside of her lip until she tastes blood. Did she take a bomb into their home?

She pictures the satchel slouched against the hallway wall where she dumped it half an hour ago. Harmless-looking. Was there anything about the way Ryan handled it, any hint it was dangerous? She remembers it hanging from his shoulder as he scaled the elevator shaft and bouncing against his hip as they ran through the building.

She remembers that moment in the lift.

'Mum.'

Angie glances over her shoulder, her body angled towards the house.

'Ryan emptied that satchel. I saw him shake it out. He let me put the shoes in myself. Would he do that if it had explosives hidden in there?'

Khan is half-listening from the car, radio in hand. 'Maybe he didn't know.'

Jules thinks about Ryan, how he moved and spoke. If he knew what he was carrying, he was either incredibly cool under pressure or incredibly careless.

Angie's eyes are fixed on the weatherboard. 'How long until your squad gets here?' she asks Khan.

'Not long.'

'Five minutes? Ten? An hour?'

The agent's lips tighten. 'They'll be here.'

'They're all caught up in the city, Khan. Tactical response, bomb squad. *Everyone*. Nobody's racing out here, not for us.'

Angie crosses back to their side of the street, dragging hair from her eyes. 'If someone really wanted to hurt us, wouldn't they have detonated it by now?'

'That depends.'

'On what?'

'On who those guys are. What level of tech they can access.'

Angie points to the dead mobile device on the car roof. 'We know they're not using the network.'

'That doesn't mean they're not watching.'

Jules twists around, eyes raking over rust-stained iron roofs and the faded orange work ute parked up by the next corner. Who the hell were *they*?

'De Marchi, don't you dare.'

Angie is headed for their front gate. Khan moves too and Angie breaks into a run.

'Mum!' Jules is on her feet and after her mother.

The agent lunges as Jules passes—'Julianne, no!'—but Jules twists away, breaking Khan's grip. She rushes through the gate, up the steps and whips open the screen door—

Angie is in the lounge room holding the satchel in both hands. She startles at the slamming door and her eyes go wide when she sees Jules.

'What are you doing? Get back outside.'

'Mum, put it down.' Fear thuds through Jules and the current buzzes in response.

'You both need to get back out here,' Khan says, breathless. She's close, on the front steps maybe. Jules won't look over her shoulder: she can't take her eyes from Angie.

'I mean it, Jules. Go.'

'No.'

'Do what you're told. This isn't a game.'

'You think I don't know that? You're the one putting yourself at risk. Do you want to die?'

'Of course I don't. I want our lives back.'

Angie glowers at her, chest rising and falling, and Jules feels it like a shockwave: the ferocity of her mother's grief and rage. The rawness of it still.

'Mum—'

'I need to *do* something, don't you get that?' Angie's jaw is tight, her eyes wild. 'I'm so sick of it, Jules. All the shit that keeps happening to us and not being able to do a thing about it.'

Jules has lived through her mother's anger. Lived through the melancholic funk that Angie slips into after a bottle of wine.

But she's never seen her like this, so reckless.

'Getting yourself killed isn't the answer.'

Angie looks down at the bag in her hands, at her white knuckles and straining tendons. Jules fizzes with the need to act but her feet won't budge. She doesn't trust herself to grab the bag *and* keep control of the charge.

'I'm not telling you again,' Khan says. 'Come out here and leave the satchel in there.'

'Mum...'

Angie turns away from Jules and pops the studs. Jules jerks back and slams her hip into the couch as her mother up-ends the satchel. The Gucci heels tumble to the floorboards, a strip of fabric caught up with them. Angie shakes the bag and something else falls out, hits the floor with a slap: a plastic ID card on a Pax Fed lanyard.

Angie bends towards it.

'Do *not* touch that. I *will* shoot you.' Khan appears in the doorway, handgun drawn. It looks huge in her small hands but she holds it with practised confidence.

Angie's fingers hover over the lanyard.

'Do you want to compromise the only piece of evidence you haven't put your prints all over?'

Angie straightens. 'Knock yourself out.' She's trying for nonchalance but Jules can see she's rattled. Khan's never pulled a gun on her before.

'One day, Angela...' The agent holsters the weapon. 'Give me the bag.' They eyeball each other as the satchel changes hands. Khan peers inside, pats it down three times before she blows out her breath. 'It's clean.'

Jules buckles to the couch and hugs the old yellow cushion against her chest. It's musty and smells of stale green tea but it's *here*. The house is safe.

Khan pulls a ziplock bag from her back pocket and uses it to pick up the ID. The agent holds it so Jules can see it through the plastic. It looks like every other ID she saw at Pax Fed today: barcode, logo and name. This one says *Eddie Baker.*

'If that's a fake, it's a good job.' Angie grips the corner of the plastic bag so she can get a better view but Khan pulls it away.

'I'll get it dusted for prints, see if we can't identify at least one of these guys.'

Jules chews on the corner of her thumbnail. Did Ryan give her his real name? Did he mean to?

'So where are we, then?' Angie asks Khan. Most of the anger has subsided, but the defiance remains. 'Is Jules a suspect for the Pax Fed attack or not?'

The agent looks over at Jules on the couch, seems to weigh up her response. 'For the moment, no. Her story checks out with the sergeant at the scene.'

'You could've said that when you got here,' Angie says.

'You know that's not how it works.'

'Yeah. I know exactly how your lot works. Does that mean I'm under suspicion or not?'

Khan gives her a tight smile. 'You'd be offended if you weren't.'

Jules closes her eyes and sinks deeper into the couch, tracing the edge of a button on the cushion. She wills the tension to leave her neck and shoulders.

They still have a home.

She's not a suspect—at least not in the eyes of the federal police.

There are no news crews in the street.

But.

She doesn't understand why Ryan was in the Pax Fed Building or why he helped her. Most of all, she doesn't understand why the driver brought her home and why the sight of him robbed her mother of words, because that *never* happens.

'Wait a minute.'

58

Khan is probing inside the satchel again, one eye screwed shut in concentration. She yanks hard. 'Got it.'

Angie moves closer. 'What is that?'

Using another evidence bag, Khan holds up a tiny silver thing between her thumb and forefinger, the size of a grain of rice. 'Audio transmitter and tracker, stitched into the seam of the bag. That's why I missed it the first time.' She turns the bug over, studying it. 'This is advanced tech. If it's working, your friends in that van have been listening in since Julianne brought it inside.'

Major Luka Voss pulls out the earbud as soon as the feed goes dead.

He's alone in his demountable office, listening through the audio file a second time, stewing over the fact Angela De Marchi thought he'd sent a bomb into her house.

It was unprofessional to let her see him. He should have gone back to the motorway. He didn't need to drive down De Marchi's street.

But he wanted to make sure Julianne got home.

No, that's a lie. He wanted to see Angela. See if she remembered him.

And she did, sort of. Enough, at least, to pull her up short. The way her forehead creased, the confusion…she knew she'd met him before.

He wondered how long it would take for her to work it out.

And he wondered if it would make today better or worse when she did.

Ryan's only half-awake. It's fifteen minutes until his alarm is set to go off. He's sprawled on his bunk, tangled in the sheet and thinking about Julianne De Marchi. Again. Watching her slide up that skirt and push down her pantyhose. He can't get the image out of his head. He feels himself stir, knows he has to find a distraction or he's going to get out of bed hard, and he'll never hear the end of it from Waylo. He forces himself to remember the way De Marchi looked at him in the van. The betrayal. The fear. Thinks about the bruises he must have left on her.

Yep, that does it. The heat leaves him and shame creeps back in.

He waits another minute before he drops over the side of the bunk and heads for a cold shower.

The Major offered no explanation on the drive back to base three days ago. Said nothing about why Ryan had to grab De Marchi when she ran, or why they took her home and sat three blocks away for the next forty-seven minutes. Gave Ryan no opening to ask questions. But the Major had plenty of his own and Ryan was careful to answer only what was asked of him.

No, he didn't know why De Marchi's interview ended prematurely.

No, he didn't see any of the shooters.

Yes, the power went out *before* the first explosion.

Yes, De Marchi let him help her.

Ryan has no clue if he's in the shit or not. A woman in a short, tight business skirt turned up later that afternoon and yelled at the Major for twenty minutes. Ryan heard it from the quad—her volume, if not the actual words. He got enough of a look at her on her way in to see she had gym-toned thighs and a shade of white-blonde hair that doesn't come from a packet. She was buffed and polished, a species of woman as foreign to him as the iridescent beetle crashing against his window last night.

Ryan is still thinking about the fallout from Wednesday on his return trip from the showers, bare-chested and barefoot, hair dripping. The doors around the common room are closed, everyone else snuffling and snoring in their beds except Frenchie; she's talking in her sleep in Arabic. Beyond the kitchen window the sky is finally brightening.

The whole Pax Fed thing makes no sense. If the shooters had a specific target, they stuffed up. The evacuation had started by the time they started firing—it would have been near impossible to single someone out in that chaos…Unless they knew their target couldn't leave with the others. Say, if that person was trapped in a lift. Plenty of space then, and time too. Time to destroy a room full of computer servers if they wanted.

De Marchi might not be so paranoid after all.

Ryan can't stop thinking about her—and not just her thighs, although he'll get back to them in a second. There was nothing in her file he didn't already know: she was convicted of arson and destruction of public property when she was sixteen, and given a suspended sentence because her old man was a dead war hero. As far as Ryan knows she only ever burned down her high school. Okay, she blew it up, which is a bit more hard-core and scored her a spot on a national watch list. But still. It's hardly enough to send a heavily armed squad after her two years later—or even have someone like him waiting in the wings.

Ryan pauses at his door, shoulders tightening at the thought of gunmen finding De Marchi alone in that lift. That's what she'd wanted: to be on her own when they got to her. For Ryan to leave so *he'd* be safe.

The irony burns.

An alarm clock goes off as Ryan steps into the room. Waylo punches it into silence without lifting his head from the lower bunk. Ryan flicks the switch by the door and the fluoro overhead sputters to life.

Waylo farts loudly and rolls over, rubbing his eyes with his thumb and forefinger. He clocks Ryan's damp hair. 'You shit the bed?' His voice is rough from sleep.

'Nah, buddy, that stink in here is all you.'

'Mate, my arse smells like roses.' Waylo throws off his sheet and sits up, stretches each arm until his shoulder joints pop. 'Kill for a decent sleep.'

Ryan rummages through his top drawer and pulls on a faded T-shirt, one of the few things he kept from the bundle he brought from home. The Mitchellstone District Footy Club tiger and the day, month and year of the Under 18s premiership are faded and peeling now, but he doesn't need the date to remember that moment the siren sounded. When he fell to his knees exhausted and ecstatic, his teammates piling on top of him, all of them battered and bruised. Back when the world made sense, before everything fell apart.

Thinking about home reminds him he needs to ring Tommy. The voice network came back online yesterday so he's run out of excuses. But he's not ready. He focuses on the state of the room instead. With the light on, there's no avoiding the mess. Two jocks and a singlet hang over the end of his bunk, drying from a quick rinse in the sink a day ago. Boots in various stages of re-lacing cover the two-seater table. The pot on the gas burner is half-full of water and the sink is crammed with dirty cups and plates. Both wardrobes are open, jeans and runners spilling out onto the carpeted floor. The room smells of sweat, deodorant, stale coffee and farts.

'Waylo, this place is a disgrace.'

Waylo slings a towel around his neck and heads for the door in his boxers, a plastic shopping bag loaded with toiletries in his free hand. 'Inspection's not till tomorrow. We got time.'

'Not if your new mate reaches out.'

The guy with the man bun—Xavier—was testing Waylo's taste for civil unrest right before all hell broke loose on Wednesday.

'I'm serious mate, I'm not cleaning this shit-sty on my own.'

Waylo pauses at the door and spins the plastic bag with his thumb and forefinger, first one direction and then the other. 'Don't be jealous, Walsh. You'll get another shot to impress the Major.' He manages half a grin before he leaves the room, favouring his left leg.

Even Waylo can't dredge up a convincing bluff this week. It's the closest any of them have come to infiltrating the Agitators or any other domestic terrorist gateway group. It's what they train for. Why they exist. Why they jab themselves with needles every day. And there's even more pressure now the Agitators have blood on their hands.

Ryan's not supposed to know what went down before the explosion. Waylo's not supposed to know about De Marchi. But neither of them is any good with rules that require lying to a mate.

Waylo was restless after Wednesday. Riled up. So the two of them sat up past midnight, lights out, talking it through. Trying to figure it all out, even though the Major had made it clear it wasn't their job to understand.

Ryan sidesteps boots and newspapers to get to the sink. He jams in the plug, squirts in detergent and opens the tap until it runs hot.

He understands why Waylo was rattled outside Pax Fed: Xavier was warning him to move further up Queen Street 'on the signal'. Waylo had no idea what the signal was—until a truck skidded sideways into the street, cleaned up two cop cars and rammed into the Pax Fed Tower foyer. The protesters bolted on impact. Waylo kept his cover and ran with them, but he wasn't quick enough. The blast threw him into a parked car, showered him with debris. He was close enough to hear the screams, see the bodies and bloodstains when the dust cleared.

The sink fills with lemony suds. A cluster breaks free, floats up past Ryan's nose.

Xavier knew that truck was coming. Did the Major? Ryan turns that last thought over, testing its shape. He wrenches off the water, stares at the suds. Tiny bubbles cling to a coffee-stained cup and burst in the humid air.

Did the Major send him into that building knowing he might not come out?

It's not until he's back from hand-to-hand combat training in the afternoon that Ryan finally makes the call. He's on his bunk, shoulders against the wall and ankles crossed. He flexes the lightweight phone in his palm a dozen times before he lets it snap flat and taps in the number.

Nobody on the farm can afford a mobile service, so he dials the home line. It rings once, twice. His palms are tacky, his tongue thick. He's surprised it still feels like this. *Pick up the phone, Tommy.*

'Hello?'

Ryan's heart trips. 'Dad?'

'No, dickhead, it's me.' Tommy laughs. 'Didn't recognise the number. You lose another phone?' Ryan blows out his breath. There's no mistaking Tommy for Dad now he's dropped his phone voice.

'I don't lose them, arsewipe, the sim gets changed every month. How many times do I have to explain this?' Relief ripples through him. 'Mum around?'

'Out in the paddock, I'll get her in a sec. Good thing you rang, she's been stressing about the Pax Attack. Were you in the city?'

Ryan finds a new blister on his heel, presses it with his thumb until it changes colour. 'Nah.' He tries hard not to lie to Tommy, but there's no way he can tell him about Wednesday. Fortunately his younger brother has a short attention span.

'You get your leave approved?'

'Nah, mate, can't get the time right now.'

'Come on, Ryno, you missed Christmas. It's my seventeenth. Macka's old man's letting us use the clubhouse and Rabbit's shouting the keg—'

'Mate, I can't help it.'

'The band's playing. Who's gonna sit in on drums?'

'What's wrong with Macka?'

'Ha ha. Did you tell the Major it's my birthday? The whole footy club's coming. Biggest party of the year.'

Ryan imagines using that argument to convince the Major to change his mind and give him leave. 'Family celebrations don't carry much weight around here.'

'Mum's gonna be disappointed.'

The pang hits. 'She'll get over it.'

Ryan hasn't been home for more than a year and he needs to get back to the farm. Not to catch up with his mates—he's not ready for the inevitable crap that's going to involve—but to see if his mum really is okay. She says she is; she says the money he's sending helps. But he can never tell over the phone.

'What about the old man? How's he doing?' The question sounds awkward and the line goes quiet.

'Doesn't say much,' Tommy says finally. 'Which is starting to scare the shit out of me, to be honest.' All the energy is gone from his brother's voice. He sounds older, the cockiness drained out of him with that one admission.

'Seeing me won't help.' Ryan clears his throat. 'Anyway, it won't matter if I'm not there. You'll be maggoted on two beers and won't even miss me.'

'No chance,' Tommy says. 'I can hold my piss better than you.'

Ryan scoffs. 'How would you know?'

'Been practising all year.'

A beat. 'You're joking, right?'

'Calm the farm, grandma. Just a few beers at the club on Saturday nights.'

'Who's buying?'

'Who do you reckon?'

Ryan rubs the back of his neck, stares down at a scrunched-up sock on the carpet. Macka's old man, Keith McKenzie. President of the Michellstone Footy Club. Supplier of booze and narcotics to underage kids for the past decade. Second-generation townie and renowned shithead.

'What'd I tell you about drinking with him?'

'Ease up, Ryno,' Tommy says, half-laughing. 'You can't pull the big-brother act when you're two states away. If you want to keep an eye on me, you better find a way to get home.'

Ryan shakes his head. The little turd is pushing his buttons. He hopes that's all it is, because the thought of Tommy turning into another broke farmer's kid smashed out of his head and throwing up behind the clubhouse every Saturday night makes him want to break something.

'Don't fret, Ryno. Party's a week away. Maybe the Major'll change his mind.'

Ryan thinks about the Major and the shitstorm he's weathering because Ryan went off-script on Wednesday. About the way the Major looks at him now, re-evaluating him.

Yeah. There's no chance Ryan's getting leave to go to South Australia for a party any time soon.

I doubt you'd recognise them or their methods.

It isn't Khan's words. It's the way she said it—off-hand, dismissive—as if there's no disputing the fact the Agitators Angie walked away from two years ago are completely different now. She knew things would change without her, but sabotage? Murder? Who have they let creep into the fold?

It's Friday night and the house smells of bolognese sauce. The front door is open, letting in the sounds of the early evening: the Bangladeshi girls across the street playing cricket in their front yard; one of the Tamatoa boys coming home with the bass thumping. A baby crying a few doors down.

Angie and Vee are on their first shiraz, dissecting the week, picking apart their favourite topics: Paxton Federation, the state of the economy and journos who aren't Angie. Jules is fussing at the stove, taking it all in but not saying much. Her skin is waxy under the harsh light of the rangehood. Angie knows she's still furious about the satchel incident. It was gutsy of Jules to come inside after her and she'd tell her that if she thought Jules wanted to hear it.

'Angie.' Vee taps a lacquered hot pink nail on the table to get her attention. 'If you want to know what's going on with that rabble, reach out to them.'

'I can't. You know that.'

'Rubbish.' Vee blows a wayward hair from her eyes. This

week she's sporting a splash of vivid purple through the black and the whole lot is twisted up on her head, the ends sticking out in all directions like a rare exotic flower. 'The Agitators are accused of attacking a building they knew Jules was inside. You have a right to demand answers.'

'That doesn't mean I can.'

Vee's been Angie's best mate since uni. She predates Jules and even Mike. She's been there for every step—and misstep—of Angie's adult life. Out here in suburbia is not her natural habitat, nor Angie's, but Angie and Jules can't afford to live any closer to the city—not since Mike died and certainly not since the work dried up—so Vee drives south to spend most Friday nights at their kitchen table. Unless there's a better offer elsewhere with a chance of sex.

'How long's it been since the last threat?' Vee asks.

Angie does a quick tally. 'Two months, three weeks, five days.' Whoever it is doesn't bother sending messages anymore, just a few seconds of impossible footage: a teenage arsonist without a flame.

'You'd think they would've made contact if they'd had anything to do with what happened this week.'

Jules is wiping her hands on a tea towel, pretending she's not listening.

Angie hasn't told Vee about the satchel or the bug. Or the fact the guy in the van was vaguely familiar. She will, but not yet. Even thinking about the driver brings a ripple of confusion. How does she know him? She's been waiting for Jules to bring it up but her daughter's been too focused on giving her the silent treatment. An argument would be so much easier. Angie knows how to handle conflict; this bruised sadness, not so much.

'It's no coincidence Jules was in the building when it happened,' Angie says.

Jules doubles her efforts with the tea towel, doesn't take the bait. Vee shakes her head.

'The only people outside this room who know what Jules can do are the ones blackmailing you. Sending in armed men after her is a big step up from threatening messages. Why go to all that trouble? I'd understand if you were leading the protest but you were here, well away from the Agitators like you're supposed to be.'

'Maybe Pax Fed made sure Jules had an interview the same day as the protest so they could set me up—'

'Oh come on, even you have to admit Pax Fed isn't the villain this time around.'

Angie raises her eyebrows, dangerous. 'Excuse me?'

Most people blanch in the face of an Angie De Marchi eyeballing. Not Vee. She's known her long enough to see through the snark. Some days Angie wishes she'd at least pretend to flinch.

'Claws in, Ange. Do you honestly believe they'd blow up their own building to get at you? You haven't written a word about them in two years.'

'You know they're behind the blackmail.'

'I don't have proof of that and neither do you. And let's face it, if they'd seen that footage, they'd be interested in a lot more than keeping you quiet.'

Angie scratches at the label on the wine bottle. 'Either way they've won again, haven't they? The media pack's already bought the story that I've been plotting against Pax Fed and that I'd put Jules in danger to strike at them. And now they're willing to believe I'd kill people to do it.' The label shreds under her fingernail.

'They have to believe it,' Vee says, gentler now. 'Otherwise they've dragged your name through the mud for no reason.'

Angie rolls the label scraps into a ball between her thumb and forefinger and flicks it into the sink. Her so-called mates in the media bought the lie that she incited Jules to set fire to the Pax Fed school lab so a gas main would explode. It was totally believable that Angie had escalated her attacks from printed accusation to criminal activity. After all, wasn't she the one leading the protests in the city every weekend? Calling the Paxton family to account for Mike's death? Accusing the army of being accomplices for the loss of soldiers in the name of shareholder profit?

Her career was dismantled in a single news cycle. Before the school fire she was a respected investigative journalist, founder of the Agitators and promoter of nonviolent resistance. Not to mention war widow. Afterwards she was a hypocrite and a criminal. A Bad Mother. No charges were laid against her but the damage was done. Her *mates* smeared her reputation and Pax Fed stepped in and blacklisted her around the country. Angie wore the lie then and she wears it now. It's that, or risk Jules being exposed.

'And here we are two years down the track and we're right back where we started: Jules is in the news, the Agitators are being blamed for an attack on Pax Fed and I'm prime suspect for pulling the strings from a distance.'

Jules flings the tea towel onto the bench. 'None of this would be our problem if I'd listened to you.'

Angie sits forward. *Finally.*

'This isn't your fault, Jules,' Vee says.

Jules simmers at Angie. 'You told me not to go.'

'Not because I thought *that* was going to happen. I knew they wouldn't be able to see past your last name, that they'd use you to get information about me.'

'And you were right as usual. You're all Bradford Paxton talked about.'

'You think I wanted that for you? I told you not to go because I didn't want those arseholes having the power to make you feel the way you do right now.'

Jules snatches back the tea towel from the bench and folds it down to a neat square. Angie spots a muscle twitch under her right eye the way it always does when Jules is smothering her anger and wishes she would just let it out. Angie wouldn't care if Jules blew the power in the entire house—even set the microwave on fire again. The kid needs to vent. Angie's convinced it's what feeds the charge beneath Jules' skin: year after year of repressed rage.

'Just say it.'

Angie raises her eyebrows. 'Say what?'

'That I'm a sell-out. I would've taken that job in a heartbeat if they'd offered it to me and you know it.'

'Of course you would,' Vee says, gently. 'A job's a job. No judgment here.'

'That's not what Mum thinks.'

Angie bangs down her glass and wine sloshes up the side. 'How do you think I feel that you had to even consider taking a job with them?'

'We have to pay our rent and eat.'

'I thought your Vet Affairs payments were going up?' Vee says.

'There's another hold-up in the Senate. Too many war widows and disabled veterans these days, Vee. We're a drain on the welfare budget.'

'Why didn't you tell me things were so tight? I'll ask around the department, see if there's any comms work we can outsource.'

'Yeah, that'll help your career.'

Vee's not long been in the job as Queensland State Manager for the Defence Department's Science and Technology Group. Her long-standing friendship with Angie means she's always working twice as hard as everyone else to prove her integrity.

'I don't care, Ange. I want to help.'

Angie pushes back from the table and drags her fingers through her hair. 'How did we get to this point? If it wasn't for the VA payments and Jules' shifts at the Souk, we'd be living on the bloody streets. I can barely scrounge enough underground freelance work to pay our rent. God, Mike would be appalled if he could see us.'

Jules' face crumples. She turns back to the stove, picks at a fleck of dried sauce on the stovetop. Wipes her cheek on her shoulder.

Shit.

Why did she drag Mike into the conversation? It never helps. It's too raw, his absence in their lives too big. More damage. It's all Angie ever seems to do.

Vee catches Angie's eye. She knows that look. They stare at each other for a full ten seconds before Vee gets up from the table and joins Jules.

'How's dinner?' She leans over the pot and waves the aroma in her direction. 'Smells delish.'

'I'm fine, Vee.'

'I know you are, sweets, but it's okay not to be. You don't always have to keep everything bottled up. Here.' Vee reaches back for the third glass on the table and holds it for Angie to fill. 'Have a drink with us.'

Jules' eyes slide to Angie. They haven't worked out if alcohol dulls the charge or makes it harder for Jules to keep track of it. Angie shrugs. 'Up to you.'

Jules accepts the wine and takes a small, measured sip. Puts the glass back on the table. 'Happy?'

Vee tucks a hair behind Jules' ear. Angie watches as Jules closes her eyes for a second. It needles her, reminds her of all the ways she's failed as a mother.

'Honey, I'll be happy when you and your bad-tempered mother get to live a normal life.'

Angie snorts. She has no idea what the future holds for her and Jules, but she's confident 'normal' won't be factoring into it.

Jules can't sleep. The last three days have left her wrung out and incapable of relaxing. The undercurrent is muted but constant, humming away like an annoying kid in the back of the class.

Her window is cracked open enough to let in the midnight air, and with it the promise of rain and a cooler day tomorrow. The afternoon cloud cover hasn't lifted and there's no hint of moon or stars. The only light comes from the TV in the lounge room. She rolls over and pulls the sheet up to her shoulder, burrows further into her pillow.

Vee's been gone for an hour but Angie's stayed up. She's out there watching the late night news, letting it flay her.

Jules exhales, rubs at burning eyes. None of this is new. Angie used to get like this before Mike died but it's worse now. For as long as Jules can remember, Angie's been fighting someone or something. Occupational hazard, her dad used to say. The difference was that her dad knew how to snap Angie out of it. Whether it was the obsessive moods—when she'd be fixated for days at a time hunting down a story lead—or those moments of despondency when she'd vent about the destruction of society by fearmongering governments, soulless corporations and narcissistic technology.

The whole planet is winding up, Mike. Can't you feel it? Something has to give.

Sometimes her dad would argue with Angie and sometimes

he'd ignore her. Other times he'd crack a joke and distract her. He always knew which approach would bring her back. Jules is still figuring it out.

It's only in the dark that she lets herself miss him.

She misses the sounds that were his alone. The laugh, those loud burps after every meal. His voice cracking a little when he talked about fallen soldiers; how he'd rage at the ref when the rugby was on TV. She misses his stubbled face and the way his eyes crinkled when he smiled. Mostly, though, she misses the hugs.

Her dad was built for endurance, for absorbing the recoil of high-powered weapons. Even after that first time she shocked him, when she discovered nobody else's body hummed the way hers did, he barely flinched. He wanted to understand how it worked so he could help her live with it, as if it was a speech impediment she had to overcome. She failed miserably. She set fires and burned him but he held her tight anyway. Coaxing her past the fear to try again.

She hadn't realised how much she relied on those hugs until they were gone.

Her throat closes and the first hot tear slips out. Jules fights the second. If Angie hears her crying it's only going to make things worse. The last thing she needs is her mother depressed. Or worse: angry. That's when she starts sending abusive messages to her old journo mates, ripping the scabs off those wounds too.

Jules lets out her breath and wipes her cheek on the pillow. Convinces herself she's in control, at least of herself. She rolls onto her back, squeezes her eyes shut and tries to will herself to sleep. No; her brain isn't interested. It's too busy picking over tonight's conversation.

The shooters must have been coming for her. If not, why were they there? They didn't hurt anyone and they didn't take hostages. Nobody's taken credit for the attack: not for the ram raid and explosion, not for the masked intruders. The one thing she does know is that Ryan was there because she was. He told her that much himself. How did she not notice it when she stepped into that lift? The way he reacted, the nervous spike in his energy. The fact he looked nothing like other Pax Fed employees. He had a *knife* in his boot for God's sake.

What was it he said to her?

You make people nervous.

She sees him on his knees in front of her, waiting to give her a boost out of the elevator car. Remembers the way he went still when she hiked up her skirt, his lips so close she could feel his breath on her thigh—

The charge buzzes and intensifies. Jules throws back the sheet and sits up, embarrassed by the flare of heat between her legs.

Get a grip.

She shakes the tension from her wrists and pushes hair from her eyes. The charge settles but doesn't completely subside. Jules swings her legs over the side of the bed, waits for the coolness of the floorboards to seep into her bare feet. Her reaction isn't a surprise, not really. She's had sex—once—with a cute gamer from school with dimples and low-slung jeans who asked her out every day for a month. They went to the movies twice before she took him home one Friday afternoon when Angie was out with Vee. He was gentle and grateful and it meant she could get 'it' out of the way without too much pressure.

Then there was a boy she really liked in the year above her, who asked her to the school formal. Total disaster. She hadn't meant to hurt Kyle. She quite liked it when his hand slipped under her dress while they kissed in a shadowy corner of the school hall—a little too much as it turned out. At least Kyle was so drunk that when she accidentally shocked him he thought it was static electricity. She hasn't come close to an intimate connection since.

Still.

76

There are more important things for her to think about than how Ryan's lips might feel on her thighs. Like, who sent him into that building? And what would he have done if she'd had less self-control and hurt him? Both are far bigger questions. And yet here she is sitting in the dark flushed with wanting.

Is this what it's like for everyone at eighteen? Or is it more intense for her because of the current? Jules blows out her breath. *This* is what happens when you don't have a life. One of these days she's going to have to find the courage to get one. Right now she'll settle for a drink of water.

She treads quietly on the way to the kitchen, hoping Angie has fallen asleep on the couch. But no, there she is propped up with cushions, fixated on the TV. Her face dances in the light of an ad showing a clutch of emaciated South Sudanese children.

'Mum, go to bed.'

'Wait for it,' Angie says, not turning her head.

Tom Paxton appears onscreen, waist-high in a field of golden wheat. Jules sighs and fills her glass from the tap. She's seen this ad a hundred times, heard her mother's response to it a hundred and one.

Angie points at the screen on cue.

'How does he think Third World countries are going to pay for all the GMO grain he wants to force our farmers to grow? Most famine is the result of corrupt regimes, not lack of opportunity or know-how to grow crops. Fix that, and half the world won't *be* starving.' Angie's in full flight, hands going. 'You know the Paxtons are going to get their legislation through, right? They're going to turn our farmers into fast-food producers or drive them off their land. Force them to buy their seed every year, not save any from the previous crop like farmers have been doing for thousands of years. And don't get me started on those fucking mutant sheep.'

It could be worse, it could be the ad for Bradford Paxton's greenhouse experiment in Pakistan. The one reliant on water from the desalination plant her dad died protecting.

Jules wipes the sink and heads for the couch. She lifts Angie's feet so she can sit down and rest them on her knees. Not for the first time she wishes she had something to offer other than a shock of electricity: why couldn't her freak ability be something that *soothed* people?

Angie is staring at Tom Paxton as the old man crushes a head of wheat between his palms and lets the breeze carry the husks away.

'When was the last time he appeared in public?'

Jules frowns. 'Isn't he supposed to be sick?'

'He didn't even make an appearance this week. He sent out the pitbull instead.' Angie means Peta Paxton, Tom's daughter. She's been the public face of the company for more than a year, although her push has been more towards military investment than the agricultural side of the business. News reports say Peta and Bradford are competing for control of the Pax Fed board, adding weight to rumours about Tom Paxton's declining health.

'Let's hope the old bastard is dying a slow and agonising death.'

'God, Mum, that's a terrible thing to say. You don't mean that.'

They've been gouged too deeply by death for her mother to wish that on anyone. Even Tom Paxton. Angie must be a little pissy—or at least pissy enough for the full measure of her bitterness to bubble up.

Angie sees her distaste and slumps back against the armrest. 'I'm sure Papa Paxton is fine. It's not like he can't afford the best medical treatment in the world.'

More emaciated children on the screen. This time it's a campaign for UNICEF. Jules squeezes Angie's shin.

'Come on, time for bed.'

Angie throws her head back and stares at the ceiling. 'I didn't tell you what happened down the plaza earlier this week,' she says.

Jules braces. Who'd she abuse this time?

'I'd come out of the supermarket and one of the UNICEF guys saw me. Somali kid, grew up in a refugee camp. Anyway, he's showing me the photos of the camps and telling me how "even the smallest contribution can help", so I get out my purse and scratch together what I can. Ten bucks—pathetic, right? But it's everything I had on me. And the kid apologises and gives me the usual spiel about how they can't take cash but I can give a monthly donation. Direct debit app. So I have to explain that I can't *afford* to commit to a donation every month because I can't guarantee we'll have it, even ten bucks.'

'Mum...'

'So I'm standing there in my clean clothes with my trolley half-full of groceries, looking at photos of emaciated babies, telling this guy I can't afford to help him. And next thing I'm frigging crying, so he starts apologising. How fucked up is that, Jules? *He's* apologising to *me*?'

'Yeah, Mum, it's totally fucked up.'

Angie lets her repeat the f-bomb, so Jules knows she's caught up in her story. Jules also knows she has to redirect the conversation right now because the image of her bulletproof mother crying in the middle of the plaza inexplicably terrifies her.

'Mum, who was the guy in the van?'

Her mother blinks and changes gears. Gathers herself into a more recognisable shape. 'No idea.'

'You knew him.'

'Yeah, but I don't know where from.'

'Where *could* it be from?'

'I'm forty-four, Jules. Do you know how many people I've met in my life?'

'Did you ever work with him? Was he a contact?'

Angie shakes her head. 'No.'

'What about the army?'

Her mother pulls back her legs and sits up, crossing her ankles. 'What makes you say that?'

A shrug. 'He spoke like Dad, like he's used to people doing what he says.'

They watch each other for a moment. Jules swallows, keeps the emotion in check.

'No,' Angie says finally. 'Your dad was wary of letting me loose on anyone connected with the military. I only ever met soldiers who served with him and that guy wasn't one of them.'

'But he used your middle name and he said it like he knew you.'

She blows out her breath. 'I know.'

'What about guys...before Dad?'

Angie's eyebrows go up, dangerous. 'You think I wouldn't remember someone I've slept with? You think there were that many?'

'No, I'm saying it was a long time ago.'

'Back in the days before your dad I spent more time in a holding cell than I did in nightclubs, so—' Her eyes go wide.

'What?'

She sits up straight, the anger dropping away. 'I know who he is.'

'Don't waste your breath.'

'Watch your tone, Major, I'm not one of your boys.'

'Then don't stand in my office peddling the same bullshit as Wednesday.'

'You were given a directive. You ignored the brief and took matters into your own hands—'

'And you failed to notify me of real and present dangers in that building. You can drive out here as often as you like but until you give me something closer to the truth, I'm not interested in anything that comes out of your mouth.'

The Major stares down at Peta Paxton. Why is this woman in his face again? Or more precisely, in his chest. She barely reaches his collarbone even with the blood-red stilettos. It doesn't stop her eyeballing him through thick mascara, all perfumed fury and too-tight jacket.

'I'm paying your wages, Major, I don't have to explain myself to you.'

He lifts one eyebrow, anger stirring for real this time. 'You might want to re-read the fine print. Your contract is only valid on the basis of full disclosure.'

She falters and he sees something shift in her eyes. *Good. Remember who you're talking to.*

'Do you still require our services?' His voice has sharper edges now, less emphasis on 'contractor' and more on 'military'.

Peta Paxton's nostrils flare and her eyes drop to his left calf. He catches her gaze, dares her to bring that into the discussion.

'No?' he says. 'Your two minutes are up.' The Major goes to his desk, opens the sit rep folder.

She stays put, arms folded and jacket bunching. It's ridiculous to have a woman like her in the same room as a man like him. What the hell is the army thinking? But he knows the answer all too well.

She takes a deliberate breath, stretches her neck to the right. Exhales and lets her arms drop to her sides.

'Bloody Bradford,' she mutters. 'I don't know what was going through his head. None of this would've happened if he hadn't let Julianne De Marchi into the building.'

The Major barks a short laugh. 'Eighteen, and she pulls off a coordinated assault like that? Impressive kid.'

'Oh come on, Major, you think it was dumb luck she was there? She and her mother are involved. They have to be. Why else would the girl apply for a job with us of all people?'

'Nobody held a gun to your head and forced you to give her an interview.'

'I told Bradford not to play games but he can't help himself. He hasn't moved beyond the fact Julianne got off on a suspended sentence for the school attack or that there wasn't enough evidence to charge her mother. I thought stymieing Angela's career was enough. It's certainly kept her quiet for the last couple of years. But no, Bradford wanted to be in the same room as the kid and watch her squirm.'

'Big man, your brother.'

'Bradford's compass is set differently to yours, that's all. He's always had a disconnect between his actions and how they're perceived.' It comes out smooth and practised, as if she's spent a lifetime explaining her brother to others. The Major makes a small noise in the back of his throat and Paxton mistakes it for an invitation to continue. 'Bradford was the kid in school biology whose frog wasn't quite dead but he dissected it anyway because that was the task. He did what had to be done. Didn't think about the frog—or how anyone would take it. Then he sat down and ate his lunch while half the class threw up. He wasn't cruel, Major, he was being pragmatic.'

The Major doesn't give a fuck about Bradford's pragmatism or his frog. 'Tell me about the special ops team.'

She blinks. 'The what?'

'The team that swept your building on Wednesday. They were military.' It's not a question. He's studied the rooftop footage and watched their retreat. It was a tactical operation.

'I didn't hire them,' she says.

'Someone sent them in. And someone gave them enough intel to plan an assault on two fronts. The power went off before the first explosion.'

'Are you suggesting I hired someone to blow up my father's building and terrorise our staff? Kill innocent bystanders on the street? Why did I need your team, then?'

The Major gives a pointed look, meaning to provoke her. 'They went after your servers,' he says. 'What did you lose?'

'Nothing relevant to your contract.' She looks around his office, at the maps and satellite photos pinned to his corkboard. 'It has to be Agitators. The federal police should've known this was coming. They're getting more funding than anyone else under the Civil Order Act, and they can't stop a delivery truck ramming the tower in broad daylight.'

The Major sits impassive, watching her. She tries to outstare him but can't hold his gaze for more than a few seconds. The arms go back across her chest.

'You don't agree? What's your theory, Major?'

He lets the seconds stretch out before he answers. She needs to learn to wait.

'It was a coordinated attack,' he says finally, speaking slowly like he's talking to a child. 'And that involves planning and collusion. There are two clear suspect groups: the Agitators and your company.'

She starts to react, stops herself.

'My unit is in a position to infiltrate the Agitators, see where that leads. You need to sort your own house.'

'We're still in business then?'

The Major doesn't miss the inflection in her voice. Peta Paxton needs him. There's more going on at Pax Fed than she's telling and he needs to determine if she's lying or being lied to. His team went in blind on Wednesday and he's not letting that slide.

'Only if you guarantee to give me any and all intel I ask for, and you leave me to run things at an operational level.'

'Of course.' There's no consideration to her response. She's telling him what he wants to hear; whatever it will take to keep him on board. This is what his career has come to: negotiating with rabbits who think they're wolves.

'You don't come back out here until this is done—unless I ask to see you—and you don't question my tactics or who I choose to use to infiltrate the Agitators. Agreed?'

Her eyes narrow. 'Who do you have in mind?'

'Are we in agreement?'

Peta Paxton's lips tighten. She wants to argue, but they both know she's already lost the advantage.

'Do I have a choice?'

Jules feels the charge stir as soon as she steps out the front gate. She shakes out her arms and takes a deep breath, walks faster.

'I told you,' Angie says, catching up.

'I'm fine.'

'Jules—'

'I'll settle down once I'm there.'

Jules has spent the past fifteen minutes arguing with Angie about accepting a shift at the Souk. Jules won. Or, more accurately, her mother backed down on the proviso Jules stays in the kitchen all day and Angie walks her to and from work.

At least there are no camera crews in the streets. Accusations about the Agitators are all over the news but the media's lost interest in Jules and Angie for the moment. Ruby—she of the ginger hair and jangly hoops—confirmed that Jules had a legitimate reason for being in the tower. The bigger news, though, was Peta Paxton breaking her silence yesterday to criticise the federal police for the lack of arrests despite questioning more than twenty protesters. None of it solves the issue of whether or not Jules was a target on Wednesday. If she still is.

Jules tries not to think about it as she heads up the street.

Ironically, the federal police surveillance Angie's always complaining about is a reassurance today. For a start there's no attempt to hide it, so either Nadira Khan is trying to rattle Angie or she wants it widely known the De Marchi house has eyes on it.

This morning it's the Kia people mover with the mismatched grey drivers panel parked opposite the Tamatoa house. The driver has the daily paper spread over the steering wheel, disposable coffee cup on the dash. He gives them a nod as Jules and Angie pass by. Angie gives him the finger.

They continue up the street under the pale morning sky. There's no sign of the storm promised for later in the afternoon. Jules and Angie turn the corner as a train flashes by, slowing for the station. They pass a group of Sudanese guys squatting and smoking under a gum tree outside the community health centre. Angie greets one of them by name and he gives her a toothy smile.

Croydon Road is blocked off for the mid-week street market. The air is already sweet with barbecuing pork, grilled corn and fish balls. The Congolese guy who sells newspapers from his pushbike at the station sometimes talks about a time, a decade or so ago, when there were jobs and opportunities, even for people like him who had broken English. But then the shit really hit the fan in the Middle East, and the war that spilled in every direction sent everyone to the wall. After that, the government pulled back on spending and the corporates stepped in. Even the CCTV cameras on every corner of the market are privately funded now.

Jules keeps her head down as they pass the top of the precinct, her fingertips itching. Too many unfamiliar faces on market day. Too many people more interested in her than they need to be. On the days she's here before the crowds, she'll walk the length of the produce stalls, asking about food she doesn't recognise: giant spiky fruits, beans as long as her arm and weird root vegetables. All from market gardens and neighbourhood backyards. None of it touched by Paxton Federation.

The Souk is on the next block. It's not an actual *souk*, it's a Middle Eastern supermarket/deli/kebab/pizza joint sandwiched between a Pacific Island grocery store and a second-hand bookstore. Azar, the Lebanese woman who owns the place, has an inexplicable soft spot for 'troubled' teens. The other kid who works at the Souk during the week did a stint in juvenile detention for a string of break and enters last year.

Jules pushes through the heavy plastic strips and gives the store a quick scan. Two women pick through a mound of flatbread on the trestle in front of the yogurt fridge, their husbands sipping coffee. Another regular, a thin-lipped blonde with four nose rings and tattoo of a cat under her ear, is tapping the glass of the cabinet, pointing to the honey-soaked pastries she wants. Azar looks up from behind the counter, paper bag in one hand, tongs in the other.

'You want coffee?' she asks Angie, and nods for Jules to go straight to work. Jules tries to catch Angie's attention to say goodbye but her mother's busy asking Azar if she's seen any reporters this morning.

Jules ducks behind the counter and into the kitchen. Washes her hands, ties on an apron and gets busy chopping onions.

Ten minutes later Angie's gone, hands full with a bag of yesterday's baklava. The urgency of the current eases almost as soon as the plastic strips slap back together. Jules lowers her guard a little and lets the steadier energy of the store slip around her, undemanding.

There's a constant stream of customers all morning. The Souk fills with aromas of chargrilled lamb and garlic; slow-roasted tomatoes and melted cheese. The air hums with chatter, most of it in English, occasional snatches of Arabic. Jules settles into a quiet rhythm, comfortable in the familiarity.

It's around midday when it changes.

Jules is slicing tomatoes when she feels it: a stab of agitation. She glances up, sees a guy in a black T-shirt and jeans at the counter, cap pulled down low over unruly blondish hair. Three-day growth. He doesn't look out of place, but his energy's all wrong for the Souk. He picks up a menu and studies it, his face half-turned from her. She reaches for another tomato, absently positions it on the chopping board. There's something familiar about him—

He shifts his weight and looks right at her.

Ryan.

The current surges. Jules catches it a heartbeat before it leaves her, crushing the tomato with the effort it takes to reel it in. Ryan holds her gaze for a long second before his eyes drop back to the menu.

He wasn't surprised to see her here: he came looking.

She picks at the pulpy mess on the chopping board. Has she made somebody else *nervous*? What about the other bloke—the driver who knows Angie—is he here?

Jules wipes juice and tomato seeds from her fingers, tries to remember what she's supposed to be doing. A quick glance—Ryan's gone from the counter. She steps sideways so she can see around the chewing gum stand. He's sitting at a table near the window, his back to the spice display. He cracks a bottle of water and takes a long drink. It's only when he's wiping his mouth with the back of his hand that his eyes slide in her direction again—and away almost immediately.

Azar brings over the docket for his order, pegs it to the twine strung across the bench and heads out to clear tables. Lamb, no onion. Jules has made hundreds of kebabs in the five months she's worked here but right now her mind has gone blank. *Focus*. She slaps down the flatbread. Hummus, lamb, tomato, lettuce—no onion (who doesn't have onion?)—tabouli, tzatziki. She puts the kebab under the press to warm it, takes a minute to steady her pulse. Alfoil. Plate. Serviettes. She stares down at the finished kebab for a second, heart racing.

Why is he here?

There's only one way to find out. Jules picks up the plate as Azar comes around the counter.

'I'll take this one,' Jules says.

Azar frowns. 'Your mother says you should stay in the kitchen today.'

'I didn't know Mum was in charge here.'

Azar gives her a flat look. 'Do you know that young man?'

Jules shakes her head and moves past Azar before she loses her nerve, willing her hands to steady.

Ryan watches her approach. He looks relaxed, arm resting on the back of the next chair, but Jules can feel from here how wired he is. She slides the plate across the table to him without breaking eye contact.

'Hey,' he says, like it's no big deal he's turned up at her work. Like he didn't throw her in the back of a van six days ago. He sits forward and drags the kebab closer. 'Thanks.'

Jules presses her nails into her palms, grapples with the charge. 'Everyone in here knows me.' She keeps her voice low. 'And there's a CCTV camera right outside.'

He blinks and then his eyes widen. 'Bloody hell, I'm not here to hurt you.' He looks around to see if anyone overheard. 'I wanted to make sure you're okay.'

'Why wouldn't I be?'

'Because you said the Pax Attack was about you.'

She keeps staring, her brain attempting to change gears. 'That's why *you* were there, wasn't it—because of me?'

'I had no idea that other stuff was going down.' His energy pushes at her but it's less agitated now. He picks up the kebab. 'You make this?'

Words desert her. What is he *doing* here?

Ryan waits a beat and then peels back the foil and takes a huge bite. Hummus runs down his chin and he wipes it away with his thumb. Jules should get back to the kitchen, back behind the safety of the counter. There's every chance Ryan is lying about not being here to hurt her. What would Angie do in this situation?

It's a no-brainer.

'Who do you work for?'

Ryan points at his full mouth. Shrugs.

'Not Pax Fed and not Agitators,' she prompts.

He shakes his head, keeps chewing.

'Cops? Feds?'

Another headshake, but he's watching her from under his cap like he's trying to figure something out. His eyes are a darkish shade of amber. Unusual.

'Why do I make people "nervous"?'

He swallows his mouthful. 'Ah...'cause you blow shit up?'

'Ryan'—he seems startled when she says his name—'why are you here?'

He puts down the kebab, runs his tongue across his teeth, checking for food. 'I told you.'

'You weren't concerned about me in that laneway.'

'Just doing my job.'

Jules thinks about how he acted in the back of that van, how he admitted he didn't know where they were going.

'The guy who was driving, he's your boss?'

Ryan considers the question. 'Maybe.'

'Did you know that he and my mum go way back?'

'Is that right?' He grabs the kebab and takes another bite but can't hide his surprise. Jules waits. He must want to know.

'Good feed,' he says, his mouth half-full. He uses the serviette to wipe his chin again as he chews. 'What happened to the taser?'

She looks out the window. There's a marked cop car slowly passing by.

'Did you toss it?'

Jules catches Azar watching them as she rings up another order and doesn't miss the look she gets. Jules moves to the next table and scoops up scraps of alfoil and paper left behind from the last customer. She doesn't want to talk about what happened in the laneway. She's a terrible liar.

'De Marchi—'

'We found the bug.'

Ryan falters. 'The what?'

'That thing in the bag with my shoes. The bug, tracking device...whatever you call it.'

He's looking at her but his mind's elsewhere. Did he not know about that either?

'Where is it now?'

'The feds have it.'

Something vibrates under the table. Ryan pulls out a flexi-phone—the latest model, which surprises her. He snaps it flat to answer it. 'What's up?'

Jules picks at scraps of lettuce next to his plate so she has an excuse to linger and listen.

'The guy in the Kia?' Ryan's eyes flick to her. 'Where?...Shit. Did he see you?...Okay. Be out in five.'

'The feds are watching our place,' Jules says as he disconnects. She's trying to rattle him but he's not fazed by the news.

'It's not only the cops. My mate saw the guy from—'

He stops as the plastic strips smack in the doorway and two local beat cops walk in, vests on, handguns at their hips and radios strapped to their chests. The woman's only been stationed locally for a month or so, but the younger one is Kyle, her date for that ill-fated formal.

'Hey Julianne.' He takes off his cap and roughs up short dark hair.

'Officers,' Jules says. Kyle's partner nods at Jules and keeps going to the counter.

Kyle tucks the cap under his arm, plants his feet. 'You and your mum holding up okay?' He's only six months out of the academy and there's no trace of the schoolboy these days; he's all cop now. He has to be: you can't be half-hearted if you want to work this community.

Jules glances at Ryan. He's sitting sideways like he's ready to bolt. His eyes flick from Kyle to the doorway, a serviette crushed in his palm.

'Khan giving you a hard time?' Kyle asks Jules.

'She's okay.'

The constable glances at Ryan, picks up on the weird vibe. 'Everything okay here?'

The tension from Ryan's side of the table comes at Jules in steady waves. Whatever Ryan was doing at Pax Fed on Wednesday, he doesn't want the cops to know.

She could do it: she could tell Kyle that Ryan was there, what happened afterwards. Jules knows Kyle, trusts him as much as she trusts any uniform cop. But Ryan doesn't seem like he'd go easily. The last thing Azar needs is a guy getting shot in front of the spice display for resisting arrest. Plus, Jules wants to know what his mate told him on the phone. She looks Ryan in the eye as she says, 'It's fine.'

Kyle moves closer anyway. 'You live around here?'

Ryan stands up. 'Nah, mate. Passing through.'

'Got ID on you?'

Ryan pats his back pocket, pulls out a twenty and shrugs. 'Wallet's at home.' He's taller than Kyle, broader across the chest and shoulders. And fit. If Ryan decides to run, there's no chance Kyle will be able to stop him without using a weapon. Ryan nods at his empty plate. 'Stopped in for a feed. Recommend the lamb kebab.'

Kyle gives him a tight smile. 'I know what's good here, mate.'

Ryan checks the street outside. He's about five seconds away from walking out the door. Jules moves in to clear the table, blocking his path. She needs to know what was said on the phone.

'You want anything else? Azar makes amazing namoura.'

Ryan's near enough to grab her if that's what he came to do. Her mouth is dry, her heart insistent against her ribs. She holds his gaze, wills him to stay. A tiny line creases his forehead.

'Maybe next time.' He steps around her before she can think of something else to say. 'Constable.' He nods at Kyle and disappears through the plastic strips.

'Anything I need to know about him?' Kyle asks, hand on his radio, ready.

Jules shakes her head. She goes to the window, presses her cheek against the glass to see up the street.

There's no sign of Ryan. He's gone, and so has her chance to find out who he is and who else is watching her and Angie.

Ryan is on his second lap of the bush track, trying to work the tightness from his shoulders and legs.

It's overcast and almost dusk, but there's enough light to finish the circuit. He's running through the melaleuca forest in footy shorts, no shirt. Sweat trails down his spine and his runners pound the hard-packed dirt track. He jogs without music, preferring the lorikeets and cicadas, still learning the sounds of this place even after a year.

Ryan goes over the conversation with Julianne De Marchi in his head again, trying to figure out why she didn't say anything to her cop mate. She wanted him to hang around, he's pretty sure of that much, but—

'Walsh.'

Ryan flinches and almost runs off the track.

It's the Major. The lorikeets are screeching so loudly Ryan didn't hear him jog up from behind.

'Keep moving.' The Major runs past and Ryan has to lift his pace to keep up. He's wearing skins and a muscle tee, moving better than Ryan would have expected given the rumours about his injuries in Syria. There's talk he's missing a foot, but if he is the replacement must be next-generation tech.

Ryan's never seen him running out here before.

It's a week of firsts.

'Anything you want to tell me, private?' The Major keeps

his eyes on the track as they jog shoulder to shoulder between paperbarks.

Shit.

The Major knows where he's been today—they wouldn't be having this conversation otherwise. Might as well be up front about it.

'I checked in on Julianne De Marchi this morning,' he says between breaths.

'Who gave you that order?'

'Nobody, sir. It's my day off.'

'Why was Waylon with you?'

Ryan brushes away an insect. Again, no point lying. 'Keeping me company.'

The Major being on the track with him is making his balls shrink a little. It's not normal. Nothing about the past week has been normal. He's seen enough of the news to know the blonde who was yelling at the Major is Peta Paxton. Has his visit today caused more strife? Ryan's never been one to fill a silence but he needs to give the Major something.

'Sir, that bloke with the man bun was sniffing around. From the Agitators.'

'Xavier? Sniffing around where?'

'Outside the De Marchi house, he did a drive-by. Waylo recognised him—didn't get seen himself, though.'

'Where were you?' The Major's breathing is steady, measured. The first rumble of thunder rolls through the clouds above them.

'At a kebab shop. De Marchi was there.'

'Which one?'

'I don't know, the one on—'

'Which De Marchi.'

Oh. 'Julianne.'

'And?'

'She wasn't happy to see me. But she could've set two local coppers on me and she didn't.'

The Major slows his pace. It gives Ryan a chance to catch his breath and get in front of the conversation.

'Sir, permission to ask a question?'

The Major says nothing for a few paces and then: 'Granted.'

'Why did we take De Marchi home?'

'It wasn't safe for her in the city.'

'How did you know she'd be safe at home?'

'The feds were already on their way to her house when we scooped her up.'

'Yeah, but...' Ryan's not used to having to think so hard before he speaks and it's tougher on the move. 'Why was it our problem?'

'Did you want her taken down by a paramilitary unit?'

'No, but...'

'Spit it out, Walsh.'

'Sir, how did you know she'd be with me when I came out?'

The Major glances his way. 'She told you about the tech in the satchel.'

'Yes, sir.'

'Then don't ask me questions you know the answer to.'

They break free of the trees and the barracks appears on the next rise. Ryan feels the first drop of rain on his cheek and decides to push his luck.

'Was it there to listen in on me or De Marchi?'

'Both.' The Major uses his T-shirt to wipe sweat from his neck as he runs. 'I needed to know what was going on in that building. And then your chivalry meant we could get surveillance into De Marchi's house without having to deal with feds.'

Chivalry. Ryan is confident that's not how Julianne De Marchi is describing his behaviour on Wednesday. He thinks about what else she told him this morning.

'De Marchi says you know her mother.'

Ryan catches the slightest change in the Major's expression but it's gone before he can figure it out.

96

'What else did she say?'

'Not much. That you two went way back.'

'Have you repeated that to anyone?'

Ryan doesn't answer. Why didn't he leave it alone?

'You talked to Waylon,' the Major says. Not a question. 'You two are a pair of old women.'

'Sir, nobody knows but us.'

The Major doesn't speak or look his way as they cover the last fifty metres, pushing Ryan to a sprint past the climbing ropes. A fat drop of rain lands on Ryan's forehead. The air trembles with another rumble of thunder. The Major slows and then stops beside the gym to stretch his calves.

The door to the barracks opens and Waylo appears, flexiphone in hand. Ryan immediately starts forward. He needs to give his mate a heads-up.

'Stand your ground, Walsh.'

Ryan stops but widens his eyes at Waylo. Waylo keeps coming, more intent on the Major than him.

'Sir.'

The Major straightens from his stretch. 'What is it, private?'

Waylo holds up his phone. 'Xavier took the bait. I'm in.'

The Major scrubs a palm against his beard and rests his hands on his hips. Looks from Waylo to Ryan and back again, calculating.

'Right-oh boys. It's time for a chat.'

The storm is in full swing when the power goes.

Jules has already lit tea lights in jars around the kitchen, so the house isn't plunged into total darkness when it happens but she flinches anyway. Angie keeps tapping away on her laptop, barely registering the change. Jules checks the street through the front window and the darkness is a strange relief; theirs is not the only house in blackness. She closes the blinds and goes back to the kitchen.

'Anything useful?' she asks, raising her voice to be heard over the rain. It's coming in sideways, hitting the house in sheets.

'Not a thing.'

The free government network is online again and her mum's been tracking chatter about the Agitators since the Pax Attack, trying to work out who else is 'in play', as her dad used to say. They can't afford a private connection, which means Khan and her team are monitoring every keystroke. Angie's found conspiracy theories but nothing credible. Nothing to explain why someone would attack Pax Fed Tower because Jules was inside.

And then there's Ryan's visit this morning.

Jules phoned Angie as soon as he left to warn her that someone other than the feds was watching them. It was enough for Angie to stake out the Souk for the rest of Jules' shift. Hardly ideal, but less stressful for both of them in the long run. Plus, Azar likes having Angie working away in a corner. She says it makes the place feel more *urbane*.

Thunder shakes the house stumps and the kitchen is bathed in a flash of brightness. Energy crackles at Jules' fingertips, stings in a way that leaves no doubt she'll need to let it go again soon.

She peers into the pitch-black yard as the wind buffets the window over the sink. She grounded the current out there when the storm was gathering, but it rebuilds much quicker when the air is charged like this.

Jules is filling a glass from the tap when she hears the banging. She and Angie lock eyes. It comes again and there's no doubt: someone's at the laundry door.

'Wait,' Angie mouths in the candlelight, already on her way to the kitchen bench. She slides out the second drawer, grabs the biggest knife they own.

'What are you doing?' Jules whispers. 'Call Khan.'

Angie shakes her head. She moves down the hallway towards the laundry, treading lightly even though there's no chance anyone outside will hear her over the storm. Jules grabs her mum's old smart phone from the bench, grateful for the shadows. She feels her way to the laundry, vaguely makes out her mother standing by the back door. They wait.

The banging comes again. Three hard thumps.

'Who is it?' Angie demands. There's no sign of the woman who wept in the plaza. This is all ball-breaking Angie De Marchi.

'Ryan.'

Jules' pulse trips. 'What do you want?'

'To get out of this rain, for a start.'

He must be soaked. There's shelter over the landing and the stairs but it's not much protection in weather like this.

'We want to talk.'

We?

Angie yanks the door open before Jules can ask. Ryan's there, a hulking silhouette. He doesn't push past Angie to get inside; he simply stands with his back braced against squalling rain.

A series of flashes illuminate the backyard. Two men are at the bottom of the stairs in hooded waterproofs. One's dark-skinned, youngish, and the other is tall enough to be the van driver. The fleeting sight sends a jolt through Jules but she keeps the charge to herself. It hurts, leaves her hands feeling wasp-stung.

'Leave your knife behind,' Angie says to Ryan.

'I don't have a knife on me. Come on, it's friggen cyclonic out here.'

'I want to see all of you. Jules, get a light.'

'No.' It's definitely the driver; Jules recognises his voice. 'Not until we're inside.'

Rain gusts into the laundry, soaks the front of Jules' shirt and jeans.

'If we wanted to hurt you we wouldn't have knocked,' the driver says.

Angie shifts her weight, hesitates another second; backs away from the door. 'Give them space.'

'Mum—'

Ryan lets the other two come in first. As soon as he follows, the wind catches the door and slams it shut. There's another flash of lightning—the three men are barely a metre away, soaking wet—and thunder peals across the sky. Jules can't separate their energy from the raging storm and has no idea what mood they've brought inside.

'What do you want?' Angie says again.

'Any chance of a towel?' Ryan asks.

'Let's see how long you're staying. If I have to ask a third time, it's going to be a short visit.'

'Angela.' It's the driver. 'I need your help to infiltrate the Agitators.'

A beat. This guy has a knack for throwing Angie off balance.

'Why?'

'Because a manipulative little grub has turned your protest group into murderers.'

'You have proof?'

'Enough.'

Jules doesn't need to see Angie's face to know her mother's going to need more than that.

'Who *are* you guys?' Jules directs the question at Ryan, but in the darkness the driver thinks she's asking him.

'Army,' the driver says.

Angie clicks her tongue. 'Bullshit.'

'Maybe not the army you'd recognise, but we're army just the same.'

'Meaning?'

'Think corporatised.'

Jules absorbs the news. Ryan's a *soldier*? A staccato flash brightens the laundry for a long second and his eyes find hers.

'Who sent you to Pax Fed Tower?' she asks when the laundry's in darkness again.

Silence. She touches the mobile in her back pocket, makes sure it's there. It's rigid and out of date but it works. She's ready to drag Angie into the toilet, lock the door and call Khan if this goes bad.

'Answer the question or get back outside.' Angie positions herself in front of Jules. 'Who hired you?'

Another gust of wind shakes the house.

'Peta Paxton.' The driver says her name like he's pulling a pin from a grenade.

It's a full two seconds before Angie detonates. 'Are you serious? Pax Fed drags Jules in for an interview to humiliate her and hires the fucking *army* to stalk her while they're at it?'

'We don't work for Paxton Federation. This is a short-term contract, fully sanctioned by the brass. Keeping an eye on Julianne was a secondary objective on Wednesday.' He makes no attempt to push further into the house. 'If we're staying long enough for an interrogation can we get out of these jackets?'

Jules tightens her grip on the doorjamb, tries to understand what it means that these strangers kept her safe on Wednesday. She comes up blank. Outside, the sky stutters and the knife glints in Angie's hand.

'Put them in the tub on your right,' she says. 'Towels are in the cupboard on your left.' There's jostling and rustling as the soldiers peel off rain-soaked coats. They hit the laundry tub with a wet slap. 'Wait here.'

Angie clamps tacky fingers around Jules' wrist and leads her down the hallway and into the candlelit kitchen.

'I'm calling Khan,' Jules whispers, sliding the mobile from her jeans.

'Not yet.' Angie snaps shut the kitchen blinds and gestures for Jules to join her by the table. 'Okay,' she calls. 'Lock the laundry door behind you and come out slowly.'

The driver emerges, hands out in front to show he's not armed. His shirt is plastered to him and his buzz-cropped scalp and beard glisten with rain. There's definitely something wrong with that left ear.

'By the stove.'

He sees where she means and nods. Behind him is the guy Jules hasn't seen before tonight. He's towel-drying thick black hair, his bare feet leaving wet footprints on the floorboards. Right now his primary interest is Angie and that knife.

Ryan comes in last. He nods at Jules as if he's spotted her at a party. The black T-shirt he had on today clings to his chest and shoulders and his hair is slicked back from his face. He's carrying one of the threadbare towels they keep for mopping up after storms. He waits for the driver to look his way before he tosses it over.

The three soldiers stand with their backs to the stove, feet apart and shoulders square. At attention. They fill the kitchen alcove. Angie and Jules are on the other side of the table, leaving

102

themselves a clear run to the front door if they need it. Angie might be impulsive, but she's not foolish.

'Names,' Angie says. 'Real ones.'

'Major Luka Voss,' the driver says. He gives his head a quick rub with the towel, not breaking eye contact with Angie. 'Former commanding officer of Security Detail 15 out of Syria, now with SECDET Q18. These two are part of my command. Julianne has been in the company of Private Ryan Walsh, *twice* now'—Jules catches the censure—'and this is Private John Waylon.'

Private Waylon lifts a hand in greeting. Ryan is waiting for something from Jules—a word, a sign of recognition—but she leaves him hanging.

'And we've met before,' Major Voss says.

Angie puts the knife on the bench, her fingers resting on the hilt. 'I remember: Brisbane Watch House during the Syrian crisis protests. It was the middle of winter in a blackout. You kept me warm, if memory serves me correct.'

Jules blinks. Angie told her this guy was arrested with her at a blockade. Her mother didn't mention anything about sharing body heat.

'Tell me,' Angie says. 'How do you go from fighting for refugee rights to fighting in the war that creates them?' But then she smiles without humour as understanding dawns. 'You were already a soldier.'

'Plain-clothes cop,' the Major says, unapologetic. 'Joined the army a month later and if we'd succeeded when I signed up, the refugee crisis would've been sorted.'

'But you didn't succeed.'

'No.'

Angie eyes him up and down. 'Why aren't you still over there? What happened to turn you into Peta Paxton's bitch?'

Ryan and Waylon exchange a startled glance.

'A suicide bomber drove a car into a market in Aleppo. I lost forty-two soldiers, half my left leg and the best part of an ear.'

Jules can't remember him limping when he came into the kitchen. Angie looks him over again, slower this time. She lingers on the mangled tissue where his earlobe should be.

'Forty-two men and women…that's a platoon.'

'Near enough. And sixty-two Syrians died on their way to prayer.' The Major's voice gives nothing away but Jules doesn't miss his stranglehold on the towel. 'SECDET Q18 is a trial counter-terrorism unit. We're given corporate ops when they align with our own objectives.'

'Really? And how do your objectives fit with Pax Fed?'

'Peta Paxton wants to protect her company from acts of terrorism. We want to infiltrate and dismantle terrorist cells— foreign and domestic.' He levels his gaze at Angie. 'Which is why we're here.'

Jules watches Angie take a measured breath—the equivalent of a ceasefire—and her fingers leave the knife hilt. She raises her eyebrows at Jules; it's the first time they've had eye contact since coming back into the kitchen. Jules gives a small nod, reassuring Angie she's got the current under control.

'What was wrong with using the front door?' Angie asks.

'Aside from your federal cop mates parked outside? You've got other admirers.'

'So I hear. Who?'

'James Xavier. He tops our list of suspects for Wednesday's attack.'

'Never heard of him.'

'He keeps a low profile but he's leading the Agitators these days. Have you had recent contact from the group?'

'No. Why would he be watching me?'

The Major wipes his hands on the towel, tosses it on the bench. Jules resists the urge to pick it up. 'Could be he's unhappy you're getting the credit for the attack and he's curious about who's giving you attention.'

The night lights up again, forcing its way through the blinds. Jules finds Waylon studying her. He has soft eyes; a kind mouth.

'Was that mob always so feral?' he asks her.

Jules remembers the frenetic energy blasting up Queen Street. 'Not like on Wednesday.' She thinks about the discarded clothes in the back of the van and the stink of scorched corflute. 'Were you at the protest?' she asks Ryan.

'Briefly.' He gestures to his mate. 'Waylo was approached by Xavier.'

Waylon nods. 'He was expecting that blast.'

'And today he made contact,' the Major says. 'Waylon's going with them to South Australia. They leave for Port Augusta tomorrow.'

'The nuclear plant? There's already hundreds of protesters camped outside the front gate. Why bother?'

'Our intelligence indicates Xavier's ambitions have moved beyond protesting. The plant's an obvious target.'

Angie stiffens. 'It's a *nuclear* reactor. The Agitators aren't going to do anything that risks radioactive fallout—what do you think the protesters are doing down there in the first place? They want to shut down the place, not ramp up the risk.'

'Are you willing to bet lives on that?'

She chews on the Major's words. 'If your boy's in, why do you need me?'

'I don't know who's funding Xavier or who else is involved. I don't know his agenda and I want to stop him before he kills more civilians. Waylon's job is to gather intel. If the Agitators are on board for whatever Xavier's got planned, we need someone with influence there to undermine him.' A drop of water slides around the edge of the Major's damaged ear and drips onto his T-shirt. 'Help Waylon get a foothold in the Agitators,' he says to Angie. 'Win back that rabble. Nobody's going to say no to Angela De Marchi, no matter how much of a grip Xavier thinks he's got on them.'

Jules sees it in Angie's eyes. The fire, the urge to be back with the Agitators. The need to be back in the fight.

And then it's gone. 'I can't.'

The Major's eyebrows twitch. 'I thought you'd jump at the chance to protect your people.'

Angie glances at Jules. The storm rages on outside, rain lashing the kitchen window. 'Apparently they're not mine anymore.'

'I'm offering you a job, Angela. Two birds. One stone.'

'You want to pay me—'

Glass shatters behind them in the lounge room.

Jules spins around to see the timber blind ripped aside. A black cylinder *thunks* onto the floor and Ryan lunges for her.

'Get down!'

Ryan hauls Jules around the table, all adrenaline and instinct. He pushes her to the floor and shields her with his body, clapping hands over her ears as the stun grenade goes off.

The flash is blinding and the *bang* fills his head, leaves him muzzy for a few seconds. Phosphorus burns his eyes and nose, forces its way down his throat.

'De Marchi,' he rasps, his eyes and nose instantly streaming. Her hands are over his now, pressing his palms tight against her ears. Rain-soaked wind rips in from outside and he blinks to clear his vision, still stained from the flash. There's more shadow than light but a candle flickers, throwing a fuzzy halo over the kitchen table. Ryan's head rings but he's been through dozens of blasts like this, knows how quickly his eyes and ears will recover; Jules and her mum are going to be a mess for a while longer. He needs to get moving because whoever threw that canister is coming.

Ryan rolls away from De Marchi, pulls the pistol from his ankle holster. His eyes sting but he can see enough to make out movement.

'Cover the back,' the Major orders. He's already up and moving, a watery shadow dissolving into the darkness.

Angie coughs and gags. 'I can't see—'

'Stay down,' Ryan hisses over his shoulder.

Something splinters at the back of the house. The laundry

door. He keeps low and heads in that direction, one hand on the wall to feel his way. Aren't the feds supposed to be parked outside?

A quick tap on his shoulder. Waylo is crouched beside him, ready. Knowing he's there steadies Ryan a little. They're armed, dosed and trained—maybe not for exactly this scenario but at least they're not pissing their pants.

The wind howls through the house, battering blinds over the broken lounge room window. Ryan clicks off the pistol safety and wipes his streaming nose against his shirt. Tries to blink away the grit behind his eyeballs. He lays a palm flat on the floorboards hoping to feel the intruders moving about in the laundry, but the whole place is creaking and shaking with the storm. Are they already up the back stairs and inside? He presses his spine flat against the hallway wall. What are they waiting for?

Another crash, this time at the other end of the house. The front door's gone too. Ryan hesitates. Was the laundry a diversion? Which way are they coming in? Should they stay here or go back and cover the lounge and kitchen?

Fuck it.

He launches himself up and into the laundry—

And right into a rifle barrel.

'Drop it.' The voice is muffled, controlled.

Ryan freezes, squints through bleary eyes. In a flash of lightning he catches a glimpse of the bloke holding the rifle, sees enough to know he's wearing a lightweight gas mask.

'Drop your weapons. Both of you.'

Crap. Ryan was hoping Waylo was still in the hallway out of sight.

Ryan raises his hands, palms out and finger well clear of the trigger, heart smashing against his ribs.

'Lose it, or lose your kneecaps,' the mask warns.

Ryan lets the pistol clatter to the tiles. Waylo's weapon follows half a second later.

'Hands on your heads. Back it up, slowly.'

Something crashes in the main part of the house. The Major?

'Eyes on me, mate.'

Ryan backs down the hallway. In the muted light he can make out a military-style vest and weapon holster. It's the same crew as Wednesday, has to be.

There's scuffling in the lounge now, swearing.

'Aaarggh, fuck!'

A shot echoes through the house. Ryan's pulse spikes. More crashing. A strangled cry, definitely female.

De Marchi.

Another shot...and then stillness. Even the wind drops.

'Clear?'

A grunt from the lounge room. 'Are your targets secure?' A new voice, male. Older.

'Yes.'

'Put a bullet in them if that changes.'

Ryan keeps moving backwards, barely feeling his legs.

'Stop. Turn around and get on your knees.'

Ryan does as ordered—and freezes.

A bull-necked bloke wearing a gas mask has a handgun to Julianne De Marchi's head. He's using her as a shield, one meaty arm clamped across her chest. Her eyes are red and streaming, unfocused from the blast. He can see from here how much she's shaking.

There's movement on the floor by the fridge: Angie is clutching her arm and gasping for breath. Her fingers are wet with blood and her face is streaked with tears and snot from the gas. The bull-neck takes the gun from Julianne long enough to point it at her mother. 'Give me an excuse to put another one in you.'

This is really happening.

The rifle barrel presses into the back of Ryan's neck. The gunman kicks out the back of his left leg and his new knee breaks the fall. Pain shoots up Ryan's thigh and into his hip. Waylo lands beside him, fingers clasped behind his head.

Ryan's pulse thuds in his ears. Is this how it ends for them?

Did he go through all that angst with his old man to leave the farm, all the tears from his mum, to die on a stranger's floor without a whimper?

He thinks of Tommy and his mum laughing at the kitchen table; his old man grinning at him from the boundary line. A sharp stab of regret. Why didn't he sort out that mess with his dad when he had the chance?

Get your shit together, Ryno.

'You good?' Ryan's gunman asks the bull-neck.

Ryan realises Angie's knife is jutting from bull-neck's left thigh. That explains the bullet in her arm. Bull-neck returns the muzzle of his weapon to Julianne's temple, pushes it into her skin. Rage stirs in Ryan's chest, hot and dangerous.

'Let the girl go, or your mate here gets one to the brain.'

The Major.

He's by the front door, so deep in shadow Ryan missed him first time around. He's got a third gunman pinned against the wall, a pistol jammed hard against the top of his head. The gas mask is gone and Ryan can see buzz-cut grey hair, a thick forehead.

'Hold your position,' the third gunman says. His face is mashed against the plasterboard. 'Wait for my command.'

Ryan's heart jackhammers. He needs to get that gun away from Julianne's head. Fragments of training pierce the panic, sharpening him. He risks a sideways glance at Waylo and they share brief eye contact. He's good to go. The guy behind them is bulkier and older than them—Ryan can tell that much by the way he moves—but if they can get his rifle, they can tip the balance in this standoff.

'Jules,' Angie rasps from the floor. 'Let it go.'

Ryan looks at Julianne's empty hands. Let what go?

'Mum…' It's barely a whisper, but it's enough for the bull-necked gunman to tighten his grip on her.

'Protect yourself.'

'What is she talking about?' Bull-neck slides his finger to the trigger.

'Jules,' Angie urges.

'I can't—'

'Do it!'

Ryan is watching when it happens: a sharp crackle and a flash so bright he has to squint against it. But it doesn't come from the sky. It comes from Julianne.

Bull-neck jerks on the spot and drops the gun without uttering a sound. Julianne squirms out from under his grip before he drops to the floor. Ryan's brain takes a second to understand and then the smell of burnt human flesh hits.

Julianne De Marchi just electrocuted the guy with her bare hands.

Ryan reacts on instinct. He ducks out from under the rifle barrel, spins on his knees and punches the gunman behind him in the gut. It's a sharp, targeted strike, and the bloke drops like a bag of shit. Ryan's vaguely aware of Waylo scooping up the rifle and Julianne scrambling for Angie.

Ryan springs from the floor, rips off the gunman's mask and smashes his fist into a flat nose, once, twice, before the guy's eyes roll back into his head. The impact hurts like hell but the brutality makes him feel stronger. He pats down the gunman: a hunting knife goes inside Ryan's boot, a handgun in the back of his jeans. The Major pistol-whips the older gunman across the back of the head and the big man buckles. He catches him before his head meets the floorboards.

They've got control—unless there are more men in the yard.

Ryan shoves aside the kitchen table to get to Julianne. She's cowering on the floor with Angie, her body angled to shield her mum. 'Come on.' He reaches for her and changes his mind. She took out a six-foot mercenary—what if she turns on him? Jules grabs a tea towel and presses it to Angie's arm. 'Mum's bleeding.' Her voice is ragged from panic or phosphorus or both.

'Angie,' Ryan says. 'We have to go, *now*.' As impatient as he is to get moving he doesn't touch either of them.

'Did you come to hurt Jules?' Angie croaks. Her bloodshot eyes are fierce and wild.

'No.'

The wind whips up again outside, brings a blast of rain into the gaping house. Angie lifts her elbow. 'Help me up.'

Julianne struggles up from the floor without support but reaches for the bench once she's on her feet.

'Here.' Ryan guides Angie to Waylo and offers a hand to Julianne, tentative. He expects her to protest—or worse—but she rests an arm across his shoulder and leans into him. She's shaking as they step around the bull-neck sprawled by the sink. Waylo crouches and presses two fingers against the man's throat.

'I think he's dead.'

Julianne stiffens. Ryan actually *feels* the buzz that rips down her arm and he almost lets go.

'No, hang on, I'm getting a pulse.'

Julianne's grip eases and Ryan takes a steadying breath. *Man up.*

The Major crosses to them, slipping a flexi-phone into his pocket. 'Van's on the way.' He nods in the direction of the laundry.

'To take us where?' Angie pulls free of Waylo and plants her feet, sways a little. Ryan doubts she can see properly—it'll take a good dousing to get her eyes completely chemical free—but she's staring down the Major regardless. Her arm is slick with her own blood.

'Back to base.'

'So you can hand Jules over?'

The Major's jaw twitches beneath his beard. 'We didn't come here for Julianne.'

Julianne's fingers tighten on Ryan's shoulder. She doesn't believe the Major. Ryan's not sure he does either. She electrocuted a hundred-plus-kilo man without a weapon—of course the Major's interested in her.

'Why the base, then?' Angie demands.

'You'll be safe.'

'Not if the army's after us.'

'We're the army and we're not after you. We need to clear out, now.'

'And then what?'

The Major checks the safety on the pistol he's carrying, barely masking his impatience. 'You can decide your next move.'

Ryan watches Angie wrestle with the offer. Her choice is to trust that the local cops will protect her and Julianne, or to take her chances with the Major. She doesn't have much time to decide: the sirens are faint but they're coming. Somebody's reported the gunshot.

'You're with us?' the Major prompts. 'Good.' He nods at Ryan to get moving. Angie hesitates for all of a second and then follows. Whatever went on between the two of them must count for something. Or her daughter's half-killed someone and she doesn't think the cops'll look the other way.

The Major leads them through the laundry—Ryan and Waylo collect their guns on the way—and outside into the rain. They follow the fence line at the side of the house and the Major scouts the road. Ryan's aware of the heat radiating from Julianne and half-expects the rain to turn to steam when it hits her.

Brake lights flash twice further down the street: Frenchie's in position. She pulls away from the kerb as soon as they reach the van. The Major opens the sliding door and they pile in: the De Marchi women first, then Waylo and Ryan. The van keeps moving, forcing the Major to jump in the back instead of taking the passenger seat. Frenchie guns the engine as soon as the door slams.

Ryan rests against the side panel as the van bounces over a speed bump. Every jolt is a comfort: they're clear and they're alive. He takes a handful of hair and wrings it out, resists the urge to drop his head and shake it like a dog. He runs through the events back at the house. Feels a stab of embarrassment. He really lost his shit there for a second.

Angie and Julianne are on the bench seat, hanging on as Frenchie takes a corner too fast. The Major and Waylo are crouched at the rear. Rain pelts the windscreen, making a racket on the roof. A few more turns and they're on the motorway heading west and it's not long before the screen slides back.

'Ah, sir?'

Ryan's head snaps up. The pitch in Frenchie's Leb-Aussie twang is off.

'What is it, private?' The Major has one hand on the seat near Angie for balance, the other holding his pistol.

'We've got company.'

'How far back?'

'Not following us. There's a woman here in the front with me, sir, with a gun in my face.'

'Angela, Julianne, are you okay?'

Angie lunges at the window, beating the Major to it. 'Khan?' She presses her face to the opening and grimaces at the sharp reminder of her bullet wound. In the orange dash light she sees the federal agent has a gun trained on the girl behind the wheel. The soldier glowers at the road, short dark hair feathered around an angular face. She's no older than Ryan or Waylon, wiry and wound tight.

'Out of the way.' The Major is at Angie's shoulder, trying to move her aside.

'Khan's a federal cop.'

'Let me talk to her.'

'Not while you're holding a gun.' Angie knocks his hand from her uninjured arm and braces for him to push her aside. He doesn't. Maybe the fact she's shot and bleeding earns her a few seconds of grace.

'*Angela*. Are you all right? What happened?'

Angie forces bleary eyes to focus. What did Khan see before she hijacked the van?

'A stun grenade came through my front window and a meat-head shot me.' Angie wipes her nose on her shoulder. Her throat feels like she's swallowed a sparkler—when will the god-awful burning stop?

'How badly are you injured?'

'It hurts like hell, but I think the bullet only nicked my arm.'

Khan lifts the gun barrel to the driver's temple. 'Is this lot responsible?'

'No, they were already inside, and they knocked first.' Angie can't see how close Khan's finger is to the trigger. She hopes the safety's on. 'They're army, apparently.'

'Do you believe that?'

Angie glances at the Major. He's crouched beside her, seriously pissed off. 'They brought Jules home on Wednesday,' she says. 'So, yeah.'

Khan lowers her gun and the girl behind the wheel blows out her breath.

'The weapon's down, sir.'

The Major waits a beat and then makes a show of handing his handgun to Ryan. Angie stays where she is for a few more seconds—she needs a feel for how far she can push him—and shuffles sideways so he can see into the cab. The wipers flick backwards and forwards in a frantic dance.

'Khan, is it?' the Major says.

'*Federal agent* Khan. And you are?'

'Major Luka Voss. SECDET Q18.'

She tilts her head as if to reappraise him. 'What's your interest in Angela and Julianne?'

The Major barks a short laugh. 'Pointing a Glock at one of my soldiers doesn't put you in charge, *agent*. If you have questions for me, you go through the usual channels.'

'Major, you were just involved in a non-sanctioned tactical raid in a suburban house during which shots were fired, and now you're fleeing a crime scene with hostages—'

'No, *you've* stumbled into the middle of a military operation.'

'Military operation? Aren't your guys guns for hire? The latest revenue-raising experiment from Treasury?'

'You might want to investigate who's funding your department before you crawl too far up your own—'

Angie bangs her palm on the wall separating the pair. 'Get over your turf pissing. Men with guns stormed my house tonight and tried to take Jules. Do either of you care about that?'

They pass an exit and Khan's face is momentarily lit up. 'They came for Julianne? Why?'

'I don't know, but that's twice in one week.'

'And *his* unit was there on both occasions. What's the story, Major?'

'That's classified—'

'He says he wants my help,' Angie says before he can finish. Her palm is again clamped over the gunshot wound. It's seeping blood and her whole arm throbs. 'I'm deciding if I believe him.'

The Major gives a low growl.

'Angie'—Khan turns sideways in the front seat—'why would anyone come after Julianne?'

Angie rubs her eyes—bad move, it's like dragging sandpaper over her eyeballs. 'Long story.'

'I need to hear it.'

The Major shakes his head. He wants answers himself, but not so badly that he'll take them with an audience. Angie wipes her bloodied hand on her trackpants and returns pressure to her arm.

'Jules,' Angie says. 'What do you want to do?'

Jules opens her mouth and her first word catches on a hacking cough. Ryan leans in as if to help but stops himself. He hovers in a half-crouch while she recovers and then settles back beside Waylon.

'Tell them the truth,' Jules says when she's regained her voice.

'Who?' Angie prompts.

'Both of them. Khan should come to the base with us.'

'Seriously?'

'You asked.'

Angie blows out her breath. If she could fix this on her own, she would; but she can't. They have to take the risk.

Nothing but shitty choices, as always.

'Can you live with that, Voss?' Angie asks.

The Major's nostrils flare. 'If Khan holsters that weapon and it doesn't make another appearance in the vicinity of my soldiers. And I want to see credentials.'

'Likewise.' Khan holsters her handgun and says something in Arabic to the driver. The girl's stranglehold on the steering wheel eases.

Angie rests her head against the side of the van, aching and dead tired. She's shielded Jules for eighteen years, helped her stay under the radar even without Mike. And now gunmen are storming her home, soldiers have seen Jules offload an electrical charge into a lump of a man, and she and Jules are going to share their dangerous truth with a privatised army unit and the federal police.

What little control Angie had left over their lives is about to be totally stripped away.

Jules knows what Ryan is thinking. Even when she couldn't see him clearly—her sight is only properly returning now—she could feel it radiating from him.

What are you?

He hasn't used those words; he doesn't need to. It's the obvious question once you've seen what she can do.

They're in the common area of the SECDET Q18 barracks. Jules is wedged into the corner of a tartan couch, picking at pilled fabric on the armrest with her feet tucked beneath her. The rain has eased to a drizzle, bringing a drop in temperature. Her hair is wet from the dash to the van and damp cotton clings to her skin. She repositions the blanket around her shoulders, avoids eye contact with Ryan. He's sitting on the floor, leaning against a bookcase filled with manuals and tapping his thumbs on his thighs. Waylon and the girl who was driving—the Major introduced her as Private Lena French—are in the communal kitchen making tea. The TV is on, volume down, and the barracks smells of socks, liniment and burnt bacon.

'You're rejoining the Agitators?' Khan says, incredulous.

'I haven't said yes or no, I'm telling you the offer.'

Angie's perched on the edge of the pool table, fidgeting with a fresh bandage. The Major cleaned and dressed her bullet-grazed arm without a word. Jules tries to swallow but her heart is taking up too much space.

'Peta Paxton is happy with you making that offer?' Khan asks the Major.

He steps away from Angie. 'It's an operational matter. It's not her concern. Or yours.'

To Angie: 'And you think Wednesday's attack and tonight's home invasion are connected, and that Julianne is the common denominator.'

Angie lifts her eyebrows at Jules. 'Do you want to explain?'

Jules shakes her head. She really doesn't. Her mouth is a wad of cotton and her right arm tingles with pins and needles. Khan looks from Angie to Jules to the Major, the moment stretching out until Ryan's tapping thumbs fall still.

'You said that wasn't the first time.' He lifts his chin at Jules. 'In the lift, you said it had happened before. Did you mean someone coming after you?'

Jules glances at Khan, uneasy.

'When was the other time?' Ryan presses.

Angie pushes off from the pool table. 'Tell them.'

Jules wets her lips, tries to work out what her mother wants from her.

'The rules have changed, Jules,' Angie says.

Jules feels her pulse in her throat. 'Yeah, but—'

'They *saw*, Jules.'

'Saw what?' Khan asks, exasperated.

Jules ignores the agent, focuses on Ryan. He raises his eyebrows, expectant.

'It was two years ago,' she says. 'At school.'

'The science lab?'

Jules hesitates. Does Angie really want her to tug on this thread and unravel their lives?

'Julianne.' Khan's tone is razor sharp. '*What* happened at school?'

Jules takes a breath and lets it out in a noisy rush. There's no going back now.

121

'When I went upstairs to get my cardigan from the lab, a guy came in behind me. He was in his twenties, maybe. I'd never seen him before. He had a gun.' Jules remembers the demand of his energy, the calculation of his stare: she'd had no doubt he was capable of violence.

Khan's mouth drops open in genuine shock—it's not an expression Jules has seen on her before. 'There was someone else in the lab? Why am I only hearing about this now?'

'I tried to get around him but he kept blocking the door and forcing me back inside. He was asking me why Mum hated Pax Fed so much, what she had on them.' Her skin crawls, remembering. 'And then he opened up the gas line to a Bunsen burner...'

'*That's* how the fire started?'

'I didn't mean for it to happen—'

'The bastard was wearing a camera,' Angie says, matter-of-fact. 'He filmed what happened and sent me the footage. Threatened to release it if I didn't back away from the Agitators.'

'Wait.' Khan holds up a palm. 'You were *blackmailed* into leaving the Agitators? Over what? Julianne confessed to lighting the fire.'

'You didn't use matches or a lighter, did you?' the Major says to her. It's not really a question.

Khan blinks, her forehead creasing. The Major waits to hear what he's already figured out. The only sounds in the barracks are the light patter of rain on the roof and an electric kettle bubbling in the kitchen. On the muted TV, a celebrity chef cracks an egg into a bowl.

'There was no taser in the laneway,' Ryan says and Jules can't tell if he's afraid or intrigued or both. She can't look at her mother and she especially can't look at Khan.

Waylon appears in the doorway carrying a tray with six cups of steaming tea. Private French has a tin of biscuits. She gives Khan a wide berth. The tray and the tin go on the pool table and

Waylon offers the first cup to Angie, teabag tag draped over the side. Angie waves it away.

'Someone needs to spell this out for me,' Khan says. 'Exactly how did the fire start?'

Jules knows she agreed to tell them, but it's so much harder than she expected. She looks to her mother.

'Certain cells in Jules' body create excess electricity,' Angie says, taking over. She delivers the news as if Jules is lactose intolerant. 'When the voltage gets too high she has to release the charge, and if it comes into contact with something flammable, like gas from a Bunsen burner—' Her fingers bloom apart to demonstrate an explosion.

Khan runs her tongue across her teeth, her eyes narrowing. 'You're telling me Julianne didn't destroy the lab as an act of vandalism on your behalf, it was to protect herself—and she did it using electricity from her own body?'

'I didn't do it on purpose,' Jules says. 'The charge is harder to hold when I'm scared or anxious. It was gone before I could stop it.' She only got out alive because the major blast didn't come until the fireball reached the gas main.

'Julianne, do you honestly expect me to believe that?'

'It's true,' Ryan says. 'She gave me a jolt out the back of the Pax Fed building on Wednesday. I thought she had a stun gun.'

'And we saw her drop a big bastard who put a gun to her head tonight,' Waylon adds. 'He barely had a pulse afterwards.'

Jules flashes hot and cold at the memory of the man on her kitchen floor.

'Show me.'

Jules hugs her knees to her chest. 'It's not a party trick. I can't always control it.'

'Show me right now or I'm charging you with perjury.'

Jules closes her eyes, remembers all the times she's failed to rein in the current: with her dad when she was trying to master it, with her friends when she couldn't. A mishap in the haunted house at the Ekka…an unexplained fire in a friend's backyard… the school explosion.

Can she do what Khan's asking? The current is background fizz at the moment and she's earthed out twice already tonight so maybe it won't be too bad, even with the swell of anxiety. Either way she has to show Khan *something* because the federal agent won't believe her unless she sees it. With Khan, it's always about evidence.

Jules opens her eyes. 'I'll try.'

Waylon deliberately steps further away and Private French does the same, even if she's not entirely sure why.

Jules holds up her right hand as if balancing an invisible plate. All she needs is to produce a spark or two. She relaxes her hold on the current for a millisecond, lets it find the path down her arm. Her fingers sting as the pressure builds and a burst of current breaks through, tiny flares of blue lightning zapping from her fingertips.

'Holy shit,' Private French whispers.

Jules brings up her other hand, tries to get the charge to curl into a ball between her palms but it's stronger than she expects. She needs to draw it back in before—

A single arc of current leaves her hands and grounds itself in the TV on the wall. The screen pops and goes blank. Jules draws the rest of the charge back to her core and holds her breath for a good five seconds until it settles.

Khan's gaze tracks to the smoking TV and back to Jules. 'How…?'

'I don't know.'

It's a few more seconds before the full weight of the truth hits the agent. 'You've lied to me, both of you, for two years. Do you know how many times I've gone out on a limb for you? Defended you whenever a new accusation was thrown your way?'

'Jules copped to the fire,' Angie says. 'What does it matter how it started?'

'The *truth* matters, Angela.'

'What would you have done with it?'

'Used it to catch whoever was in that lab threatening your daughter, for a start.'

'And then what? We don't know who sent that guy or if he even knew what to expect when he cornered Jules.'

'Did it occur to you that I might be able to find out?'

'You work for a federal agency.'

'So?'

'Who do you think made her this way?'

Khan laughs, flinty. 'Ah, the conspiracy theory: the government's to blame.'

Unease ripples through Jules. Khan's questioned them, kept them under surveillance and disagreed with Angie's politics, but she's never accused either of them of outright lying. Jules knows the agent's anger is justified but it stings anyway.

'Jules generates dangerous levels of electricity. That's not a genetic anomaly, Khan, that's engineered.'

'Who would do that to her, Angela? Who?'

Angie draws a breath to reload and the dread rises again for Jules. That older, familiar unease of knowing she was made *wrong*.

'The defence force.'

There's a spark in the room's energy. Jules can't pinpoint who set it off, but it's not Angie. She knows her mother's spikes as well as her own.

'Jules is different *genetically*,' Angie continues. 'Mike and I created her the old-fashioned way—so that means whatever gene makes her the way she is had to come from me or Mike. And nobody's tampered with my DNA.'

'You think the army did something to your husband?'

'He was getting jabbed every week on that first tour in Afghanistan—'

'The ebola vaccine,' Khan says, impatient. 'In the early days it had to be administered weekly.'

125

'Anything could've been in those syringes.'

'I'm no expert, Angie, but I don't think genetic engineering works like that.'

Jules' mum shakes her head. 'Why is it so hard for you to believe our soldiers are being used as guinea pigs? What do you think this corporatised army is all about?' She gestures to Ryan, Waylon and Private French. All three find somewhere else to look. The Major says nothing, gives nothing away. Jules glances at Ryan and is relieved to find him fixated on the carpet rather than her, thumbs again tapping.

'Let's work our way back to that issue, shall we?' Khan rubs the corner of her eye with a finger, careful not to smudge her eyeliner. 'The most pressing issue is identifying your intruders.'

'Sir, permission to speak?' It's Waylon, slouched against the bookcase, cup of tea in hand. 'Those guys tonight can't have known what our girl here can do or they would've taken her down first.' Waylon looks to Jules. She doesn't answer but he's right: there's no way anyone who's seen that video would get close to her.

'Which means they're guns for hire, not the main game.'

The Major nods. 'Agreed.'

'They could be connected to Xavier. Why else was he casing the house earlier today?'

'Xavier?' Khan asks.

'An Agitator,' Waylon says. 'I saw him check out the De Marchi place today.'

'What were *you* doing there?'

Waylon nods at Ryan. 'Walsh had the guilts over Wednesday.'

Ryan looks over his shoulder. Jules can't see his expression but whatever it is it gets a laugh out of Waylon. How are these guys even functioning after that stun grenade? Jules' eyes are still burning and weeping even after repeated rinsing but these two—it's as if they weren't in the same room as her.

'Do you have a full name for your Agitator?' Khan asks.

'James Clay Xavier.' The Major gives her a flat smile. 'He's not even on your radar, is he?'

'A photo would help.'

The Major doesn't move.

'Don't be a dick, Voss,' Angie says. 'Khan might have information and we need all the help we can get.'

'You might. We don't.'

'Do you know who hired those mercenaries? No? Then I guess you do.'

The Major inhales slowly. Exhales even slower. 'Walsh,' he says finally. 'Get the PF6 file from my office.'

Ryan's up from the floor and out the door without a backwards glance. Jules is stuck on the Major's words as the door clicks shut. *PF6*. If PF is for Paxton Federation, maybe six is the number of private contracts the army has taken with them. Was PF1 the mission that sent her father to that desalination plant in Pakistan? Or were there contracts even before that?

Khan touches the butt of the gun holstered at her ribs. She studies Jules, shakes her head and turns away. It hollows Jules out a little more. Waylon and French sip their tea in silence.

Ryan returns five minutes later, a fat manila folder tucked under his arm and his T-shirt patterned with raindrops. He hands the file to the Major and exchanges a look with Waylon that Jules can't decipher. The Major slaps the folder onto the pool table and flips it open, pulls out a page.

'That's him?' Angie takes it and holds it away from her, as if the distance will help. 'Someone needs to tell him the man bun's been gone for a decade. Do you know this guy?'

Khan doesn't need to touch the photo. 'He's high on our list for Wednesday but we haven't been able to charge him. The CCTV in Queen Street went down when the truck hit so we've only got media footage to go on. It's patchy at best.'

'What name do you have?' Waylon asks.

'James Clay Xavier.' Khan's unapologetic. 'I wanted to be

127

sure we were talking about the same person.'

'What's your intel?'

Khan glances at the thickness of the army file. 'We know he dropped off the radar after being arrested at an anti-nuclear rally three years ago. No job, no Centrelink file, no bank accounts.'

Jules runs her fingertips across her palm, still warm from the current. 'Can I see him?' she asks quietly.

Angie brings the photo to her, turning it around when she gets close. The image is slightly grainy and the guy's hair is different but she knows exactly who he is. Coldness creeps over her.

'Do you know him?' Angie asks, surprised.

Jules meets her mum's gaze when she answers.

'He's the guy who threatened me in the lab.'

The first glass of whisky goes down a little too easily. He takes his time on the second.

The Major is alone in his office picking over the PF6 file again. The only light in the room is from the lamp bent over his desk like a curious bird. A moth flutters in and out of the glare, crashing into the bulb.

Waylon and Walsh are sleeping and French is on watch. Khan called for a ride into Brisbane an hour ago, but only after photographing the Major and his credentials and threatening to have him arrested if the De Marchis weren't there in the morning. Angie and Julianne are in the spare bunks next to the kitchen.

Given what the Major now knows, he probably should have found somewhere more secure. He's never seen anything like it: the girl's a walking defibrillator.

Why wasn't her complete skill set included in the intelligence compiled for this job? Either the army doesn't know about Julianne De Marchi, or it does and the Major isn't in that circle of trust. Which would piss him off enormously, especially if Michael De Marchi was part of an earlier incarnation of Operation Resilience. Not to mention it would have been handy to know Julianne's full capabilities before he sent Walsh into Pax Fed Tower last week.

The Major takes another sip of whisky. He's got operational

decisions to make and he needs to make them before the rest of SECDET Q18 return at 08:00.

The face on the desk goads him from half a dozen photos. The Major has long suspected Xavier was more than a protester with a chip on his shoulder, but a stalker and a blackmailer? He walked into a public school and spooked Julianne into showing her hand. Twenty-two kids were injured in the explosion. Was that planned or unforeseen collateral damage? Either way, Xavier knew enough to take a camera and use the footage to drive Angie from the Agitators, giving him free rein to take over the group and redirect Agitator anger to deadlier violence. It's a lot of effort for a lone radical.

He spreads out the photos. The set of Xavier's shoulders, the calculating stare, they're the same in every surveillance shot, whether he's working the crowd at a protest rally or climbing out of the Agitators' dust-caked bus. There's no trace of self-doubt about him.

The Major thumbs through the file again, his mind working. Does anyone at Pax Fed know Xavier's blackmailing Angie? There's a link between the Agitators and the company—Peta Paxton admits it or at the very least acknowledges someone on her side is leaking information to the group. Without an insider, there's no way Wednesday's attackers could have known Julianne would be in the building.

The Major had wanted Angie back in the Agitators mostly to help Waylon's infiltration, partly to see if she had the influence to redirect that ragtag mob away from further violence. But that was before he knew there was a connection between her and Xavier. Before he saw the effect that piece of news had on Angie. Now he's not sure if she can stay focused long enough to be of use.

His bigger concern is the tactical assault unit they encountered tonight at the De Marchi house. He knows those guys. They were part of Z12 before the unit was decommissioned fifteen months ago. He'd heard rumours half the squad had turned merc but had assumed that meant foreign contracts, not domestic.

It hasn't taken long for this job to get messy. Big fucking surprise. He throws back the rest of the whisky.

By the time he's re-read the file it's close to midnight and the rain is all but gone. The night is noisy with cicadas and he almost doesn't hear the knock when it comes.

'Sir, it's Walsh.'

'Enter.'

Walsh opens the door and steps in, looks sheepish. 'Sir, she insisted.'

Angela De Marchi steps around him. 'We need to talk.'

Walsh is barefoot and bleary-eyed, wearing nothing but a pair of old footy shorts. Obviously well into his sleep cycle when Angie came calling. He should have sent her back to her room but no, he brings her here. Bloody teenage boys. It doesn't matter how well you train them, they never know how to say no to a demanding woman.

'Dismissed, Walsh.'

Walsh ducks his head and disappears.

The Major gestures to the chair across his desk. Angie sits down, watches him sweep together the PF6 file and tuck the pages back inside the folder. Long hair falls from a loose knot on her head and there's a pillow crease on her cheek, but her eyes are alert. She's come to him in trackpants and a fitted singlet that highlights every dip and curve of her breasts. He can't tell if that's intentional, but he hasn't missed that she still wears her wedding band.

'At least now I know why you didn't call me after the watch-house,' she says.

The Major leans back, tries to read her mood. 'I didn't think you'd go for a bloke in uniform. I was off the mark there.'

A tight smile. 'You lied about who you were. The uniform wouldn't have come into it.'

131

Outside, the cicada chorus intensifies. The Major wonders how much she recalls from that night. He remembers the way she paced the cell like a wild cat, snarling at the cops until even the drunks and addicts cringed away from her. And then the lights went out and he found her in the corner, fuming and vulnerable. They'd been in the same paddywagon, so she didn't question it when he sat with her. They talked about the protest and the injustice of the Syrian refugee crisis, and complained about the cold until the duty cop tossed a couple of scratchy blankets into the cell. His job was to get intelligence on the protesters' next target, but he lost focus the instant she slipped onto his lap and pulled the blanket around them both. *She* kissed him. In his memory, she tastes of Mentos and pear cider.

'You know why Jules is the way she is, don't you?' she asks.

The Major picks up a paperclip, pushes it out of shape with his thumb. 'I'm a soldier, Angela, not a geneticist.'

'But you'd know if there were trials involving infantry in the field.'

'There's nothing I can tell you.'

'Because you don't know or because it's classified?'

'The end result's the same, isn't it?'

Angie props her knees on the edge of his desk. She probes the bandage on her arm, winces a little. 'I'm not leaving this room unless you tell me what you know.'

The Major sets his glass to one side. It's obviously a thing with her: the need for conflict. She eyes him. He gives her the moment and then he straightens the paperclip and sits forward.

'I don't know why Julianne can electrocute people.' It's the truth. His own body is testament to the advances of science, but he didn't know genetic manipulation like hers was even possible. 'You must have found out something over the years. Doctors, tests?'

'I couldn't dig too deep without drawing attention to Jules.'

'Bullshit, Angela, you're an investigative journalist.'

132

She tilts her head. 'Do you have kids, Voss?'

'No.' Two ex-wives. No kids.

'Then you won't get it.'

'Humour me.'

She blows out her breath and slides lower in the chair. 'You have no idea what it's like watching your clever, happy kid withdraw from the world because she's scared of herself. Mike figured out she could earth the charge when it got too much, and that helped for a while. But every time it got away from her she'd pull back from her friends—us too, sometimes. Mike was the only one who could talk her around, move her past the fear. He was always there for her—until the day he wasn't. I've tried to fill the void but I'm no replacement for her dad.'

For a second the Major sees beyond the bluff and the snark, the hint of a softer shape.

'And then that fucker turned up at her school.'

The Major taps the paperclip on the desk. 'Who told Xavier about her?'

'I don't *know*, Voss. Don't you think I would've done something about it by now if I did?'

The Major splays his fingers on his desk. 'I'm in two minds about sending you south with Waylon.'

'Yeah? Well, I'm in two minds about going.'

He doesn't believe her for a second, not after her reaction last night, but he lets it play out.

'For the last two years I've been living under the threat of that footage being released if I go near the Agitators—and you want me to front up to an Agitator rally under the nose of the prick who's blackmailing me?'

'It's a risk whether he's there or not. Your call. We'll do what we can to block him uploading or sending data files—that's the best I can offer. But if I allow you to go with Waylon you have to keep your head.'

She sucks her lips in between her teeth until they turn pale.

They spring back with a sound like a soft kiss. 'How credible is the threat to the nuclear plant?'

'Credible enough.'

Angie lifts her eyebrows, waits.

'Our intel points to an attack this weekend.'

'By the Agitators?' she asks in disbelief.

'We've picked up chatter about explosives headed for the Anti-Nuclear Assembly. Xavier and the Agitators are on their way to the same location. Join the dots.'

'So arrest him and stop this madness before it gets out of hand.'

'We don't have enough on him and neither do the feds. We need to know who he's working with. You drive him off too quickly and the whole lot of them will go underground.'

'What makes you think the sight of me won't do that anyway?'

'We've been watching him for a while. He thinks he's the smartest guy in the room. He'll want to know why you're back—even more so if he's your blackmailer—and he'll probably reach out to whoever's pulling his strings. We've never been close enough to get personal surveillance tech on him. That's Waylon's job. Yours is to fast-track Waylon's integration to undermine Xavier's grip on the group.'

Angie looks past him to the whiteboard, to the aerial maps of the nuclear plant and radioactive waste storage silo. She lets out her breath and her attention settles on his glass. 'Got another one of those?'

The Major opens his bottom drawer and pulls out the bottle and spare tumbler wedged between the personnel files. He pours Angie two fingers of whisky, slides the tumbler across the worn timber desk. She rolls it around on its base—her nails are plain, short and chipped—but doesn't take a drink.

'I'm not leaving Jules behind.'

'You're not taking her with you. Too risky.'

'Why is that more risky than sending me in?'

'What if he does more than threaten her this time?'

Angie lifts her glass and lowers it again. 'I notice you're not concerned about him hurting me.'

The Major can't pick if she's genuinely offended or not. 'Waylon will have your back.'

'And who's looking out for Jules? I'm not leaving her on this base and she can't go home. I've talked to Vee—'

'Who gave you a phone?'

'Ryan.'

Walsh. Bloody hopeless. 'Who's Vee?'

'Veronica Ng. A friend.'

He remembers the name from Angie's file. She's tied up with the Defence Department's Science and Technology Group.

'She wants Jules to stay with her.'

'Does she know what Julianne can do?'

Angie measures him for a long moment. 'No.'

She's a bad liar.

'There's another option,' he says.

'I'm all ears.'

The Major takes a slow sip of whisky and tells her. It's a lot more risk than he'd usually consider but he has a narrow window if he's going to get Angie back in with the Agitators before they roll out to South Australia. Angie absorbs the plan. When she finally lifts the glass to her lips, he knows she's in.

'It's not the worst idea.' She knocks back the drink in one hit. 'But Jules is going to hate it.'

'Are you serious, sir?'

'When was the last time I made a joke, Walsh?'

Ryan blinks. 'Never, sir.'

It's 06:00 and the Major has them assembled in his demountable office: Ryan, Waylo and Frenchie are standing at attention along the wall, hands clenched at their sides; Angie and Julianne sit in steel chairs with their backs to them. Outside, the first flush of dawn stains the sky. Ryan feels oddly out of sync. He's heavy with sleep and a good two steps behind the conversation. He checks how Julianne's faring. She's wearing the same T-shirt and jeans she had on last night; the shirt's out of shape and she's trying to force it to sit straight, stretching it in one direction and then the other when she thinks nobody's watching.

The Major is seated at his desk, waiting for Ryan to accept the news.

'You're granting my leave,' he manages.

'I thought you wanted to see your family?'

'I do.'

'Officially, that's what you're doing. Unofficially, you're on the clock.'

Ryan shares a quick glance with Waylo and Frenchie. Maybe they're keeping up. Nope—blank looks there too.

'Orders, sir?'

The Major nods at Julianne. 'Keeping your house guest safe.'

Ryan frowns, uncomprehending.

'You're taking her to South Australia.'

'Ah—'

'No, he's not,' Julianne says and turns to her mother for backup.

'Yeah, Jules, he is.'

Understanding dawns for her the same time it does for Ryan: the Major and Angie made this decision without them.

'You're unbelievable,' Julianne says to her mother.

'For wanting to keep you safe?'

'For agreeing to any of this without talking to me.'

Angie swivels sideways to face her. 'What's to talk about? I'm getting on that bus with Waylon today. I can't take you with me and I'm not leaving you behind. Ryan's family is east of Port Augusta. You'll be close by and out of immediate danger while we sort out what's going on at the Anti-Nuke Assembly.'

'We agreed I would stay with Vee.'

'It's not a negotiation, Jules. This is the only way to keep you safe.'

'Since when do you trust anyone in the defence force?' She gestures to the Major. 'You think *his* priority is your safety? You told me this morning there's a risk Xavier wants to set off a nuclear meltdown. Why would you want to be anywhere near that?'

'The plan is to stop it.'

'Julianne,' the Major says. 'Private French and I will shadow your mother and Waylon. We won't let anything happen to her.'

Frenchie shifts her weight and Ryan knows his mate's shitting herself at the pressure of a one-on-one assignment with the Major.

'And I get no say in this?' Julianne folds her arms.

'I don't know how else to protect you. Come on, Jules, it's a paying job. I thought you'd be happy.'

'Don't make this about money. It's hardly a long-term solution.'

'It might be if I can get out from under the blackmail and take back the Agitators. You could go to uni—'

'The Agitators have no corporate sponsors left, no online advertisers. Who's going to pay you to run campaigns for a suspected domestic terrorist organisation?'

'I can turn things around.'

'How? I'm a liability for you and anyone who gets near me.'

'Jules—'

Julianne stands up so fast the metal chair rocks backwards and threatens to topple. Ryan reaches for it out of reflex, breaking rank. Julianne spins around, locks eyes with him. 'Don't you touch me either.'

He lowers the chair back to the floor and stands to attention. Keeps his mouth shut.

'Tell me: what would you have done if I *had* started a fire at Pax Fed on Wednesday?'

Ryan glances over at the Major. The Major gives a curt nod. What does that mean? Permission to lie or permission to tell her the truth?

He shrugs. 'I'd have taken necessary measures to neutralise the situation.'

When in doubt, quote the ops manual.

'You would have hurt me?'

'Not unless you were an immediate threat.'

'*How* would you have stopped me? With that knife in your boot?' She's openly furious and Ryan can't help but wonder what's going on under her skin. Does it really matter what might have happened on Wednesday? He's dragged her out of a deadly situation twice since then.

'Would you have *killed* me?'

'Walsh had authority to use lethal measures if necessary.' The Major is matter-of-fact. 'It was a contingency in an extreme situation, given your history for bringing down buildings. Standard operational protocol. Don't take it personally.'

Jules stares at him. 'Don't take it personally? You want me to trust my life to someone who was willing to take it a few days ago.'

'I wasn't *willing*,' Ryan says. Fuck, when did this become about him?

'What do you want to do, Jules?' Angie demands.

'Stay with Vee.'

'And what happens when those men with masks and guns storm her house and shoot her and then you?'

Julianne steps around the chair and goes to the window, stares out into the breaking morning. Angie holds up her hand to stop Ryan or anyone else speaking—and surprisingly the Major lets her. Julianne stares at the quadrangle outside the Major's office, punctuated with puddles from last night's storm. Ryan knows every centimetre of that rough bitumen. He's sweated on it, bled on it, had it imprinted in his shoulders and knees and forehead. Right now he'd rather be face down out there than cornered in this conversation.

'Does Khan know about any of this?' Jules asks her mother.

'She signed off on it twenty minutes ago.'

Ryan feels the prick of insult: Julianne has more faith in a fifty-five-kilo federal agent than in him. He needs to get his shit together and own this.

'Sir, when do we leave?'

'You're on a Hercules out of Amberley at 16:00 hours. I'll have transport sorted in Adelaide by the time you touch down at Edinburgh Air Base. Your orders are to get home and stay with your family until you hear from me. You keep your head down, and hers.'

Now's probably not the time to tell him about Tommy's party on Friday night.

'How do I explain De Marchi?' He's acutely aware of her eyes on him, accusing.

139

The Major rises from his chair. He's taller than everyone in the room except Ryan. Out of habit, Ryan's eyes find the mangled skin around his ear.

'You tell them she's part of a multi-agency investigation and your job is to keep her safe until we need her back in Brisbane. You do not mention Port Augusta or this operation.'

'But—'

'You use your brain, Walsh. Figure it out.'

He *is* using his brain. It's finally awake and sorting through everything that could go wrong.

He's taking Julianne De Marchi to his family home. Her turning up on social media isn't the problem: the district's been without wi-fi and functional optic fibre since the price hike seven years ago. But what about the mercs who are after Julianne? Does he need to be looking over his shoulder? Is his family at risk? Ryan can't voice his concerns without questioning the Major's orders or sounding like he's not up to the job.

He knows he should be happy. Tommy will be stoked to see him and his mum will cry and then pretend she didn't. And his old man…the thought of facing his dad brings a tight knot to his gut but he'll worry about that when he's at the farm gate. The bigger worry is Julianne. Not only keeping her safe, but keeping others safe from her if she loses control.

And from the look on her face right now, he's the one most at risk.

Jules is sitting outside the Major's demountable office wishing she had more skill at summoning the charge on command. That would give them all something to think about.

She's on a bench under a flaking gum tree, eyes fixed on the boom gate separating the SECDET Q18 compound from the main base. Her mother left an hour ago with Waylon and a borrowed swag. They're catching a train into the city and then heading south again by bus to the Agitator rendezvous.

It's a sticky morning and the cicadas are already loud. Inside his office, the Major is bashing away at a keyboard. He's as violent a typist as her mother. Occasionally he glances up to make sure Jules is outside his window. She picks at a splinter on the edge of the bench, replaying the last moments with her mum.

Angie had *hugged* Jules. It was quick and all elbows and Jules was too busy managing her anxiety to appreciate the gesture.

And her mother's parting advice? *If anything goes wrong, do what you need to do to stay safe.*

What could go wrong being stuck out in the middle of nowhere with a guy who was prepared to kill her a few days ago? How is she meant to ground herself without causing damage or being seen?

Jules isn't surprised Angie's grabbed the first opportunity to wrest back control of their lives. But putting herself in the path of a potential nuclear meltdown and trusting the army to keep them safe? Rejoining the Agitators in plain sight of the guy threatening to expose Jules? It's beyond reckless.

Jules drags a finger across her eyelid, hoping the Major knows more than he's telling. Even with the sweat beading on her top lip it's a relief to be outside and away from him. His tension is tightly contained but it still sets Jules on edge. She's been scanning the compound all morning, looking for a safe point of release if she needs it. It's a new base, so there's less steel than she'd hoped. So far the best option is the chin-up bar in the open-air gym. It's exposed, but it's metal and bolted to cement so at least she won't set it on fire.

A fly does a drunken loop and lands on her knee as Khan's unmarked sedan passes under the boom gate. Jules catches a glimpse of purple hair in the passenger seat and Vee's out before the engine's stopped. She's wearing a batik-dyed halter-top, silk pants and four-inch fuchsia slingbacks: an explosion of colour in a sea of concrete and khaki. She strides over and pulls Jules from the bench and into a hug, wrapping her up in a heady mix of vanilla-bean body lotion.

'Mum's going to get herself killed,' Jules says into Vee's shoulder.

'No she's not.'

'You could have talked her out of it.'

'Julianne,' Khan says, not pausing as she passes with a bunch of shopping bags. 'You know better than anyone that your mother makes her own decisions.'

Vee brushes her fingertips along Jules' arm. 'If your mum can keep her temper she'll be fine.'

Jules pulls back. 'Please don't treat me like a child. The army is sending a counter-terrorism unit to South Australia to stop an attack in three days' time, so don't tell me Mum will be *fine.*' A bubble of panic rises up. 'What am I supposed to do if something happens to her? Nobody here seems to have given that much thought.' Her throat burns and she steps out of Vee's reach as the sound of movement comes from the Major's office.

'Ladies.' The Major fills the doorway. 'Agent.'

Khan stops at the top of the stairs to his office, nods in Vee's direction and makes introductions.

'Always a pleasure to have departmental staff on base,' the Major says, in a tone that suggests the opposite.

Vee climbs the steps to his office, her heels clicking on the deck. 'Major.' They shake hands and he goes back to filling the doorway, intimidating in black T-shirt, camo pants and combat boots. He glances at the bags in Khan's hand.

'Glad to see you're using your time wisely, Agent Khan.'

Khan gives him a flat look. 'Julianne needs clothes. Veronica obliged.'

Jules knows from the logos on the bags that she can't afford Vee's choices.

'I'll be on-charging, of course,' Vee tells the Major. 'You can pass the cost on to Pax Fed with the rest of your invoice.'

'Is personal shopping part of your official ministerial capacity as well, Ms Ng?'

Khan hands the bags to Jules while Vee and the Major continue to snipe at each other. Jules takes a cursory look through the contents, counts three T-shirts, two pairs of jeans, a hoodie and new runners; undies and toiletries and a black cocktail dress and matching ankle boots. Vee can't help herself.

'Take this too.' Khan turns her back on the Major and presses a flat silver disk into Jules' palm. 'So I can find you if I need to.'

Khan cares enough to keep track of her, but not enough to look her in the eye. Jules puts the disk in her pocket with tacky fingers. It's bigger than the device Khan found in Ryan's bag.

'I'm sorry we lied to you,' Jules says quietly.

Khan's nostrils flare. 'No you're not. You've had dozens of opportunities over the last two years to tell me the truth.' She shakes her head as if disappointed in her own gullibility. 'I thought we'd reached a point of trust.'

'We had,' Jules says. 'But this thing I have…Mum was trying to keep me safe.'

'That's worked out well, hasn't it?'

Jules doesn't want to argue with her. 'Thanks for not walking away.'

'I can't walk away, Julianne. It's my job. *You're* my job.' She walks down the stairs, leaves Jules alone on the Major's deck.

The reality of the situation forks through her: she's about to leave the state with a complete stranger and Khan has all but washed her hands of her. The current bites at her fingertips, searching for release. 'I need to earth out,' she says, dropping the bags and hurrying for the workout area.

'Not there.' The Major comes down the stairs behind her. 'Follow me.' He strides towards a windowless building. Jules changes direction, focusing on containment and vaguely aware that Vee and Khan are crossing the quadrangle with them.

The Major taps in a code and lowers his face for a retinal scan. There's a beep and the sound of locks turning. He goes in first, flicking switches until a bank of fluorescent lights sputter to life. Jules steps in after him and falters. Everything is concrete: floor, walls and ceiling. Chains hang down in the middle of the room and more chains are bolted to the floor. Set aside in one corner are speakers on stands and a stack of spotlights.

'Use the chains on the floor,' the Major says. The door clicks shut and all traces of natural light disappear.

Jules continues to the middle of the room and drops to her knees. It's deathly quiet now. Even the cicadas are distant static. She cradles the heavy chain links and forces herself to hold the charge a while longer, like her dad taught her. *You control it, Jules, not the other way around.*

'When you're ready, Julianne. You can't do any damage.'

Jules takes a long, slow breath. *Concentrate.* But it's hard. The place feels like a dungeon and stinks of fear, and something even more sour and nasty. Her skin fizzes and stings. She thinks about her dad again, how disappointed he'd be that she's no better at this than she was at fifteen.

There's a loud *pop*—a bright flash—and the current grounds out somewhere beneath the concrete. It's like sneezing: the relief is instant. She sits back on her heels and the chain clanks on the floor. The air is instantly sharp with ozone.

'Is that it?' The Major asks, coming closer.

'Give me a minute.'

Khan is rooted to the spot by the door. 'Did that hurt?'

Jules wipes her palms on her jeans and holds them up. 'No permanent damage.'

'Not even a blister?' The agent has momentarily forgotten her anger.

'No.'

'Bloody hell.' The way the Major says it—impressed and fascinated—makes her stomach dip.

'And that, Major Voss, is exactly why Angie De Marchi has let a blackmailer have the upper hand for so long,' Vee says, crossing the floor. 'Because men and women like you won't be able to help themselves when they understand what Julianne can do.'

'Men and women like me?' His fascination evaporates.

Vee sits on her heels next to Jules, careful not to let her silk pants touch the grimy concrete. 'There are two types of people who would be interested in Julianne De Marchi.' She helps Jules up and steadies her by the elbow. 'Those who'd study her, and those who would use her as a weapon. I think we know where you sit on that spectrum.'

The Major levels his gaze. 'And what kind of interest does Defence Science and Tech have?'

'The department's not aware of what Jules can do.'

'You sure?'

'There's nothing on her in the system and I certainly haven't brought her to their attention.'

'But your lab rats would be in the loop if there was anything

145

other than ebola vaccine in the shots given to Mike De Marchi two decades ago.'

'The Afghanistan files are classified, Major.'

The Major measures Vee, his expression unchanging. 'Is that what you've been telling Angela?'

Vee's energy shifts from its familiar shape to something spikier. 'It's the truth.'

'Bullshit.'

'Major, I'm not going to dignify—'

'Is he right?' Khan interrupts. 'Did you find something?'

'Nothing relevant to this discussion.'

'I'm not asking out of curiosity, Veronica. I need to understand who knows what.'

Jules sees it then, the shadow of guilt. She pulls free of Vee's grip. 'What do you know?'

Vee runs her tongue across her teeth, hesitates, and then exhales through pursed lips. 'Okay. Look, *something* went on with troops in the Middle East in 2013, but honestly Jules, I haven't been able to get answers on what. The initiative wasn't approved by Canberra and it was shut down as soon as the minister got wind of it. I haven't been able to confirm if your dad's unit was involved—'

'But?' Khan presses.

Vee glances at Jules. 'It appears there was corporate sponsorship involved.'

The sweat on the back of Jules' neck chills because she *knows* what's coming next. It's Khan who says it.

'Paxton Federation.'

Vee nods, eyes not leaving Jules. 'It's taken me eighteen months to get this far—'

'You have to tell Mum.'

'Not until I know beyond a doubt it's relevant to your dad.'

'You should've told her Pax Fed did *something* unofficial with the army.'

Vee shakes her head. 'Think about what she'll do with that information. I'm trying to look out for both of you and the best way to do that is to protect your mother from herself.'

Jules pictures Angie standing in their lounge room clutching that satchel. 'You should've told Mum. She's taking risks because she's frustrated by endlessly hitting brick walls and now it turns out that you're one of them.'

'Please, Jules.'

Jules shrugs away from her and heads for the door. Khan catches her eye on her way out, and *yes*, she's well aware of her hypocrisy.

It doesn't make the weight of Vee's choices any lighter to bear.

Angie picks at the edge of her thumbnail, which is torn and snagging anything it comes into contact with. She rips it off in one go, taking a chunk of skin with it.

'You have a thing for pain, don't you?' Waylon asks as she sucks on the side of her throbbing thumb. They're heading out of the city. The bus is almost empty and they've claimed the back seat. Angie ignores him. Waylon takes off his cap and wiry black hair springs out in all directions.

'You need a haircut, Waylon.'

'Gotta look the part, Angie.' He flashes her a grin.

She snorts. 'What are you going to tell Xavier when he asks how you know me?'

He gives an easy shrug. 'You did a story on foster kids back when you were working for the *Courier-Mail* and you took a shine to me. We stayed in touch over the years. You even brought your husband and daughter along to a family day to meet me. You're the reason I got interested in the Agitators in the first place.' He doesn't miss a beat, as if the story is well worn.

'Who made up the part about the family visit, you or Voss?'

'Me. You talk a big game but I reckon you're a soft touch deep down.'

'Stick around, kid,' she says. 'Watch and learn. Why did we lose contact?'

'I dropped off the radar.'

'Doing what?'

Waylon fiddles with the leather band on his wrist. 'Stupid shit. Stuff I didn't want to talk to you about. Still don't.'

There's some truth there, Angie thinks. 'When did we reconnect?'

'Julianne saw me in the crowd on Wednesday. She told you, and you tracked me down through my old case worker.'

'Why?'

'You're worried the Agitators have been set up for the Pax Attack.'

'Shouldn't you have asked Xavier before you brought me along today?'

His grin widens. It's a beautiful smile: obviously his weapon of choice when he's straying from the truth. 'Why would I? You're Angela De Marchi.'

The bus pulls in at Buranda Station. Two teenagers in school uniforms get on. Waylon watches them drop their bags on the rack behind the driver and flop into seats. The smile fades and his fingers stray to the leather band again. At some point it must have been a neat braid but now it's tatty and frayed, held together with a series of knots.

'Did you make that?'

His gaze lifts to confirm what she's talking about and then slides away. 'Mum did, when I was little.'

'You two are close?'

'Used to be.' Waylon shifts so he's sideways in his seat. 'So, how much do you hate soldiers? Do I need to sleep with one eye open?'

The swerve in conversation throws Angie for a second. 'I don't hate soldiers, I was married to one for twenty years.' She rests her knees on the back of the seat in front of her. 'What I hate is the bastardisation of the Australian Defence Force. Corporate interests dictating where and how our troops serve. This operation of yours is a classic example.'

The bus gets moving again. Waylon's still looking at her. 'What happened in Pakistan? The real version.'

Angie scuffs the heel of her boot over a wad of old chewing gum. 'Mike's unit was redirected from protecting a village to protecting assets owned by Paxton Federation because the company was co-funding military operations in the region. He didn't sign on for that. He was willing to risk his life for people who couldn't fight for themselves. He was willing to die in the service of his country. He wasn't looking to give his life for shareholder profits.'

'He was a good bloke?'

Angie swallows and looks away. Fragments of memories rise up. Of laughter and drunken singing. Of angry words and make-up sex...Mike crying when Jules was born...feeding her a bottle in front of the TV watching rugby...taking her to her first day of school, both of them in uniform. And then that call in the dead of night. The cold fingers in her chest squeezing her heart until it was the size of a walnut.

She shuts down the memory before it dismantles her.

'Mike wasn't the saint everyone's turned him into. But, yeah, he was a good bloke.'

Mike was a soldier. He went to work with a rifle on his back and a handgun strapped to his thigh and she'd expected him to live forever.

'Waylon, roll up your sleeves.'

He gives her a nervous grin. 'Wanna see my guns, Angie?'

'Sure.'

'Nah, I'm shy.' He starts to lean away but she's too quick. She pushes up the right sleeve of his T-shirt. His black skin is bare. 'What are you looking for?'

'What shots are they giving you?'

A shrug. 'Nothing out of the ordinary. Vitamins, vaccinations, you know the drill.'

The bus pulls in at the next interchange. Passengers move

off and on. Angie leans in closer to Waylon. 'You think it was vitamins that let you boys withstand a stun grenade last night?'

He scratches the tip of his nose, doesn't answer.

'Don't tell me there's not something else going in your supplements regime.'

He gives her that lazy smile. 'Whatever it is, it helps me keep this'—he lifts his shirt to show off his abs—'so no complaints from me.'

Angie shakes her head. If she pushes Waylon hard enough he might cave, but now is not the time. First she has to deal with Xavier. She's been daydreaming about what she'll say when she's face to face with him; the ways she'll undo him that he won't see coming. Voss sent her off with another warning to set aside her agenda until the threat to the nuclear plant is sorted. But Angie's confident she can do both.

And she's got three days to prove it.

The ride to the Amberley RAAF Base takes about forty minutes. Jules faces the window almost the entire way, trying to shut out Ryan's incessant tapping on his knees. The rhythm changes regularly but that doesn't make it any less irritating.

Their driver takes them straight to the airfield, stopping only for checkpoints. An ancient-looking grey monstrosity waits on the tarmac. Its back end is wide open, with a ramp leading up into it that sets off a nervous flutter under her ribs. She wasn't completely tuned in when the Major was going over the flight plan, but they're not going in that, surely?

Ryan's staring at it too, grinning.

Jules climbs from the Land Rover and leans back in for her bag. 'I'm glad you're enjoying yourself.'

'That's a C-130 Hercules,' he says as he gets out, as if it should mean something to her. 'I've never been in one.'

Jules hoists the bag over her shoulder and slams the door to end the conversation.

They meet their pilot, a weathered man with pockmarked cheeks and bright eyes. He runs them through the safety routine as they shrug into their jackets and then leads them up the ramp into the back of the plane. It's a gutted whale with shelving and red netting.

Jules falters. 'Where do we sit?'

The pilot gestures to one side. *Oh.* The shelves are the seats.

Someone else takes Jules' bag as she sits down. She isn't paying enough attention to say thank you: she's too busy buckling herself in and making sure the seat is securely bolted to the plane.

A whine starts up outside and the engines rumble to life. Through a small window she can see props turning over. Ryan hands Jules a headset and puts on his own. She hesitates—her trembling fingers are going to give her away—but she lets go of the seat long enough to slip the earphones on and adjust the mic over her mouth.

'It'll get loud in here.' Ryan's voice crackles in her ear. He points to the cockpit and taps his earphones to let her know the pilot can hear them too. Good. Less chance she and Ryan will talk during the flight.

'Let me check your belt.' He waits for her permission before he leans over and pulls the strap to test the buckle. She keeps her hands by her sides, tries not to think about him on his knees in the lift. Focuses instead on the fact he had a knife in his boot and the reason it was there. The anger rekindles, brings the wall back up. She's starting to understand why it's Angie's default mode.

'All good,' Ryan says. He settles back, lengthens his legs. 'It'll be easier if you relax. The Hercs are slower than a commercial airline. We're going to be strapped in here for a while.'

It's not the news she was hoping for.

They taxi out to the runway, the engines vibrating through the floor and seats. Jules can't tell if it's that or anxiety that's feeding the current under her skin. She did enough at the base to keep it in check for a few hours but she can't afford to drop her guard. The ramp starts to close and Jules exhales. It will be better when she can't see the—

The ramp stops moving. They straighten onto the runway.

'Aren't they going to shut that?'

Ryan leans forward to see past her. 'Not yet. The Captain thought he'd give us the full show.'

153

The engines build to a roar and the plane picks up speed. Within seconds they're hurtling along, everything shuddering and shaking as the ground rushes past. Jules is pushed sideways in her seat by the force—and then they're not on the runway anymore. She watches the tarmac drop away, her heart hammering in her throat.

'Did the Major mention we're not landing when we get to Adelaide?'

Jules tears her eyes from the gaping mouth at the back of the plane. Ryan gestures to the cables running the length of the opposite wall and the straps flapping in the wind. Her nose and fingertips sting from the sudden cold.

'The co-pilot will fit our chutes mid-flight.'

She stares at him. 'I don't care if this thing is on fire and you have a gun to my head, I'm not getting out until we're on the ground.'

Ryan laughs—he's having a ball, the bastard. 'I'm kidding. Bloody hell, you have no sense of humour.'

She squeezes her eyes shut, presses herself back into her seat as hard as she can. 'Imagine what my life's been like these past few years. See how much of a sense of humour you have then.'

A beat. 'We've all had shit to deal with.'

'I'm pretty sure mine's different to yours.'

'It's still shit though, isn't it?'

She tries to imagine what could possibly be so tough in his life. He's fit and healthy, hot in a scruffy kind of way, and has a paying job in a covert army unit. Yeah, he's been dealt a terrible hand.

Jules opens her eyes as the plane banks and she immediately squeezes them shut again. They stay that way until a new voice speaks in her ear.

'Last chance to enjoy the view, folks. We need to close up before we climb any higher.'

Jules takes a peek and her breath catches. A patchwork of

154

green is spread out below, punctuated by squiggles of rivers and creeks. If her seatbelt lets go now she'll tumble straight out the back and make a crater in one of those paddocks.

'You should have said you were scared of flying.'

The ramp finally resumes closing and Jules waits until it's sealed tight and her eyes have adjusted before she answers Ryan.

'I'm not scared of flying. I'm scared of a thousand-metre drop.' She fixes her eyes on the opposite wall, refusing to let him see her relief.

'The Major said you were okay before we left the base. Are you?' He doesn't sound quite so smartarse now. 'You can't lose it up here.'

'No shit, *Walsh*.' He's making it easy to stay annoyed at him.

She closes her eyes again, tries not to think about all the things that could go wrong up here, on the ground, and on that bus when Angie meets Xavier. Has she seen him yet? How did he react? Maybe he's already released the damning footage. There's no way Jules will know until they land. If Xavier has uploaded the video, Angie will have nothing to lose and God knows what she'll do then.

'Are you worried about your mum?'

Jules opens her eyes. 'A little.'

'I reckon she can handle herself.'

'Not as well as she thinks she can.'

'Waylo's good under pressure. He'll keep an eye on her.'

The engine drops revs and Jules' heart climbs back in her throat until she realises the pilot has powered down to cruising speed. She takes a deep breath, lets it out slowly.

'I was never going to follow that directive.'

Jules turns her face away from him, clocks that the ramp is sealed tight. 'The one that said you could—' She stops, remembering the pilot and co-pilot can hear every word.

'Yeah. I wouldn't have taken that option.'

'It's easy to say that now.'

A pause. 'You're pissed off at the situation, I get that, but don't take it out on me.'

'No, I'm pissed off at *you* because you didn't tell me what you were really doing in that building.'

'When would I have done that? When we were halfway up that ladder or when I was holding you over the elevator shaft?'

'You could've told me in the van.'

'Yeah, you were totally in the mood for that conversation then.' He clears his throat loud enough that she hears it through the headset. 'How can I protect you if you don't trust me?'

'I didn't ask for your protection. All I need is somewhere to stay while my mother runs off to fight a war she can't win.'

'Fine.'

It didn't take long to exhaust that poor excuse for an apology.

An hour passes without another word. Jules spends the time breathing deeply and concentrating on holding the charge behind her ribs. It's constantly changing shape but she has a reasonable grip. The vibrations are steady now and the hum of her own energy has fallen in sync with it.

She's feeling reasonably settled when Ryan unbuckles his belt and stands without a word or a glance her way. A few tentative steps and he gets his balance enough to walk to the tiny window on the other side of the plane. Jules waits for a commentary on the view but he maintains radio silence. After a minute, he moves towards the front of the plane.

'Captain, permission to come up top?' His voice sounds strange in her ear after its absence for so long.

'Permission granted.'

Jules has no idea if the approval extends to her but there's no way she's undoing her seatbelt.

Alone, she feels dwarfed in the yawning space. She imagines these seats packed with soldiers, adrenaline-fuelled energy roiling against the hull. Her dad must have flown in planes like this when he was deployed, strapped in with his platoon on the way to battle. He didn't know what it was like to live with her charge, but he understood nervous energy. Mike De Marchi said there were only two types of people in the world: those who could control their fear, and those who couldn't.

It's only now that Jules wonders which type she's going to find on Ryan's farm.

She's chewing over that thought when Ryan returns a while later. He sits down without speaking and she realises she didn't hear a word of conversation from the cockpit—the pilot must have switched off her headset while Ryan was up there.

'Is there anything I need to know about your family?' she asks, partly to find out the answer and partly to see if she's on air again. He doesn't respond and when she turns to check if he heard her she finds him with his head resting back against the netting, staring up at the curved hull.

'Ryan.' She bumps her knee against his.

'What?'

'It would be good to know something about your family before we turn up at your place.'

'Like what?' He stays fixated on the ceiling.

Great. It's going to be one of those conversations.

'Who lives there?'

'Mum, Dad and my brother Tommy.'

'How old is Tommy?'

'Seventeen this week.'

Is that why he'd applied for leave? 'What do you farm?'

Another pause and Jules notices his fingers have curled into fists on his thighs. 'Wheat and sheep, but it's hard to grow anything in a dust bowl.' She waits for him to say more. It takes so long she thinks the conversation is over, but then: 'The old man won't touch GMO grains or New Gen Prime Lamb Merinos, so now he's got no access to emergency relief funds, a bank loan, or the new inland pipeline. Bloody tough to run a farm with no water and no cash flow.'

'But that legislation hasn't gone through yet.'

'It doesn't need to. The old man's one of only a handful in the district who hasn't signed on to Pax Fed's so-called voluntary scheme. Nobody's channelling resources to a property where the farming practices are "unviable".'

Pax Fed: ruining families across Australia.

'How are your mum and dad surviving?' she asks.

'They're hoping there's a market for traditional spelt wheat if we can get in a decent crop and it rains. And if the wind doesn't blow bloody GMO seed from the rest of the district onto our land.'

'What about the sheep?'

A defeated shrug. 'Half the flock was gone when I left home last year, shot before they starved to death. I don't know what's left now, nobody wants to tell me. I have no idea what I'm going back to.' He picks at a thread on the seam of his jeans. 'If the Paxton legislation goes through we won't have a choice—grow their grain and sheep or lose the farm.'

We've all had shit to deal with.

Jules runs her fingers through her hair. 'Do they know we're coming?'

'Safer for everyone if we just turn up.'

'Will that be okay?'

Ryan meets her gaze but his mind is elsewhere, maybe already on the farm. Wherever it is, it's not a happy thought. 'I guess we'll find out.'

Jules is shifting about, trying to get more comfortable, when the plane drops out from under her. She panics and grabs the seat between them until the plane steadies.

Ryan puts his hand where hers was and leans in. 'You good?'

'Yeah, sorry—'

The plane dips again, more violently and this time she grabs his wrist.

'Hang tight, folks,' the pilot says, his voice fuzzy in the

headset. 'We're in for a bumpy ride for a few minutes. Nothing this old girl can't handle.'

The charge is stronger now. Ryan shifts into the seat next to her and threads his fingers through hers.

'This is nothing. Mick's flown in war zones dodging missiles.' Ryan relaxes his thigh against hers, rests their joined hands on his leg. Her mouth is bone dry but she manages to swallow and nod. Another drop, and this time the engine changes with it. Her heart's thundering, palm sweaty against Ryan's. He has to be worried she's going to electrocute him but he doesn't let go.

He brushes his thumb over her wrist, lightly. Jules closes her eyes again, breathes through the fear.

'You into music?'

'Uh huh.'

'What do you listen to?'

Jules tries to find a meaningful answer but it's hard with the blood rushing in her ears and the noise of the plane. 'All sorts of stuff.'

'Like what?'

She thinks about what's on the old mobile she and her mum share and finally manages to name a few acts.

'Not bad,' he says. 'I'm more an old-school guy myself: drums and guitars. Loud.'

He rattles off a list of his favourite bands, some she's heard of, most she hasn't. The bumpy ride lasts longer than a few minutes but he doesn't miss a beat, even when the plane drops hard enough that the netting above them slaps against the hull. Ryan talks about gigs he's been to since moving to Brisbane, discovering bands in dodgy suburban pubs. It's the most she's heard him speak. Jules focuses on his voice, tries to block out everything else. The whole time he holds her hand in his, unflinching.

He falls quiet when the plane is back on a steady course, but makes no move to untangle their fingers. It's only when the pilot announces their descent that she turns her head and finds him watching her. It's strangely intimate to make eye contact while they're touching and she gently extracts her fingers. She flexes the joints and wipes her hand on her jeans.

'You keep seeing me at my worst.'

Ryan shrugs. 'Next time I'm losing my shit in a small dark space you can hold my hand.' He raises his eyebrows, tentative, and she manages a small smile in return. It's hard to stay annoyed at him. He's the only person aside from her parents to touch her when she's been afraid, knowing what could happen.

Even Vee's never done that.

'He must know I'm here by now.' Angie fidgets with her wedding band, turning it one way and then the other.

Waylon shrugs. 'Makes sense he kept his head down in the city. Nobody outside this rabble is supposed to know he's in charge.'

The bus is packed. The initial buzz at having her on board has calmed and conversations have dropped to a hum. Cool air blasts down from the vents and does nothing to calm her. Waylon is sideways in his seat, his back to the aisle and one knee tucked against his chest.

The Agitator convoy is two hours from Brisbane, heading west out of Warwick. Four buses, two Kombis, eight sedans. All covered in spray-painted slogans and stickers: anti-nuclear, anti-GMO, anti-government. There's no attempt at subterfuge. Whatever they're doing, they're happy for the feds and anyone else to know exactly where they are and where they're headed.

The convoy was waiting on the service road a block south of the Hyperdome. Angie's plan had been to scope out the crowd, find Xavier and see if he gave himself away when he saw her. But as soon as the Agitators boarding the nearest bus spotted her, they herded her on board, hungry to know why she was back. It meant she and Waylon had to trot out their cover story sooner than they'd planned. It also meant she'd lost the element of surprise.

Angie pulls out a bottle from the seat pocket and takes a long drink. The water is tepid, tastes like hot plastic. She'd thought coming back would feel different. *Better.* Maybe it's because none of the faces are familiar. In the two years she's been gone, her old crew has either moved on or been pushed out. She didn't keep in contact with them—her doing, not theirs—so she has no idea when and how it happened. But her status with the Agitators hasn't changed. This crew—younger, harder and angrier than hers—sees her re-emergence as validation of their cause. It took less than two minutes to understand why: they think she's stayed away because of the threat of jail, and she's come back because Jules is old enough to fend for herself if Angie gets locked up. They think she's that callous.

Maybe she's made the wrong decision getting on this bus. Jules was seriously pissed off at her when she left. In any other situation, Angie would be happy to see her daughter fire up, but not like this, not when they're so far apart. Why can't Jules understand Angie's doing this for her? It's the only thing she *can* do.

She's trying not to think of Jules too often because it brings an unfamiliar clutch of panic. She has to believe her daughter will be safe with Ryan. The kid clearly has protective instincts, and Khan is breathing down Voss's neck to keep Q18 accountable for her safety.

Voss.

Angie can't get a read on him: too many years in the military have perfected that stony façade. But she knew him before the wall existed and he knows it. It's been two decades since she's thought about that night in the watch-house, and now she can't shake it. Undercover or not, he surprised her. It was his lips and hands she measured everyone else against until Mike came along and made her forget.

But there's no point trying to reconcile the man Voss was with the soldier he's become; the soldier is the one she has to deal with.

Gum trees flash by outside the bus, branches swaying. They clear the forest a kilometre later and the bus is buffeted by winds gusting across the plain. There's chatter on the two-way radio up front. The driver, a freckled woman with short blue hair and shoulders as wide as the Major's, has a curt conversation over the air that Angie can't pick up.

The bus starts to brake and Waylon straightens to see out the back window.

'They're all slowing,' he says. 'Okay, we're pulling over.'

Angie nods. 'Good. Let's get this over with.'

Waylon shakes his head at her eagerness. 'Be cool, Angie.' He leans down as if to tie his bootlaces, and adjusts the knives strapped beneath his cargo pants.

The bus veers onto gravel with a hiss of brakes. A puff of dust rises up from the roadside and is whipped away in the wind. Waylon is watching something behind them. 'Here he comes,' he says quietly. Angie leans away from the window, refusing to let Xavier catch her looking. The door opens and Xavier appears at the top of the steps. The bus falls silent.

He's younger than Angie expected, but stocky like his photo. His hair is tied in the usual topknot but his beard is trimmed to his jaw. He's wearing a muscle T-shirt with a peace sign, showing off black and grey tatts on both shoulders. His eyes rake over the passengers until he locks on Angie. Everything in her tightens. *Here we go.*

'Angela De Marchi.'

He smiles and the hairs on the back of Angie's neck stand up.

'This is perfect.'

The breeze is cool when the back of the Herc opens at Edinburgh. Outside, the dusk sky is bruised purple and lights are coming on around the base. Ryan is first out of his seat, pulling their luggage from storage at the front of the plane. He's back in South Australia—home—and yet he feels out of place because he's on a military base without the rest of Q18.

He hands Julianne her bag, digs around in his own and swaps his heavy jacket for a hoodie. She's ditched the headset and unclipped her belt but hasn't made it out of the seat. She let go of his hand twenty minutes ago and he can still feel the softness of her skin against his. He doesn't know if it was the contact or the conversation that distracted her; either way, it worked. It would have been easier if he could have let her listen to all the tracks he was describing, but maybe he and Tommy can play a few for her instead. He thinks about the drum kit waiting in the shed at home, runs through the songs he wants to practise.

Julianne is massaging the backs of her thighs to get the circulation moving and Ryan resists the urge to offer her a hand. He also stops short of helping her up. It's only going to set her off again if he treats her like she's helpless, especially now he's seen that she's not.

A sedan with darkened windows pulls up at the end of the ramp. The driver climbs out and signals to them to get in. He's in civvies, but his greying hair is crew cut and his movements precise.

'After you,' Ryan says.

Jules hoists her bag over one shoulder. There's no smile but her mood has definitely improved.

They clear the base and drive towards the city. The driver doesn't give them his name or use theirs. It's Monday and the heaviest traffic is heading in the opposite direction, but they don't take the bypass so there's no avoiding the gridlock at Gepps Cross. Ryan's been here a hundred times: the crossroads that for him have always marked the start of the city. He's never lived in Adelaide but he knows its grids and main roads thanks to countless weekend trips to watch or play footy, or to hang out at the cricket—first with his old man and later with his mates. And then there were the months he spent training at Footy Park before draft camp...

There it is, the sting of regret he thought he'd outrun. It's stronger now he's back, burns almost like it did a year ago. He's not aware he's tapping until Jules nudges his elbow from the back seat.

Fifteen minutes later they're far enough off a major road for Ryan to have lost his bearings. The streets are narrower and the blocks alternate between corrugated iron industrial sheds and tiny houses. They pull up in front of a house that looks exactly like the ones either side: low-set brick with a stone and wrought-iron fence. The only difference is the heavy-duty roller shutters on all the windows. Ryan cracks the car window to get a better feel for the place. Stale brine taints the breeze and muted sounds come from the neighbours: a surround-sound shoot-out on one side; dramatic classical music on the other.

The driver hands Ryan a bunch of keys with a car remote, a bottle opener and a miniature plastic Darth Vader.

'There's transport in the garage and food in the kitchen. The code to get you in the house is your army ID. Entry is a one-time-only deal. You can keep moving or stay the night but be gone by sun-up. Clean up after yourselves and don't touch anything in the spare room.'

'Yes, sir.'

'Tell Voss the car needs to make its way back to me by the end of the month.'

Ryan collects their bags and has barely closed the boot when the sedan pulls away. The tail-lights disappear around the corner and the street falls still. The TV gun battle is over and the night soundtrack fades to distant traffic and the symphony seeping through the bricks next door.

It's a single-car garage with an antique roller door. It takes Ryan three goes before he finds the right key on the bunch. Jules fidgets beside him, repositioning the bag on her shoulder and rubbing her arms against the cold. The door finally gives and a tiny white hatchback stares at them. It's a four-cylinder hybrid. Seriously? Ryan does a lap and kicks the tyres. At least it's not self-drive. And once he's on the A1, he'll still be at the farm gate in less than three hours, even in this shitbox.

He's not ready.

'How about we stay tonight?'

Jules drops her bag inside the garage. 'We're supposed to go to your place.'

'We will, tomorrow. I'd rather arrive during the day.'

'Why?'

'Mum'll crack the shits if we turn up in the middle of the night. If we get home in the morning, she'll at least have the day to get the shed ready.' He can't tell Julianne that his old man is likely to be half-tanked already and will be fully loaded by the time they arrive. Not really the first impression he wants her— anyone—to have of his family.

He finds the keypad by the door into the house, taps in his code.

The house is sparsely furnished: a hard plastic setting in

the kitchen—plus a dartboard and plaster scarred by wayward shots—a bedroom with bunk beds and a bathroom with a shower missing the screen.

Ryan's more interested in what's in the next room along the hallway. He could smell the gun oil from the garage. The door's not locked, so he opens it and flicks the light. His breath hitches.

The walls are lined with floor-to-ceiling lockers, shut tight and padlocked. Military chests are bolted to a rough concrete floor. Ryan moves closer and peers through the diamond-shaped ventilation holes. *Holy shit.* He works his way around the room. The lockers are stacked with assault rifles, handguns and grenades. RPGs. Nerve and smoke canisters and gas masks. That explains the window shutters.

He thought these places were a myth: suburban caches of weapons, stockpiled around the country for use in the event military bases are attacked or compromised. The Major must have serious clout for Ryan and a civilian to be given access. It makes the Browning pistol he's got tucked in his duffel bag seem like a toy.

Ryan hooks his fingers through the grille and thinks about the rest of Q18. He should be with his unit. He shouldn't get to go home when they don't.

'I hope you're not hungry.' Julianne's voice comes from the direction of the kitchen. She didn't follow him into the spare room, which is probably a good thing. He takes one last look around the room, turns off the light, and carefully closes the door.

'This is all there is,' Julianne tells him when he walks into the kitchen. On the bench are two tins of baked beans, a loaf of frozen bread and a super-size bag of Twisties.

'Do we have a toaster?'

There's nothing on the laminated benchtops, not even a kettle or a microwave. Julianne opens two cupboards before she finds plates and a newish toaster. When she plugs it in he guesses they're staying.

'I'll hunt around for bed linen,' he says.

It's only when he's made the lower bunk that a small, hot thrill flashes through him: he and Julianne are going to spend the night in the same room. He starts to fantasise how that might play out—and then wakes up to himself. Nothing's going to happen in an army safe house or anywhere else.

He gets the distinct impression he's not her type: meaning that her type is someone who doesn't have authority—albeit briefly—to maim and kill her.

The Major is at a picnic table in the dark.

He's near a boxy motel on the outskirts of Coonabarabran, sitting far enough from the neon Vacancy sign and the lights of the highway to be out of sight. The evening is cool and heavy with the promise of morning dew.

On the other side of town, the Agitators are bedded down at a caravan park. He wonders if Angie's sleeping in the bus or on the ground, or if Waylon's used his ops cash and shouted her a cabin. Waylon's a sharp lad, but he's even softer than Walsh when it comes to mother figures.

The Major stretches out his legs and settles into the moment. It's good to be away from the city. Out here there's nothing to breach the stillness...even on base it's never like this. He can almost hear the *whomph* of chopper blades in the distance, feel the dry desert air. The smell here is different but for a heartbeat he's back, his unit intact and his body whole. His fingers drift to his shoulder, to the rope of scar tissue running down the front of the joint, and his foot aches. Not the one he has now, the one he left over there.

A white sedan slows on the highway and turns into the motel car park, grille and headlights caked with insects. It pulls up outside room six. Nadira Khan gets out first; scans the car park. The driver follows, a young New South Wales copper on full alert.

Khan peers into the darkness where the Major said he'd be but he's too deep in shadow to see. She hasn't changed from her city clothes, which is a surprisingly rookie move: nothing says *cop* out here louder than a suit jacket. He lets her wait half a minute more to test her nerve. She stands her ground, refusing to blink first.

'Over here.'

Her eyes sharpen in his direction. She says something to the constable and the lad takes up sentry point at the back of the car. She crosses the car park and into shadows.

'Good flight?' He knows full well she came in on a supply plane.

A shrug. 'Where's Private French?'

'Sleeping. She's first shift behind the wheel tomorrow.'

A road train changes gears on the highway, building speed as it heads out of town.

'Xavier's made no attempt to release that footage since he saw Angela this morning,' Khan says. 'Or made any other threats.'

The Major leans back, elbows resting on the table. 'The blackmail is a bluff, probably always was. In which case we can assume Xavier's not serious about exposing Julianne.'

'Or he's under instructions not to. There's growing evidence to support a link between Xavier and the men who stormed Angela's house last night.'

The Major knows where this is headed but he's not holding her hand to help her get there. 'On what basis?'

'Xavier made a phone call today. The number was routed through two satellites and a dummy exchange. Black ops style.'

He ignores the bait.

'Xavier's a nobody—no known associates, no criminal record beyond that one arrest.' Khan sits on the opposite end of the bench. 'He doesn't have the clout or the funds to hire a mercenary crew, which means someone else is calling the shots. And they are connected enough to use military-level communications to evade surveillance and tracking.' She twists her shoulders to stretch out her back. 'Major, we agreed to work together. That involves sharing information, and not only when it suits you. If you can't do that, I'll call in my own backup and run this as a full federal operation.'

The Major scoffs. 'Those men had army equipment and were army trained. It doesn't mean they're still army.'

'Do you know them?'

'No,' he lies. He can sort this without the feds sticking their noses in.

A car hurtles past on the highway into town, windows down and bass thumping. Khan watches it pass and settles back against the table. 'Do you have ears on Xavier yet?'

'Waylon's working on it.'

'Have you picked up anything from his feed?'

'Nothing useful. Xavier made a show of meeting Angie and as far as I can tell she didn't stab him.'

The agent clicks her tongue.

'She's got more self-control than you think, Khan.'

'With someone who pushed her out of the Agitators and threatened her daughter? Major, you're hilarious.'

The car with the bass is coming back. It slows by the turn-off and swings into the motel car park, a dark purple coupe with spoilers and black rims. It passes under the vacancy sign and the front seats are momentarily lit up. The driver and passenger are focused on the constable. They're wearing balaclavas.

'Get down,' the Major yells, a split second before a semi-automatic rifle barrel appears out of the passenger window and opens fire. The young copper ducks behind the white sedan, scrambling as bullets slam into the car and room six, breaking glass. The driver fires in their direction before the Major can get off a shot and he and Khan dive to the ground. The driver searches the darkness as he accelerates, trying to pinpoint their position. The semiautomatic keeps unloading into the motel.

The coupe is between the Major and the building now and he has no idea if the constable's been hit. He rolls over and fires three rounds, shattering the coupe's rear window. Khan empties her clip into the car. She takes out the left rear tyre and the coupe fishtails through the car park.

The room six door bursts open. French sprints after the shooters in singlet and silk boxer shorts, firing as the car slides back onto the highway, tyres howling. The passenger sticks his upper body out the window and fires another round, but the car's all over the place and the shots spray wide. And then the coupe's gone, disappearing up the highway in a trail of smoke and sparks.

The whole attack lasted less than thirty seconds.

'Constable!' Khan runs to the bullet-riddled sedan and helps the young copper to his feet. The lad's tyres are shot to shit: no chance of a pursuit. He's lost his hat and his knees are dirty but otherwise he's uninjured.

'They weren't locals.'

'How can you tell?' Khan asks.

'Our blokes wouldn't know where to start to get their hands on that sort of weaponry, mostly sawn-off twenty-twos in this part of the world. I've never seen that rice rocket before and I've chased 'em all.'

He slides into the sedan and calls in the shooting.

French jogs back to them. Blood streams down her left arm.

'Sir, what the hell?'

'Injury report, private.'

French lifts her arm to get a better look. 'Glass fragments, sir, from the motel window.'

Khan holsters her weapon and dusts off her pants.

'Do you still need me to sell the case that these mercenaries are connected to Xavier?'

The Major ignores her. He's more interested in the holes peppering the timber-clad motel. There's not a single stray bullet: each one has lodged in the front wall and door of room six. Not room five, not room seven. And all of them are above head height. Even the unmarked cop car: the bullets hit tyres and panels away from where the constable took cover.

Khan stands with him, her eyes following the same path. 'Almost respectful, one might say. A polite warning between professionals.'

He ignores the implication.

'They know we're following the Agitators,' Khan says.

The Major checks the clip in his pistol.

'They know *you* are. Let's hope that's all they know.'

They clear the outskirts of Adelaide as the first strains of dawn lighten the eastern horizon.

Jules has adjusted the passenger seat so she's not wedged under the dash, and Ryan's slid his back as far as it goes and still barely fits under the steering wheel. The language is getting worse every time he bumps his knee on the console. Jules is bleary-eyed from the early start and a night of broken sleep. It's been at least a year since she's slept in a bed other than her own, let alone with a six-foot soldier in the room.

They played darts until nearly midnight. At first she'd thought Ryan had let her win the opening game. But the way he grinned after beating her in the next, she knew it was on. He was way too competitive to pull a throw, let alone a game. They played best out of three, then best out of five. It was three-all when Ryan reminded her they had to be up and gone before the sun in the morning.

Jules had showered first—awkward and self-conscious in a strange bathroom—and was tucked under the blanket in her T-shirt and undies by the time Ryan came in. The light was out but she heard his zipper slide and his jeans hit the floor. Jules lay there wondering what he might say to her under the cover of darkness, imagining him half-naked on the bed above her. He'd been checking her out all night—she'd caught him more than once—but he'd made no attempt to flirt. Unless trash talking counted; there'd been plenty of that through six games. She didn't even know if she wanted him to make a move. At the same time it was all she could think about.

It felt like a time-out: a stepping away from the urgency that had brought her here. A beat where she could be in the moment, wrapped in unfamiliar sheets in an unfamiliar house, daring herself to go with whatever might happen.

She'd waited, the current humming. Wanting and not wanting. Remembering Ryan's voice in her ear during the flight and the way his thumb found the soft part of her hand when the plane shuddered; the effort it took not to unload the charge into him. Now there he was, centimetres away. She'd wondered if he was trying to figure out what to say to her, if he was imagining kissing her.

Then he started snoring.

Relief. Disappointment.

A minute later, annoyance: he was so *loud*. How did he not wake himself with that racket?

Jules knows he got a good rest last night—she heard it—but this morning he's been slouching around like he hasn't slept. And that was before his army-issue flexi-phone vibrated with a message. He read it and muttered something about the operation being on track. That was it.

Ryan is fiddling with the radio again, skipping from station to station. A blast of syncopated dance track...a country-pop chorus. A woman screaming over a harp. None of it's working for Ryan and the snatches of music aren't helping Jules find her calm. The time-out is officially over.

'Did you say something about breakfast?' she asks.

He flicks off the radio, his eyes on the bitumen. 'Port Wakefield's not far. We can grab something there.'

As promised, Ryan pulls in at a truck stop. It feels like they're miles from water—there's no hint of blue in sight, only low dusty hills—but Jules can smell the salt on the air, and seagulls squabble between the diesel bowsers. She hugs herself against the chill and follows Ryan inside.

They find a table near a man wearing a singlet and shorts despite the fact it's only fourteen degrees outside. He's hunkered over a plate piled with oversize chops and chips, his backside spilling over his seat. Ryan glances at the meal and away, shoulders tightening. His energy is dull and brooding, so different from last night.

'Are you all right?'

He stares past her to the highway and unease swirls. There must have been more in that text.

'What's happened?'

Ryan doesn't answer.

'Is Mum okay?' She taps a nail on the table like Vee does. '*Ryan.*'

'What?' He shifts his gaze and comes back to the table, finally registering the question. 'She's fine.'

'What's going on with you?'

'Nothing.'

Jules raises her eyebrows at him. He lets his breath out through his nose. 'It's nothing to do with you or your mum or this job. Okay?'

She waits for the spike in his energy, some sign that he's lying, but there's nothing. Maybe his mood really is about going home.

'Okay,' she says.

Their food arrives and they eat in silence. They're back on the road twenty minutes later, driving north, treeless hills on one side and a patchwork of brown paddocks on the other. Hectares of freshly ploughed dirt, the occasional crumbling stone farm shed. They pass a salt lake tinged pink and a string of small towns with sun-bleached wheat silos and fading red rooftops. Everything is dead or dying.

'It looks totally different in winter when it's all green,' Ryan says as if seeing the countryside through her eyes.

176

They round a sweeping bend and there's a change in the horizon: objects sprouting from low hills like splintered toothpicks. It takes another kilometre before Jules realises what she's seeing: a trail of wind turbines, hundreds of them. The highway loops around until the towering structures are parallel to the road. Only half are turning; the others are frozen in place like petrified insects. The charge stirs, as unsettled as Jules in this foreign landscape. Nothing here is familiar: even the cloudless sky is smudged and streaky, and Ryan's mood isn't helping.

She slides lower in her seat and brings her knees to her chest, makes herself small. She's never travelled with someone she doesn't know. Even now, riding in a car with Ryan and knowing that he *knows* about her, Jules feels unstitched, like she might flutter apart without warning.

An uncomfortable truth is taking form: she's less together without Angie.

Ryan drops his speed to sit behind an oversize semitrailer hauling two gleaming water tanks. He sticks out the car's nose into the oncoming lane, prompting a tiny flare of panic.

'You're not thinking about overtaking?'

'In this gutless heap?' He checks the clock on the dash. 'There's no rush, we're making good time.' He doesn't sound happy about it.

They reach a passing lane a few kilometres later and Ryan guns the engine and swings out. The sedan shudders and Jules' pulse picks up—sudden acceleration does that to her—but the charge stays steady. By the time they crest the hill, they're in front of the semi and rocketing along. Ryan stabs the radio button and crackling static fills the car.

Ryan searches until he strikes a thumping beat with funky banjos. It's an old tune, one her dad used to play, and Ryan's eyes light up. 'Dan Sultan. Bonus.' He cranks the volume and taps along on the steering wheel. His lips twitch as if he knows the words and he's trying not to sing, but then the chorus hits and

177

he's mouthing along about hanging with his cousins and texting for loving. The speedo creeps over a hundred and twenty. Jules' pulse keeps time with the drums and her skin buzzes but it's not anxiety driving the current: it's exhilaration.

The next track is newer, a mess of driving guitars and rasping vocals. Ryan keeps tapping and now his left foot's going. The smallest nod of his head. By the second chorus there's barely a trace of tension in his shoulders. Everything about him is fluid.

They clear another hill. On the plain below is a smear of civilisation, a towering smoke stack rising out of it like a middle finger, and then the highway has flattened and they've passed the turn-off to Port Pirie. Beyond the sea of saltbush the smoke stack dominates the skyline, flanked by silos, industrial sheds and cranes, and a huge ship that looks docked on land.

Ryan points in the general direction of the stack. 'If the Major hadn't offered me a job, I'd have been lining up for one over there.'

'At the port?'

'Not if I could help it. Smelters would've been my choice.'

Everyone in the country knows that half the ships coming into Port Pirie carry radioactive waste. From this distance Jules can see a radwaste cask being offloaded onto a freight train—a giant cotton reel packed with spent fuel rods on their way north for 'temporary' storage at Port Augusta.

'What about the farm?'

Ryan works his jaw. He's about to say something and changes his mind. He shifts in his seat, straightens his left arm so his wrist hangs over the wheel and stretches his neck to one side. The tension springs back. 'No future there.'

Like Angie, Jules is good at reading body language. Unlike her mother, she knows when to respect it.

She draws her knees even closer, stares out the window at the hulking industrial landscape and wonders how much darker Ryan's mood will be when he actually gets home.

'Why haven't you taken credit for the Pax Attack?'

The kid with the bristled scalp shakes his head at Angie. 'It's hard to make a statement from behind bars.'

It's not a denial, but it's not an admission either. The kid—Ollie—has claimed the seat in front of her two days in a row and now he's followed her to a picnic table at the rest stop, eager to talk.

The Agitator convoy is north of Dubbo and taking its first break since breakfast. The buses and Kombis are parked outside the toilets, hidden from the highway by a patch of gum trees, and the Agitators are clustered around concrete picnic tables and benches. Their main topic of conversation is the shootout at the motel across town last night.

Angie's more interested in last Wednesday. 'What was the point of blowing up Pax Fed Tower if not to get the credit?'

Ollie straddles the bench. He says he's an Environmental Science grad. From a distance, with his small frame and freckled skin, he looks like he should be in high school. Up close, though, his eyes are sharp and full of secrets.

'The outcome's the point, Angie, not the credit.'

'Which is?'

'Chaos. Making the bastards nervous.'

Angie's grip tightens on the bench. 'Which bastards in particular?'

'Pax Fed, the government, anyone selling off our future: they all need a wake-up call. Last week was only the start.'

Angie rips a splinter from the timber, tearing another fingernail with it. She hasn't wanted to believe the Agitators were responsible. *Hadn't* believed it.

'You knew it was us, right?'

She squints against the glare to mask her bitterness. 'I thought the group was being framed.'

'You didn't think we were capable of it?'

'Agitators have never been killers.'

He scrubs his palm over his bristles. 'People weren't supposed to die.'

'You blew up a gas main in Queen Street. What did you think was going to happen?'

'That wasn't the plan. We didn't know—'

'Who's *we*?'

'*Us*. The Agitators.'

'Who planned the attack?'

Ollie's eyes flick to Xavier. He's beyond the buses, lotus-style in the dirt, watching a fuel tanker rumble down the highway. A girl—fair skin, short skirt and bruised shins—sits on her heels capturing the moment on a vintage SLR camera.

'How long's he been in charge?'

Ollie shrugs. 'He was already running the group when I met him at the anti-GMO rally in Brisbane last July. We hung out and he got me on the team. I'm in charge of coordinating transport.'

'Who's funding this trip?'

'Don't worry, we've got money in the bank.'

Interesting. In Angie's day, the Agitators were financed by corporate sponsors, crowd funders and like-minded businesses wanting to advertise on the group's online channel. They were never flush, but there was enough to keep the site running and pay Angie a modest wage. Most of that income disappeared

180

when Angie left. Jules was right: nobody's going to touch the group now, not after Wednesday's body count. If there's money in the bank, it's coming from another source.

Across the car park, Waylon lopes out of the unisex toilets with a hand to his nose. Angie told him long-drop toilets weren't for city boys. He sees her with Ollie and frowns. Changes course away from them.

'Why the gunmen?'

Ollie's piercings catch a ray of sunlight. 'That was a Pax Fed security team, had to be.'

'Is that Xavier's theory?'

'It makes sense.'

'And what does he think happened in town last night?'

Ollie shields his eyes. 'You think that was about us?'

'I have no idea. That's why I'm asking.'

All Angie's heard is the chatter around the campsite: that shots were fired at a local cop during a drive-by incident. A *drive-by*. In Coonabarabran. Thank God Jules isn't here.

'Maybe the feds want it to look like we're causing problems so they can lock us up in the middle of nowhere,' he says.

Angie scoffs. Her Agitators weren't fans of law enforcement but they were never paranoid. 'I doubt it.'

There's movement at the rest stop. The protesters are breaking from their clusters and moving back to the buses. Angie stretches her legs and worries her torn nail, breathes in dry, dusty air. A crow caws mournfully on the side of the highway.

'What's the plan at Port Augusta?'

Ollie's eyes flick to Xavier. Angie's blackmailer hasn't risen from the dirt, his gaze still fixed on the highway.

'Are you here to lead or follow?' Ollie asks.

'That depends.'

'On what?'

'On whether I think the current leadership has a strategy, or this group is simply careening from one cock-up to the next.'

Xavier rises from the ground and Ollie is instantly on his feet.

'I promise you there's a strategy.' His lips flatten to a hard smile and there's nothing childlike about it. 'It's going to put us on the world stage, Angie. And you'll be right beside us when it happens.'

He leaves her on the weatherworn bench, blood prickling where her fingernail should be and a thorny, unnamed fear vining around her gut.

Ryan turns off the highway and winds his way through bald, thirsty hills. They're always brown in autumn, but after spending a year in Queensland he sees them for their ugliness. It's not his landscape anymore.

Then they clear the pass and Mitchellstone appears below, a grid of iron roofs and dirt roads, and Ryan eases off on the accelerator. He's coasting down the hill when he finally feels a tug for home that has nothing to do with the town or the farm. It's the scribble of gum trees winding down from the hills and cutting through properties across the plain. He and Tommy have their own spot on the creek out the back of their top paddock. That's what's calling him now.

Ryan seriously considers avoiding the main street—seeing the guys is going to be tricky enough without handing them the gift of what he's driving—but he decides that's a bit dramatic. Instead he pulls his cap low and slides down in the seat as far as his knees will allow, ignoring the sideways glance he draws from Julianne. It's weird cruising through town in a stranger's car, like returning to the scene of a crime in disguise. He passes the tennis courts and town hall, the servo and the butcher. The road that leads to the footy oval and netball courts. Then the pub, two churches—side by side—the cop shop and the CWA hall.

Ryan keeps his eyes on the bitumen but he can't miss the dirt-caked ute out the front of McMahon's store: his mum's in town with the dogs. He nearly touches the brakes. It would be easier to see her here, away from the farm and his old man. But stopping would mean their conversation would be overheard and the whole district would know he was home, and he's not ready for that either.

He keeps driving.

It's a weekday so everyone should either be out in the paddock or—in Stevo and Trine's case—over the range at the nuclear plant. The new power station's not popular in most parts of Australia but it's given a few of his classmates some cash in their wallets. Something they weren't getting ploughing dirt and herding starving sheep.

Julianne's been quiet since they turned off the highway. He likes that about her: she's okay with silence. She's taking it all in, head turning from side to side, eyes hidden behind her truck-stop-bargain sunnies. He's curious what a city girl thinks of his one-pub town, but not enough to ask.

He turns into Creek Road and even in a lightweight sedan with skinny tyres he finds the sweet spot on the gravel. It's barely rained since he was last here, and the surface feels the same through the steering wheel. Every corrugated bump, every section where the verge is too soft.

Ryan slows at the old plough and veers onto the dirt track. It heads up into the foothills, not much more than wheel ruts between two barbed wire fences. The paddocks here are thick with ghost gums and stubbled grass. The flock's already chewed everything edible to the ground.

'Are we in a hurry?' Julianne's voice sounds thin.

Ryan checks the speedo. Sixty. He's driven this road hundreds of times, in wet and in dry, knows what speed to hit each bend to avoid spinning out or meeting a strainer post.

'This is how I drive around here.' His mood's lifting, he can't help it. A quick glance at Julianne. 'You okay?'

She nods.

'Hang on.'

They hit the dip at fifty and they're airborne for a split second. The hybrid bottoms out on the other side and Ryan grins. The Major's mate would shit himself if he could see his car now.

Julianne is hanging on to the doorhandle and the dash, feet apart on the floor. 'You're a lunatic,' she says. Her eyes are wide but she's not scared. It's the same look Tommy got the first time Ryan did donuts in the paddock in the old man's ute.

'Wait till I bring you back up here on the bike.'

He rounds the last bend and remembers the car he's in, so his usual handbrake slide is out of the question. He slams on the footbrake and they come to an abrupt and untidy finish in the clearing. Ryan waits until the dust cloud overtakes them before getting out. He stretches his shoulders and rolls his neck.

'Where are we?'

Julianne is out of the car, wrapping her hoodie around her as she takes in the towering ghost gum and dry creek bed, hemmed in by scrub and sky.

'This is our place—mine and Tommy's.'

Ryan kicks off his boots and hobbles across loose stones to the creek. He's gone soft after a year of wearing boots all day. He skirts last winter's fire pit and picks his way over the smooth rocks until he reaches the middle of the creek bed. Even bone dry, there's something steadying about standing barefoot in this place. He puts his back to Julianne so she can't see him close his eyes and breathe in the tang of the bush. He lets the quiet settle on him.

This is home.

When he turns around she's running her fingers over the wide trunk of the gum and the markings he and Tommy have carved into its skin over the years. Words they were never allowed to use at home. Drawings of giant penises. Initials of girls they'd wanted to bring here. Ryan can feel Julianne's disapproval and instinctively knows it's not about the dick pics.

'That gum was here before I was born and it'll be here long after I'm gone,' he says, treading carefully to avoid three-corner jacks on his way back to his boots.

'So it's okay to deface it?'

Typical tree-hugger. It's survived drought and bushfires, been eaten by grubs and shat on by a thousand galahs. A few scratches are the least of its worries. Ryan laces up his steel caps and reaches for the rope wound around a knot on the trunk. It drops out to hang out over the deepest part of the creek. A stagnant puddle is the only clue it's seen water at all this year.

'There used to be enough rain to fill that waterhole every winter, but we haven't used the rope for years.'

'What do you do up here aside from vandalise trees?'

He shrugs. 'Talk shit. Hang out.'

Ryan got drunk here for the first time when he was fifteen. He and Rabbit stole a bottle of rum from the footy club and drank it with flat coke until they threw up. The bottle was only half-full, which was probably why they didn't end up with alcohol poisoning. He got laid for the first time under this same tree a year later, in the passenger seat of Missy's hatchback. She was three years older and they were both drunk. She'd taken the lead, made him wait. It was awkward in that cramped space, but she was on a mission and made a big deal about how long he'd lasted. In hindsight it wasn't that impressive, but at the time he'd been full of himself. They'd done it a few more times before Missy officially hooked up with Nunnie—she was strictly a one-man woman—and the two of them stayed friends. Something he'd got worse at as he got older. There'd been other girls and other cars, but that first time was seared into his memory.

Ryan sneaks a look at Julianne. He imagines her half-undressed in his car—not the hybrid, his old man's Monaro—face flushed, wanting him, her hands on him—

He turns away, well aware of where his blood's rushing right now.

Julianne wanders down to the creek and sits on a flat rock, cross-legged, and tips her head to a cloudless sky. Ryan dusts off his hands and is on his way to the car for a bottle of water when he hears the trail bike lower on the track.

Julianne jumps up, looking to him for direction.

'It's okay, it's Tommy.' He frowns as he says it. His brother should be at school.

'He's not expecting me. Might be best you stay out of sight until I tell him what's going on.'

She looks around. 'Where?'

'Behind the tree, only for a sec. He won't hear a word I say otherwise.'

The bike's closer now, revving hard as Tommy accelerates for the dip. Julianne disappears behind the gum. Ryan props himself on the back of the hybrid, hears Tommy change down coming into the bend. His heart's a little bigger than it was a minute ago. It's been a year since he's seen Tommy and he hasn't let himself miss his brother until now.

Tommy takes the corner tight, like he always does, handling the Yamaha beautifully—

It's not Tommy.

No...wait. *Shit*, he's grown.

Tommy grins as soon as he sees Ryan. He slides the bike to a stop a couple of metres away and drops it, engine still running.

'What the fuck, Ryno!' He leaves the bike in the dirt and grabs Ryan in a man-hug. A quick back slap and they're apart again, but it's enough to confirm Tommy's grown in the year Ryan's been gone. Two years younger, and he's almost caught up to him.

'What's with the bum fluff?' Ryan says.

'It's my beard, bro.' He touches his chin, self-conscious, and is immediately *Tommy* again.

'Needs work.'

They grin at each other.

'You're early. Party's not until tomorrow night.' He leans down to kill the engine and the stillness returns.

'What are you doing home this hour of the day?' Their mum's always insisted Ryan and Tommy both finish Year 12. She didn't care if they planned to spend the rest of their lives driving a tractor; she wanted them to know how to think. Ryan's not sure she understands how school works.

'We got a lot going on. Spud Laidlaw's dropping off the ram tomorrow arvo so the ewes need bringing up today or tomorrow and we haven't got the seed in yet. I was sowing the house paddock when I saw the dust up here. I figured I'd better come and see who's poking around.'

'What's the old man doing through all this?'

Tommy's grin fades and it brings a stab of unease.

'Having a bad day.' Tommy rubs at his soft whiskers. His hair's finer than Ryan's, fairer. It's shorter too, and sticking up in all directions after being on the bike.

'What's that mean?'

His gaze slides away. A white cockatoo shatters the silence with a shriek further along the creek. 'He drinks himself stupid and sleeps out in the shed sometimes. He's pretty useless the next day. But it's only every now and then.'

Anger curls up like smoke. 'How's Mum with that?'

'She used to crack the shits and they'd fight for a few days. Now she lets him go. Waits for him to come good.'

'Bloody hell, mate, why didn't you say something?' Ryan knew his dad was drinking more but not that it was keeping him from working.

'What's the point? It's not like you can come home whenever you want.'

'What sets him off?' But Ryan knows the answer as soon as he asks.

'Seeing Maxie Barclay in his shiny new tractor, running into a pipeline maintenance crew at the pub, watching the Paxtons

188

on the news...take your pick.' A nervous glance to read Ryan's mood. 'Mostly it's the days your money goes in the bank.'

Ryan leans against the car, all the air going out of him. He wishes Julianne hadn't heard that.

'How's the seeding going?'

'Don't do that. Don't change the subject every time I try to talk about it. Your money's the only thing keeping food in the fridge some weeks. That's what guts Dad so badly, but without it we'd be—'

'*Tommy*, I've got someone with me.'

His brother falters, looks around. 'Where?'

'Julianne,' Ryan says over his shoulder and she emerges from behind the tree. She doesn't say a word or raise a hand, simply waits for the reaction.

'Ryno, you brought a *girl* home?' Tommy's instantly alight again. It's like a switch, this ability of his to flip from big kid to grown-up and back again in a heartbeat. He moves past Ryan, offering his hand. 'I'm Tommy, this dopey bastard's brother.'

Julianne hesitates—the greeting's not what she was expecting—but she takes his hand. 'Julianne De Marchi.'

Tommy blinks. 'I thought you looked familiar.' He studies her for a second. 'You look different from the photo they're showing on TV. What are you doing hanging out with Ryno? Better question: what are you doing in Mitchellstone? There's gotta be a million better places to hide out.'

'What makes you think she's hiding out?' Ryan asks.

'Why else would she be here?' To Julianne: 'The news is saying you and your mum blew up Pax Fed Tower. That true?'

She shakes her head, her eyes never leaving him. 'I was in the wrong place at the wrong time and my mum was sitting at home watching it all on TV.'

'I've got no beef with someone hitting Pax Fed or knocking those Agitators on their arses—no offence—but people getting killed...'

'I know.'

'So-o. Why are you with Ryno?'

She raises her eyebrows at Ryan to answer. Fair enough, it's his family.

'Julianne's helping out with a cross-agency investigation,' he says, trying to say it the way the Major did. 'She needs to drop out of sight for a bit. The Major thought I should bring her home for a few days.'

'Yeah,' Tommy says. 'Nobody would come looking for her in this shithole.'

'That's the plan.'

Ryan takes a closer look at Tommy's sweat-stained T-shirt, tanned neck and callused hands. His brother's been doing the heavy lifting for more than a day here and there.

Tommy claps his hands together. 'Gemma's coming over for a jam tonight. Can you sing? Play?'

Julianne frowns but Tommy jumps right back in.

'That's cool. We'll find something for you to do.' Tommy picks up the bike and straddles it. 'You coming home now?'

'I saw the ute in town.'

'Mum's getting aspirin for Dad. She won't be far away.'

Ryan does a lap around the Yamaha as if he's checking whether or not Tommy's been taking care of it. But he's not seeing the bike. He's seeing the homestead and his old man, and he's still not ready.

'Ryno, you can't stay up here. Not in *that*.' He gestures to the hybrid. 'Please tell me that's not yours.'

'Don't insult me. It's a loaner.'

'You following me back down, then?'

Ryan wishes his insides didn't squirm every time he thinks about turning into the long driveway and seeing his dad for the first time since the fight. The need to patch things up doesn't seem so urgent without a rifle muzzle pressed to the back of his head.

And now he's bringing Julianne De Marchi into this mess.
Taking a lit match into a woodshed.

Tommy kickstarts the bike, waits for a response.

Ryan exhales and gestures to the track.

'After you.'

Ryan's tension comes at her in waves, setting off her pulse. It's like being trapped inside a thunderstorm. He's rigid in his seat and strangling the steering wheel, eyes fixed on Tommy fish-tailing ahead of them, showing off.

In any other situation she'd let Ryan work through his own drama—rule number one of living with Angie De Marchi is to give her space when she's stewing—but his mood is affecting hers. And if things are as dysfunctional as it sounds at the Walsh farm, she needs to be in control when they arrive.

'Is there any chance you could chill a little?'

They're back on the wide gravel road, clear of the creek and the trees. 'If you wanted chilled, you should've gone with Tommy.'

Maybe she should have. He's a damn sight easier to read than his brother. Physically, Tommy is a younger version of Ryan, but there's a lightness to him, despite the obvious issues at home.

'Sometimes the current reacts to other people's energy and yours is not ideal right now,' she says.

He glances sideways. 'You can *feel* my energy?'

'It happens when someone's worked up enough. I can't always deflect it.'

He grinds his jaw. 'What do you expect me to do about it?'

'Vee says the best way to get tension out of your body is talk it out. Or yell at the sky.' Actually, Vee says good sex is the best form of stress relief but Jules keeps that tip to herself.

'What do you do—talk or yell?'

'Neither. I offload mine into the ground.'

Jules appreciates the irony of passing on Vee's advice: she's never taken it herself. Releasing the charge is one thing: the thought of letting go in any other way feels like surrendering too much of herself.

The hybrid feels like it's floating as they speed past vast bare paddocks. Jules can't see Tommy for the dust his bike is stirring up. She can taste it through the vents, though, coating the back of her throat.

'You and your dad don't talk at all?'

Another sideways glance. An impatient sigh. 'No.'

'How come?'

'We had a fight.'

It's like pulling teeth. Jules takes a slow, calming breath.

'I made a choice he didn't like,' Ryan says finally.

'You joined the army?'

He hesitates. 'Yeah.'

Jules can see it was more than that but she wants to get to the heart of the issue before he shuts down again.

'And now you send money home.'

He doesn't answer but he doesn't have to. They both know she heard what Tommy said.

'How can you afford that?'

A stiff one-shouldered shrug. 'The army feeds me and gives me a bed and I'm not much of a drinker. As long as I've got enough cash to catch a band occasionally I'm happy.'

'Why's your dad angry if you're helping out?'

'Because I'm doing what he can't.'

Ahead of them, buildings start to take shape. Steel sheds of various sizes, old stone barns with thatched roofs, a tall silo. Two rows of rigid pine trees form a line between the gate and the homestead.

They slow. Ryan follows Tommy over a livestock grid and into the driveway—Jules' bones judder as Ryan takes it too fast—and then they're speeding between the pines. Jules catches flashes of a stationary tractor in the paddock on the right. Hooked to it is an alien-looking piece of machinery, a long row of claws resting on dry soil. The homestead is all bullnose iron and weathered stone, red brickwork framing windows and two fat chimneys punctuating the roofline. It's tired and faded, but the house stands proud. It wasn't always a struggle here.

Tommy stops at a gate near the back of the house. Ryan keeps driving. He passes chook yards and an empty stable, and weaves around a large gum tree peppered with white blossoms. Ahead is a corrugated iron shed and empty stockyards, a shearing shed maybe. Before they get there, Ryan veers into a carport and parks beside a low, wide car covered with a tarp. He pulls on the handbrake and sits for a long moment. The engine ticks as it cools and the quiet closes in.

'Can you do this?' Jules doesn't mean to whisper.

'Yeah. Can you?'

'Yeah.' It's a lie, but adding to his stress right now won't help either of them. Maybe it'll be better when they're not in a confined space. They leave the hybrid and walk to the house. Ryan's eyes flick to a shed with a glass sliding door and vertical blinds. Jules can hear muted music: heavy metal.

'My room,' Ryan says. 'That's where the old man's passed out.'

'You want coffee?' Tommy asks. He's sitting sideways on his bike in the shade of a pine tree, one knee on the fuel tank. He watches them approach, looking for an excuse to smile.

'Yeah,' Ryan says. 'And then I'll give you a hand in the paddock.'

Tommy tilts his head and squints one eye, like he's trying to figure something out. 'Are you two together?'

'No,' Jules says quickly, not looking at Ryan. She pushes up the sleeves of her hoodie and pulls them down again past her knuckles, feels heat flare in her cheeks.

Tommy shakes his head. 'You've lost your game, Ryno.'

'Shut up and put the kettle on.' Ryan punches him lightly on the arm and both brothers turn to the road at the sound of a car.

'Twenty bucks says the first thing Mum does is burst into tears when she sees you.'

'You're on,' Ryan says. 'She'll go crook first.'

Jules feels a flutter of nerves and notices Ryan run his tongue over his teeth and check his shirt. If he hasn't been home for a year, does that mean he hasn't seen his mum in that time either? The thought of not seeing Angie for that long entices and terrifies her in equal measure.

The ute barrels over the grid and heads for the house in a puff of dust. Jules sidles further into the shade of the pines. All she can make out of the driver is an Akubra hat and sunglasses. Ryan's mum skids to a stop behind Tommy's bike and is out of the car as soon as she cuts the engine, leaving the drivers door open.

'What's wrong? Are you okay? Why didn't you tell me you were coming?' She's striding to Ryan, barely notices Jules. Two kelpies—one rusty brown, the other a patchwork of black and white—are out of the ute and scuffling around Ryan's feet, whining. He bends down to pat them, not taking his eyes from his mum.

'I'm fine, Mum.'

She stops before she reaches him. Even at this distance, Jules can feel Ryan's energy settle. It could be the dogs or it could be his mum. She's wearing faded jeans and a navy shirt with the sleeves rolled above her elbows. She takes off her sunglasses to look him over. 'Ryan James—'

'Seriously, Mum, I'm here for work. *Army* work.'

She folds her arms, tests his words for truth. While Angie is all angles, Ryan's mum is all curves. Her blonde hair is tied

195

at the nape of her neck, long enough to sit over her collar. She looks to Tommy. 'That true?'

'He's got protective duty on Julianne De Marchi, so he's brought her home to show her the glamorous life of us farm boys.'

Ryan's mum finally acknowledges Jules and the recognition follows. She knows exactly who Julianne De Marchi is. 'Hello Julianne,' she says, her voice neutral. 'Have you spoken to your father yet, Ryan?'

'No.' In the shed, the last song has finished and the next one hasn't started. 'But he's obviously doing a bang-up job.'

'Please don't start. Can I enjoy having you home for a full minute before we get into that?'

He lets out his breath. 'Does that mean you're happy to see me?'

'Of course I am. I can't believe you're standing here in front of me.' Her voice breaks on the last word and her face crumples. 'Now look what you've done.' She waves him to her. 'Come here.' They meet halfway. She barely reaches his shoulder and he has to lean down so she can get her arms around his neck. The dogs settle at their feet, tails wagging. Her hat falls off and Tommy scoops it up, brushes off the dirt.

'I missed you,' Ryan says to his mum. 'Even the nagging.'

She laughs into his shoulder.

Jules should turn away—it's a private family moment and she's an intruder—but she can't stop watching. They're so easy with each other. A longing for contact, for *connection*, rises up so strong it jolts the current to life. She digs her hands into her pockets and concentrates on reeling it back from her hands. Her body's never responded like that to loneliness before.

'Come on,' Ryan says to his mum. 'I'll tell you what's going on while Tommy makes us coffee.'

Jules follows Tommy inside, leaving Ryan with his mum and the dogs on the verandah. The kitchen's almost the size of Jules' entire house but once she gets over the high ceiling and long bench, she realises it's not that different from her own: threadbare tea towels, mismatched cups drying in the sink rack, a toaster missing two out of three knobs and an old fridge rusting at the corners.

She takes a stool and waits for Tommy to start up a conversation. It's only after a minute of silence that she realises he's trying to listen in on the murmuring voices outside. When the kettle grumbles to life and makes that impossible, he props his elbows opposite her on the bench and drums his fingers on the speckled surface.

'How's Ryno doing?'

Jules glances at the back door.

'I don't mean today,' Tommy says. 'Is he doing okay in Brissie? Girls, mates? We talk on the phone but he never gives much away. You know what he's like.'

Strangely enough, she's starting to think she might, at least as far as his capacity for deep and meaningful conversations goes.

'He seems to get on well with his roommate.'

'Waylon, yeah, he sounds like a solid guy.' Tommy frowns. 'And you two have never hooked up?'

Jules feels the heat again. Not all of it in her face. 'We only met a few days ago.'

'I guess that means you'll be sleeping in the house with us.'

Jules blinks. Is that the choice: sleep in the shed with Ryan or here in the house with complete strangers? She hadn't thought that far ahead.

'You want to see the spare room?' Tommy's out of the kitchen before Jules can say no. She'd rather Ryan's mum was giving her the tour, confirming that she's welcome.

'You coming?' he calls from further in the house.

Jules passes through a dining room—the table and corner desk are buried in haphazard stacks of paperwork—and finds Tommy halfway down a wide hallway. The walls are hung with watercolours of varying sizes, rural landscapes mostly, and the occasional rooster. The signature is the same on all of them.

'Mum used to paint,' Tommy says, offhand. 'Right, here's where you'll be sleeping.' He goes in and cracks the blinds. Jules stays in the doorway so she can take it all in: wall-to-wall footy posters, framed photos and jerseys, shelves of trophies and a fat bunch of medals hanging off the handle of a cricket bat. A double bed is pushed up against one wall, the only clue the room was once something other than a sporting shrine.

Jules picks up a statue of a cricketer, sees Tommy's name engraved on its base.

'Are these all yours?'

'I wish. They're mostly Ryan's. He left them in here when he moved out to the shed.'

Jules recognises Ryan in one of the larger photos, leaping high over a pack of footy players, his fingertips first to the ball and his face open, expectant.

'Didn't he tell you?' Tommy says. He's holding a football now, handballing it to himself.

'Tell me what?'

'Ryno was set to be the number one draft pick in the AFL the year before last. Hands-down favourite. And then he blew out his knee at draft camp, and I mean blew it *totally*. No club wanted to touch him until he'd had the surgery and they could see how he pulled up. Problem was Mum and Dad didn't have private health insurance—who does these days?—so they couldn't afford the sort of op he needed. I think it gutted Dad more than Ryan. That was the start of it, really.'

Jules has moved on to the next photo: two rows of straight-backed boys in black-and-yellow striped jerseys. She finds Ryan in the centre of the front row—guarded but smiling—with his hands clenched on his knees. A prominent '(c)' sits next to his name. *Captain.*

'His knee's fine now.'

He didn't have any trouble scaling the elevator shaft or chasing her down the laneway last week.

'It'd want to be,' Tommy says. 'Voss turned up two days after it happened and recruited Ryno right where you were standing in our kitchen. Offered to pay for his op and rehab in return for five years of army service and monthly pay.' Tommy spins the footy in his hand. 'Ryno knocked him back at first. He'd only planned to leave the farm to chase the footy dream. All he ever wanted was to play for the Crows, you know? He was awesome to watch, too. *Smart.* Quick and fearless, read the play beautifully. Never a smartarse on the field.' Tommy's smiling, remembering. 'Then the bank knocked us back on a hardship loan because Dad wouldn't plant a GMO crop—after he'd already said no to a discounted herd of Pax Fed's extra-meat sheep. *That* was a fun night.'

Jules has a flash of Angie clutching an empty glass and ranting at newsreaders, calling them *lazy* and *puppets* and promising to expose the lot of them when she got her life back. Jules has had a few fun nights of her own.

'Dad didn't want Ryno to leave, said the public hospital surgery on his knee would be enough to keep him mobile, but we all knew he'd never play footy again. He was an elite athlete. He never would've coped not being able to play in the local league, let alone at AFL level. Whatever the army's done, it's got him running again. He reckons his beep test is almost up where it was at draft camp. I know he's not playing footy but he's fit enough if he wanted to. That's gotta help his headspace.'

Jules sits on the edge of the bed and touches one of the medals. Ryan joined the army to support his family.

'Do you know what he does for Major Voss?' she asks Tommy.

He shrugs. 'Some secret squirrel shit.'

She runs her fingers across a crocheted blanket draped on the end of the bed. It's made up of blue, red and gold squares and must be football-related because nobody would put those colours together as decor.

'I guess you miss having him around.'

Tommy flicks one of the medals. 'Every day.' He fidgets with the cords on the blinds, staring out the window. 'But you know, it's—ah, crap.'

He drops the cords and hurries past Jules.

'Dad's up.'

Ryan is on his feet on the verandah.

'You look like shit.'

He's not saying it to pick a fight: his dad looks terrible. Bloodshot eyes, three-day growth and the shuffle of a man with a sore head. He's managed to get his hat and boots on, though, so he's not totally useless. His dad props at the house gate, says nothing.

'Bloody hell, I come home for the first time in a year and find you sleeping off a bender in the middle of the day while Tommy's busting a gut trying to keep this place alive.'

The bleary eyes harden. 'You don't know what you're talking about.'

Ryan's aware of Tommy hovering at the back door, staying out of it. The dogs haven't moved from under the table.

'I know Tommy's got the seeder hooked up, trying to get something in the ground in case it rains.'

'It's not going to rain. That'd involve something going right.'

'What about bringing the ewes in and having something for Spud's ram to do when he drops it off tomorrow?'

'We've barely got a hundred head left.'

'So? There's no future for the flock at all if they're not in lamb come spring.'

'Well, fuck me, son. How have we coped without you and your decades of farming wisdom this past year?'

'All right, you two, that's enough.' Ryan's mum is up from the table and on the move.

'No, Shell, I'm not having him strolling back here telling me how to run my farm.'

She touches Ryan's arm as she heads down the step—her way of telling him to shut up.

'Ryan's here for a few days so you'll have plenty of time to growl at each other.' She reaches the gate and makes a show of recoiling. 'God, Jamie. Go have a shower and shave, and put those clothes straight in the wash. I'll get the aspirin.'

'I'll do a few hours in the paddock first.'

'No you won't. Ryan's brought a guest home and it'd be nice for you to look and smell a whole lot better when you meet her.'

De Marchi.

Ryan checks the back door and finds Tommy there alone. 'Where's Julianne?'

Tommy leans into the house. 'She was here a second ago.'

Oh shit. Ryan pushes past his brother, hurries through the empty kitchen and into the hallway. The front door's open. He breaks into a jog, aware Tommy is right behind him.

'What's up?'

Ryan doesn't answer. As soon as he's on the front verandah he sees Julianne kneeling in the yard, gripping the bottlebrush farthest from the house.

'De Marchi—'

Crack.

The trunk bursts into flames.

Julianne scrambles backwards on her hands and feet to escape the heat. Her eyes snap to Ryan, panicked.

'What the hell was that?' Tommy says and bolts for the garden hose.

'I'm sorry,' Julianne says, breathing hard. 'I didn't know where else to go.'

Ryan's beside her in the dirt, not game to touch her. He's

202

sweating already: the fire is scorching. 'Finished?'

She nods, fixated on the flames consuming the tree. Tommy's hosing it, using precious water from the underground tank. The air is heavy with ozone and burning sap.

'Tommy, go keep the olds distracted.' Ryan takes the hose from his brother. 'Don't let them come out here.'

'They're going to smell it.'

'Not if you get them in the kitchen. I need a minute.'

'What happened?'

'We'll explain later.'

'Promise?'

'Yeah, Tommy. *Go*.'

Tommy sprints back into the house, banging the front door shut behind him. Ryan wrenches off the tap. The fire's taking too much water; he has to let it burn itself out. The flames are contained and there's no wind to carry embers so hopefully they've done enough. The leaves of the bottlebrush are gone, its bare branches wet and blackened. A few lazy flames lick the higher limbs but they've got nowhere to go.

'I didn't know what else to do,' Julianne says. 'You were so worked up, I could feel it from inside the house.'

'Is that normal?'

'No.' She drags a loose hair from her face. 'Mum's the only person who affects me like that.'

What does that mean?

He helps her up. 'We should've stopped on the way here so you could offload,' he says. 'I was too busy planning that fight with Dad to think about it.'

'I can't stay here.'

'It'll be fine.'

'Your brother saw how the tree caught fire.'

'Tommy's cool—'

'He *saw* and you said you'd explain it. Nobody's supposed to know, Ryan.'

'Seriously, if I tell him to keep it to himself, he will.'

Ryan starts at the sound of boots on the concrete verandah, approaching from the other side of the house.

'Hang on, Mum,' Tommy says loudly.

Ryan's drawing a blank on how to handle this. His mum rounds the corner and pulls up short. 'Why is my bottlebrush a smoking ruin?'

'I'm really sorry,' Jules says, stepping forward. 'It was an accident.'

Ryan stares at the back of Julianne's head. She's going to confess but he has no idea to what.

'I'm not good with conflict and I came out here to get away—'

'Do you have any idea what happens if there's a fire this time of year?'

'It was our fault,' Tommy says, jumping down from the verandah to stand with Ryan and Julianne. 'We surprised her while she was playing with this.' He pulls out a miniature black cigarette lighter. 'Open flame, dry leaves,' Tommy continues. 'But it's all sorted. I'll hang on to this little baby and we'll be fine. Right, Julianne?'

She nods, slowly.

Ryan's mum does a lap around the bottlebrush, staying far enough away to avoid the ash-stained mud. 'Did you leave any water in the tank?'

'Yeah,' Tommy says. 'We didn't use any more than Ryan does in the shower.'

Ryan shoves Tommy, attempting to play along. When did his brother learn to think this quick on his feet? His mum looks from Tommy to Ryan. She knows something's up.

'Julianne.'

'Yes, Mrs Walsh.'

'We've got enough going on in this house without me worrying about you setting off a bushfire.'

'I understand.'

'Ryan tells me it's safe for you to be here. I want to trust his judgment but he doesn't always think straight around pretty girls with long legs.'

Ryan throws his mum a look that she ignores.

'I'm not here to cause drama,' Julianne says. 'I totally understand if you don't want me to stay.'

Ryan's mum clicks her tongue the way she does when she's being misunderstood. 'I didn't say you couldn't stay; I'm asking you not to set anything else on fire. Deal?'

Julianne breathes out. 'Okay.'

His mum takes one last look at the smoking bottlebrush and shakes her head. 'This should help things no end with your father.'

'What happened last night, Major?'

'Your merc unit paid us a visit. If they had a kill order, it was a sub-par effort.'

'Stop calling them that. They're not *mine*.' Peta Paxton's irritation is hushed over the line.

'Somebody's paying their wages.'

The Major is at a remote servo, talking on his phone away from the pumps and charging stations. French is filling up the van and Khan's inside searching for something that might pass as coffee.

'What makes you so sure it's the same men?'

'Same weapons, same skills.'

'How does that tie them to me?'

The Major stretches his neck to one side, feels the pull of the tendon. The breeze coming off the plain chills the late afternoon sun. Everything around him is tired and faded: the sign on the highway, the peeling adverts above the pumps, the dry carcass of a roo being picked over by two crows.

'Major—'

'They had access to your building, they knew when the power was going out and they had a clear exit. It was an inside job, and now they're shadowing the Agitators cross-country and warning off anyone who gets too close. They're an assault team providing protective duty.'

'And I know nothing about it.' A calculated pause. 'Have you learnt anything about Wednesday's attack?'

'Nothing I can tell you.'

'I'm subsidising this operation—'

'Xavier's been linked to an imminent energy security threat, Paxton. Your needs come a distant second.'

She huffs into the phone. 'I can't believe you put Angela De Marchi on one of those buses. Does she know Xavier?'

'There's no connection. Anything else?'

A beat. 'Where's Julianne De Marchi?'

A four-wheel drive towing a caravan slows on the highway and the crows scatter from the carcass. The Major waits for the vehicle to pass and Paxton reads it as stonewalling.

'Major, she may not be safe.'

'Last week she wasn't safe from us.'

'That was a precaution, this is different. She's disappeared and someone is going to considerable lengths to find her. If it's the mercenary unit, she's in real danger.'

'Why would mercs track an eighteen-year-old girl?' But the Major knows the answer and he's starting to suspect Peta Paxton does too. He watches French walk into the servo to pay, passing Khan on the way out with takeaway cups.

'I can't answer that, but whoever is looking for her hacked our surveillance footage after the attack and downloaded one of the last camera feeds before the power went.'

At the van, Khan rests the cups on the dash and gestures for him to wind up the call. The Major can guess what's coming, but waits for Paxton to say it.

'It's of Julianne in the lift with one of your soldiers. If she's under your protection, Major, you'd better stay sharp.'

Angie misses her bed.

She'd forgotten that protest road trips are all about sleeping under a cold night sky and being eaten alive by insects, or being wedged in a bus seat—or on the floor—with people who haven't showered for two days. Last night she was on the bus. Tonight, with that extra day of unwashed armpits, she's rolled out her swag next to Waylon's under the trees. Right now he's on the other side of the camp, flirting with Xavier's photographer.

The convoy is an hour south of Broken Hill. Angie had expected to spend the night in town, but no, they kept driving to a rest stop. At least this one has toilets and they've got the site to themselves. A semitrailer slowed not long after they arrived. The driver took one look at the buses, changed gears and kept going. Smart move: truck drivers and environmentalists tend not to play well together. Not that Angie's convinced of the environmental cred of this crowd.

The Agitators are clustered around Tilley lamps, sharing trail mix and energy drinks and writing anti-nuclear signs with fat black markers. Between the buses and Kombis there must be at least two hundred people in the convoy. Angie hasn't switched on Waylon's lamp, preferring to sit in the gathering dark to get a better feel for the mood of the group.

'This is a waste of time.'

'He's got a strategy and it involves placards. Keep writing.'

Two men sit on logs about ten metres from Angie, their voices carrying on the motionless desert air. They're in their early twenties with hard mouths and tattooed knuckles. Both are chain-smoking hand-rolled tobacco. The new breed of Agitator.

'It needs to be *big*,' the guy on the right says. He's balancing a placard on bony knees, a texta in one hand and cigarette in the other. 'We've had our heads so far up our arses fighting the war against idiots that we've dropped the ball. The farmers are starving, the military's up for sale and we're building nuclear power plants and radioactive waste dumps.' The other guy nods along—it's a well-worn spiel, but he's on board with hearing it again.

'The bastards will sit up and take notice after Saturday.'

'You know what's going down?'

'Nah, but Xavier'll make it count.'

A mossie buzzes and Angie slaps at her neck. The two men turn and peer into the shadows. She holds her breath until their interest returns to the placards.

Angie feels around for her water, needing to wash away the bitter taste in her mouth. They're using her rhetoric—the inspiration for anti-violent resistance—to justify violence. There's nothing else about this group that belongs to her, only her words, twisted and made vile for a new agenda. She chugs a tepid mouthful and screws the cap on so hard the plastic grazes her fingers. Above her the night is clear and stark, an ocean of stars.

A figure emerges from the lead bus. Stocky build, man bun, arrogant gait. He checks the faces in each cluster of protesters, sweeps a beam of light over the spaces between them. He's looking for Angie. She waits, watching the way the Agitators grow wary when he passes, as if they're not quite convinced he's tame.

When he reaches her, she raises a hand to block the glare. 'Who are you after?'

'You.'

She puts her back to him and finds her own torch. She shines it straight at his face and feels a flash of satisfaction when he squints against it. 'What's up?'

'We need to talk.'

Angie leaves her torch on, forcing him to keep his face turned as he lowers himself to the ground.

'Hang on a sec.' She reaches for Waylon's lamp.

'We don't need a light.'

Angie turns it on as bright as it will go. He's kidding himself if he thinks he's getting away with another faceless conversation. He sits cross-legged, his back straight and hands resting on his knees. The soles of his feet are hard and cracked and his toes hairy. He's broad enough to block her view of Waylon.

'Why didn't we stop in town?'

'And miss inconveniencing our escort? Where do you think the coppers are laying their heads tonight? Not in a comfy bed, I promise you.'

A marked police car has been following them since they left Coonabarabran. Angie hasn't caught sight of it since they set up camp but it won't be far away. Neither will Voss and Khan, assuming the Major's plan is still on track.

She and Xavier watch each other in the lamplight. He's clever and calculating but there's something else, something darker that blurs his edges.

'What's your big plan?'

He raises his eyebrows, feigning surprise. '*My* plan?'

'You're in charge, aren't you?'

'Unless you want to be.'

She shakes her head. 'This is your show. I'm just along for the ride.'

'And why is that?' His smile is quick and flinty. 'Why now?' Stubby fingers stray to bare toes. He absently pulls at a tuft of hair—a nervous habit?

'The Agitators are being blamed for killing people,' Angie says. 'You think I wouldn't care about that?'

'As Ollie explained to you, the truck was part of our plan; the gas line and casualties were not.' The words are correct but the tone is off. He doesn't care about the people who bled and died in Queen Street.

'Jules was in that tower so I need to know what's going on.'

'Tell me why you walked away from the Agitators.'

Is he serious? 'Because some arsehole blackmailed me.'

He blinks once, twice. He was *not* expecting the truth. Neither was Angie until it was out of her mouth.

'Blackmailed you over what?' She can see his mind working, trying to read her and the situation. He has no idea what she does and doesn't know, and the temptation to rip off the scab here and now is overwhelming. But he's also violent and unpredictable and Angie doesn't know how expendable she is, or how far away Voss is if Xavier loses his shit.

'Who's blackmailing you? Angie—'

'It's not your problem or your business.'

'Do you know who it is?'

'No.' She's not much of a liar but maybe he won't notice.

'Why take the risk of being seen with us?'

'Because I'm suffocating on the sidelines and I can't do it anymore,' she snaps.

Xavier flinches...and then he relaxes. There's no fake confusion, no toe-hair tugging. She's angry enough that he's bought the half-truth.

'Are you going to tell me the plan or not?' she demands.

Xavier pretends to think about it for a moment. 'When we get there.' He rises from the ground and Angie watches him weave his way back to the lead bus. It's only when her face starts to hurt that she unclenches her jaw.

On the other side of camp, Waylon says something that makes the blonde photographer laugh and then takes the long

211

way back to Angie, keeping a healthy distance between himself and Xavier.

'You all right?' He sits down and checks her over as if the conversation might have left a mark.

'Of course I am. I see you've made a new friend.'

'Yeah.' His eyes stay on Angie for another second before he glances back across camp. 'That girl thinks Xavier's some kind of badass.' He grins. 'Of course, she might have a slight crush on me now, too.'

Waylon taps his ear as he speaks: confirmation he's placed the audio device. Angie raises her eyebrows. *Where?* Waylon slides a finger inside his boot and his grin widens. He's put a bug in one of Xavier's discarded shoes.

Angie exhales. The first part of their job is done. Now she has to hope Xavier calls whoever's paying the bills here and the Major overhears.

Otherwise she's just eaten shit for nothing.

'You're like one of the X-Men.'

'Because I'm a mutant?'

'No,' Tommy says, eyes bright. 'Because you have a superpower.'

It's after dinner and Jules, Ryan and Tommy are out in the shed, which is Ryan's old bedroom. Most of the floor space is taken up with music equipment: a drum kit, guitars on stands, amps, pedals and endless leads. Tommy tunes a guitar while they talk. Ryan is plugging in leads and staying out of the conversation.

'It's a gift,' Tommy insists.

Jules straightens her fingers and tucks them under her thighs. She's still jittery over what happened in Ryan's front yard today and the fact Tommy saw it.

'My dad used to say that too.' He told her she was special: it's why he bought her comics before she was old enough to read them. She believed him in the same way she believed in Santa Claus. Jules let go of both lies when she was eight, the year she blistered his wrist, blew the lights on the Christmas tree and set the carpet on fire. 'But what I have isn't a power and it's definitely not a gift.'

Tommy clicks a pedal off and on. 'You can make things burst into flames with your bare hands.'

'What's the point if I can't control it?' Jules is wrapped in the crocheted blanket from the spare room, wedged in a beanbag and shivering against the chill rising through the concrete. There's a pot-belly stove against the far wall, cold and dark. It doesn't look like it's been lit recently and there are no signs of that changing tonight. She pokes her fingers through gaps in the crochet stitches and draws the blanket tighter.

'You need more practice, that's all.' Tommy looks to Ryan for backup, but his brother's pulled up a stool to the drum kit and is spinning drumsticks between his fingers.

'Hold that thought,' Ryan says and launches into a rapid-fire drumroll on each skin before settling into a groove. The beat shakes her bones, thuds inside her skull.

Tommy leans in and yells: 'Gemma's gunna be here soon.'

Gemma is Tommy's best mate—has been since kindy. Gemma plays bass. Gemma's a townie. Gemma's never been Tommy's girlfriend; it's not like that with them.

Tommy talks about Gemma a lot.

'She's keen to meet you, *Jules*.' He grins and walks over to Ryan, flicking the guitar lead out of the way behind him. It was Ryan's idea to go with the name he's heard Angie use rather than something fake, although the first time Ryan called her Jules it did strange things to her pulse.

Nobody's telling Gemma who Jules really is. They're relying on the fact she looks different now from the photos on TV. Her face is leaner than when she was sixteen, her lips fuller. Her eyes will give her away if anyone looks too closely but, as Tommy keeps saying, nobody's going to expect to see her in Mitchellstone. Her hair is tucked up in a slouchy beanie—not her thing, but Ryan's mum thought it would help with mis-direction—and she's wearing make-up, so maybe it'll work. Jules sighs and burrows deeper into the beanbag. The buzzing beneath her skin is a bassline to pounding drums and stretched nerves.

It's past seven and a smear of orange lingers in the sky. The light lasts so much later here than it does in Brisbane. Jules is exhausted after a long day of static agitation, spent mostly on the back verandah watching Ryan's dad pull the alien-looking seeder up and down the paddock. Jamie Walsh is out there in the dying light now, sowing with the headlights on. He climbed into the tractor while his wife was coming to terms with a smouldering bottlebrush in her front yard. She'd stared out at him for a few tense seconds before shaking her head and sending her sons to check on fences in the hills.

Jules spent the afternoon on the side verandah, trying not to be overwhelmed by the endless space and stillness. She knows the rhythms of the city: the constant soundtrack of people, traffic, trains and birds. The quiet here is unnatural. This afternoon she tried to picture growing up surrounded by dirt, sky and dry creek beds instead of concrete and graffiti. Briefly—and not without a prick of guilt—she imagined what it would be like to have a mother who worked the earth and shared hugs as readily as Michelle Walsh.

Always, her thoughts led to Angie. There's a part of Jules— that sharper edge hidden beneath the charge—that wants Angie to *be* Angie and take back their lives. But then she remembers where her mother is headed and why, and all she wants is her mum back safe.

Fear wins. Again.

Ryan slows his tempo on the drums and Jules finds him watching her as he plays, his face calm and shoulders loose. The shed door opens and Ryan doesn't miss a beat when a girl walks in. She's wearing ripped jeans, faded Converse sneakers and a flannelette shirt, carrying a long square case in one hand and a bottle of lemonade in the other. Her short blonde hair has pink tips. Ryan finishes on a cymbal and grabs it to bring the room back to quiet.

'Hope you've been practising, Gemini,' he says. He's trying to sound gruff, but the warmth in his eyes gives away that he's happy to see her.

'Hope *you* have, Ryno,' she says, grinning. 'We don't want to embarrass you tomorrow night.'

He laughs and it's the closest Jules has seen him to being unguarded. 'You worry about yourself.'

'We'll see. Where's the city chick?' Gemma looks around and spots Jules in the beanbag. 'Hey,' she says and heads in her direction. 'I'm Gemma.'

Jules struggles to get up from the floor. Gemma puts down the guitar case and grabs her by the wrist. The contact startles Jules but the charge is in check. It helps that Gemma is warm and steady.

'That beanbag's a greedy bastard. Never lets go.' She smiles at Jules, all dimples and smudgy green eyes. Her eyebrows have never seen tweezers, but she's got that novo-punk look going on and it's working for her.

'I'm Jules.'

They shake hands. Gemma's fingernails are trimmed short, painted black with silver stars. A tendril of barbed wire is inked around her wrist. She eyes the beanie. 'Only someone with your cheekbones could pull off that hat in this shed.'

'Oh...' Jules' fingers stray to her head. She feels conspicuous, like she's turned up to the wrong party in fancy dress. 'My hair needs a wash.'

'You're in good company. Check out the grunge twins over there.'

Tommy's watching the exchange, pleased with himself. He grins at Gemma and bends a string against the fretboard to make the guitar wail. She shakes her head at him and unpacks a black bass.

'Oh hey, Macka knows Ryno's home. I saw him at the servo running home from training. He's gone to get his guitar.'

Jules looks over at Ryan in alarm.

'Macka's our other member,' Tommy explains. 'He's terrible on drums but holds his own on rhythm. He's usually a no-show on Thursday 'cause the big sook can't handle training and jamming on the same night.'

Ryan extracts himself from the kit and gestures for Jules to join him near the ensuite bathroom.

'Macka's harmless,' he says. Behind them, Tommy and Gemma are tuning up, heads bent together.

'What if he recognises me?'

'Gemma didn't, and Macka has a shorter attention span than Tommy even. Can you do me a favour?' He reaches into his back pocket without waiting for an answer. 'I want to play with these guys without worrying about missing anything from the Major. Can you hang on to this? It's on silent, but keep it out of sight. Nobody has mobiles out here these days.'

Jules takes the flexi-phone and folds it between her palms. 'Do you think this is what the Major had in mind?' She nods at the band.

Ryan shrugs. 'It's a small town and I can't pretend I'm not home. How would that look?'

'Have you been rehearsing that line for the Major?'

He blinks. 'You're tense.'

'I can't imagine why.'

'Are you in the right headspace? These are our mates...'

Great. He thinks she goes around electrocuting people when she's in a bad mood.

'If nobody threatens me, they'll be fine.'

'That's not what I meant.'

'Yeah, it was.' Jules shoves his phone into her hoodie and returns to the beanbag, wondering if she should retreat to the house before Macka arrives. Maybe Ryan's right to be concerned: it's not like she's had a lot of experience hanging out with people she doesn't know.

Macka turns up before she can decide if she's staying or going. He's dressed in a grey school jumper, footy shorts and striped socks pushed down to his work boots. He's gripping a beat-up electric guitar by the neck. A waft of cigarette smoke follows him inside.

'Fuck me, look what blew in with the westerly.' His voice is rough and he walks with the hunch tall guys tend to, as if they're always navigating doorways too small for them.

'Shit, Macka, you eaten anything since I left?'

'Can't fatten a thoroughbred.'

'Or a mongrel.'

They bump fists over a cymbal.

'How's the knee?'

'Did a twelve beep test last week.'

'Shee-it. Not too shabby for a broken-down midfielder.'

Jules has no idea what a beep test is but from Macka's reaction she's guessing twelve is impressive.

Macka shifts his weight. 'You know Rabbit's gonna be at Tommy's party?'

'Shouting the keg, I hear.'

'He's captain now.'

Jules sees the split-second shadow darken Ryan's features, feels the spike in his energy. 'Someone has to be.' He looks past Macka to Jules. 'We've got company, by the way.'

Macka spots Jules as soon as he turns around. 'Oh.' He pulls up short. His cheeks are hollow and his eyes bleary. 'Hey.'

'That's Jules,' Tommy says. 'Ryan's date for the party.'

Jules waits a beat—decides to let Tommy's ad lib slide—and raises a hand for Macka's benefit.

'You plugging that thing in?' Tommy says and Macka turns away, no hint that he's recognised Jules.

A few minutes later after a song choice debate that Ryan wins, they kick off with an up-tempo bluesy number. They're rough, and Ryan makes them play the start three times. When he's happy, Tommy steps to the mike and belts out the opening lyrics. His voice is strong and husky, like a two-pack-a-day smoker. It surprises a laugh out of Jules. Tommy misses her reaction because he's too busy watching for cues from his brother. They all are: Gemma, Macka and Tommy, eyes on Ryan at every transition. They're all grinning by the end.

Tommy nods at Gemma and they start up a new song, vintage pub-rock, Tommy back on the mic singing about how he doesn't care if he's broke as long as he's still getting laid. Ryan laughs out loud as Tommy sings, and for a heartbeat he looks like his younger brother: light and happy. Gemma rolls her eyes at Macka, and Jules *feels* how relaxed they all are with each other, their rhythm and energy woven together.

'Jules, you want to join in?' Ryan asks when the song ends. The memory of laughter warms his eyes.

'I can't sing or play.'

'You can manage a cowbell.'

Tommy's grin widens and Gemma hands Jules a metal cowbell and a drumstick. 'Hold it at the top and hit it with this. Easy.'

'When?'

'Keep your eyes on me.' Ryan tells her.

The beanbag rustles as Jules crosses her legs and sits straighter. It's ridiculous how much she wants to do this.

Ryan counts them in and they launch into a rock number, faster than anything they've played so far. Jules is gripping the drumstick with clammy fingers, ready. Tommy's singing some-thing raunchy, but she barely registers the lyrics because she's waiting for Ryan's cue. He widens his eyes in warning, then nods his head. She hits the cowbell on the beat. It's crazy loud but she keeps striking it in time with Ryan's head bobs. He jerks his head sideways to signal her to stop, all the while smashing out the drum line. His eyes flick to the rest of the band as they play through the verse and then back to Jules. There's the signal.

This time she holds the beat without his guidance. It's only a cowbell but she's making music in time with the rest of the band.

Ryan nods for her to keep playing and works over the kit, hands a blur and legs pumping, while Tommy grinds out a guitar solo. She strikes the bell harder. Faster. The impact reverberates up her arms and into her chest. Gemma and Macka surge with them, chasing the beat, and it's like nothing Jules has ever felt.

Ryan starts to wind down and they follow. She stops a beat before the rest of the band, and then it's Ryan drumming on his own, finishing up with a controlled run. Jules' pulse is racing and the charge is going with it, but not pushing—it's a different brand of adrenaline. This is the rush that comes with thumping music and speeding cars.

'Bloody hell, Ryno,' Macka pants when they're done. 'You're off the chain.'

Jules can see Ryan's pleased with the three of them—and himself. 'Nice work on the cowbell.'

She smiles and it catches him by surprise. His mouth softens in a way that sends warmth flooding through her and when she drops her gaze the heat spreads deeper. It takes a few seconds for the flush to subside, and it's only then Jules notices the current has faded too—without her wrestling with it or releasing it into the earth. How did she do that?

She's still trying to understand what happened when her pocket vibrates.

Ryan watches Jules cross the floor, tuning out Tommy, who's mucking around with an AC/DC riff. He's buzzing from playing and from that moment just now with Jules. She followed his lead and kept the beat. She was *into* it. Ryan can't tell if it's that or the fact she's wrapped in his Crows blanket that's turning him on the most right now.

She's on her way to him because his phone's gone off—he can tell from the crease in her forehead and the way her hand is in her pocket—but for a second he pretends it's something else.

He spins his stool so he's side-on to the drum kit. He pats his thigh and raises his eyebrows. She falters, glances at Macka and gets it. At least Ryan assumes she does, because she perches on his knee and drapes an arm around his shoulder. In the moment, with the beat still in his blood, Ryan runs his palm up the outside of her thigh and pulls her closer. She stiffens and he feels the tiniest sensation from her fingers digging through his T-shirt. He can smell camphor from the blanket, and the lime and coconut handwash his mum buys.

'The phone,' he whispers, as if that was his sole motive for drawing her further onto his lap.

He sees the pulse jump in her throat. Is she okay with his hand on her leg or is she about to shock him? Either way he can't take his eyes from her lips, imagining how they'd feel, how her tongue would taste—and then stops, realising she's going to feel *him* in a second if he's not careful.

'Bloody hell, you two, can't you wait till we're done?' Macka plays a few dirty notes on his guitar. Jules ignores him and leans closer, hiding the phone from the others. She bends her head to his ear and his grip tightens on her thigh.

'Are you going to look at this?'

'Ah...yep.' He takes the phone. 'Pretend you're talking to me.'

He wakes up the screen, totally distracted by her breath on his ear and the overwhelming impulse to slide his hands under her shirt and touch her skin. It takes a second to register that the message is in code. Another second to focus enough to understand what it means.

'What's it say?' Jules whispers.

He squeezes her thigh in response—any excuse really. 'I need to call the Major but it's operational contact, not an emergency.'

'Are you sure? What if it's something to do with Mum?'

'It would be a different code.'

They make eye contact for the first time since she sat on his lap and his heart does an unexpected duck and weave.

'Did you zap me?' He's more startled than alarmed.

'No, but slide that hand any higher and I might.'

Ryan eases his grip. He's considering apologising when she leans in and kisses him. It takes him by surprise but he responds without hesitation. He keeps it PG-rated—no tongue, no more hands—and it's over too soon. She's already on her way back to the beanbag, his phone again in her pocket. He should have said something, done more with the moment.

Macka wolf-whistles and Jules gives him a look that says: *Grow up.*

Ah.

She was keeping up their cover. Good thing he didn't get too carried away or he would've made a total dick of himself. Across the room, Jules raises her eyebrows at him. Is she after a reaction or is this for Macka's and Gemma's benefit? He has no idea what's going on so he shrugs at her—like, *Macka's a tool*—and counts in the next song.

Ryan wraps up the session an hour later. He waits until Gemma and Macka are headed into town before he goes outside to make the call. Tommy knows about the phone but Ryan doesn't want him to overhear a conversation with the Major.

Jules follows Ryan from the shed. The driveway's lit up, but they're far enough in shadow that nobody will see them from inside the house. Ryan's aware of her closeness and is still trying to figure out that kiss.

'You need to make the call,' Jules says, impatient. Clearly he's the only one who's unfocused. Ryan hits dial and puts the phone on the opposite ear to where Jules is standing. The Major answers on the first ring.

'Are you in a life-threatening situation, private?'

'No.'

'Then don't ever take that long to report in again.'

'Yes, sir.'

The rest of the call isn't a conversation: it's a briefing and an order. Ryan listens, nods to the night, and waits for a question that requires a response. His world narrows to the voice in his ear.

'Is that clear, Walsh?'

'Yes, sir.'

The entire exchange lasts less than two minutes. When it's done, Ryan pockets his phone and stares out into the darkness.

'What did he say?'

Ryan probably shouldn't tell her. He heads for the light and the sliding door, but doesn't open it, watches Tommy scribbling notes on a lyric sheet instead.

'Stop figuring out how to edit the conversation and tell me.'

He drums his fingers on the doorhandle. 'Someone's hacked surveillance footage from Pax Fed Tower and the CCTV camera outside that Lebanese joint you work at. They're trying to ID me.'

Jules glances over her shoulder to the road. 'The mercenaries?'

'Most likely, but the army keeps our details locked down. It won't be that easy for them to find me.'

It's what the Major promised his family when Ryan signed on: that his role with SECDET Q18 wouldn't put them in danger. That was before Ryan went off-script twice in the past week—and got himself filmed both times.

'But you're a bit famous, right?'

How does she—

Tommy. The little shit showed her the room, told her the story. 'Only if you're a hardcore AFL fan and you cared about the draft eighteen months ago. If not, it'll take a while without a name.' Unless they have access to intelligence databases and facial recognition software...

Jules rubs her arms. Cold, self-conscious or spooked, he can't tell.

'What else did Major Voss say?'

'Not much beyond the usual nagging.'

The screen door to the house bangs open and Ryan's mum appears at the gate.

'Julianne, you might want to use the bathroom before Tommy comes inside. I don't know what that boy does in there but it takes him half the night. Come on, I'll show you where everything is.'

Jules hesitates and Ryan tries to catch his mum's attention. He never should have told her he was on protective duty with Jules: she's taking his job too seriously. The burning tree incident might also have something to do with her vigilance.

'I had fun tonight,' Jules says. 'I didn't expect that, so... thanks.'

'Any time,' he says, not sure if she means the music or the kiss, and wishing he knew how to keep her out here. His mum stays at the gate as Jules passes. *Now* she wants to make eye contact with him.

'What?'

'You know what. Keep it in your pants. Don't complicate things.'

The screen door slaps shut and Ryan breathes out his annoyance. There's no way Jules missed hearing that.

'I thought you and Jules weren't a *thang*,' Tommy says when he's back in the shed.

'You're the one who told Macka she was my date for the party. We were playing along.'

'I don't know, bro. Looked pretty convincing to me. Maybe you should make an effort, see what happens.'

Ryan flicks off the lights over the band gear. 'You *making an effort* with Gemma?'

'I'm taking my time, doing it right. You, on the other hand, have a small window of opportunity.'

'You don't think trying to hook up with Julianne De Marchi is a high-risk manoeuvre, given what she's capable of?'

Tommy grins. 'Yeah, but what a way to go.'

He's got a point.

Once Tommy's in the house, Ryan puts his dad's smart phone in the speaker dock—music is all it's good for—and scrolls through his blues collection. Jamie Walsh never picked up an instrument but he raised his sons to appreciate every form of the blues, from John Lee Hooker to Stevie Ray Vaughan and Joe Bonamassa. He had a playlist for every occasion. Back before the bank knockbacks and burning sheep carcasses. Back when Jamie Walsh cared about things other than battles he couldn't win. Ryan's old man doesn't listen to the blues anymore; those wailing guitars cut too close to the bone. If this morning's soundtrack is any indication, his dad's moved on to Moldovan thrash metal.

Ryan cranks up the volume until Robert Johnson's slide guitar fills the shed. The tractor was silent just now so the old man's finally knocked off, but Ryan has no desire to see him.

He's tired of picking over the carcass of their exchange this afternoon, worrying about how much worse things are here. What he wants is to think about something else for a while. He digs around in his bag until his fingers find the false bottom and the leather pouch hidden beneath it.

The fluoro in his bathroom is too bright but Ryan needs to see what he's doing. He unwinds the tie around the pouch so he can lay it out flat on the sink. He slides out a vial and syringe, tries not to think about the fact he's doing this at home.

The Major gave him next to nothing over the phone. Ryan's put his family at risk by bringing Julianne here and his commanding officer acts like it's a routine assignment. It's not. Nothing about this op is routine.

Ryan draws the contents of the vial into the syringe, drops his jeans and lowers himself to the tiles. He props against the dead gas heater on the wall and stretches out. It's always easier sitting down. He jabs the needle into his thigh—it burns the way it always does—and he's about to deliver the dose when footfalls reverberate through the bathroom floor, picking up speed.

Shit.

Ryan fumbles for the knife in his boot—he can't hear a thing over the guitar—and then Jules appears in the doorway, face flushed and eyes wide. He lowers the blade, relieved it's her and not a gunman catching him with his pants around his ankles. And a needle sticking out of his leg. His relief evaporates.

She stares at the syringe for another beat, breathing hard, and turns and strides out of sight. *Fuck.* He gives himself the shot and gets to his feet, listening for the sliding door to slam. Instead, the music shuts off and she's on her way back, her steps hard and angry. He zips his jeans before she reappears.

'It's not what you think,' he says.

'I *thought* you were hurt. You were on the tiles.' She folds her arms tight over her breasts. She's in the jeans and hoodie she had on before, but now she's wearing his mum's old slippers.

226

'I'm not a junkie—'

'I worked that out from the fact you're pumping it into a muscle and not your veins.' She nods at the pouch on the sink. 'What is it?'

He thinks about lying, decides to go with a half-truth. 'Booster shot.'

'For what?'

How much is he supposed to tell her? 'It helps with fatigue and muscle recovery.' He unfolds a medical waste bag and drops the used syringe inside, zips it shut.

'And your nervous system.' Jules blocks the bathroom doorway so he can't leave without asking her to move or pushing past. 'Mum and I were a mess for hours after that flash bomb but you guys were fine.'

'We weren't *fine*.'

'You could see and breathe.'

'If we hadn't been able to, we might all be dead right now.'

That makes her pause, if only for a second. 'What else does it do?'

A shrug. 'Improves immunity, speeds up metabolism.'

'Really? And everyone in the army is injecting themselves now?'

Another decision. 'Only us. We're the "proof of concept".'

'There's no government funding for military medical research, I know that. So who's paying?'

'How would I know?'

Her eyes widen in disbelief—mocking him—and for the first time he catches a glimpse of Angela De Marchi in her.

'You have no idea what they're doing to you, do you?'

'It's the army, De Marchi. I do what I'm told.'

Her gaze drops to the pouch on the vanity. She grinds her jaw while she thinks. 'The contract work you do with Pax Fed... what else do they get for their investment?'

He knows what she's getting at. 'Not that.'

'How would you know? Have you asked?'

'Why would I?'

'Because you're injecting it *in your body*.' She throws her hands up in exasperation and walks away. 'Another mindless soldier.'

Why is she so pissed off at him?

Jules scans the shed, looking for something—

Crap.

'Use the heater. It hasn't had gas for years.' He steps out of the way. 'And I'm not mindless. I needed a job and this was the only one on offer.'

Jules drops to her knees and grabs the cold metal grille, eyes blazing. 'Would you have taken it if you'd known you'd be working for the company ruining this farm? How would your dad feel if he knew?'

'You're judging me? Tell me again why you were in Pax Fed Tower last week?'

She opens her mouth like she's going to answer, but then clamps her jaw shut and the heater flashes blue and white. It's all over in a split second but the force of the charge leaves the hairs on Ryan's arms standing. And now there are scorch marks on the wall.

'The moral high ground doesn't pay the bills,' Jules says. None of the heat is gone from her anger. She uncurls her fingers from the grille and notices the black smudges on the wall. Exhales with frustration.

Ryan doesn't come any closer. He's not convinced she's done.

She closes the lid of the toilet and sits down, leaning forward to rest her elbows on her knees. Her hair falls in a curtain around her face and he watches her calm herself, slowly inhaling and exhaling. His own anger falls back into line.

Pax Fed is only part of the reason his family's in the mess it's in, but De Marchi's barb has stuck. His old man would totally lose the plot if he knew where this month's money came from.

It shouldn't upset Jules this much, though; no matter how much she hates Pax Fed.

'De Marchi, why'd you come back out?'

'Tommy beat me to the bathroom...' Jules tucks her hair behind her ear so she can see him and then shakes her head. 'It doesn't matter.'

Understanding and regret arrive at the same time: she came back because of the kiss. Nothing is going to happen now, not with frustration and accusation taking up all the space between them.

'Right.' Ryan leaves the bathroom, ignoring the tight wad in his gut.

'Can I borrow your phone?'

That pulls him up short. 'Who do you want to call?'

'Khan.'

'I'll take you wherever you want to go. You don't need to call her.'

'I don't want to go anywhere; I want to talk to Khan.'

He takes out the phone and taps it on his thigh, no idea if she's authorised to use it. He hands it over anyway and waits for her to leave so he can go back in the bathroom and shut the door.

Julianne De Marchi thinks he's a mindless grunt who's sold his soul to the devil. He needs to finish getting rid of the evidence that she might be right.

'Julianne. Is everything all right?'

No.

'Have you heard from Mum?' Jules is wedged into the beanbag staring at the bathroom door. She can hear Ryan in the shower on the other side.

'Not directly, but as far as I know she's keeping it together.'

Jules almost laughs at the irony. Her mother is exercising self-control while she's sitting here with her fingertips burning. She's never released the charge in anger before. It was a different shape, easier to grip, and it's still churning under her rib cage stronger than it should be. She's annoyed that Ryan is willing to be a lab rat for the army but not enough to set her off this badly. What is it about him that does this to her?

'Is this phone secure?' Khan asks.

'The Major called Ryan on it, so I guess so.'

A beat. 'What did he say?'

'Someone's stolen video surveillance of Ryan, presumably to figure out who he is, to get to me.' The reality of the words sinks in and her breath shortens.

'The footage tells them Ryan's been shadowing you, nothing more. Did Voss say anything else?'

'No.'

Khan hesitates, as if he should have. 'He won't be impressed you're using an army phone,' she says instead.

'You don't have to tell him.'

'Oh, I think I will, in the spirit of inter-agency cooperation.'

The way Khan says it tells Jules all she needs to know about how the cooperation is going—but at least Khan is talking to her. Jules glances at the bathroom door. 'Do you know if corporate military contracts involve anything other than guns for hire?'

'Such as?'

'Bio-genetic experiments.'

'Julianne, now's not the time to buy into your mother's conspiracy theories.'

'Ryan's admitted his unit is trialling a drug that helps them recover faster. Someone has to be paying for that research. Is it something Pax Fed would be involved in?'

The line goes quiet while Khan thinks. 'Peta Paxton's been lobbying the Pax Fed board to increase investment in military interests for a while now, but there's resistance. She barely got the numbers to engage forces in Pakistan and even the Q18 experiment has been controversial—particularly with her brother.'

Jules sees Bradford Paxton across the interview table. Humiliating her, enjoying it. Her skin crawls at the memory.

'Tom Paxton's looking to one of his children to replace him on the board,' Khan continues. 'There's only one seat at the head of that table and Bradford's pinning his ambitions on the Priority Agricultural Practices Bill. I can't imagine him supporting trials to make better soldiers. He's not going to approve anything that might give Peta an edge.'

'Would the Major tell you who's funding the Q18 medical trial?'

Khan gives a short laugh. 'The Major doesn't like telling me the time.' Jules can feel her turning the idea over all the same. 'Leave it with me.'

There's a moment of silence and the gnawing worry from earlier in the day returns. 'Can you promise me Mum's safe?'

'Xavier knows she's on the bus and hasn't threatened her or

231

attempted to release your video. Waylon's right there with her—'

'What about when they get to Port Augusta? How will she be okay if there's a radiation leak?'

'It won't get that far.'

'It's meant to happen on Saturday and you don't even know how he plans to do it or who's helping him.'

'We will, Julianne. Give us time.'

Jules ends the call with trembling fingers.

In the bathroom, the shower shuts off and Jules hauls herself to her feet. She drops the phone on Ryan's bed and heads for the door, needing to be gone before he comes out.

She wants to believe Khan. She and Voss are so sure they can stop whatever Xavier's got planned, but Saturday's the day after tomorrow. And neither the feds nor the army have a strong track record in getting it right when it comes to protecting De Marchis.

Almost there.

Angie stretches her cramped legs into the aisle and feels the blood return to her knees. The Agitator convoy is barrelling down the highway beside Spencer Gulf. The nuclear plant dominates the horizon, steam pluming from two giant cooling towers and power lines strung out across the plain like spider webs. Beyond it, Port Augusta hunkers between sand hills and salt-bush, straddling the top of the gulf. The old coal power stations are long gone, along with the two-hundred-metre stack that once stood sentinel over the sun-faded city.

The sheer size of the plant is enough to bring a quiver to Angie's chest, a primal response to the sight of a monster capable of devouring the landscape and everything in it. A monster Xavier wants to wake.

The sight of it at least signals the end of the longest, shittiest bus trip of her life. She's over the endless sitting and inescapable body odour and pretending she doesn't want to shove Xavier's head in a compost toilet. Tired of watching every word, careful not to slip up in case someone's listening. Tired of worrying about Jules and having no idea if Khan or the Major have learnt anything useful about Xavier or the men who stormed her home. Wishing she had something to show for the ride other than sore legs and the taste of dust.

Xavier is riding the final leg of the trip on Angie's bus. He climbed on board after the morning break, gave her a wave and took the seat nearest the door. There's no getting off now until he says so.

'What's that?'

Waylon leans across Angie to get a better look at the field of solar panels flashing in the sun and the stadium-sized greenhouses beyond them. He's on the aisle, keeping himself between her and the rest of the bus.

'That, young Waylon, is the definition of irony.'

Waylon gives her a dry look. 'I'm gonna need a little more detail.'

Angie rubs her eyes and wishes she'd had a decent sleep. 'What you're looking at used to be the most promising sustainability project in the world. The Sun Farm. Pioneering sustainable horticulture using salt water and sunshine.' She taps the window. 'They take water from the gulf and desalinate it—use the water on the greenhouse crops—and the whole lot is powered by solar.'

'Cool.'

'Yeah, it was. The original plan was to develop a system for Third World countries that have low rainfall—not much fresh water—but access to sea water. Brilliant idea. And then the government changed, they cut off the funding and the corporates swept in. Pax Fed outbid Wesfarmers with all their usual bullshit about feeding a starving world and made it part of the Happy Growers empire. In the end, all they've done is supply tomatoes and capsicums to high-end restaurants so cashed-up diners can feel good about being sustainable.' Angie pauses as an older, dustier anger grips her. 'Then the government turned its attention to that nightmare'—she points to the reactor—'and built the world's largest radioactive waste storage silo right next door, underwritten by foreign investment. Another brilliant revenue-raising strategy.'

Waylon's watching her with an expression she doesn't recognise. He's serious and intense, on the brink of telling her something. But then he blinks and the moment's gone. He

234

stretches his arms above his head and twists until a shoulder pops. 'I don't know how you keep track of all the things that piss you off. Must be exhausting.'

It surprises a half-laugh out of her. 'It's a full-time job.'

The bus slows and then comes to a complete stop on the highway. A woman in high-vis is blocking traffic so workers can mark lines on a new overpass. Angie's surprised it's taken this long to separate the road traffic from the nuclear freight line. It's been an accident waiting to happen.

'Where's the protester camp?' Waylon is trying to see past her.

'You'll see.'

A few minutes later and they're moving again, the convoy forming a single lane to crest the overpass.

'Bloody hell...'

The Permanent Anti-Nuclear Assembly has been camped in a bare paddock near the nuclear plant since before they started building it a decade ago. In the beginning, a hundred or so protesters set up camp and kept the vigil. Angie was part of that first push, bringing the Agitators south to lead roadblocks and nonviolent opposition. She knew numbers had been building in recent years. She'd heard the size of the protest camp was at record levels when the plant went online. But even she wasn't expecting this.

There must be more than a thousand people jammed in that paddock.

From the top of the overpass she can see the protesters are massing in front of a stage at the western end of the camp. There are banks of speakers and a mega-screen, all of it new since the last time she paid attention to what was happening down here. Even from this distance the place feels overcrowded.

'How come nobody's moved them on?'

'No government's wanted the hassle. There's never been any real drama over the years, just the occasional skirmish. There's a cyclone fence around the camp and even if you breach it, there's a good half a kilometre of saltbush between the fence and the plant. See those towers?' Angie points to the structures along the plant's security fence. 'Snipers.'

She rests her face against the glass, takes in the panorama. The Happy Growers sun farm, the nuclear plant, the protester camp—and the gleaming radioactive storage silo. Modern Australia in all its glory. That sense of unease claws again.

'I've got your back, Angie.' Waylon says it quietly, eyes focused beyond her on the camp.

'I can look after myself.'

He nods. 'I know. I've got your back anyway.'

The road returns to ground level and her view is limited to a line of portaloos and washing strung along the camp fence. The bus doesn't get a chance to pick up speed before it swings into a dirt road and is waved through a boom gate. The convoy stays at walking pace, passing tents of all sizes and a row of outdoor showers. It's a conspicuous entrance. Deep inside the camp, the crowd parts to let the convoy through, faces upturned to see who's onboard. Angie shrinks back from the window.

'Angela De Marchi, are you ready?'

'For what?' She kneels on her seat to see Xavier hanging on to the luggage rack to keep his balance. His eyes are flint-like.

'To change the future.'

Theirs is the only bus to pass through a second barricade and continue on to the side of the stage. Xavier is out the door first and everyone else fills the aisle to follow. Waylon doesn't push in with them, forcing Angie to wait.

'Move,' she says. Good, bad or otherwise, she wants to know what's coming.

Waylon holds his ground for another beat and then leads her down the bus aisle.

Xavier is waiting outside. The sun is bright but the breeze coming from the gulf brings a shiver. On stage, two girls with acoustic guitars are harmonising about a nuclear winter. Xavier blocks Angie from following the Agitators into the crowd.

'You're with me.'

'And I'm with her.' Waylon's tone is conversational, friendly even, but his stance is unmistakably don't-argue.

Xavier eyes him coolly. He and Waylon have barely spoken on the trip and it's only now Angie remembers Xavier personally recruited him. Whatever he saw in Waylon in Queen Street he sees now. He nods, a second before a flash of pigtails, plaid and denim descends from the side of the stage holding a clipboard.

'We had no idea you were coming!' the girl says to Angie, loud enough to be heard over the frantic strumming onstage. Her eyes are bright as she hugs the clipboard to her chest. She looks from Xavier to Angie and back again, bounces on her heels. 'This is amazing!' She hugs Xavier—she's enthusiastic, he's awkward—and adjusts her headset. 'Are you ready?'

Angie frowns. *Ready for what?*

She follows the pair up the stairs, her gut churning. They wait out of sight behind a stack of speakers. This mob at least looks like the Anti-Nuke Assembly she remembers: dreads, tie-dye, sun-browned faces. Less like the crew on Xavier's buses with their prison tatts and scarred hands, currently positioning themselves in the front rows. Angie picks at her torn thumbnail and ignores Waylon's attempts to catch her attention. Xavier shakes out his bun and reties it. Hangs his sunnies from his T-shirt. Changes his mind and puts them on again.

The girls finish their song and exit the opposite side of the stage.

Angie's heart rate picks up. Xavier speaks to the clipboard girl and she turns away to relay his direction into her headset. A few seconds later, the screen onstage lights up and the crowd cheers. Angie sucks in her breath. It's her. Old footage of Angie standing in this camp eight years ago. The storage silo behind her, newly constructed and gleaming under an unforgiving summer sky. The nuclear plant seven years in the future.

Onscreen Angie comes to life, her eyes fierce and face sun-reddened.

> In 2015, Australia took back the low-level radioactive waste we sent to France for processing in the 1990s. I said it then: it was the thin edge of the wedge.

The camp crowd falls silent.

> Because it didn't stop there. France offered to pay for us to take its intermediate-level waste and our government said yes. Good for the economy, our leaders said. And now we've agreed to take high-level radioactive nuclear waste, not only from France, but from any other OECD member country that can afford it.

Onscreen Angie points to the hulking silo behind her.

> That's where it'll all be stored until our government finds a hole in the ground deep enough to bury it. The Spencer Gulf Safe Energy Storage Facility. *Safe energy*, what a joke.

Angie stares down the barrel of the camera.

> We need to stop this madness—

The picture pauses, leaving onscreen Angie's face frozen mid-rant.

Real-life Angie is barely moving either. Is that what they've been using to fire up the Anti-Nuke Assembly: her old vlogs? In a heartbeat she knows where all this is leading. A quick look between the speakers, and she spots a pack of journos and camera crews crammed near the stage.

Shit. Xavier is on his way to the microphone. The crowd is hushed, expectant.

'Angela De Marchi warned us eight years ago about the dangers here. What's changed since then?'

'Nothing,' someone calls out from the front row. It's one of the guys Angie overheard talking at the campsite.

'Exactly.' Xavier takes the microphone from its stand and holds it away from himself to clear his throat. 'That radioactive waste is in so-called temporary storage. The long-term plan, still, is to bury it—but nobody can agree on where. Now we've got tonnes of nuclear waste arriving at Port Pirie each year, coming up that freight line. Our own nuclear power station has gone online. They're talking about building another in Victoria. When is it going to end?'

Xavier makes a show of pausing to look out over the mass of protesters.

'Most of you don't know me, so let me tell you why I'm here.' A beat. 'When I was fourteen and my sister was five, my parents moved us to Honeymoon. The uranium mine had just reopened. It was the only work they could get. Once I finished school, I joined them underground.'

Xavier worked with uranium? Angie glances at Waylon. He's fixated on the Agitators' leader.

'We were retrenched five years later and by the time my sister was diagnosed with leukaemia, there was no way to prove a link to the mine. That meant no compensation and no help with medical costs.'

Xavier licks his lips and wipes his hand over them. Angie's trying to spot the signs of performance but if it's an act it's a good one. He straightens, shields his face against the sun.

'Successive governments have failed to make good decisions for our nation, and families like mine are paying the price. We need to send our so-called leaders a message. We have to do things differently. Nothing changes if *nothing changes.*'

The Agitators in the front row are whistling in support, stirring up the crowd.

Xavier points to the cameras. 'The eyes of the nation are on us. We have to be more than a ten-second grab. We need action. Are you with me?'

More of the crowd is cheering now, shouting and rattling placards.

'We can change the trajectory of this country.' He paces from one side of the stage to the other like an evangelist, fuelled by the response. 'And we're not doing it alone.'

Xavier flings his arm out in Angie's direction and her skin prickles.

'Come on out, Angela De Marchi!'

The entire camp erupts and Angie steps out from behind the speakers. It's barely a conscious decision: the crowd's elation is irresistible. The moment overwhelms her, pins her to the spot. The adrenaline, the euphoria...For a good ten seconds, she stands there, halfway to Xavier, basking in the glow of a thousand people cheering at her. *For* her. She's been silenced for two years, defamed and disempowered. But these people want to hear from her. Her work still means something. She's vaguely aware of Waylon prowling at the side of the stage and keeping out of sight of the cameras.

'*Are you with us?*' Xavier asks.

The crowd roars. Angie needs to say something meaningful, not waste the moment.

'Then be ready to act!' Xavier shouts.

The crowd erupts again, this time in triumph. Angie looks around, confused. Four guys are carrying guitars and a set of conga drums onto the stage. They've got plaited beards and shaved heads and are famous enough that even she knows who they are. They're all the crowd wants now.

Xavier gestures to Angie to make way and her understanding hardens to anger. He has no intention of letting her speak to this crowd. Of course he doesn't: the two of them aren't actually in this together.

Waylon gets between them before they reach the stairs. 'You want to make it any easier for him to shift blame to you?' he mutters. Angie's head pounds in time with the conga drums and she can't look at Waylon because she knows he's right.

Xavier's primed this crowd for civil unrest and now the world knows she's up to her neck in it with him.

Ryan sprints down the road, easily beats Tommy for the mark. He turns and boots it back to Macka, hitting him on the chest with a satisfying thump. It's late in the afternoon but there's enough light left to see the ball.

'That's it, I'm going up the other end,' Tommy says and shoves Ryan in the shoulder before he leaves.

Ryan glances at the front verandah where his mum and Jules are sipping beer from frosted glasses. He can't hear them talking because the galahs are screeching in the trees but they seem to have plenty to say to each other.

Macka boots it long again and Ryan runs backwards, takes the grab. He returns the kick, putting the ball high so Tommy can take a hanger over Macka. His brother marks it and then wrestles with Macka, laughing.

Ryan can almost let himself believe that if he came home it would be like this, like it used to be. Coming in from the paddock tired and satisfied; leading the team out onto the field, his mum and dad cheering from the back of the ute; Michelle and Jamie Walsh being the first couple everyone looked for at the footy club on Saturday night.

But those days are gone.

Still, it was good to be out there today. He and Tommy brought the flock down from the top paddock and Spud Laidlaw turned up with the ram and a truckload of hay. Jules helped transfer it to their shed and then rode out in the back of the ute and helped bust up bales and spread the feed. She worked hard, breaking a sweat and stretching her shoulders every time she cramped.

Ryan kept a close watch. At first it was to make sure she wasn't on the verge of setting the dry feed alight; then because he liked the way she was putting her back into it, as if it mattered to her too.

She helped with the fences too, and Tommy took her to the house when she needed a break mid-morning. Ryan stopped tensioning the wire to watch her climb onto the Yamaha. She held on to Tommy when he opened the throttle and it took Ryan a second to identify the tightness in his chest: he'd never envied his brother before.

Jules has barely spoken to him since the bathroom incident but the chill between them is thawing. There's nothing like a big day in the paddock to unravel tension—unless it involves his old man. He won't make eye contact or acknowledge Ryan but at least he's sober and functioning. His dad's finished the seeding, fixed the pump to the sheep trough and chopped a stack of wood, even though it's nowhere near cold enough for a fire. Anyone would think his old man was trying to make a point. All Ryan cares about is the work's getting done and Tommy or his mum won't have to do it.

It's five o'clock and they're killing time before they go into town to set up for the party. Ryan needs to get his head right so he can deal with Rabbit and Keith McKenzie and anyone else who wants to give him shit tonight.

'All right boys, off the road,' his mum calls out. 'Someone's coming.'

Ryan checks over his shoulder and sees churning dust against the darkening sky.

'Yeah, I need to get going.' Macka snatches up his cap from the side of the road and jams it on his head. 'What time's soundcheck?'

Tommy knocks the peak into his eyes. 'Set up at six, run through at six-fifteen.'

'Pissed at seven-thirty.'

They bump fists.

'The party doesn't start until eight, gentlemen,' Ryan's mum says. 'So don't let me catch either of you anywhere near that keg until then.'

'Yes, Mum.'

'Ryan, you're responsible for keeping an eye on your brother.'

Ryan ambles through the front gate. 'You're the one letting a seventeen-year-old have a keg for his birthday.'

His mum looks over at Jules. 'What else do you give the kid that has everything?' Her lips twist before they can form a smile. The two women share a moment and Ryan's struck by how Jules gets it, this bind they're in.

A late-model ute hurtles past, spitting up stones. A maintenance crew from the inland pipeline. Ryan and Tommy watch it flash by, another reminder of what they can't have as long as their old man keeps saying no to Pax Fed. The new desal water supply is out of their reach without a bank loan for the connection fee.

'Right-oh.' Ryan's mum stands up. 'I'll go see where your father is. See you in an hour, Macka. That gives you plenty of time for a shave.'

Macka comes into the yard and glances at the blackened bottlebrush—twice—and lopes towards the driveway. Tommy handballs the footy to Ryan as he follows, leaving him and Jules alone on the verandah.

Ryan absently spins the footy in the palm of his hand. 'Big day today, you must be knackered.'

Jules brushes wheat dust from her arms for about the tenth time and he can tell she's itching for a shower. 'It's helped with the current. Maybe that's the trick: wearing myself out.'

'You never played sport?'

She gives him a flat look. 'Think about it.'

Ryan bounces the footy with one hand and guides it back onto his palm. She gestures at the ball. 'Do you miss it?'

'A bit.'

Like he would miss breathing. He couldn't even watch footy for the first few months after the injury. But he loved the game too much to stay away and by the start of round one last year he was in front of the communal TV in the Q18 barracks, doing rehab exercises while the Crows flogged Fremantle.

'Is your knee strong enough to play now?'

'At AFL level? Maybe. But the army wants its pound of flesh for another four years so there's no point worrying about it.' Being good enough and not being able to play is the thing that crawls across his chest at night and steals his breath.

Jules lifts her glass and changes her mind, reties her hair instead. A few loose strands settle on her collarbone, dark against sun-pink skin. Ryan absently wonders if she tans or peels.

'Have you heard from the Major today?' she asks.

'Not a word.'

Macka's quad bike starts up in the driveway, scattering the birds from the trees. Ryan should think about getting cleaned up himself.

'Julianne,' his mum calls out from inside the house. 'You need to see this.'

Ryan and Jules exchange a look and hurry to the kitchen where the flat screen is showing news footage of the protest camp at Port Augusta.

> Angela De Marchi, former leader of the Agitators and a suspect in last week's attack on Paxton Federation Tower, received a hero's welcome at the Anti-Nuclear Assembly this afternoon.

Angie steps onto the stage and falters, clearly stunned by the crowd's frenzied reaction to her.

Jules gapes at her mother. 'What is she *doing*?'

244

Ryan searches the screen for signs of Waylo. 'She must have a plan.'

'Planning is not in my mother's skill set.'

The footage shifts from the crowd to the stage. Xavier's front and centre.

The man now identified as James Xavier arrived with De Marchi and urged the crowd to escalate its resistance efforts. While his intentions remain unclear, local police and security at the Port Augusta Nuclear Plant and Spencer Gulf Safe Energy Storage Facility are now on high alert in the wake of De Marchi's appearance.

'Can you phone Waylon and find out what's going on?' Jules asks. Her voice is thin.

'I'm not authorised.'

'What about the Major?'

Yeah, right. 'That's not really the way it works.' He moves closer. 'Do you need air?'

Jules drags her eyes from the TV, understands what he's asking. 'I'm okay.' His mum is watching them, curious. The story changes to an update on the injured hamstring of the Crows ruckman. Jules exhales. 'I left my glass outside. I'll go get it.'

Ryan's mum nods in Jules' direction after she's left. 'What is it between you two?'

'What do you mean?'

'I've never seen you like this with a girl. Considerate. Caring.'

He gives a short, humourless laugh. 'Thanks.'

'You're different with her. You're not doing that infuriating aloof thing you do around girls you like. You're more...yourself.'

He wonders what his mum would think if she knew how they met. 'She's had a rough go of it lately.'

The screen door closes and Jules is coming back up the hallway. Ryan's mum leans across the kitchen bench and touches his arm. 'Then make sure you're part of the solution and not the problem.' Ryan nods. Wonders how he's supposed to tell the difference.

Xavier: *Relax.*

Caller: *You and I have a vastly different understanding of the term 'low key'.*

Xavier: *You wanted her to be all over this. What's the problem?*

Caller: *You needed to wait until afterwards to redirect attention.*

Xavier: *None of it changes the outcome.*

Caller: *If she's filmed elsewhere when you breach the fence, she'll have an alibi.*

Xavier: *Trust me, when it happens, she'll be there.*

Caller: *Stop saying that.*

Xavier: *'Trust me'?*

Caller: *I don't like it when you go off-script.*

Xavier: *That's when things get interesting.* (A chair scrapes.)

Caller: (Pause) *Are we on speaker?*

The call goes dead.

'You know who that is, don't you?' Khan asks, grim. The federal agent is beside the Major, earpiece in. She overheard Frenchie saying she'd picked up something from the mic in Xavier's shoe and insisted on listening in on the feed. The Major really wishes she hadn't, because of course he recognises the caller's voice as well as she does.

And it complicates his life no end.

'You're with Ryno?'

The guy leans in to shout the question, empty glass in one hand, the other gripping the bar as he waits to be served. Jules nods, trying to avoid inhaling his bourbon breath.

Tommy's party is in full swing. It's between sets for the band and the filler music is just as loud. The footy club is packed—the whole town must be here—and almost everyone's at the bar shouting at each other. Jules is queuing too, waiting for Ryan to get back from the toilet. The lights went down two hours ago, so there's even less chance of her being recognised.

'He's always had killer taste in women.' The guy grins, all dimples and crinkling eyes. He's tall, blond and buff, wearing a T-shirt that shows off his chest and shoulders. Everyone at the bar makes room for him. He's *that* guy.

'I'm Dan O'Hare.' He hands off his glass so he can shake her hand. His palm is cool and lightly callused. Another farmer's son.

He gives her the sort of once-over that's meant to be flattering but never is. Jules wishes she hadn't worn the fitted black dress and ankle boots. She'd wanted to wear jeans but Ryan's mum insisted: she said Jules' legs would distract people from trying to work out why her face was so familiar.

'What can I get you?'

Dan crowds in every time he speaks and Jules resists the urge to lean away. She can't stand strangers in her personal space, dimpled or not.

'A beer for Ryan.'

Jules needs to keep her wits about her. She's already numb from a glass of shiraz. She's fairly sure getting drunk at a party is *not* part of the Major's or Khan's strategy to keep her safe, although in any other circumstance Angie might approve. Jules stops that train of thought: she can't allow herself to think about Angie tonight. She's tense enough as it is and the hot, fuzzy energy of the room isn't helping.

'What about for you?' Dan presses.

'I'm fine, thanks.'

'That you are.' His smile widens before he elbows his way to lean over the bar. 'Keithie!' The bony-faced barman has bags under his eyes and cigarette-stained teeth. Macka's dad. He sees Dan and nods.

Jules scans the bar for Ryan and Tommy. They said they were coming back before the next set but that doesn't mean much. Not with so much alcohol in the place and not when everyone wants a piece of them. Tommy's loving the attention. Ryan, not so much. He's been on edge all night. Even his drumming's different for this crowd: faster, angrier. Tommy, Macka and Gemma have had to play furiously to match his intensity.

Jules has only been clubbing twice—both times with Vee— and it was nothing like the vibe in the footy club. This feels like a throwback to last century. The guys are at the bar and the girls are grouped on the dance floor, squeezed into little black dresses and breakneck heels like Jules'. The older crowd is spread across tables at the back of the room. Ryan's dad is pouring a round of beer; two empty jugs clutter the space between him and Spud Laidlaw. Spud's eyes are bright, his curly hair tied back and his beard trimmed. He spots Jules and tips his glass, recognising her from the farm even without Ryan at her side. Jamie Walsh, on the other hand, has barely spoken to Jules except to grunt what she assumes was a greeting at breakfast this morning. Tonight, though, he's loud and animated and well on the way to drunk.

Michelle Walsh is on the next table over, deep in conversation with a woman wearing a shiny gold dress and showing a startling amount of glittery cleavage. Ryan's mum is nodding and smiling but she's distracted. Her eyes keep flitting to her husband and then around the room in search of her boys.

Gemma nudges Jules in the ribs. She's still flushed from the last set—either from exertion or from the way Tommy's been singing to her all night. She's punk-rock hot in black leather pants and matching halter top, her pink-tipped hair tied up in short spiky pigtails and a new ring through her eyebrow.

'You know that's Rabbit, right?' Gemma says in her ear.

Jules glances at Dan. He's shouting at someone further down the bar, pointing and giving instructions. Dan O'Hare...*Rabbit*. Of course.

'He's the one paying for the keg,' Jules says.

'Yeah, and if Ryno sees him cracking on to you, it'll be on for young and old.'

Gemma pulls her out of the crowd to a dry bar. 'They used to be best mates but they fell out right before Ryno joined the army. It's going to be bad enough when Ryno finds out Missy is with Rabbit. I thought Tommy was going to tell him but I'm guessing that hasn't happened.'

Jules has no idea who Missy is, let alone if Tommy and Ryan have talked about her.

'Ah, crap, here's Ryno.'

Ryan is making his way around the edge of the room, eyes roaming the crowd until he finds Jules. He's dressed for the gig rather than the party: jeans and faded grey T-shirt.

'Here you go. You look like a white wine girl.'

Rabbit is carrying three beers and a glass of wine. He puts them down with expert ease, ignoring Gemma. Ryan has almost reached them, his expression darker now.

Jules pushes the wine away. She didn't ask for it and there's no way she's drinking anything she hasn't seen being poured. She *feels* Ryan behind her—thunderous, agitated—and makes room for him at the table.

'Ryno.' Rabbit says it loudly and nods at the glass on the table. 'Drink up. My shout.'

Ryan's fury slices through the buzz of the crowd and lifts the hair on her arms. It can't be about Rabbit talking to her: they're only *pretending* to be together. A tall brunette squeezes through the line at the bar to join them, holding a jug of beer above her head.

'Ryno, hey!'

She offloads the beer and seems about to go to him before changing her mind. Rabbit loops an arm around her and his fingers settle on her hips. He locks eyes with Ryan and then leans in and kisses her neck. She doesn't push him away and something new flickers across Ryan's face. Hurt.

This must be Missy.

Jules doesn't know what Missy was—or is—to Ryan, but he picks up the beer and downs it in four gulps. Gemma widens her eyes at Jules, urging her to say or do something. It's a natural reaction; she's meant to be Ryan's girlfriend. Jules has zero practice in that role—with him or anyone else—and she has no clue what's going on between these three. But she can feel Ryan's energy compressing. So she does the only thing she can think of at short notice: she slides her hand into his back pocket and squeezes his backside.

Ryan looks at her, surprised. He puts down the empty glass. Jules leans in and his arm comes around her. She doesn't mean to glance at Missy and is surprised by what she finds: gratitude. Whatever this is, Missy doesn't want to rub Ryan's nose in it.

Rabbit raises his glass. 'Here's to *our* women.'

Ryan stiffens—he's about to lash out—and Jules instinctively slips between him and the dry bar. His gaze flicks away from her and back at Rabbit, his grip tightening as if to move her aside. Jules slips her hand under his shirt and runs a palm across his stomach. *That's* got his attention. He searches her eyes and she makes a small circle with her thumb inside his jeans. It's sexy and teasing and she knows he's lost interest in Rabbit by the way his lips part. He understands this is for show but there's expectation now, need. Her own response is a fast-spreading fire.

She leans in and he bends his head to hear.

'Do you want to go outside?'

He nods. She leads him away from the table before Rabbit can get another hook into him. Ryan's fingers thread between hers as they weave through the crowd, his skin warm. The charge stirs, a distant distraction.

They push through the glass doors and into the night. The cold air is a slap in the face but it's too late for a jacket. Ryan takes over, heading away from the floodlit oval and around the side of the clubhouse. The doors close behind them, muffling the music.

As soon as they clear the corner Ryan pulls her to him. Jules has a second to catch her breath and then his lips are on hers, hungry. She wraps her arms round his neck to keep him there. She feels the heat from his body, tastes beer on his tongue. Her whole body is buzzing, nerve endings alive and the heat coming in waves.

Ryan walks her backwards until she's against the wall, kissing her hard. One hand cradling the back of her head and the other guiding her by the hip. He slides up her dress so he can position his leg between hers. The contact sends a ripple of pleasure through her and she squeezes her thighs to intensify the sensation. Ryan's breath quickens. His mouth is on her neck, his hand cupping her breast through her dress.

The charge is building, burning through the alcohol haze. Jules ignores it. She's done this before without hurting anyone. That was slower, gentler, but it doesn't matter. She's got this.

Her fingers are in his hair. She's not feeling the cold. She can feel *him*, hard. She reaches down and traces the length of him through his jeans. Ryan presses closer. He runs his palms up the outside of her thighs and takes her dress with it, bunching it around her waist. The current surges through her, stinging her fingertips. More demanding than Ryan's touch. *Oh no.*

Not in control. Really not.

Jules tears her lips from his. 'Ryan...' She concentrates hard on reeling in the charge, but she's left it too late. Ryan's nuzzling her neck, pushing down her underwear.

'*Ryan,*' she pants, palms pressed to his chest. 'Slow down.'

He covers her mouth with his and his hand is between her legs—

The charge leaps into Ryan from her fingertips before she can stop it. It strikes him hard, throwing him backwards. He doesn't even have time to swear before he hits the dirt.

Dickhead. *Dickhead*.

Ryan rolls to his hands and knees, trying to catch his breath. She said no and he didn't stop. What did he think was going to happen? His chest is on fire and his hard-on well and truly gone. Jules has got herself together and straightened her dress. He can't see her face but he doesn't need to.

He picks himself up from the dirt. He had one job to do here—keep Jules safe—and he's managed to fuck that up. The only threat she has to worry about here is him.

'Ryan...' Jules hasn't moved from the wall.

Dickhead. No discipline. That's what his old man always says. It's what the Major says too. Julianne De Marchi is never going to trust him. Why should she?

'Ryan—'

Jules doesn't finish because a lanky silhouette with rounded shoulders slips around the corner. 'Ryno? You got your pants on?'

'What do you want, Macka?'

'Mate, I think Tommy's about to do something stupid with my old man.'

Ryan's already moving. 'Where?'

'By the oval.'

Jules follows them.

'Go back inside.'

'No.' She walks past him after Macka. He doesn't have time to argue because as soon as he clears the clubhouse he sees Tommy huddled with a handful of mates under the scoreboard. Keith McKenzie's in the middle of them, his face lit up by the field lights.

Macka melts into the darkness, not wanting his old man to know he's been telling tales. Ryan sticks to the shadows as he approaches.

Let it be dope.

He sees the glass pipe in Keith's hand and rage explodes across his chest.

'What the fuck, Tommy.'

Tommy looks up, mortified. 'I wasn't going to, honestly.'

'Back off, Ryno,' Keith says, breaking clear from the pack. 'It's his present.'

'You're giving him black resin? We not dying off quick enough for you, Keith?' He stops his hands from tightening into fists.

'Settle down,' Keith says, laughing, 'I'm helping your little brother escape his shit life for a while.'

'The only shit he needs to escape is you.'

'Ryno, I wasn't going to take a drag, I swear.'

Ryan eyeballs Keith McKenzie. 'You don't know anything about his life so why don't you shut your mouth?'

'I know your old man's going to lose everything when that legislation goes through. And for what? His fucken pride? He could've saved your farm a dozen times over in the last five years but he never will because he won't admit he's wrong.'

The music throbbing from the clubhouse swells louder for a few seconds. Someone else is coming out. Ryan has a quick look and his chest constricts. It's his old man and Spud. Both drunk. Jules moves further away from the light.

'Get the fuck away from my boys,' his dad says, slurring.

'I tell you what, Walsh, you start paying for your drinks and you can give me orders.'

254

'Fuck you.'

Ryan watches his father approach with uneven steps. Does he stop this? What if his old man turns on him? The last thing their family needs is half the town watching the two of them go at it—at Tommy's party, no less.

Ryan's head thuds double-time and his shoulders are strung too tight. Tommy is silently begging him to intervene and Ryan shakes his head. 'Stay out of it,' he mouths at his brother.

His dad stops a few paces from Keith. Back in the day, Jamie Walsh threw a good punch. But tonight, beaten down by life and full of piss, he's not in any state to pick a fight. 'You hear me, Keithie? You don't come near my boys.'

'Your boys?' Keith's laugh is harsh. 'They don't want nothing to do with you, Walsh. Tommy gets wasted *here* every weekend to get away from you, and Ryno joined the fucken army to escape.'

'Dad, that's not true—'

Tommy doesn't finish because their dad charges Keith McKenzie. He barrels into him and they both end up in the gravel under the scoreboard, two middle-aged pissheads scuffling and throwing wild punches.

A circle forms. Tommy knows better than to interrupt a fight in Mitchellstone and moves in with everyone else. Ryan grits his teeth. Somebody needs to break this up before their mum comes out and sees it.

'Let 'em go, Ryno.'

It's Rabbit, joining the circle. Most of the senior team has followed him outside and Ryan knows exactly where their loyalties lie.

'Your dad's had a beating coming for a while.'

'My dad's had it coming? Yours was the first to bend over for Pax Fed and the banks. Now they tell you what to plant, what to breed and when to take a shit.'

'Fuck's sake,' Rabbit snaps. 'Nobody bent over. We made good business decisions—'

'You buckled at the first sign of pressure and everyone else had to fall into line or get sent to the wall.'

'We all had choices.'

'Nobody had a choice after your old man sold out.'

Under the scoreboard, Ryan's dad and Keith McKenzie are still laying into each other. Nobody's talking, it's all grunting and smacking flesh when one of them lands a punch.

Ryan's had enough. He breaks formation and Rabbit grabs him by the elbow.

'I said don't—'

Ryan's well aware of how many blokes are around Rabbit but he goes anyway: a quick, sharp blow to the throat that steals Rabbit's air and sends him to his knees. Ryan has a fleeting moment of satisfaction before three blokes jump him. The same mates who piled on top of him in celebration three years ago are now throwing punches at him. They're all a blur. He head-butts the full-forward, elbows the rover in the guts, and lands an uppercut on the half-back before someone takes out his new knee. Two defenders pin his arms long enough for Rabbit to get up and take a swing, which lands square on his eye socket. The night turns white and his head splinters.

'That was a cheap shot, Ryno,' Rabbit wheezes without irony.

Ryan's eye throbs, the blood rushing to it. More scuffles have broken out around them. Not everyone was happy to see him outnumbered.

'Stay back Tommy, or you're next,' Rabbit warns and then he frowns at something behind Ryan. 'Come on, gorgeous, you don't want to get involved—'

Ryan feels a twinge of voltage before the two defenders drop to the ground either side of him. Rabbit lunges at Jules and drags her towards the light under the scoreboard. Ryan tries to get up but his head is three sizes too big.

'Where is it?' Rabbit's rough, trying to see what's in her hands.

Bad move.

'Show me—'

There's a flash of light and he's juddering on the spot. Jules lets him twitch for a good few seconds before he drops to a heap on the ground.

'Holy crap,' Tommy says, hauling Ryan to his feet. Ryan's trying to see his old man through the mass of brawling bodies and finds him back on his feet, mouth bloodied, dragging Keith McKenzie around in a headlock.

A gunshot splits the night and everyone hits the ground, Ryan with them. He scrambles around to locate the shooter, heart thrashing. Sinks to the dirt with relief.

'Break it up now or I'll arrest the lot of you.'

Senior Sergeant Beth Horrocks manages to scare these blokes, even in a gold dress and sparkly cleavage. The Smith & Wesson helps.

Ryan's mum is behind her, surveying the scene—men and boys, bloodied and bruised, climbing back to their feet. She holds up a palm at Tommy and Ryan. 'I don't want to hear it. Julianne, are you all right?'

Jules nods.

'The three of you go home. I'll take your father to Beth's and get him cleaned up.'

'You're taking him to the cop shop?' Tommy asks.

'I'm taking him to *Beth's*. Unless he resists and then, yes, he might spend a few hours in the cell. Gemma's sober. She can drive the Monaro and you can leave Macka to sort the band gear.'

His mum frowns at the three sprawled-out footballers coming to in the glare of the field lights.

'Why have they all wet their pants?'

Angie can't tell if she's playing Xavier or he's playing her, and it's killing her not knowing.

It's why she and Waylon have hiked under a crisp sky to a service station on the outskirts of Port Augusta to find a landline. The contact hub will be a monitored connection on an ancient network, but it won't be Xavier or his cronies listening in.

'Why hasn't Voss made contact?'

She and Waylon linger outside the halo of light on the deserted concourse. The night is tangy with brine and Waylon sighs with the frustration of repetition. 'We'll only hear from him if my orders change or something goes pear-shaped.'

'Something *has* gone pear-shaped. Xavier's made me the face of whatever he's got planned here—and don't go on about me making that easy. He was setting me up whether I stepped onto that stage or not.'

'Yeah, well, at least now you've got more clout to influence his mob when the time comes.'

'How? I don't know what he's going to do and he's been avoiding me all afternoon.'

'He'll tell you when he's ready. He's the kind of tool who needs to brag to someone.'

'You're taking all this in your stride, Waylon.'

His silhouette turns to her. 'We've got a job to do and so far we're getting it done.'

'Fine. Do your job and fix the light over that contact hub.'

She catches a hint of smile in the moonlight, which only fans her irritation.

Waylon screws the suppresser on his pistol, takes a moment to steady himself and fires. There's a pop of tinkling glass as the light winks out.

Angie jogs from the saltbush and skirts the bowsers. Waylon hangs back, covering her. She takes the handset from the hub cradle, swipes the pre-paid card and holds her breath. The dial tone crackles but at least the screen works, even coated in grime from years of tapping fingers. She tries Khan's number first. It rings out.

Angie disconnects and wipes her palms on her jeans. Khan could be out of range. She won't answer a number she doesn't recognise. Nothing to worry about.

Angie fishes out the number for Ryan's farm. It's in code—every second number is two lower than the actual digit. She taps it in and waits, her agitation growing when it rings out twice. Her scalp prickles. Did Jules even make it there?

Voss didn't give her his number, but Angie needs to talk to someone. She dials Vee.

'God, Ange, I've been worried sick.' Vee's wide awake despite the late hour. 'Tell me that stunt at the camp wasn't your idea.'

'Of course it wasn't.'

'Have you heard from Jules? Or Khan or Voss?'

'Total radio silence so far.'

A beat. It's the type of pause Vee takes when she's got bad news to deliver.

'What have *you* heard?'

Vee doesn't answer and the silence is long enough to trap the breath in Angie's throat.

'*Vee*—'

'The government shut down an unsanctioned corporate pilot project twenty years ago involving our soldiers in Afghanistan.'

259

It comes out in a rush. It's not what Angie was expecting and it takes her a few seconds to change gears.

In the silence, Vee pushes on: 'Pax Fed was in the mix but I can't prove Mike's unit was involved. I didn't want to tell you until I knew for sure—which I need to stress I *don't*—but I told Jules it was a possibility on Wednesday and I wanted you to hear that from me.'

Angie stares at a line of graffiti scrawled on the perspex in streaky black texta, backlit by the concourse lights: *#PortAguttaGlowsInTheDark*. She can't see Waylon but she can feel him watching her from the shadows.

'When did you find out?'

'About a month ago.'

Angie De Marchi is well acquainted with incendiary rage. The sensation building right now is slower and much, much colder.

'I thought you'd be yelling at me by this point.'

'Because you lied to me?'

'I haven't lied. I don't have any proof.'

'You didn't trust me enough to tell me you *might* have something: the only lead in a decade. I'm so sick of you thinking you have to save me from myself.'

'Somebody has to. What happens to Jules if you get yourself killed because you can't let this go?'

'You're not her mother, Vee, I am.'

'Then act like it.'

Angie slams her palm on the Perspex. 'I may not hug her like you do, or take her shopping and clubbing, but that doesn't mean I don't love her. I need to know who did this to her—'

'So you can punish them?'

'So I can give my daughter a *life*. She's eighteen and she's shut herself off from the world because she's scared she's going to hurt someone.'

Vee doesn't respond and Angie knows she's giving her room

260

to seethe. Managing her. Air brakes hiss on the highway: a semi slowing for the station.

'What else haven't you told me?'

'Angie, I didn't mean that you don't love Jules. All I meant was—'

'*Is there anything else?*'

Vee exhales like she's winded.

'Pax Fed has poached the top senior geneticist from Queensland Uni for a short-term offline contract. It only happened this morning and nobody's supposed to know about it.'

'They have their own geneticists.'

'Theirs specialise in genetically modified grains. Professor Mian's an expert in human bioengineering.'

Angie puts her back to the concourse. The nuclear plant looms half a kilometre away, its cooling towers dressed in twinkling lights. Somewhere to the east of that monster, beyond the silo and the moonlit fields of the sun farm, Jules is meant to be safe. But how can she be when Pax Fed is paying the unit that's supposed to protect her?

'Where is the geneticist now? The government tracks our top scientific minds, right? So you should know. Or are you going to feed me more sugar-coated crap?'

'Ange...' Vee sighs. 'The professor boarded a flight late this afternoon. She's headed to South Australia.'

'What'd you do with the taser?' Gemma asks as she guns the Monaro out of the clubhouse car park. The engine's loud and meaty, hungry for speed. Ryan's in the back with Jules. Ordinarily he wouldn't let anyone else drive but his left eye is so swollen he can barely see out of it.

Jules hesitates. 'I, ah...'

'You don't want to know,' Tommy says from the front, saving Jules from lying.

Gemma glances at Tommy. 'Right.' She finds Ryan in the rearview mirror. 'We should've told you about Missy and Rabbit. Sorry.'

Jules shifts position on the leather seat and Ryan can't look at her.

'What happened with Nunnie?' His voice is flat.

'He went to Queensland last year looking for rousting work and didn't come back. She waited six months. That's a big effort for Missy.'

Ryan stares out at the town flashing by. Everything's in darkness except the pub. His face throbs and his knuckles are raw but he's sobered up. And at least those fuckers didn't wreck his knee. It's sore, but it took his weight when he got up.

'Missy and Ryan go way back,' Gemma explains to Jules.

'You were a couple?'

Ryan glances at her, surprised she's interested.

'Friends with benefits,' Tommy says.

'Mates, first and last.' Ryan sees Rabbit's hands on Missy. 'And she can do better than that cockhead.'

Gemma puts her foot down as soon as they get out of the town and the Monaro eats up the road. It doesn't smell like his dad's car anymore. Right now it reeks of make-up and hairspray.

Tommy and Gemma don't get out when they pull up by the shed.

'It's still his birthday,' Gemma tells Jules and her gaze slides to Tommy.

Ryan taps the drivers headrest to get Gemma's attention. 'About bloody time.'

Tommy's watching Gemma with bright eyes, not game to open his mouth. The drama at the club is all forgotten for now. It's the best gift Gemma could give Tommy and Ryan loves her for it.

'Don't prang Dad's car.' Ryan gets out and stands on the opposite side of the driveway to Jules, watching the Monaro roar back towards town. He needs to lie down, but from the way Jules is lingering he knows his night's not over yet. And if there's one thing the army's taught him, it's how to take his punishment.

*

Jules left her borrowed jacket at the clubhouse but she's not feeling the cold. The midnight air fizzes on her still-warm skin and the current crackles beneath it.

'I thought V8s were illegal,' she says.

Ryan follows her gaze to the tail-lights fading in the dust. 'Only if you get caught on a public road and you have a local copper who cares.' He sounds exhausted.

'That car's a bit hard to miss.'

'Gemma will switch over to electric before they head up to

the creek. They won't want the whole town knowing where they are.'

Ryan's energy is a swirly mess. They need to talk about what happened earlier, but not out here.

'Can we go inside?'

He blinks with his good eye. 'In the shed?'

'Unless you want me to stay in the house on my own?'

'Might be safer,' Ryan mutters and unlocks the shed anyway. He fumbles until he finds the lamp and soft light brightens the space, not quite reaching the corners. Jules closes the door and is instantly aware of how alone they are.

Ryan takes a hand towel from the bathroom and goes to the beer fridge, finds an ice tray in the freezer. He puts a handful of ice in the towel, twists it into a half-decent pack and presses it to his eye socket. Jules hovers by the door, grappling for a way to break the silence.

'How's your dad? Did you get a good look at him?'

Ryan shrugs, one hand on the fridge. 'He's not too banged up. Fat lip, some bark off his arms. He'll be sore when he sobers up but he had the best of Keithie at the end there so his pride's intact. Until Mum got stuck into him.' He clears his throat and then meets her gaze, his expression guarded. 'Thanks for not making me piss my pants.'

It's not the opening she was expecting, but she'll take it. 'It's more luck than anything.' That's not quite true: she fully intended those other boys to end up in the state they did.

'I don't usually drink.' He lowers his arm so she can see his face when he speaks, beat up as it is. 'Being with everyone again, seeing the way the whole town looks at my old man, and then Missy and Rabbit. It's no excuse for not stopping when you told me to.'

'I didn't tell you to stop,' she says quietly. 'I asked you to slow down. The charge was building and I didn't have a grip on it.'

'Because I was going too fast.'

'No, because *I* was.' She exhales. 'I don't have a lot of experience with...I got carried away and ignored it.'

'I should've stopped.'

'Yeah, you should have. I should've been more aware of what was going on with me.'

She lost track of everything else the second his mouth was on hers. He was reckless but so was she. She would have gone there, crushed against the bricks, if the charge hadn't interfered. The idea of it thrills and shames her in equal measure and a sobering thought strikes her. Is that how he sees her? The type of girl you do against a clubhouse wall?

*

Ryan knows there's something else he should say, something to keep her talking but he has no clue what it is. He's never had a conversation like this with a girl before.

'I'm sorry.'

She presses pink lips together. Some of her lipstick survived those hungry kisses. 'Me too.'

He'd thought maybe they were bridging the gap, but the way she says it widens the distance again. He should have apologised before now.

The throbbing in his eye intensifies. He sits on the bed, exhausted when he shouldn't be: the fight barely lasted a minute. He rests his elbows on his knees, presses the ice against his face. What a mess the night turned out to be. Tommy huddled over a meth pipe with Keith McKenzie, his old man drunk and embarrassing himself, his mum taking charge like it's business as usual. He reaches down one-handed to unlace his boots. The lump rises in his throat, unbidden, and his good eye wells. What is he getting teary about? He hasn't cried in years, unless you count the grand final win, and he's not breaking the drought with Jules in the room.

A weight sinks on the mattress and he lifts his head in surprise. He was so preoccupied keeping his shit together he didn't hear Jules cross the floor.

'Was Tommy going to smoke that pipe?'

Ryan focuses on the laces and presses the icepack to his good eye in case it's still leaking. 'I don't know, he's got a lot on his shoulders. I'm in no position to judge.'

'I don't think he would have. He'd be too worried about letting you down.'

Ryan laughs, short and harsh. 'I let him down by leaving.'

'Ryan…' In his peripheral vision he sees her hand move to the doona between them. 'Would the situation be different if you hadn't joined the army?'

He scratches at a fleck of dried mud on his boot. They'd miss the money, but he'd be *here*. He knows it wouldn't save the farm. It might save Tommy from turning into their old man, though.

'You're doing the best you can with tough choices.'

'But I keep making the *wrong* choices. I messed up with Dad, with looking out for Tommy, with you.' He risks a look at her. She's close enough for him to see the mascara smudged into the creases around her eyes. Ryan can't undo the past year, but he can fix things with Jules. He needs her to know he's not a prick who disrespects women. 'You're smart and you're beautiful and I've spent the past week fantasising about what it would be like to be with you. And when we started up, you were so into it that all I wanted was *more*, but that's not the way I wanted it to happen.'

Her mouth softens. Finally he's said something right.

'And then you took down those idiots at the oval. You shouldn't have put yourself at risk.'

'If I hadn't stepped in, you'd look even worse than you do.'

'That bad?'

She screws up one eye like it pains her to look at him. 'It's not pretty. How badly does it hurt?'

'A bit.'

Jules shifts sideways to face him and his pulse does a weird skip. She waits a beat and then leans in and kisses him softly. He resists the urge to reach for her. She breaks contact but doesn't pull back.

'Can we get into bed?'

Ryan blinks, a little dazed. 'Is that a trick question?'

He runs the back of his fingers lightly across her thigh, testing himself. The feel of her skin stirs him, but it's nothing like that blinding need at the clubhouse. Maybe all she wants is for him to hold her and that's fine by him. It's better than he deserves.

'Do you want something to sleep in?'

She frowns, genuinely surprised. 'We're going to sleep?'

He falls a little in love with her right then.

*

Jules' fingers tremble as she slips out of her dress and boots in the bathroom. The conversation with Ryan was more intimate than anything that passed between them against that wall. It's intoxicating to say what you want, and she wants to be with Ryan, there's no getting around it. Not in the way they were at the footy grounds—that was too frantic, too impersonal—but how it was just now on his bed. Honest.

It's tricky for him to be home with his family, she sees that. He loves them so deeply it's bending him into a different shape and the longer they stay here the harder it's going to be for him to leave. Jules is sure there were moments tonight he even forgot why he was back.

Jules catches sight of herself in the mirror. Her make-up is smudged and her hair wild: she looks like her mother after a big night and it brings a stab of anxiety for Angie.

But her mother is exactly where she wants to be. And whatever's happening in Port Augusta, Jules can't help from here, so why shouldn't she allow herself a brief moment that's not about Angie, or the current, or paying bills, or any of the other forty-nine things she frets over every day?

She ties back her hair and tests the charge. It should be barely there after her efforts tonight but it's steadily humming away. Not quite compliant, but manageable—although her ability to manage it only matters if Ryan wants to share more than a doona. She's shocked him twice now. He may not want to try for a third time.

*

While Jules is in the bathroom, Ryan locks the sliding door and closes the curtain. He strips down to his jocks and T-shirt, checks there are condoms in his top drawer (just in case) and gets into bed. It's all a bit weird: he's never been with a girl in his own bed.

When Jules reappears he can't help but laugh. 'I hope you don't think that's going to dampen my enthusiasm, because I gotta be honest: it's having the opposite effect.'

She's wearing his old Tigers guernsey and footy shorts, and it's about the sexiest thing he's ever seen.

'It was all I could find.'

He lifts back the doona and makes room. 'Tommy pilfered everything else when I moved out.'

She climbs in and snuggles against him. He rests his cheek on the top of her head, feels the weight of the night lift from him.

They kiss for a while, slow and deep. When Ryan takes a breather to check how she's doing, she plants butterfly kisses around his swollen eye and her fingers snake down the length of his stomach to grip him through his jocks. He remembers the last time he was in this state.

'Are you sure?'

'Yes.'

They help each other out of their clothes, taking their time. Ryan teases her, enjoying the way she arches to meet him every time his lips leave her breasts. He runs his palm across her stomach and hips, learning the landscape of her, and when his hand slides lower she falls completely still. Ryan checks himself, ignores his own building need. He takes her hand and positions it over his. 'Show me what you like.'

Her cheeks flush pink but she doesn't look away and then she guides him, sets the rhythm. It's slow and purposeful. Her pressure falls away: she's trusting him to get the job done.

Ryan takes his time—another first. Her head is back and eyes closed, lost in his touch. He can't stop watching her mouth. He changes tempo, ad libs a little and she seems to like it. Her grip on his arm tightens. It takes a while, but they get there. She arrives with a surprised gasp and a rush of colour. He keeps his hand in place while she rides out the sensation, swears he can feel the charge pulsing through her. Another small sound of pleasure escapes her and he almost loses it.

She looks at him, unguarded, through heavy lids, and the intimacy of it strips him bare. She rolls onto her side to face him properly, reaches down to see how he's doing.

He's doing *fine*.

'Condom?'

He wets his lips, doesn't want to sound overly prepared. 'There could be one in the top drawer.'

Jules leans over and finds it right where he left it.

'There are other things we could do,' he says.

She concentrates and carefully tears the packet open, takes out the rubber. 'I want to do this.'

Ryan wants to watch her but as soon as her hands are on him again he closes his eyes, feels her roll the latex down. Her fingers aren't practised, but they're meticulous.

They kiss again and Ryan draws her on top of him.

'You're in charge.' He says it partly to minimise the chance of electrocution, partly because she's been doing a stellar job so far.

'You're not worried?' Her hair falls in a curtain to frame her face.

He wets his lips. 'A little.'

Jules guides him into position—it takes a few attempts—and lowers herself onto him. He gasps. He's aware of it immediately: her entire body humming.

'You can feel that?' she asks.

He sits up and wraps her legs around his hips, locking her to him. 'Is it normal?'

'For me, yeah.' She gives a secret smile and pushes gently against him.

Maybe it's the fact she's naked. Maybe it's the fact his own need is overwhelming. But right then, Ryan is happy to trust his life to her.

It's after 05:00 when the knock comes.

The Major opens the door holding a coffee mug, confirms Peta Paxton's alone. At least she had the sense to lose the suit: she's in black jeans, business shirt and designer sneakers. Without heels she barely reaches his chest, but it doesn't stop her eyeballing him.

'I've endured two flights to get here, Major. Can I come in, or are we having this conversation in the hallway?'

The room is above a public bar in Port Augusta. French is in the van keeping watch in case Paxton's been tailed. Khan is next door, earpiece set, listening in. There was no avoiding her involvement after that audio playback. The rest of Q18 are an hour out of town, on their way.

'Nobody put a gun to your head,' the Major says.

'You've requested to terminate Paxton Federation's stake in this contract. It is necessary to have this conversation in person.' She's momentarily distracted by the fact he's in a T-shirt and skins.

The Major gestures to the only chair in the room. Paxton doesn't take it. 'Are you going to tell me what's going on, or do I need to file a lawsuit for breach of contract?'

He finishes the instant coffee and holds her gaze long enough to unnerve her.

When he can see she's understood who has the power in the

room he says: 'Your brother wants Julianne De Marchi dead. Why?'

Her outrage takes a second too long to surface. 'That's a ridiculous accusation. What gives you the right—'

He slams the cup on the windowsill and she has the sense to snap her mouth shut. 'It's too early in the morning for bullshit so let's skip our usual dance. I know your brother's hired a dipshit to set up Angie De Marchi for whatever's about to go down here. I know that dipshit's being shadowed by a paramilitary unit that only someone with your brother's resources can afford. That means your brother orchestrated that clusterfuck in Brisbane last week, the sole aim of which was to get to Julianne De Marchi, and when that failed he sent them to her home.' The Major gets in her personal space. 'So tell me: why is Angie De Marchi a threat and why does your company want her daughter dead?'

She takes an involuntary step back and bumps into the chair. 'What makes you so sure they were there to hurt Julianne?'

'They're a kill squad, Paxton. That's what they do.'

She takes a long, deep breath and sits down. Whatever her game is she needs him or she'd already be out the door.

'Paxton Federation has no interest in harming Julianne.'

'But your brother does.'

A minute shrug. 'He thinks she's in his way.'

'How does a teenage girl get *in his way?*'

Paxton massages the side of her long neck. 'He needs his new legislation to get through the Senate without amendment. Anything that threatens our reputation could influence that outcome. Paxton Federation might be a generous government funding partner, but that will mean nothing if our reputation isn't squeaky clean.'

'No shit. He's carpet-bombed Angie De Marchi's career so your lot have a clear run to peddle your GMO propaganda. Where does Julianne come into it?'

Paxton glances at the door, runs a manicured fingertip over

one eyebrow and then the other. Huffs out her breath. 'You'll remember there was a short-lived period when the West thought the key to the war on terror was to weaponise soldiers?'

'A brainless idea, then and now.'

She ignores him. 'Our military research arm was in its infancy then. We were experimenting with mitochondrial mutation and nanotechnology. My father believed the solution wasn't in turning the human body into a weapon but in increasing resilience and recovery time, and he needed test subjects. We were in such early stages of trials there was no way we'd get official government approval for human subjects, so a deal was done off the books to use randomly selected soldiers serving in Afghanistan.'

*Mother*fuckers. Veronica Ng's information was good.

'Who was the genius who selected the husband of an investigative journalist as a random test subject?'

Paxton gives him a taut smile. 'An actual genius. A geneticist with no understanding of the world beyond a microscope.' She straightens the rings on her fingers.

'What happened?'

'There were promising results, but the defence minister got wind of it and shut us down. My father was told to bury the records if he ever wanted to be in business with the government again. Our agricultural unit was on the verge of securing approval for the first of the new wheat strains so my father did what he had to for the good of the company.'

The Major walks to the window and back, struggling to contain his temper.

'I've always believed in that research, if not the exact method,' Paxton continues. 'It's why my team spent years officially developing a new variation in the lab, why I've pushed so hard for your unit to trial the latest iteration as soon as we had approval. Operation Resilience is legitimate and you know it works, you've seen the results.' She glances at his calf.

The Major grunts. The Q18 boys might not know the

scientific name for what they're taking but they do at least know what effect it's meant to have. And they knew about the trial before they signed on. Unlike Mike De Marchi and the men and women targeted in Afghanistan.

'When did you know about Julianne?' he asks.

'When did *you*?'

His nostrils flare, slow and deliberate.

She's too far from shore now to swim back and she knows it. 'We kept tabs on the returned soldiers, especially when they had children of their own. To be honest, we were more concerned about female test subjects passing on genetic anomalies, but none of the offspring showed signs of being affected by the trial.'

'Until De Marchi's kid.'

'It wasn't a big issue. She had some mitochondrial inconsistencies but as far as we knew, there were no external signs. My father insisted the family be left alone.'

The Major pours himself a glass of water from the jug by the TV. Doesn't offer one to Paxton. 'What changed?'

'Mike De Marchi was killed in action defending one of our assets in Pakistan. It's the greatest irony of all: if he were alive, none of this would be a problem. Angela had led protests against us, but she led them against everyone. After her husband died, she put all her energy into attacking our company from every direction. Our government support started to waver. I wanted to ride it out, but Bradford panicked. He thought she must have known about the trial and was going to expose the company. He needed to know if anything had changed with Julianne so he sent that "dipshit", as you call him, into the school.'

'You knew about Xavier?'

'Not until afterwards and I certainly didn't have a name.' She uncrosses her knees, crosses them again. 'Bradford's paranoia went off the charts after the school incident. He was convinced our company wouldn't be safe until Julianne was out of the picture, but Dad forbade it.'

'Did your old man see what she did in that lab?'

Paxton's eyes widen. 'You've seen the footage?'

The Major weighs up the situation, decides to show his hand. 'I've seen the real thing.'

She stares at him. 'When?'

'Julianne took down a six-foot soldier who put a gun to her head on Tuesday night.'

Paxton sits forward. 'Did she mean to? How did it happen?'

And there's *her* hand. The Major smiles. 'I thought you weren't interested in Julianne De Marchi.'

'Of course we're interested in her. The fact she can generate and conduct electricity without it harming her—we have no idea how that's even possible. There's a chance it can be replicated in the lab, but—' She stops.

'You knew what she was capable of so why did you agree to let her in the building last week?'

'I didn't, that was all Bradford. He wanted to see what Julianne would do under pressure. I had no idea he had a mercenary unit in the building—he didn't tell me. There was a chance he'd push her too far; that's why I needed at least one of your soldiers nearby. I didn't know Bradford wanted her dead.'

'Then you're very naive. His bill goes up to the next session of the Senate. Why hasn't your father stepped in?'

She rubs the corner of her eye, careful not to poke herself with a red fingernail. For a split second he catches a glimpse of, what—it can't be grief?

'My father is not well, Major. Bradford's had control of the board for the last six weeks and I'll take over next month for eight weeks. After that, Dad will decide who succeeds him as chair.'

The Major grunts. He'd like to waterboard the lot of them. 'You two are buying military units to pit against each other because you're fighting for your old man's approval?'

'Please don't compare me to my brother.' She runs her

tongue across her teeth. 'Regardless of what's going on between Bradford and me, Julianne De Marchi isn't safe. Bradford's destroying all traces of the Afghanistan trials. The servers that were shot up on Wednesday stored the only remaining copies of the early Op Res files. They were never saved to the cloud, which means Julianne and her DNA are the only physical evidence left. Bradford's not going to stop until she's gone.'

'What about Xavier? Is your brother going to put a bullet in him too? He's seen what Julianne can do.'

'I don't know what the deal is between those two and, truly, I don't care. But I want Julianne safe.'

'She's safe where she is.'

'Major, you do understand that protecting Julianne De Marchi was never in your contract? She's not part of this operation.'

'She is if I say so—and nothing in our conversation tonight convinces me otherwise.'

Sweat beads on her top lip. This is not the way she wants this conversation to go. 'Z12 has identified the boy you sent in on Wednesday. If she's with him, she won't be safe for long.'

The Major doesn't react. Two decades of feigning respect for pin-dick commanding officers has honed his poker face. 'Who told you it's Z12?'

'I've followed the money trail, Major. There's only so much you can hide without a requisition order, especially at board level. I can help you keep her safe.'

She's been a step ahead of him all this time, playing him for her own ends. But she might not be lying. If she's right and Z12 has identified Walsh, there's a shitstorm of trouble headed for the family farm.

Is he prepared to take the risk she's bluffing?

Ryan's snoring wakes her.

Jules is curled up beside him, wearing only her undies and the footy jersey. The shed is cold and dark but she can see he's on his back, one arm across his chest. A sliver of sky is visible through a break in the blinds: the sun's not far away.

She's heavy with sleep and a sensation that takes a moment to identify: a lazy contentment. Jules replays the end of the evening again, warms at the memory. She resists the urge to wake Ryan. There's something she's ready to do and she'd prefer to be alone. She slips out of bed and rifles through Ryan's bag, finds a pair of running skins. She puts on a bra under the jersey, and slips into Ryan's parka and her ankle boots. It's a ridiculous combination but she's not planning on being seen.

The sliding door catches in its tracks—Ryan doesn't stir— and outside the air is dewy and sharp with eucalypt. Faint light stains the horizon, enough to let her find her way past the chooks and towards the shearing shed.

Yesterday, Jules sat on the verandah and watched the sun come up, wrapped in her doona and cradling a cup of tea. The vastness beyond the shearing shed called to her in the half-light, but she didn't want to face it with an audience. Yesterday, everyone else was up and about at this hour.

Not today. This morning nothing moves: not the trees, not the chooks roosting in the hen house, not even the dogs. The

Monaro and Michelle's ute are back but the house is dark.

Her boots crunch on fallen twigs, loud in the stillness. The closer she gets to the shearing shed, the stronger the smell of sheep shit and lanolin. The shed is elevated and she can see that even the dry grass underneath has been eaten to the ground. The sheep huddle together in the paddock, asleep on their feet.

Jules rounds the corner of the yards and startles at a figure in the dirt.

Ryan's dad is sitting against a timber support staring out at the paddock. A shotgun sits across his lap.

'Go back to bed,' he growls.

His face is puffy and bruised, his top lip split and crusted with blood. Jules glances back at the house, uneasy. Does Michelle know he's out here? The energy coming from him is erratic, pulsing in fuzzy waves. Is he still drunk?

'Do you want me to get someone?'

'No.' His eyes are fixed on the horizon. The soil in the yard is churned up from a hundred small hooves. Jules glances at the herd in the paddock, the dread building.

'You're not going to shoot those sheep, are you?'

He laughs—a horrible sound. 'Not today.'

Jules takes in his grip on the shotgun, the way he's slouched in the dirt like he doesn't care how he'll get back up, and understanding hits her like a slamming door: he's watching the sun rise and then he's going to do something truly awful with that gun.

She needs Ryan but she can't leave his dad here alone. What if he pulls the trigger as soon as she goes? The charge surges, but it's useless from this distance and if she handles this badly he might shoot *her*.

'Give me the gun.' The words are hollow. 'Please.'

He ignores her. She takes a step closer.

'Mr Walsh…Jamie—'

He lifts the shotgun in her direction. 'Don't.'

Jules freezes. It takes a few seconds to drag her eyes from the barrel but when she does, she recognises the grief in his battered face: a desolation that runs dark and deep enough to erode his capacity for reason. Jules has seen the shadow of it in her mother.

'Go.'

She doesn't move.

'*Go.*' Jamie turns the weapon on himself and wedges the barrel under his jaw.

Oh God, no. He's going to shoot himself right now if she doesn't do something. The shotgun bites into Jamie's stubbled chin.

'Please don't do this. They need you.'

A sharp laugh. 'No they don't.'

'They do. You're their dad.'

'They'll survive. You did.'

Jules falters. 'You don't know what you're talking about.'

The change in her voice snags him and bloodshot eyes meet hers.

'I miss my dad every day. *Every* day.' She taps her fingers over her heart. 'I lie to myself that I'm doing okay, that he's still with me. But he's not *here*. I can't talk to him or hug him or laugh with him. I can't miss him the way you miss someone when you know they're coming back.' The yard blurs and she blinks her eyes clear. 'I keep expecting him to walk around a corner or lean in my bedroom doorway but he's never coming back. That's what you want to give Michelle and your sons? A life of misery and resentment? If you do this they'll never get over it.'

He glares at her, his jaw working and his finger too close to the trigger.

'My only consolation is knowing my dad would have never left us by choice. He went down fighting.' Her voice breaks on the last sentence.

'I don't have any fight left.'

'You do. I saw it last night. So did your boys.'

His nostrils flare and his mouth tugs down, wrestling with her words.

'Ryan loves you. You don't get that angry with someone you don't care about. Trust me, I know.'

His face scrunches and his eyes well. A tear rolls down his swollen cheek and drips onto the barrel. 'Ah, fuck.' He lets out an anguished sob and lowers the shotgun.

Jules whimpers with relief. She sinks to the dirt with him. A hundred metres away, his family sleeps on.

'Six generations on this land,' he rasps. 'And when that legislation goes through, the government's going to take it from me and sell it to Pax Fed.' The shotgun rests on his lap, his finger clear of the trigger. He sniffs and stares out at the horizon. 'I shot and burned a hundred and twenty-two sheep last month. I couldn't feed them and I couldn't sell them, not even for pet food. The government's taken our dam water but won't give us access to the new pipeline. The banks won't loan us money between harvests because Pax Fed tells 'em our farming practices aren't *financially feasible*.'

Jules wipes her cheek on the sleeve of Ryan's parka. 'Why don't you grow what they want?'

He shakes his head, as much to himself as to her.

'How much of our grain and meat do you think'll make it to Third World countries? It'll go to the highest bidder.'

He sounds like Angie and for a second Jules misses her mum so much her heart hurts. Impulsive, ball-breaking Angie, who Jules hopes will always be too angry at the world to ever let it defeat her.

A white cocky screeches from a tree along the road and Jamie closes his eyes. The bleakness is getting a grip again. His energy is less erratic, but hazy enough to be unpredictable.

Jules crawls forward.

'How about you give me the gun?'

Ryan hears the shot from the bathroom.

It sounds like a .22 rifle, not a military weapon, but that does nothing to calm his panic. *Where is Jules?* He cuts short his piss and jams on jeans, jumper and boots. Grabs his service pistol from his duffel bag.

The shot came from the sheds, he knows that much.

He sneaks a quick look between the blinds—the driveway is clear—and slips outside. The chances of a mercenary firing a .22 are slim, but he uses the cars as cover as he makes his way through the yard, listening for movement before he runs into the open.

When he hears a voice it's closer than he expects. He can make out enough to know it's Jules and that she's upset. Ryan sprints around the side of the shearing shed—

—and pulls up short, confused.

Jules is standing with his dad's shotgun, chamber open and barrel pointed to the ground, her face streaked with tears; his old man is propped against a bearer post with his head in his hands.

'What the...?' But he understands quicker than he'd like.

Shock paralyses him for a full three seconds before a far stronger emotion hits. 'You were going to top yourself and you were going to do it here so Mum could find you? Or Tommy? You selfish, useless—'

'Ryan.' Jules steps in front of him, forcing him to look at her. 'Give him a minute.'

Ryan vaguely registers that Jules is wearing high-heeled boots in the shearing yard. Blood thunders through him. What if *he'd* found his dad collapsed on the ground with his brains sprayed up the side of the shed? The thought of it makes his gut lurch and he stumbles away from Jules to dry heave. He stays hunched over after the spasms stop, holding his weight on his knees.

'I let off the shot. I needed you and I didn't want to leave him alone.' Jules stays back, giving him space.

'Did you shock him?'

'No, we talked.'

Ryan lifts a hand to wipe spittle from his chin and finds he's trembling. The reality is pressing in: his dad was going to kill himself. Might in fact be dead now if Jules had stayed in bed.

'Bloody hell, Dad.' His voice breaks. 'What were you thinking?'

The house door slams and two sets of feet pound their way down the driveway.

'Jamie! *Jamie!*' Ryan's mum rounds the corner at full pelt, not stopping until she skids to her knees by his dad. 'You bastard.' She's pushing him in the chest, her voice hoarse. A piece of paper crushed in her fist. 'You *bastard.*' She shakes it in front of him but he can't see because his hands are clamped over his face. 'This is all you've got to say to me?'

Tommy crouches inside the yard. He seeks out Ryan, bereft. The dogs have come with them and they stick close to Tommy, bellies on the ground and tails wagging nervously.

Ryan's mum has fistfuls of their dad's shirt. She's shaking him and sobbing, and Ryan can see how broken she is. That she's been broken for a while watching her husband come apart.

'Ah, Jamie...' She wraps her arms around him and pulls him to her. His dad resists at first but then he drops his hands and holds her tight, burying his face in her neck. His whole body heaves.

Ryan kneels in the dirt and drops the handgun. It's like someone's punched through his rib cage and ripped out his heart with rough hands. Yesterday means something else now. *This* is why his dad worked so hard: it's been in the back of his mind for a while. All the sledging last night, the punch-up with Keith McKenzie, it pushed him over the edge.

Jules lays a hand on Ryan's shoulder. He's not sure how long they stay like that: him with Jules, Tommy with the dogs, and his mum and dad clinging to each other. Eventually the sun breaks the horizon.

'We should get them inside and make a cup of tea,' Jules says quietly.

'Tea's not going to fix this.'

She squeezes his shoulder. 'It won't hurt.'

Ryan leaves Jules to offload her charge into a star picket while he detours to the shed to put away the guns. He sees the notification as soon as he picks up the phone: a missed call from the Major. He shoves the phone in his back pocket and heads to the house.

His dad wants to kill himself. He can't deal with the Major right now.

'You should call him.'

'I will after breakfast.'

As much as she wants to know why the Major's making contact, Jules doesn't push Ryan. She's cooking scrambled eggs, concentrating so they don't stick to the pan. The urgency of the current has eased, leaving her drained and exhausted and ready to fall back into bed.

Ryan pops the toaster and tosses the hot slices from hand to hand. He drops them on the breadboard and wipes his palms on his jeans. On the other side of the bench, Tommy digs a knife into the butter.

'I wish I could hear what they're talking about,' Tommy says in a voice Jules barely recognises. His eyes are red and his cheeks blotchy.

Michelle and Jamie are on the back verandah on their second round of tea. Jules can mostly make out Michelle's voice—angry, anguished—and every now and then Jamie says something too low to hear. At least they're talking.

Ryan rests his hands on the benchtop. His knuckles are grazed from brawling, and his eye a plump purple mess.

'Hey…' She touches his shoulder.

He stares out the window, breathing hard and trying not to be swamped.

'It's not your fault,' Jules says quietly.

Ryan swallows hard, and then he hangs his head and lets out a strangled sob. Tommy flinches. Ryan clamps a hand over his mouth so the next one doesn't carry to the verandah. His grief fills the kitchen and Jules absorbs it with him. Tommy watches his big brother buckle, his own face twisting and ticking. Ryan weathers the onslaught and then lets out a shuddering sigh. When he finally lifts his face, there's no effort to mask the hurt.

'He thought I was ashamed of him,' he says to Tommy and wipes his eyes with the back of his hand.

'What did you say to that?'

'I told him he's a stubborn prick.'

Jules switches off the gas and brings the pan to the bench. 'Your dad thinks you've lost faith in him. If you show him that's not true he'll keep it together.'

Ryan tears off a piece of paper towel and blows his nose into it. Tommy shakes his head. He wants to believe it but he's scared to hope.

They all eat together on the verandah, faces turned to the newly risen sun. Out in the paddock the sheep make their way to the trough in a haphazard line, dust drifting up behind them. Michelle is washed out and tear-streaked, eating one-handed because she won't let go of Jamie. He's doing the same, fingers laced through hers, hanging on with a fierceness that breaks Jules' heart.

When everyone's done, Jules stands up to stack the plates.

'Julianne, what exactly are you wearing?' Michelle asks, eying her up and down.

'Oh...' The fact she's dressed in Ryan's footy shirt and skins gives away where she slept last night. She looks at Ryan for a clue on how to handle the conversation but he grabs the plates and disappears inside. What a hero.

Michelle watches the door slam and then offers Jules a tired half-smile. 'I'm not entirely sure the boots work with that outfit.'

Jules is fumbling for a response when tyres rumble over the

sheep grid at the top of the driveway. The dogs race up the fence, barking. It's more than one vehicle—

Ryan bursts out of the back door, rounding the side of the house and bolting for the shed.

'Everyone get inside. *Now*.'

Black vans with dark windows, three of them, speeding towards the house. *His house.*

Ryan snatches the handgun from the duffel bag and races back across the driveway. He hurdles the gate and flattens his back to the house, clicks off the safety, breathing hard.

Can he take out a merc unit on his own? He's barely fired a weapon away from the shooting range, but he's a good shot, right? He sucks in a deep breath and pokes his head around the corner. The first van skids to a halt ten metres from the house gate.

There's no way he can protect his family and Jules from these guys. How did they find them? How many of them can fit into three vans? They're tactical, which means they'll be coming at the house from all directions. The moment grinds down to his staccato heartbeats. A car door opens.

Do it. Step out from the house and unload the clip into these bastards.

Do it.

Do—

'Stand down, private.'

It takes time for his brain to change gears. Ryan stays pinned against the wall for another five seconds before he checks around the corner. It's long enough to confirm who's standing beside the open drivers door, and his legs almost give out.

'If you answered your bloody phone you would've known we were coming.'

Ryan clicks on the safety and steps around the corner to face the Major and Frenchie. The Major takes in the state of his face, says nothing. He's come armed: his Browning is holstered on his thigh. Ryan presses his own gun against his leg to hide his tremors.

'Where's De Marchi?'

'I'm here.'

Ryan glances over his shoulder and realises she didn't go inside with the others.

'Julianne, get in the van,' the Major says.

Ryan tries to see who's in the other two vehicles. 'Is the whole unit here?'

'Get your family, private. They're coming with us.'

'Why?'

'You're on thin ice, Walsh.'

Ryan scans the road, his pulse erratic. The op's gone pear-shaped and his family's not safe. But his old man needs space and time to sort himself out *here*, not be bundled into a van and taken God knows where because Ryan didn't think hard enough about what it would mean to bring his work home.

'It's not a good time for them to be away from the farm—'

'I don't give a shit, soldier. I gave you an order.'

Ryan fingers the butt of his pistol. If he raises the weapon, his career in the army is done. He might also wear a bullet for his trouble.

The screen door opens behind him. 'What's going on?'

The Major takes in the sight of Ryan's dad: dishevelled, dirt-covered and bloodied. Ryan's mum and Tommy flank him.

'I need you all in Port Augusta. It's not safe for you to be here today.'

Port Augusta?

'Why isn't it safe?' Ryan's mum demands.

288

'That's classified.'

'That's not good enough. Ryan?'

Ryan stretches his neck to one side, jittery from adrenaline and still rattled from the thought his old man was ready to eat a bullet.

'For how long?' Ryan asks.

'A day. Maybe a night.'

The Major shifts his weight. It's barely noticeable but it's enough for Ryan to know the Major's agitated, because that man never moves without intention. This is serious shit.

His dad gives the Major a baleful glare and Ryan steps between them. The mercs must be on their way. Why else would the Major bring the entire unit across the ranges?

'I don't like this arsehole coming on to my property and giving me orders.' His dad's trying to muster the energy for an argument, but he left it all at the back of the shearing shed.

'This is shitty timing,' Ryan says to his mum, 'but the Major wouldn't be here if he didn't need to be.'

'Is this about what's happening at the nuclear plant?' Tommy asks.

The full reality of the situation smacks into Ryan. The longer it takes Q18 to get back to the protester camp, the longer Angie and Waylo have no backup.

'I don't know, but we need to move.'

Jules wraps the parka around herself, trying to hide the fact she's in Ryan's footy gear. 'Is Angie all right?'

The Major levels his gaze at her. 'Did you see her on the news?'

'That was twelve hours ago.'

'Her status is unchanged.'

It's army jargon, but it seems to reassure Jules.

The Major follows Ryan into the shed to get his kit while everyone else scrapes together an overnight bag in the house.

'What did I tell you about returning my calls?' The Major's

eyes rake over Ryan's busted face. 'Did your old man do that?'

He hates that his commanding officer thinks that about his dad. 'I got jumped by some wankers at the footy club.'

The Major's nostrils flare. 'The footy club?'

He repacks his pistol. 'It was Tommy's birthday.'

'And you took De Marchi?' The Major gives him the kind of stare that makes his balls crawl up into his belly. Ryan ducks into the bathroom, tosses Jules' party dress into his wash basket in case the Major goes in there too.

'Where are we taking my family?' He asks it more to distract the Major than because he expects an answer.

'A motel.'

'And us, sir? Me and Julianne?'

'Happy Growers.'

Ryan pauses, halfway bent over to pick up his T-shirt from the floor. 'That's a Pax Fed facility.'

'Are you questioning me, Walsh?'

'No, sir.'

But the news turns his gut queasy. The last time Jules was in a Pax Fed facility she was lucky to get out alive. Him too.

The Major directs Ryan's mum and dad and Tommy to the second van. They've left food and water for the dogs and checked the gates. Ryan watches the van door slam shut and realises he didn't say a proper goodbye to his family. Jules waits beside him, fidgety. Close enough that he can brush his knuckles across hers. He'd hold her hand but that'd be a red flag to the Major and probably result in them being separated.

Frenchie is waiting in the back of the lead van. It's got bench seats on both sides, adapted for military use. It smells of oiled leather and pine air freshener, in better nick than most of the vehicles they knock around in.

Frenchie nods at Jules. 'You're with me.'

Jules has changed into her own jeans, T-shirt and hoodie. She sits next to Frenchie and tucks her hands between her knees. Ryan can't tell if she's anxious or afraid, or if it's his nervous energy that's unsettling her. He needs to calm himself or he'll make the trip worse for her than it needs to be. Maybe it really is nothing to worry about. Ryan tries to steady his pulse. Something's not right about the way Frenchie's sitting.

The Major climbs in and takes the seat next to Ryan and as soon as Ryan glances at him, Frenchie makes her move.

Too late, Ryan sees the syringe sink into Jules' neck. He reacts on instinct, punching Frenchie hard in the jaw, before the Major grabs him by the throat, slams him back into the seat, and presses a gun barrel to his kneecap.

'Calm the fuck down.'

Jules wilts in her seat. Ryan watches, helpless, struggling for air against the Major's grip. The pressure eases as soon as he stops straining, but the Major's rough fingers stay in place. So does the gun barrel. Frenchie rubs her jaw and glares at him. She carefully extracts the needle from Jules and repositions her head so it won't bump against the window when they take off.

Someone climbs into the cab and starts the engine. The van rolls forward, leading the convoy around the gum tree and back up the driveway. Jules lolls against Frenchie as they bounce over the grid, her jaw slack.

Ryan would take a bullet to his new knee if he thought he could get Jules out of here. But that's not going to help her or his family, so he keeps his hands splayed on his thighs and his eyes forward.

He's out of options. As usual.

Angie is off-centre as soon as she steps into the donga and it takes a few seconds for her to figure out it's the floor that's tilted—not her. She reaches for Waylon to steady herself.

Ollie came for them five minutes ago. Angie's unclear why Waylon was included in the summons and there was no chance to figure it out with Xavier's errand boy escorting them across the camp.

The man himself is seated at a table under a bank of television monitors, wearing yesterday's T-shirt.

'Grab a seat.' He gestures to two folding chairs opposite him and nods for Ollie to leave. Ollie, ever obedient, disappears outside and closes the door behind him.

Xavier watches Angie sit down. The air conditioner above them rattles and hums, pumping out a lukewarm breeze. Angie has lived this moment a dozen times in her mind. She was primed to leave Xavier in no doubt how she felt about being used as a prop until Waylon, in that annoyingly calm manner of his, suggested she'd keep him wrong-footed if she didn't take the bait. It's the only reason she's holding her tongue now, and the effort is making her teeth itch.

Waylon spreads out on the folding chair, legs apart and arms loose in his lap. 'How long were you at Honeymoon?' he asks Xavier.

'Five years,' Xavier says. 'You?'

An easy shrug. 'About the same. A few years after you, I reckon.'

Angie tries to hide her surprise. Is that the truth?

Xavier sits forward. 'Your mum worked in the mine, right?'

'She drove a truck. We left before I started school. I don't remember much about the place.'

'What about your dad?'

'No idea. He didn't go north with us.'

A beat. Then: 'How's your mum's health?'

Waylon's fingers brush the tatty leather wristband. 'She passed eight years ago. Lung cancer.'

Xavier's mouth quirks down. 'I'm sorry. Radiation exposure?'

'Hard to know. She was a chain smoker.'

Xavier checks Angie. 'You didn't know.' It's not a question. Apparently she can't stay quiet and also keep a poker face.

'I don't talk about it,' Waylon says, not meeting her gaze. 'If you haven't been through it you don't get it.'

Angie doesn't know his specific brand of loss, but she understands something of grief. Did Waylon not trust her enough to tell her? The sting surprises her.

'Did your mum get treatment?' Xavier asks, more interested in Waylon's story than Angie's reaction.

'At the start. But we didn't have health insurance, and she didn't respond to the drugs.'

'What was the prognosis?'

'Forty-five per cent.'

If Waylon's mum had come in at fifty per cent she would have qualified for ongoing treatment in a public hospital. Another piece of genius economic rationalisation.

'Were you there at the end?' Angie asks, breaking her silence.

He nods. 'She was in a hospice in Alice Springs.' Waylon runs his fingertip along the edge of the laminate table and Angie sees the scars he hides beneath that practised nonchalance. He needs to get his armour back up before Xavier digs any deeper.

293

'Xavier,' she says. 'What about your sister? How is she?'

She does *not* want to empathise with this bastard, but she needs to know.

'She's in remission.'

'She made the percentage?'

'Yeah.'

Waylon rests a boot on a knee. 'You joined the Agitators for her.'

Xavier leans forward, everything about him sharpening. 'If we can't recognise the danger of uranium before it comes out of the ground, how are we ever going to see the danger after it's been spent? The power station, that silo…We've lost sight of the threat. Nothing changes if *nothing changes.*'

'So you keep saying,' Angie says. 'What is it we're going to change?'

'We're going to remind the world what we're playing with here.'

'Cute sound bite, Xavier. Now tell me what you've got planned. You've put me front and centre—'

'Where else would you be?'

'How about in the loop?'

He gets the full force of an Angie De Marchi eyeballing, and falters. It's a small victory.

'What do you think would happen if a thousand people swarmed over the camp fence and marched on the nuclear plant?'

'They'd get shot.'

'With rubber bullets.'

'Which bloody well hurt.' Angie copped one in the leg in Brisbane a decade ago. The bruising was horrific and she limped for a month.

'Your mates in the media will start speculating on what *might* have happened if we'd made it to the plant,' Xavier presses. 'We'll get everyone talking about the risks again. The promise of jobs and reliable electricity has drowned out the hard lessons of

Chernobyl and Fukushima. This country needs a scare.'

Waylon pushes back his chair and stands up. 'That's it? We're going to charge at the plant with placards? I thought you said we're going to *change* things.'

'We will,' Xavier says, surprised at his anger.

'You're no different to the rest of them. I thought you had some balls but you're weak as piss.' He heads for the door.

'Hang on, mate.' Xavier's up and after him. 'Hang *on*.'

Waylon stops and turns, hands shoved in his pockets. 'What?'

'I'm not like the rest of them.' Xavier positions himself between Waylon and the exit. Angie stays in her chair, fascinated. He wants to *impress* Waylon. Bloody hell, the kid's playing him like a piano.

'You have to trust me that there's more.'

Waylon considers him. Runs his tongue across his teeth. 'Like what?'

'I can't tell you, but it's going to be big.'

Push him, Angie thinks. He wants to tell you.

There's a bang on the door. 'It's me,' Ollie calls from the other side.

Xavier hesitates a good three seconds. 'Come in.'

The door swings open. 'There's someone asking for Waylon,' he says. 'A woman. Didn't give her name.'

There's no hesitation, no catching Waylon off guard. 'Is she a cop?'

'You expecting one?'

Waylon grins, sliding back into himself. 'Always.'

It disarms Ollie. 'This chick looks more like an accountant. And she has a Syrian accent.'

Khan.

Angie forces herself to stay in neutral. The muscles in her face are instantly heavy with the effort of not reacting. Khan should be with the Major. What is she doing at the camp?

'Is she at the main gate?' Waylon asks.

'Yeah. Nobody gets in unless they've been vouched for.'

Angie curls her toes in her boots until her feet ache. There's no way she can sit here playing mind games with Xavier while Waylon meets with Khan.

'You coming?' Waylon asks her. She tries for an agreeable shrug, not wanting to give away her eagerness.

Xavier steps aside so they can leave. 'Everything's set for after dark. Come see me before dusk.'

Even out of the donga and back on flat ground, Angie's off-kilter. She should care more about what Xavier's got planned for tonight, but all she can think about is Khan and the fact she's risked blowing Waylon's cover by reaching out.

It can only mean one thing.

Jules is in trouble.

The Major hates tomatoes, always has.

The Happy Growers packing house is empty and the conveyer belts silent but the smell is everywhere. He keeps his breathing shallow as he crosses the floor. Julianne De Marchi trudges in front of him, groggy. She's pissed off, but not so much she's forgotten he's armed. Walsh, for obvious reasons, is outside with the rest of Q18.

The Major finds Peta Paxton in the lunchroom where she said she'd be. The smell of stale coffee at least masks the tomatoes. Two tables have been pushed against a wall and crammed with an electron microscope and a bunch of equipment he doesn't recognise.

'You have an interesting definition of "safe",' the Major says.

Peta Paxton stands in front of the window, framed by a field of silver panels. 'You said she would be unconscious.'

'What can I say? It was a strong dose.'

'Give her another one.'

'She doesn't need it. She'll be harmless for a while yet.'

The girl in question glares at him, bleary-eyed from the shot.

Paxton clears her throat. 'Julianne, have a seat please.'

Julianne doesn't move. Paxton gestures to the door. 'Thank you, Major Voss.'

He very deliberately checks over her makeshift lab, slower this time. Yet again, she's fallen short of their agreement for full disclosure. It shouldn't irritate him as much as it does. Of course she manipulated him: she's Peta Paxton. But she's grossly overestimated his capacity to indulge her.

'Where's everyone who works here?'

'I sent them home.'

'How long do you think it will take before your brother finds out you're here?'

'It doesn't matter. I told you: this farm is our sustainability flagship. Bradford's spent a decade convincing the market our produce won't be affected by the nuclear plant. Its reputation means too much to him to risk an incident here. This is the safest place she can be.'

'What if you're wrong?'

'Your team will protect us.'

Unbelievable. She can't see an issue with setting soldiers on each other. He needs to stop this rot.

The Major doesn't acknowledge Julianne as he leaves the room. He strides across the packing house, repressing the urge to throw something. He's almost at the other side when French appears between the machinery, her jaw still red from Walsh's fist.

'Sir,' she says, 'we've got new audio from Waylon's feed.'

'And?'

'Khan's been in contact with Angela De Marchi.'

Jules needs to keep herself in check because right now the only advantage she has is that Peta Paxton thinks she's harmless.

Peta Paxton is wrong.

The charge is crackling beneath her skin, and Jules can't figure out if the Major lied or if he believes the injection short-circuited her. Either way she needs to hide the truth.

Her legs are shaky. She grabs a chair—cheap, hard and plastic—and drags it to the opposite side of the lunchroom, as far as she can get from the lab equipment. It barely makes a sound on the tiled floor. She sits under a poster about the importance of good hygiene, tries to grasp the significance of the Major's conversation.

Jules didn't see Ryan when she came to but she heard him arguing with someone outside the van. It was his energy—raging and violent—that jolted her from the fug. He's out there now fretting for his family, anxious for her and stretched to snapping point.

Peta hovers near the door. In real life, she's slimmer in the hips and her skin is shinier. Her eyes, though, are just as shrewd as they appear on TV. She glances at her flexi-phone once, waits a beat, and then glances again. Only a Paxton could access a voice and data signal so close to the Anti-Nuke Assembly—a known tech black spot.

'I had you brought here to keep you safe.'

'From who?' Jules grips her elbows. The room hasn't quite come into focus.

'Julianne...' Peta presses together cherry lips and then puffs them out. 'I know what happened at the school.'

She *knows*? Jules forgets to exhale for so long that Peta's face blurs into a platinum halo. Did the Major tell her?

There's a soft knock. Peta snatches open the door and a short woman dressed in a kaftan and black leggings hurries inside, dark curls swept back from her face by a tiger print headband. For a confused moment Jules thinks she's a Happy Growers staffer, until her eyes lock on Jules. The appraisal is detached, perfunctory.

'Good,' the visitor says to nobody in particular.

'Julianne, this is Professor Mian.'

'Professor of...?' Jules' tongue is unwieldy and she sounds drunk.

'Cytogenetics.'

The professor's suitcase squeaks as she wheels it across the room. She hoists it onto the table nearest the window and takes out syringes and vials, lays them in a neat row. Jules watches it all as if underwater. Everything is sluggish: her thoughts, her movements.

The professor snaps on latex gloves and frowns at the equipment on the bench. 'Somewhat...low tech. But I can make it work.' She picks up a syringe and approaches Jules. Stops a few steps short and looks over at Peta.

'She's been dosed,' Peta says. 'I'm told it will render her inactive long enough for you to do what you need to.'

Peta's words penetrate the murkiness. It's everything her dad was afraid of: she's about to be turned into a lab rat. The professor raises her eyebrows at Jules, testing her receptiveness. 'I need a small amount of blood and tissue to run preliminary tests. That's it.'

Jules folds her arms, hiding the soft skin inside her elbows.

'No.'

The other woman's brow flattens. 'No isn't an option.'

They face off.

'What will you do with the results?'

'That's for the Paxton Federation bioengineering team to decide. I'm here as an independent go-between from a purely scientific perspective.'

Jules stares at the tiger stripes on the professor's headband. This doesn't seem entirely real. How did she go from kneeling in the dirt at the farmhouse with a shotgun to sitting in a Pax Fed facility staring down a kaftanned cytogeneticist waving a needle at her?

'We're all interested in learning why your body generates such extreme amounts of electricity. I've never seen anything like it.'

It's a second or two before understanding dawns. The professor has seen the footage, which means Peta Paxton has too. But that makes no sense.

'May I?' the professor is losing patience. 'Don't you want to understand?'

Of course Jules does. She also wants to unload a blast of charge into both of these women, but then what? The Major's turned on her, Ryan's outnumbered and she still has no idea what's actually going on.

Jules loosens her arms.

She's thinking clearly again for the first time since she came to. Something's taking shape here and if she wants to find out what, she's going to have to play along. And that means letting the professor stick that needle in her.

Ryan grinds his boot heels into the dirt. He's on watch, needing to do something but having no idea what. He's so restless he can't even keep a beat in his head.

Why won't anybody tell him what's going on? Frenchie keeps making eye contact—bruised jaw and all—but she's either too pissed off at him or too wary of the Major to talk. And now she and the Major have disappeared into the surveillance van without a word, which could mean anything.

He should have returned that missed call. If he'd known what the Major was planning, he could have got ahead of it—sent his mum, dad and Tommy to Spud's place while he and Jules took the back road to Port Pirie and got in touch with Khan. There's no way the federal agent would let Jules be turned over to Peta Paxton. What is she even doing in Port Augusta?

They should have run.

Not that they would have got far. Not in the hybrid, with its gutless electric engine and smart-tracker, and the Monaro would have been too conspicuous, even with the V8 switched over. And who knows what intel the mercs have on him, how much more danger his family would be in if they weren't with Q18.

So around it goes again, the same set of questions, excuses and answers, all leading back to this point: Ryan staring at the Happy Growers packing-house doors in the glaring sun, waiting for orders. Waiting for something to happen. Feeling utterly useless.

His gut twists at the memory of vans hurtling down his driveway, the thick hot fear that he couldn't protect his family. If it had been the mercs instead of Q18...But it wasn't them, it was his own unit. And it was one of his mates who stabbed a needle in Jules' neck.

The cool breeze coming off the gulf does nothing to douse the burn. His mum and dad and Tommy are holed up somewhere in Port Augusta. He has no idea how his old man is coping—there was barely time for eye contact after the Major turned up. Ryan checks his handgun for the fifth time. Apparently he can still be trusted with a loaded weapon.

The van door slides open and the Major calls him over.

'You are on my shit list, Walsh, make no mistake. Get into your chest rig and get your head right because I need you on your game. We've got threats on two fronts and your job is out here. Stop worrying about what's happening in there.'

'I can be in the packing house—'

'You're not listening to me. The threat, when it comes, will be external. I'll leave you with nine soldiers. Get your team on point so you've got eyes on every entrance and every approach.'

Where are you going? Ryan doesn't ask it out loud because the Major's leaving him in charge of the watch and he doesn't want to jeopardise the post. If he takes the western side of the packing house, he might be able to see where Jules is being—

'Walsh,' the Major says, snapping him back. 'It was a sedative.'

Ryan squints, takes a second to catch up.

'I wasn't in a hurry to be twitching on the floor in my own piss if Julianne was unhappy with our destination.'

Ryan's relieved. But why didn't the Major dose her again when it was obvious she was coming to? Did he want her conscious by the time he handed her over?

'They'll come after dark,' the Major says, scouring the solar panels. 'Z12. Decommissioned.'

'Those blokes are ex-army?' But Ryan knew; deep down they all did. 'Who's paying them?'

'The other Paxton. The pencil neck.'

A frown. 'How does that work?'

'It doesn't.'

Ryan has more questions but he doesn't have enough standing with the Major to voice them. He's lucky he's been given this much airtime.

'You and your team are all that's between those soldiers and Julianne until I get back. Your orders arc to protect her and Peta Paxton. Don't shoot to kill unless the threat escalates. Get up high and get a feel for the topography.'

He doesn't need to be told twice. Two minutes later Ryan's on the packing-house roof watching the Major's van pick up speed on the road to the highway. He breathes in saltbush and endless sky, wonders if Jules can feel his energy from up here. He walks a slow circle, orientating himself.

It's all laid out in front of him: the solar panels stretching to the new railway line, a straight piece of track to the nuclear waste storage silo. On the far side of the line is a wide swathe of saltbush, power lines and the ramshackle protester camp.

Z12 could come at Happy Growers via the rail line. They could come through the saltbush. Or they could drive right up the road and smash through the security checkpoint, be here en masse in a matter of minutes.

But this, at least is simple: Ryan doesn't care if these guys are ex-army. He doesn't care about orders. If any one of them threatens Jules, he's putting a bullet in them.

'Khan, give me your gun.'

'No.'

'Waylon?'

'What she said.'

Angie gives them both a filthy look and resumes pacing the fence, dust kicking up around her. It's been four minutes since Khan finished relaying the conversation she overheard last night in the hotel. Three minutes since Angie learned Jules has been handed over to Peta Paxton at the sun farm. Khan knows this because Jules is carrying the tracker Khan gave her.

Angie wants to scream.

Brad Paxton sent Xavier to the school to threaten Jules.

She can barely form Bradford's name without danger of bursting an artery. And Peta Paxton is saying she'll protect Jules?

What a crock of shit.

The truth is a blunt knife: the Paxtons are responsible for Jules' charge. And now they have her.

Screw Major Voss.

Screw the army.

Screw Paxton Federation.

Angie's mind swivels from one threat to the next, unable to focus on any target long enough to form a strategy—short of arming herself and shooting her way to Jules.

'I can't set foot on the sun farm, Angela, it's a direct command from Canberra.' Khan says it again, as if repetition makes the news more palatable. 'Neither can Waylon. His orders are to stay here, you know that.'

'I don't want your company, I want your gun.'

'If you were getting enough oxygen to your brain, you'd know how ridiculous that request is. Angela, *breathe*.'

Angie twists away so Khan can't grab her through the fence as she passes by on another lap. They're on the northern side of the camp, out of sight behind a last-century bus spattered with bugs. Mount Brown shimmers blue-grey in the east, as dead and parched as everything else here.

'Angela—'

Angie stops abruptly and a plume of dust swirls around her legs.

'Do you have your gun *on* you?' she asks Waylon.

He looks at her sideways. 'Why?'

'Because I want to give Xavier something to think about.' She can't access the Paxtons, but she can get to the bastard who set all this in motion.

Waylon waves away a blowfly, glances at Khan. 'Okay.'

They leave Khan fuming: the federal agent's not authorised to enter the protest camp any more than she is the sun farm. Vouched for or not.

Angie stomps her way under a rope strung with washing, avoiding the cluster of ripe portaloos on her way back to the donga. Two guys in singlets and boardies step into her path. One look and they clear the way without a word. Angie toes an empty drink can out of her path. Maybe this is what it's like for Jules, this sensation of being eaten alive from the inside. What was she thinking, trusting Jules to the army? And for what—so she could confront Xavier and punish him for blackmailing her? Will it be worth it?

She's about to find out.

Xavier flinches when the door smacks open. He's alone, his flexi-phone lit up like he's recently ended a call. *Smug bastard.* Angie pushes aside a chair and rushes him.

'Hey—!' He scrambles back from the table as she launches herself across it. She collects him and they tumble to the floor in a tangle of arms and legs. Angie lands on her hip and elbow, grunts at the impact but doesn't let go. Xavier's stronger, but slow. She jumps on his chest and pins his arms with her knees, grabs him around the throat. His eyes bulge, panicked, and he thrashes beneath her. She's got him, though, she's—

Xavier gets an arm free and punches Angie hard in the ribs. It knocks her sideways. She kicks before he can strike again, her heel finding solid gut. She lashes out again but this time he catches her foot and flips her onto her back. He's on his knees looming over her, his neck mottled and breathing ragged. Angie plants her other foot on his chest to hold him away as she scrabbles backwards, trapped between the table and the wall. She reaches for a chair leg, grappling...*Got it.* Angie uses all her strength to fling it at him. Xavier sees it coming and lets go of her foot to catch it. He gets a better grip, lifts it above his head—

'Not happening.'

Waylon's behind Xavier, gun pressed to the back of his skull. He drops the chair.

'Get up.'

Xavier hauls himself to the table, breathless.

'Shit, Angie,' Waylon says. 'You nearly had him.'

Angie stays on the floor, back to the wall and chest heaving. The ebb of adrenaline has turned her legs to linguini. For a long moment she and Xavier eyeball each other, both pulling in air.

'What's that look for?' she demands.

'I don't understand—' A hacking cough steals the rest of the sentence.

'You're on Bradford Paxton's payroll, you prick.'

Xavier stops massaging his throat.

'I know he's paying you to turn the Agitators into a national threat. Great job: you've destroyed any vestige of credibility we had as a nonviolent voice of reason.'

'You're wrong, Angie,' he rasps. 'I joined the Agitators to give them a *real* voice. Actions speak louder than words.'

'Are you that bloody-minded? You're clearing the way for Pax Fed to write its own legislation without a whimper of protest. People *died* in Brisbane.'

'I'm not apologising for getting the nation's attention. You should know better than anyone: words on placards only get you so far.'

Angie brushes grit from her hands. The lino is filthy. 'Pressuring the corporates is the only point of influence we have left—they'll only change their practices if public perception affects shareholder profits. Governments can be bought and voters manipulated, but the bottom line will always count. That's how we keep these deadshits accountable: public pressure. Not bloodshed.'

'It's not working.' Xavier sucks in a short breath. His windpipe's not yet back to full strength. Long strands of hair are loose from the scuffle and he flicks them back from his face. 'That time bomb'—he points in the direction of the nuclear plant—'is going to destroy this country long before Pax Fed does, and nothing short of a disaster is going to get people to understand that human lives are more important than affordable power.'

'So you sold your soul to Bradford Paxton to further your own cause?'

'I took advantage of an opportunity to step up the fight.' He wipes his chin and glowers at her. 'And to keep my sister alive.'

Waylon lowers his pistol. 'She was under fifty per cent, wasn't she?'

Xavier's nostrils flare. 'She's in remission because Paxton paid for genome therapy.'

'I didn't think that was publicly available.'

'It's not—that was my price. What would you do? She was fourteen and dying. She was weak, anaemic, constantly bleeding from her nose and gums. Untreated leukaemia is a cruel way to die, Waylon.'

Waylon clicks the safety on and off. 'How did Bradford reach out to you?'

Xavier wets his lips, eyes on the gun. 'One of his guys bailed me out after an anti-nuclear protest in Sydney. We met in the back of a real estate office in Blacktown and he offered me work, odd jobs. When he told me to join the Agitators I jumped at the chance. '

'I bet you did,' Angie says. 'You traded my daughter's life for your sister's.'

'What are you talking about?'

'Bradford has hired a military unit to come after Jules. They've tried twice already in the past two weeks.'

'Why would he do that?'

'Because you showed him what she can do, and then you used that footage to drive me out of the Agitators.'

He stares at her. '*That's* what you were blackmailed over?'

'Waylon.' Angie nods at Xavier. Waylon reintroduces him to the business end of the gun.

'It wasn't me.'

'Jules recognised you.'

'I was there, sure.' Another fit of hacking, more short breaths. 'Bradford wanted me to threaten her and film her reaction, see what she'd say. I had no idea what she was capable of. I gave the camera and file to him immediately afterwards and he sent in his tech goons to track down and delete every trace of it. I'm telling you, it wasn't me. It must have been him or one of his lackeys.'

Angie straightens her legs one at a time and waits for the stiffness to ease. It's Bradford Paxton, then. He's her blackmailer. Always has been.

'What happened to Julianne to make her like that?'

She feels the weight of Xavier's gaze.

'None of your fucking business.'

They sit in bruised silence, the hum and wheeze of the air-conditioner filling the void.

Waylon shifts his weight. 'What's really going down tonight?'

Xavier shakes his head. 'You don't want to know.'

'Yeah, I do.' He levels the gun at Xavier's left eyebrow, his hand steady.

'I thought you wanted to change things, make a statement for your mum?'

'I want that plant decommissioned. I don't want it in meltdown.'

Waylon steps close so he can press the barrel to Xavier's sun-blasted forehead.

'I'm not playing cops and robbers, mate. Talk.'

Xavier's face is flushed and the tendons tight in his neck. 'You can shoot me but it won't stop what's coming.'

Angie can't tell if he's bluffing. Waylon meets her gaze: neither can he.

'Hand him over to Khan, let the feds figure it out,' Angie says.

Xavier's eyes darken. 'You're working with the feds?'

'Don't you question my choices. I wasn't left with many, thanks to you and that arsehole you work for. Waylon?'

Waylon's thinking it through. He glances at the door and shakes his head slightly. 'We stay with Plan A until we hear otherwise.'

Typical bloody soldier. He assumes the Major is listening in, and won't hand Xavier to the feds without an order. That doesn't help Angie get Jules away from Peta Paxton. How is she supposed to do it without help? It's not like she can storm the sun farm by herself—

The idea hits, so obvious she can't believe it took her this long.

'What are you thinking?' Waylon raises his eyebrows but the Major's probably listening in and there's no way she's telegraphing her plans to him. He's already sold Jules out once. She's not giving him a chance to do it again.

'I tell you when you need to know.'

The public bar is gloomy, even with the sun lingering over the gulf.

The leader of Z12 sits two stools down from the Major. It took a handful of calls through back channels to track down the unit captain, and it's a testament to the Major's contacts that this bloke has agreed to meet. Both men crane their necks to watch horses race on the screen above the bar. The captain waits until the barman drifts out of earshot before he speaks.

'Thanks for not cracking my skull on Sunday.'

'You gave a kill order. I should have left you in a pool of your own blood.'

'I didn't know it was you until we were inside. Once I did, tactics changed.'

'So I should thank you for the soft touch at the motel?'

The captain tips his glass in the Major's direction. 'The beer covers it.' He waits for the Major to take the lead. The former Z12 leader might not be army these days but he still respects rank, which counts for something.

The Major holds off until the next field of horses leap out of the gates.

'Why the contract on the girl?'

The captain keeps his eyes on the thoroughbreds. 'National security risk. Why are you protecting her?'

'Because she's not.'

'I have a pride-sore corporal who would disagree. Is that your directive, to protect her?'

The Major thinks about the geneticist he let into the lunchroom with a suitcase full of syringes. He doesn't answer, and the captain sips his beer.

'What do you want, Major?'

'Do you know what your boy's got planned?'

'What boy?'

'The one you've been escorting across the country.'

The Major takes an earpiece from his pocket and puts it on the bar. The captain waits a beat before he reaches for it. As soon as it's in place, the Major taps play on his flexi-phone. It's the conversation they picked up an hour ago between Xavier and Angela. French edited out Waylon's contribution and the reference to the visitor at the gate. When it's over, the captain stares down into his beer. 'That stupid little fucker.' He empties the glass in three gulps.

The Major repositions his good foot on the bar stool. 'The Paxtons have turned us into their attack dogs. The two of them are in a pissing contest and we're on the leash doing what we're told.'

'Everybody's still breathing.'

'The national interest's coming a distant second though, isn't it?'

The captain picks up a coaster, taps the edge on the bar. Turns it round, does the same to the next side, and the next. 'What do you think's going to happen here, Major?'

'We can end this right now. Stand down and let my unit do its job.'

The captain laughs. 'I break this contract and I don't get paid. Tell me where the girl's hiding and we'll finish it quick and clean. No collateral damage.'

The Major's not in the mood for games. 'I heard you've already got intel on that front.'

'What intel? Details on your ops are sealed tighter than a duck's arse.'

The Major drains his beer. That bloody woman. Z12 doesn't know where Julianne is—hasn't since she left Brisbane.

'What's your priority: the girl or the ratbag?'

'I've got the resources to cover both,' the captain says. 'And if you play this smart, we can both do our jobs and go home with a clear conscience—and in one piece.'

The Major doesn't miss the glance at his foot.

How did it come to this? Two war veterans pitted against each other on conflicting contracts—one army-sanctioned, one strictly commercial.

'No, mate, we can't. Not if you take out a civilian and that clown in the camp does more than lead a protest across the scrub.'

'Then we're in for an interesting evening.'

The Major stands up and pockets his change. 'Looks like it.'

The solar panels tilt to follow the path of the sun, changing from silver to orange as the sky fades and then bleeds purple. Jules watches the darkness come until all she can see is her own reflection in the window. She barely recognises the girl with the unruly hair and smudgy eyes.

The lunchroom is cold and stale, like it's never breathed fresh air. Jules has consumed nothing but bottled water for the past few hours, but it's not hunger that's making her fingers tremble. Sunset has brought a fresh bout of anxiety, gnawing its way through her paper-thin defiance. She picks at the band-aid inside her elbow. The only thing keeping her from a full-blown panic attack is the hope that Ryan is close by.

Professor Mian is preoccupied with blood and tissue samples, flitting back and forth between the analysis machine, microscope and tablet. Peta Paxton reads her phone and then disappears for hushed conversations on the other side of the door. In between calls, she fumbles in her handbag until her fingers find reassurance that whatever she needs is still in there.

The only time Peta has spoken to Jules has been to fire random questions from the opposite side of the lunchroom. Jules has consistently ignored her. Instead, she's stared out at the dying light, fretting about her mum and Ryan and knitting the current into a tight ball beneath her ribs.

What are the tests going to show?

What will Pax Fed do with the results? With her?

Peta's fingers are back in her handbag when her flexi-phone vibrates. She snatches it from the bench and lets it spring flat in her palm. She stares at the device, tapping a lacquered nail on its edge. A quick glance at Jules and she pockets it.

'This is taking too long. What have you found?'

Professor Mian double-taps the tablet and massages her left shoulder. 'Julianne's mitochondria is abnormal and her ATP levels are off the charts.'

Peta gives her an impatient stare.

'ATP. Adenosine triphosphate: it's produced by mitochondria. In very simple terms, it creates energy by becoming ADP—adenosine diphosphate.'

Peta bunches her eyebrows. 'Make it simpler.'

'The building blocks in Julianne's cells create energy at a level far beyond normal human capacity. I'll need to refine my tests to understand how it's a byproduct of the Afghanistan trials, but it's deeply fascinating. Do you have any tissue samples from her father for comparison?'

Jules turns in her chair. *What did she just say?*

Peta aims a black look at the professor and Jules sees the truth in the pinch of her lips. It takes all the oxygen from her. It shouldn't shock Jules, not after everything that's happened, but it does. She's never bought into Angie's conspiracy theories, not really. Even with Vee's admission that Pax Fed sponsored *something* it shouldn't have two decades ago, there was no evidence it related to her or her dad.

Over the years she's quietly convinced herself the charge is the product of a random genetic mutation. Nothing more. It's the tiny thread she's held on to: that she was made wrong but it's nobody's fault. Even the blackmail—she had to believe it was opportunistic rather than part of a more complicated web. That guy—Xavier—was as surprised as she was when the charge sizzled from her fingertips.

316

But she's been lying to herself. Of course somebody made her. *Paxton Federation* made her. Does Bradford know too?

Oh God. She's going to throw up.

Jules stumbles to the lunchroom bench, vaguely aware of movement elsewhere in the room. She grips the bench and heaves once, twice, until a rush of water spatters into the sink—the contents of her empty stomach. She retches again, her whole body straining until the spasm releases her. Spit dribbles down her chin and her cheeks are wet with tears. One final, spine-straining heave and she slumps over the sink, weeping and aching from the effort.

Nobody speaks.

The current dances beneath her ribs but it's restrained, as if waiting for her to pull herself together. Jules takes a wet breath and wipes her chin. She unfurls her spine from over the sink and then wrenches on the tap to wash away the bile.

Another deep breath and she turns. 'Did you mean for me—'

The question dies on her lips. Peta Paxton has a handgun—small, shiny and deadly. The Prada handbag is on the bench, gaping like a dead fish. Jules' stomach quivers. It's the second time she's stared down a gun barrel today, only this weapon was always meant for her. It's the talisman Peta's had to touch each time she's come into the room.

'Stay where you are.'

'Are you going to shoot me?'

'If I have to.'

The charge surges, zapping under her skin on the race to her fingertips. Jules clenches her jaw to reel it in, fighting the pull of the earth. Any sign of a spark and Peta will squeeze the trigger.

And Jules doesn't want to die.

She turns out her arms, a supplication. 'I've let you take your samples. I'm not a threat to you.' *Not from this distance, at least.*

Peta shifts her weight and readjusts her aim. Her bracelets

jingle. Professor Mian is flat against the wall, one hand over her chest and the other clutching her tablet. She eyes the door.

'If you've known about me all these years, why the interest now?'

Peta offers a thin, unhappy smile. 'Because after the attack on our headquarters last week you're the only evidence left.'

'Evidence of illegal bio-engineering trials.'

'Those trials provided research data that has since helped with advances in cyto-bionics. It's saved limbs and given wounded soldiers back their lives.'

There it is. The truth from her own lips.

'Not my dad's.'

'He gave you a gift none of us anticipated, and if we can understand how that happened we can—'

'Turn soldiers into human transformers?'

'No, Julianne. We can stop wars.'

Jules stares at her. 'You think my cells can do what the greatest minds in history have failed at for thousands of years?'

'They could open up new possibilities for how we train and deploy soldiers.'

'And how much will that cost the army?'

Peta straightens her shoulders. 'Once I'm chair of the board—'

There's a rapid-fire knock a second before Private French enters. Her gun is drawn and she raises it at Peta as soon she's through the door.

'Lower your weapon.' French sounds a little out of breath. 'Hand it to me, safety off.'

Peta only hesitates a second before doing as she's told.

'Where was that?' French asks, pocketing the handgun. She glances at the handbag. 'You're a piece of work, woman. You good, Julianne?'

Jules slides to the floor on wobbly legs. The charge is testing her grip and she's going to have to ground it—soon. But first she has to wait for strength to return to her limbs. Jules closes her eyes and pushes her fingers into them, feels her pulse against her eyelids. The weight of the day presses down.

Jamie Walsh with a shotgun jammed under his jaw.

Private French plunging a needle into her neck.

Professor Mian taking her blood.

Peta Paxton ripping the scab from her life.

A fresh longing for Angie hits Jules: a punch that nearly doubles her over. Her mum is across the railway line but she may as well be a thousand kilometres away.

Does Angie know she's here? Has Khan been able to track her? Is Ryan pacing outside or did he throw another punch and get locked up somewhere?

The only way she can reach any of them is to get out of this room.

And she's going to have to do it herself.

The loudhailer is tacky in Angie's palm, even though the breeze has turned icy.

She's bundled in a fleece hoodie, beanie and scarf, waiting out of sight of the hushed crowd. A thousand protesters are crammed in front of the stage with solar torches strung around their necks, jostling each other with placards and trying to keep warm. There's a single spotlight on stage, enough for Angie to be seen when she's ready. Waylon stands close in the shadows. Xavier jiggles on the spot from nerves or cold or both.

'I need to know the plan, Angie,' Waylon says, agitated.

'You're about to find out.'

He leans in. 'I need to know *before* this mob does.'

She shakes her head. 'Xavier's the only one you have to worry about.'

A sharp whistle snags Angie's attention. Ollie's on the opposite side of the stage giving Xavier and Angie the thumbs-up: the fence is ready. Ollie thinks they're working on Plan A. Xavier checks his watch for about the ninth time in ten minutes.

'You won't be able to control what happens once they're out there,' Waylon says in her ear.

Angie ignores him. The mob's ready to march on the nuclear plant. Ollie put the word around twenty minutes ago and the response was immediate. Angie doesn't know what else Xavier has planned for tonight—his 'big statement'—but that's the Major's problem. She's been half-expecting cops or soldiers to breach the gate before now. But they've been left alone, which means either Waylon's audio isn't working and the Major doesn't know what's happening this side of the fence, or Bradford Paxton's got more clout than his sister and Q18 has been ordered to stand down. Do the Paxtons have a clue about what Xavier intends to do tonight?

She tightens her grip on the loudspeaker and walks onstage, signalling for the crowd to stay quiet; the plant security team is already on edge with all the movement in the camp. Angie glances at the cameras trained on her from the front row.

'I know what you've heard about our plans tonight,' she says. Even with the breeze at her back, the loudhailer doesn't carry as far as the PA system. The protesters hold still to hear her. 'But I need your help. Pax Fed has my daughter. They've got her right over *there*.'

A ripple goes through the mob. The protesters know where she's pointing. Giving up Jules' location is a gamble and if Angie's judged this wrong, there'll be no undoing the damage. But if she's right she'll force Khan's hand. The feds won't leave Jules at Happy Growers under the threat of civil unrest.

She wets her lip and tastes the brine in the air. 'That's where I'm going tonight, to get her—'

The hailer is pulled from her mouth before she can finish.

'You didn't tell me about Julianne,' Xavier says between his teeth. Waylon hasn't come onstage but she can see him pacing at the edge of the spotlight, fists bunched.

'I thought you knew, given you're so thick with the Paxtons.'

The mood of the crowd has slid sideways, nervous anticipation replaced by a swell of outrage. They know she's not finished.

'De Marchi. De Marchi. *De Marchi*.'

The chant intensifies. It gets under Angie's skin, sets her alight. She needs to get them moving while they're primed. She jerks away from Xavier and lifts the loudhailer again.

'If you march on the nuclear plant you'll get shot. Help me storm Happy Growers instead. Let's show Pax Fed they can't take whatever they want from us. Are you with me?'

Angie knows from the response that she's got enough followers to make it work.

'Then come on!' She bolts for the opposite stairs, away from Waylon and Xavier. The first wave swarms around the stage and carriers her towards the back fence—there's enough ambient light to see a yawning gap where it used to be. The wire has been prepped by Ollie, cut and peeled back to save skin and clothing. Angie peers over her shoulder but there's no sign of Waylon or Xavier in the bobbing faces behind her.

The frontline protesters surge through and fan out on the other side, trampling paths between the saltbush. It's hard to tell whether they're headed for the plant or the sun farm because a bottleneck has already formed and Angie's been herded into the middle of it. The pace has slowed by the sheer volume of bodies trying to push through.

She stumbles along with the tide. Muttered apologies turn to curses as the protesters crush together. Angie's jabbed in the neck by a placard, elbowed in the ribs. Someone shoves her and she stumbles into a woman carrying a solar torch above her head. The light disappears. Angie loses her beanie and her gunshot wound flares every time she's bumped. She doesn't care; she has to get through the fence. She has to get to Jules.

But she's not moving. The crowd on the far side has the tide now; her side is an eddy trapped against the riverbank. She needs to get *through*.

Fingers clamp around her wrist and a body wider than hers shoulders protesters aside without apology, making a path. Even in the dark Angie knows it's him. She ignores the instinct to wrench free of his touch, too relieved at moving forward. Angie lets Xavier drag her through the throng. More elbows, a few stomped toes, another placard in the side of her head and she's through the gap and stumbling between clumps of saltbush.

Xavier is checking his watch again, hauling her towards the railway line one-handed. Her jeans snag on dry branches. A siren starts up and spotlights wash the world in white: the snipers at the plant are in place, ready to pick off protesters. Angie squints against the glare and lifts the loudhailer.

'Second target. *Second* target!'

Xavier drags her clear of the throng and the spotlights but he's heading south, *away* from the sun farm and the surging mob.

'Let me go.' Angie tries to pull free. His fingers only dig harder into her skin. His attention is fixed on the railway line, searching for something.

'Let me *go*.' She jerks her arm free with such force that she loses her balance and lands on her knees in the dirt. The loud-hailer tumbles away from her and Xavier scoops it up before she can reach for it.

Angie scrambles to her feet and takes off towards the crowd—the protesters are already a good fifty metres away. She yells to them but the siren drowns out her voice. Where's Waylon? He should have caught up by now. All she'd wanted was to get clear of the fence before he—

She's yanked off her feet by the hair and hits the ground hard enough to drive the air from her lungs. Xavier looms, and Angie's vaguely aware they're under power lines. He grabs her by the scruff of her jacket, still holding the loudhailer in his other hand.

'You disappoint me, Angela,' he says, and slams the hailer into the side of her head.

'Sir, Angie has deviated from the mob. She's headed south on foot with Xavier.'

The Major grunts. Walsh has rejoined him on the roof of the packing house and has his finger to his ear, trying to hear the feed relayed from the van. The Major watches the horde of protesters stumble about in the scrub, backlit by the nuclear plant. Best he can estimate through binoculars there are around three hundred of them headed his way instead of towards the nuclear plant. They've passed the power lines, but to reach the sun farm they have to get over the two security fences flanking the track and then find their way through the field of solar panels.

'Does Waylon have a visual?'

Walsh turns his face to the camp. 'We're waiting on confirmation.'

The Major keeps his eyes on the scrub. What a rabble. The guns waiting for them here are loaded with real ammo, not rubber bullets. And in any case, more than half of them have stuck with the original plan to charge across the flat to the nuclear plant, even with the saltbush lit up like daylight.

That's not his problem.

His problem is Peta Paxton.

It took all of two seconds for her to decide the best option was to put Q18 at risk defending a company asset rather than changing location. But then Paxton Federation's long had form for that brand of decision-making. Just ask Mike De Marchi. Paxton's also convinced Z12 is lying in wait to snatch up Julianne the minute they leave the sun farm, and she's not ready to give up her prize.

The Major has spent the last five hours planning contingencies, and Angie De Marchi's stunt to send the protesters his way adds a new degree of difficulty. He's got Z12 prowling out there somewhere and he's still unclear on Xavier's primary action.

'Sir,' Walsh says. 'We've got a vehicle approaching via the main entrance.'

The Major finds the security booth in his binoculars as a sedan pulls up. He sharpens the focus on the drivers side.

Oh for fuck's sake.

It's Bradford Paxton.

The siren is loud in the distance, like a wartime air raid alarm.

Jules has no idea what's happening outside but Peta Paxton is spooked. A quick exchange with Mian, and the professor lost all interest in her tablet. She dropped an empty vial in her haste to pack up and now keeps crunching the glass underfoot as she moves between the tablet and the lab equipment.

Jules needs to get off the floor. The current is surging and stinging, demanding release. She uses the bench to haul herself up and fumbles for a bottle of water. A couple of mouthfuls to wash away the last of the bile.

By the exit, French lifts a finger to her ear and then seeks out Jules. 'I'll be back.' She disappears.

'What's going on?' Jules asks and Peta Paxton looks up from her phone. She's as far away from Jules as she can get without leaving the room.

'The camp is marching on the power station.'

Is Angie out there in the scrub with him?

Is this it—Xavier's big move?

The blind is up but all Jules can make out is the reflection of Professor Mian bent over her screen, saving data. The plant and storage silo are on the other side of the sun farm, so there's nothing out there to see anyway. But anyone out there can see in.

A spike of adrenaline propels Jules to the window on rubbery legs. She grabs the twist of cords and flattens herself against the wall so she's out of sight while she separates them.

'Julianne—'

'Do you want to make it easy to get shot?' For an intelligent woman, Peta Paxton is acting extremely dumb.

Jules gives a hard, panicked yank and the blind slaps to the sill. Another jerk and the louvres shut against the darkness. It won't stop bullets, but it will make it harder to find a target... unless the mercenaries have thermal imaging sights.

The siren drones on and the charge is becoming almost unbearable. Fiery pinpricks at her fingertips. She pulls one arm across her chest and then the other, the way she's seen Ryan stretch, and feels the muscles give a little.

Professor Mian clears her throat and straightens her kaftan. 'I can pick this up again when you find me space in a fully equipped lab.'

'Have you saved everything?'

'Only to the tablet. Your data network has gone down.'

Peta gestures to the suitcase and the tablet. 'Leave all that.'

Professor Mian falters. It takes her a long moment to decide her safety's worth more to her than the data and equipment, then she leaves without a backwards glance. She bangs her hip on the doorjamb on the way out.

Peta's phone buzzes and she answers with a forceful tap, eyes on Jules. 'What?' She licks her lips while she listens. 'Send him in.' Peta shakes out her wrists and her bracelets jangle. Whoever is coming, Jules has to act before they get here. Peta's not a large woman: Jules should be able to push past her without using the current. She heads for the door.

'What are you doing?' Peta says, alarmed. Her energy is erratic, anxious, but Jules can't tell if it's about *her* or whoever is about to arrive—

The doorhandle turns and Jules freezes. She's missed her chance and now she's stranded in the middle of the lunchroom.

'After you,' Private French says from outside.

Bradford Paxton steps through the door and Jules' heart gives a confused little hop. He's dressed in suit pants and polo-neck jumper, his dark hair and beard trimmed shorter than when she last saw him. The energy he brings into the room is as cold as it was at Pax Fed Tower.

French follows him inside.

'He's unarmed,' the soldier promises Jules.

Bradford stops a good two metres from his sister. 'I take it you're aware the Anti-Nuclear Assembly fence is down and there's a plague of crusty ferals swarming your way?'

'Of course I am,' Peta says.

Jules looks to French. 'The protesters are coming here?'

The private checks the safety on her handgun, and nods. Jules exhales. *Angie knows she's here.*

'You think this keeps her safe, bringing her to my facility?'

Peta bristles. 'It's *ours*, and yes, I do.'

Jules can feel the uneasy swirl of energy between them. They're physically similar—long neck, narrow shoulders— but there's nothing about their mutual proximity they find comforting. Peta has to work to act aloof; Bradford's detachment is effortless.

Peta shifts her weight. 'I can't believe you've set your dog loose on a nuclear facility.'

'Don't be so gullible.' Bradford strolls to the nearest lunch table—two away from Jules—and sits at the head as if he's in a boardroom. 'Do you honestly think I'd risk the viability of my crops here? His only job is to lead the Agitators to the point of no return and silence Angela De Marchi.'

'Angela was already silent. It's your paranoia that's the problem. As usual.'

Another piece falls into place for Jules.

'You're a sore loser, Peta. Dad made his choice. You need to move on.'

'Dad may have prioritised agricultural investment, but he

still approved long-term funding for my research. He knew the advances we're making.'

The way Bradford rolls his eyes suggests this is a well-worn argument, and one he thinks is long won. 'Yeah, and he would've dropped it like a hot brick if he'd known you lied about destroying the Afghanistan research.'

Peta shakes her head. 'Either way, you were told to leave this alone.'

'Things change.'

'When?'

'Dad understands the importance of the bill and what it means for the future of our company. What it means for the world.'

'Dad has Alzheimer's, Bradford, he doesn't know his name most days.'

'Peta'—Bradford shakes his head as if embarrassed he has to spell it out—'Dad knew what I was going to do last week.'

'Did he understand you wanted to have an eighteen-year-old girl executed in our building?'

Bradford raises his eyebrows as if it's a rhetorical question, and not a particularly interesting one. For a few long seconds, all Jules can hear is her own breathing. The moment stretches out like frayed elastic. More puzzle pieces are falling, falling... and when they click into place the current bites into every nerve ending in her hands.

'Dad can't give you permission, he's legally incapable. Does the board know?'

'Listen to yourself. We have the opportunity to eliminate human starvation within a generation if every piece of arable land in Australia is used effectively.'

'Like you give a shit about that. All you care about is being the one to solve a problem nobody else has been able to.'

He shrugs, not disagreeing.

'And what if you succeed? The next war will be over food

329

rather than oil or religion. You'll still need armies, you always will, and I'm helping make better soldiers.'

'As long as your program is legal you'll always have my support for funding. But that'—he points to Julianne—'is the biggest risk to both our futures. Is deconstructing her DNA worth losing everything? Your work will be worth even less than mine if our friends in Canberra find out about her.'

Peta's gaze slides to the suitcase and tablet beside it. She doesn't look at Jules.

'Are you going to let the mob out there overrun this place?' she asks.

'My security force won't let them get that far. But a little chaos can work for us tonight if we use our heads.'

Jules understands exactly what his so-called security force will do to her and Angie in the 'chaos'.

Peta taps her forefinger on her lips while she thinks; the gesture is vague and dismissive. Is that all the consideration their lives deserve, a lacquered nail on a collagen lip?

Jules can barely breathe because the fear, as always, is suffocating.

And she's done with it.

She's sick of always being afraid, of always being held together so rigidly she can never simply *be*. After all the hiding and pretending and mistrusting herself, Jules has ended up here anyway, alone and vulnerable. But not helpless. She's not without skill to manage this current that flows through her: she proved that last night.

And now, what's left to be afraid of?

The anger rises and she leans into it. The charge snakes up her spine, zapping between sinew and bone and surging to her fingertips. She lets it break across her skin, sizzling blue-white lightning strikes that leave her feeling wild and raw...and *free*.

'Julianne—' Peta stops, eyes widening at the sight of her hands. 'Private, do something.'

Private French raises her gun. 'De Marchi, you need to calm down.' She doesn't sound particularly calm herself. 'Nobody's going to hurt you.'

Bradford is out of his seat and backing away, his spindly fingers outstretched behind him to feel for the kitchen bench. 'Shoot her.'

'No,' Peta says. 'Let me think.' Her eyes flick to the lab equipment, to the tablet and the suitcase filled with vials of Jules' blood and slides with tissue samples. No matter what she's indicated to her brother, Peta wants that evidence.

Jules moves closer to it.

'De Marchi...' Private French warns.

Jules cups her hands as if carrying water and the lightning strikes curl around themselves to form a ball. Her breath catches. *This* is what her dad wanted—for Jules to set aside her fear and own the current. The terrifying beauty of it momentarily arrests her. She's so wired she feels weightless.

'*De Marchi.*' Private French raises her gun.

Jules pauses near the table, straining to keep the charge in her palms. The Paxtons bump shoulders, their energy flowing together instead of against each other. United in fear. They're frightened of her.

'Just shoot her,' Bradford snaps at the private.

Jules cradles her beautiful ball of crackling light. Lifts it towards the lab equipment. Without Professor Mian's results, Peta needs Jules alive.

'Don't you dare,' Peta says. 'Julianne—'

Jules releases the charge. The current arcs in the air to earth out through the nearest grounded object: the table and everything on it. The electron microscope and tablet spark and pop, and the suitcase bursts into flames.

Jules steps away a split second before a final violent short takes out the power.

'Do *not* move.' Private French steps forward, finger on the trigger. Her face dances in the light of the blazing suitcase. 'Where's the fire extinguisher?'

Bradford searches under the sink. He doesn't care about the safety of anyone in this room bar himself: all he's worried about is protecting his facility. Jules flexes her fingers, waits for him to get closer—before thoughts of what she might do to him are cut short by a new sound in the compound.

Gunfire.

Bradford's mercenaries are here.

Ryan ducks for cover behind a stack of crates. He's inside the packing house waiting for his sight to adjust to the sudden blackness. He's listening hard, trying to figure out if one of the shooters has come in behind him; checks for zip ties in his chest rig just in case.

The absence of light doesn't freak him out, not with so much space to breathe in. Ryan briefly thinks of the lift and that moment of heart-splitting panic when the dark closed in. Jules kept it together then—and again later when she was hanging off the side of the elevator shaft, terrified. It's only now that he understands how much control it must have taken for her to not ground the charge. She would have killed them both if she'd lost it on that climb.

Another round of gunfire, outside and close. The reality of the moment thuds through him: Z12 is here and he has to get Jules out before they reach her.

His earpiece buzzes with urgent reports. There are three shooters in the compound, more closing in on foot. The concrete is cold under his fingers but his blood pumps hot as he counts off another five seconds and peers around the crates. Shadowy forms take shape in the gloom: conveyer belts and sorting stations, stacks of styrofoam boxes.

It's as good as his sight's going to get. He scampers across the concrete, handgun drawn, eyes sweeping ahead of him.

Something hits the wall in the lunchroom.

'Stay where you are!' It's Frenchie, strung tight.

Ryan runs for the lunchroom door—

Thump.

A shadow crash-tackles him to the ground. His shoulder crunches on the concrete as the mass of muscle lands with him, grappling to pin his arms. Ryan's gun clatters away in the dark. He reacts with fists and knees, breathing in a bitter tang of sweat and gun oil. The merc is shorter than Ryan, and he's fast. They wrestle on the ground, grunting and panting, both searching for a submission hold. Is this the guy who held a rifle to the back of his head last Sunday night? No. That bloke would have put a bullet in him already.

Ryan wraps his legs around stocky hips and rolls the merc onto his back, clamps an arm around his neck. The guy ducks his chin and jams fingers between his throat and Ryan's arm, but Ryan is too strong. He's locked in the hold, squeezing to slow the blood flow to the other man's brain, careful not to crush the airway. The merc thrashes for a full six seconds before going limp.

Ryan doesn't have much time before the guy comes to. He drags him to the nearest conveyer belt. Zip-ties him to the steel leg and gags him. He relieves him of his knife and handgun, scoops up his own weapon and crouch-runs for the lunchroom.

There's another crash inside and he can smell smoke. The voices are quiet in his ear...*shit*. His earpiece is gone. He presses his back against the wall, clicks off the safety and catches his breath. The door to the lunchroom is ajar, orange light flickering inside.

'Frenchie?' he says through the gap.

'Paxtons at three o'clock,' Frenchie says from inside the doorway. 'They're not armed. Your girl is, though.'

Ryan nudges the door with his boot in time to see Bradford Paxton rush at Jules. He has a split second to take it all in—the fire, the black smoke, Jules with her hands covered in snapping blue lightning—and lifts his gun.

'No,' Frenchie hisses and knocks his arm down. 'He's going for the fire.'

And he's too close to Jules. Ryan moves after him, gun raised.

'Heads up,' Frenchie says.

Ryan reacts in time to see an airborne plastic chair. He bats it aside with a forearm and registers Peta Paxton by the sink.

'Get the Major,' she barks.

'He's busy.'

Ryan turns back in time to see Bradford blasting the fire with dry powder. Jules is watching him, strangely calm. Is she in shock?

'Jules, are you okay? *Jules.*'

The charge in her hands shorts out and her eyes meet his. 'Is Angie out there?'

'Yeah, somewhere. We have to go.' Acrid black smoke gathers and curls against the ceiling.

'Open the window,' Frenchie says.

Ryan nods. It's the best option if they move quickly. 'Give me a hand.' He wants Jules away from Bradford. If Frenchie wasn't in the room Ryan would have pistol-whipped the prick already.

Jules draws up the blind and Ryan opens the window. It takes a double thump with his palms but the screen gives.

Frenchie switches on her torch before Bradford puts out the last of the flames. 'The window is for the smoke, soldier, not you.'

'They're coming for Jules. We're not staying.'

'You're not leaving without the order. Ah, shit, Walsh. Don't point that at me.'

Ryan keeps the gun on her. 'Is it clear on this side?'

'I'm not helping you get yourself court-martialled.'

'Is it clear?'

A beat while she listens to her earpiece. 'Far as I can tell.'

Ryan holsters the gun and is half-turned to the window when Bradford lunges at him with the extinguisher. Ryan ducks on reflex and before he can recover, Jules steps into the space between them.

'Get back—'

Bradford doesn't finish because Jules unloads her charge into him on his backswing.

Bradford twitches and jabbers and his eyes roll back into his head. It's horrible to watch but Jules can't look away. She reels in the current but he keeps quivering on the floor, spittle dribbling down his chin in the torchlight.

'Shit, Walsh, go if you're going, before she kills him.'

Private French is right: another dose into his chest and she *could* kill him. Bradford curls into himself, moaning. Does she *want* to? The stink of urine fills the lunchroom and revulsion shudders through her.

She wants to hurt him. But end his life? She'd never be able to carry that.

In the corner by the sink, Peta Paxton is silent.

A burst of gunfire erupts close by. Not random semi-automatic firing but targeted shots inside the packing house.

'Come on.' Ryan's touch is tentative, as if she might turn on him too.

They spill out the window with the smoke. Outside, the breeze is bracing. Jules hears shouting in the distance over the siren and takes off in that direction.

'Jules, wait—' Ryan catches up and grabs her before she can round the corner of the packing house. He pulls her behind a stack of crates and puts his finger to his lips. He's got a knife in his other hand. 'Trust me?'

She nods.

He lifts the cords hanging from the neck of her hoodie and cleanly slices off the knotted ends, tosses them into the dark. 'Surveillance tech. The Major bugged you while you were unconscious. Frenchie's been listening in all afternoon.'

His chest rises and falls and he doesn't move away. Jules rests her head against his collarbone while she finds her breath. He gives her a few seconds and then lifts her chin so he can see her.

'Are you okay?'

Jules has no idea how to answer so she tells him the only thing that matters: 'They're here to kill Angie.'

'And you.' He reaches behind him. 'Do you know how to use one of these?' He presses a gun into her hand. It's rough and heavy, a soldier's weapon.

'No.'

The last time she held a handgun she was at an army shooting range with her dad. She was fourteen and he wanted her to learn, but the recoil set off the current. It was a once-only visit.

Jules attempts to give it back but Ryan traps her fingers around it. 'That's the safety. Leave it on until you want to fire.'

'Don't you need it?'

'It's not mine.'

Jules chews her lip, nods to herself. If this is what it takes to get to Angie, she'll do it. She lifts the hem of her hoodie and tucks the gun down the back of her jeans. The metal is a shock of cold against her skin.

Ryan checks around the corner. 'We're clear.'

He leads her between the packing house and the endless solar field. It's like running along the outskirts of an abandoned city. If they're going to get to the railway line, they'll have to run through it—

A blast bucks the ground, sends Jules sprawling. She lands on her hip and barely registers the shock of impact before Ryan's hauling her up and into a gap between greenhouses. She recovers beside him as the solar panels flicker orange.

'What was that?'

'Grenade. The Major called in another favour from our mate in Adelaide. The gear arrived this arvo.' He checks his handgun. 'If we run out into that paddock now, the Z12 guys will pick us off. We need to keep cover for as long as we can.'

He squeezes her wrist. 'Shoot anyone carrying a weapon: our guys are suited up.' He taps his vest. 'Put two in the chest. No head shots.'

Jules is a soldier's kid so she understands the double-tap principle; that doesn't mean she can deliver it.

They sprint between the greenhouses, the sky above them a sickly tangerine and the air slick with burning fuel. They're more than halfway along when Ryan fires two loud shots in rapid succession. He keeps sprinting with his weapon raised.

Jules spots the target at the end of the alley: a black-clad soldier slumped against a huge water tank. Ryan takes his weapons and headset and probes his vest to confirm the shots. Satisfied, he steps back.

'Sorry, mate.'

He fires into the soldier's calf to keep him down. The gunman mewls, finds the strength to clamp a hand over the wound.

Ryan leads Jules to the cover of a second water tank, equally high and wide. The stench of smoke is stronger here and there's a blast of heat on the wind. They hedge their way around the tank and Jules finally has her bearings. They're back to where they came in earlier today: the compound that forms the nexus between the greenhouses, work huts and solar fields.

Jules catches her breath, counts three black vans, two SUVs, a white sedan and a silver hatchback. One of the SUVs is engulfed in flames. The heat is ferocious. Metal pings and cracks, and glass shatters. The tyres are melting faster at the front, giving the burning beast a weird tilt.

The passenger window of the van she arrived in is missing. It must have blown out in the blast.

'Will the other cars go up?' Jules covers her mouth with her T-shirt to keep out the fumes.

'Not unless someone drops a grenade in them.'

A generator starts. Spotlights flare, illuminating the compound. Jules and Ryan stay close to the water tank, in shadow as four figures emerge from the packing house. Two of them have balaclavas and rifles; the other two are Bradford and Peta Paxton.

What happened to French?

The soldiers spread out as they close in on an SUV. Peta glances around the compound—is she unnerved to find no sign of Q18?—and bolts for the hatchback without a word to her brother. The gunmen keep their eyes on the shadows, unconcerned when she slams the door and starts the engine. Bradford strides for the SUV with the confidence of a man who's never stared down a gun barrel.

The weapon is in Jules' hand before she's thought it through. The safety clicks off without a sound. She doesn't want to kill Bradford, but she wants him to remember he was here. Jules takes a steadying breath and takes aim, the current giving her arm an unexpected lightness.

Ryan sucks in his breath. 'Jules, no—'

She squeezes the trigger.

The recoil slams her shoulder into the steel tank and she almost drops the gun. Ryan drags her around the curve of the tank a heartbeat before bullets slam into the metal. Tyres spin in gravel—Peta's gone.

'Help me with cover.'

Ryan takes point using the rifle. Jules' heart punches her ribs, the charge a swelling orchestra beneath it. Did she hit Bradford? She lifts the gun again—she's shaking now, from the recoil and adrenaline—and stares into the night on the dark side of the tank, braced for a rearguard attack.

Everything is loud. The siren blaring across the salt flats. Voices shouting and car doors slamming in the compound.

Another round of bullets *thwacks* into the tank, forcing them further back. Vehicles leaving. More sirens, this time from the direction of the highway.

Ryan repositions the rifle butt against his shoulder. 'If we can reach one of those vans, I can get us out of here.'

'What about Angie?'

He's stopped listening, already focused on what he needs to do. 'Wait here.'

He crouch-runs across the compound and grabs the drivers door handle of the first van. It snaps back under his fingers. Locked. Boots crunch on gravel and he spins around. Three figures rush at him from the shadows, assault rifles drawn. One of them is French. She must have fled the lunchroom before the mercenaries reached the Paxtons.

Ryan doesn't resist. He holds his rifle out in front of him and French takes it. 'Where is she?'

'I don't know,' he shrugs.

He's not giving Jules up but he can't help her from there. Alone by the tank, Jules flexes her fingers and tries to think.

All he needs is a distraction, enough to make a run for it.

The vests.

Jules tries to steady her hand but her shoulder aches where it slammed into the steel tank. She lifts the gun anyway, aiming for French's chest.

Cold metal kisses the skin under her ear. 'That would be unwise.'

For a big man, the Major can be frighteningly quiet.

'Give it to me before you hurt yourself. And my safety's off, so I wouldn't advise using that other weapon of yours either.'

Her fingers are slippery. The Major takes her gun, keeps his in contact with her neck.

'You two...' he mutters. 'You're doing your best not to see the night out.'

'Major—'

'Save it.'

He prods her forward and into the light. Ryan's on his knees, hands behind his head. His eyes meet hers, bitterly frustrated. He might disobey an occasional order but he's not going to take on his own unit. Jules drops to her knees beside him without being told and the gravel bites through her jeans. Heat radiates from the burning SUV, warming her face and neck.

Two Q18 guys grab fire extinguishers from the vans and douse the SUV. The sirens are closer. Beyond the railway line there's sporadic gunfire. Someone is shooting at the protesters with real ammo.

'Major, I need to find Angie.'

The Major grunts. 'Another De Marchi problem I have to sort.'

'Please—'

'You need to worry about yourself right now. Your mother can look after herself.'

Jules opens her mouth to disagree when the ground rumbles. It's another explosion, big enough to rattle the glass in the SUV behind her. It's come from the west, either from the nuclear plant or the protester camp.

Oh God, where is she?

Angie lurches into consciousness to find the world a violent blur, her bones rattling as she's thrown from side to side. She reaches out to brace herself. It's only then that she realises she's strapped into a car's passenger seat.

She sits up and the night comes into sharp focus. They're bouncing through the scrub in a four-wheel drive ute, Xavier murdering the gears in search of third.

'What the...'

Ahead of them, a power line tower is toppling sideways in slow motion, cables snapping one by one. The saltbush burns where the tower's feet have been uprooted, and beyond it the nuclear plant winks out. The searchlights are gone. The siren silenced.

'Ollie,' Xavier says by way of explanation.

Angie tastes blood in her mouth. 'What's the point? The plant has a generator.'

'And when that fails...'

The plutonium rods overheat and the plant goes into nuclear meltdown.

'Ollie's not getting to the generator,' she says. 'He won't get near the plant, even in a blackout.' The thought that he might is a cold fist in her belly.

Xavier grips the steering wheel and stares ahead. 'Not without another distraction.' He reefs the wheel and heads for the railway line. It's pointless, because there's a prison-grade cyclone fence protecting it, as sturdy as the one hemming in the Anti-Nuke Assembly camp. They won't get past it unless...

Ollie's been busy here too. There it is, a gap wide enough for a single vehicle.

Xavier has to brake hard to fit through, changing ham-fistedly down to first gear. The jagged wire scrapes the duco on both sides and they're halfway through when something heavy lands in the tray of the ute. Angie twists around to see a figure crouched there, struggling to stay upright. Waylon. *Thank God.*

Xavier grimaces in the green dash light and guns the ute, swerving left and then right in the soft sand, trying to throw him out. When that fails, he grinds back up to second and veers up the verge, onto the railway track. Angie's jaw bangs on her shoulder as they judder over the sleepers. They're heading towards the highway. She assumed his plan was to ram-raid the plant via the railway line, so this option makes no sense.

'What are you doing?'

Xavier doesn't answer. Meaty fists white-knuckled on the steering wheel, eyes fixed ahead. He pushes the engine harder. Waylon staggers forward and manages to grip the roll bar behind the cab, finally steadies himself. He presses his face to the back window.

'Get out of there,' he yells at Angie. 'Look!'

Ahead on the track, a single bright light punctuates the darkness in the distance. Is that—

No, no, no.

The only trains on this line are loaded with radioactive waste. Angie tastes ash. 'Xavier, there's a train coming.'

He hunches further over the wheel.

'You're a lunatic.' She reaches for him—

His elbow flies up and her head snaps back. The night splinters again.

'Hey, *hey!*'

Angie's vaguely aware of Waylon banging the butt of his gun on the back window. Her cheek throbs in time with the impact, shards of white forking through her skull. She tries to sit up, can't. Her head hurts too much. She fights to stay conscious because the truth is taking shape in the fug. Xavier knew a train was coming; he's been checking his watch all night. The march on the plant was the first distraction, this is the second. Xavier is going to derail a shipment of radioactive waste by driving this ute into an oncoming train. With both of them in it.

Her heart climbs into her throat. She rests her aching head against the window and tries the door: it's centrally locked. She fumbles for the button to open the window. Nothing. She's trapped. A horn sounds. The train driver's seen them. Why didn't they brake when the tower went down?

'I have to get to Jules,' she says, pulling on the doorhandle again.

'You need to be with me.'

The light on the track is brighter, closer. The horn blasts, longer this time. Waylon bangs again and Angie cranes her neck to see him pointing the gun at the rear window, eyes frantic.

'Why?' She's pleading now. Praying for Waylon to shoot. Anything to get this ute off the tracks.

Xavier doesn't look at her when he answers.

'Because if you're still a threat after tonight, Bradford Paxton's going to stop paying for my sister's treatment.'

'Go,' the Major orders. '*Now*, before we have company.'

Two of his soldiers disappear to investigate the explosion. Three more head in opposite directions to guard the perimeter and the other four are already on their way to give Bradford Paxton's war dogs something to think about other than shooting at unarmed protesters. French takes point a few metres away.

The night has gone to shit in spectacularly unexpected ways.

He didn't have the resources to stop Z12 extracting Peta and Bradford from the lunchroom. He had no imperative to intervene anyway, given they left willingly. Both of them. *Fucking Paxtons.* Of course they'd stick together. The Major has never believed the adage about blood being thicker than water but maybe there's something to it. Or maybe it's a mutual fear of shareholder losses.

And as for Walsh...

'What was going through that tiny brain of yours when you took De Marchi out of the lunchroom?'

Walsh lifts his head. 'She wasn't safe.'

'What is it you think we've been doing here all afternoon?'

A defiant half-shrug. 'Whatever Peta Paxton tells you to do.'

The anger is instant. 'Careful, private. You're still a soldier in the Australian Army until I say otherwise.'

'What does that even mean? We're shooting at ex-soldiers and dropping grenades on Australian soil. How does that work, *sir*?'

'It doesn't matter how it works. Your job—your *only* job—is to follow orders. But that's never been your strong suit, has it Walsh?'

French clears her throat. 'You got this, sir? I should check the audio and police channels.'

The Major grunts. Weak as piss, the lot of them. These kids can't handle a bollocking—not even watching a mate wear one.

'Go.'

French slings her rifle over her shoulder and disappears into the tech van. The Major paces in front of Walsh and Julianne, his phantom foot throbbing.

'You think you're hard done by, don't you, Walsh? Giving up five years to get yourself a new knee?' He stops and yanks up the leg of his pants. 'What do you think that cost me?'

Walsh stares. No smartarse comeback this time.

'It cost close to a decade and responsibility for *this* shit show. So save me your sob story.'

A heavy pause, and Julianne says: 'Is that cyto-bionic?'

'From the knee down.'

'Supplied by Pax Fed?'

'No.'

'Bullshit.'

She sounds so much like her mother it throws him for a good three seconds.

'Their nanotech helped speed recovery,' he says. 'That's it.'

'You benefited from the illegal testing done on my father.'

A train horn sounds again in the distance, loud enough to cut through the gunfire on the salt flats.

'How was I supposed to know that?'

'And you're comfortable with them getting away with it? What they did to my dad? To me? What they still want to do?'

The Major grinds his jaw. If she wants him to take on the Australian military and Paxton Federation, she can think again. He's not Angie De Marchi.

The train horn comes again. More insistent. Police sirens swell closer. There's only one road off the sun farm, and without a Paxton on site to talk down the local law enforcement, this scenario is going to be tricky to explain. Where the hell is Khan? *This* is what he needed her for.

'Sir—' French bursts out of the van. 'Xavier's on the freight tracks. Waylon and De Marchi are with him. He's—'

The night splits with the sound of screeching steel followed by an almighty crash that reverberates through the earth.

'Oh fuck,' French says, aghast. 'They've hit the train.'

It doesn't stop. The scream of twisting metal and the earth-pounding thuds as wagon after wagon jackknifes.

Ryan redlines the van, bouncing over saltbush. Wind whips in through the open window, swirling chewing-gum wrappers on the floor and sliding icy fingers down the back of his jumper. Jules is in the passenger seat, silent and pale. Broken glass litters the carpet and the cab stinks of burning upholstery from the Z12 SUV bonfire.

They're smashing through scrub as the carnage mounts ahead of them. Freight wagons spear towards the sky and topple sideways, radwaste casks bolted to them. If one of those casks has a breach there won't be a safe place within a hundred kilometres, but all Ryan can think about is Waylo.

His mate would not have stayed in that ute. No way. Unless he couldn't get Angie out…Ryan's focus flits from the road to the track, knee jiggling.

'We don't know for sure where Angie and Waylo were when it hit,' Frenchie says. She's in the back of the van, dominating the rearview mirror and trying to convince herself as much as him. She and the Major are hanging on with one hand and reloading rifles with the other. Ryan caught sight of a Steyr 882 fitted with a grenade launcher. They're done playing games. If Z12 gets between them and the crash site, all bets are off.

Ryan's gone bush to find the most direct route to the wreckage but what are they going to find when they get there? He's scared to look at Jules. She hasn't spoken since they left the compound, even when they jolted over a washout or rabbit warren. He finds another hole now—he can't see them in time—and his head meets the roof. The other two bounce around in the back but nobody complains, not even the Major.

Ahead of them, momentum carries the train in a slow, tired slide. Less spectacular but no less horrifying. Dust plumes up around the locomotive and wagons. There's no sign of Xavier's vehicle. Ryan's headlights find the cyclone fence bordering the track. He stomps the brakes and the van shudders to a stop. He kills the engine, leaves the lights on. 'Cutters?'

'Got 'em,' French says.

They don't wait for the dust to clear before they're out of the van. Ryan peels back the wire as Frenchie cuts, and the Major goes through first. Jules is stone-like in the van with her hands tucked between her knees, staring at the train. It's still sliding, centimetre by centimetre.

Ryan opens her door. 'We have to go the rest of the way on foot, come on.'

'What if she's dead? I don't...I can't...' Jules curls in on herself and Ryan reaches across to undo the seatbelt. He takes her face in his hands and makes her look at him.

'What if she's not?'

Jules takes a shaky breath and wipes her cheek on her shoulder, lets him help her from the van. He guides her through the fence, metres from a wagon with its axles in the air like an overturned beetle. The wreckage has finally come to rest. Twelve freight wagons: twelve steel radwaste casks packed with spent fuel rods.

Frenchie is already jogging up the line, the Steyr on her back and a first-aid kit in hand. The locomotive must have jumped the tracks after impact and careened down the embankment, sliding onto its side and setting off the chain reaction pile-up.

God knows how the driver's fared in all that. The point of impact was east, closer to the highway, and Ryan leads Jules in that direction, following the Major. His commanding officer sweeps the saltbush with the torch beam.

Ryan sees it a second before the Major calls out: a vehicle on its roof in the scrub. He hangs on to Jules until they're close enough to smell diesel.

'Wait here,' he says.

Even without the benefit of a torch, Ryan can see that the headlights, bumper and grille have been ripped away and the engine shunted sideways. The passenger-side front panel is a mangled mess of twisted metal, the front wheel bent sideways like a broken wing, the cabin crumpled into itself. Fear uncoils under his ribs. Nobody could have survived that.

Jules waits beside the tracks, arms around herself, framed in the moonlight by a jackknifed radwaste container.

The Major jimmies open the passenger door. It groans as he forces the hinges. Ryan squats down, his legs numb and heart thrashing. He doesn't want to see. But he has to. He has to know.

The Major shines the light into the cab—

The relief sets Ryan on his arse. There's a solitary figure inside. He wouldn't have recognised Xavier without the beard and man bun. The Agitator leader's face is covered in blood and gore, a glint of bone where the skin has peeled away from his cheek. He hangs in his seatbelt, blood dripping down loose strands of hair. His right arm dangles at a weird angle, the shoulder dislocated or broken. Ryan fends off an onslaught of nausea.

The Major climbs into the cab and presses fingers against Xavier's neck. 'He's dead. Search the track.'

Ryan scrambles to his feet and catches the torch the Major tosses to him. 'They're not in the ute,' he yells to Jules.

She takes off before he can get back up the bank to her. 'Mum. *Mum*!' She's stumbling around the wreckage, screaming into the dark.

Ryan forces himself to go slower so he can scan the saltbush. If Waylo and Angie managed to jump before impact, they can't have landed far from the track, but they could be either side of the train. He vaults over a coupling between wagons and makes his way down the other embankment. The salty night air is overlaid with diesel and grease.

He sees the fallen power-line tower a few hundred metres away—closer to the camp—and the spot fires burning around it. It's only now he realises the nuclear plant is dark as well as silent.

More sirens on the highway, speeding from Port Augusta. The cops who'd been closing in on Happy Growers must have doubled back, because they're now turning into the track from the main road. They're only minutes away.

'Walsh.'

French is standing on the high end of a radwaste cask holding the Steyr like she intends to use it. It's almost as tall as she is, but he's seen her in action on the range. He knows how well she handles it.

'You find the driver?' he asks, springing up beside her to get a better vantage.

'Yeah. In shock, but stable. Lacerations, concussion.' She lifts the rifle to her shoulder and checks the night-vision scope. 'Z12 are incoming. Eight o'clock. Scrub buggy, no lights. Two hundred metres out, heading for a break in the fence. They must have cut it earlier.'

Ryan strains to see or hear the vehicle but the Z12 soldiers are running electric and they're too far away for him to see without tech. The cop car keeps coming up the track from the opposite direction, back end sliding out as it manoeuvres around the wagons.

'Orders?' he asks.

'They're not getting near this train. I've got this. Find Waylon and De Marchi. We've got under a minute before those cops get here.'

352

'What about our guys?' The gunfire has stopped, but the rest of Q18 are still out in the scrub. As far as Ryan can tell, the protesters are all headed back to the camp. A radioactive train wreck will have that effect.

'They're coming in at nine o'clock covering the flank. I can see them, Walsh. They're clear.'

He hesitates, adrenaline burning through him. It feels wrong. It's one thing to put a shot in a vest at twenty metres; something else to fire a grenade into a buggy full of ex-soldiers. 'You can't fire on them, not from this range. The margin for error's too great.'

'Not my call.'

Ryan scans the track to the south, his mind racing. 'What if they're retreating? To intercept the protesters they had to go bush from the sun farm like we did. They're in range and haven't fired. They could be trying to get out of the way.'

French drops to one knee and takes aim through the scope.

Ryan peers down the track beyond the locomotive. He can finally make out a vague buggy-size shape about a hundred metres away. It scrambles up the bank—Ryan braces for French to loose a grenade—and then the buggy bounces over the rails and sleepers and down the other side. Tail-lights wink as it races through the scrub towards the solar field. No shots are fired.

French stands. 'Go,' she snaps, but he can hear the relief. 'Deal with the cops.' She drops down to the eastern side of the train as the patrol unit slides to a stop in the churned dirt. The passenger door opens and Ryan shows his hands, ready to dive for cover if the Port Augusta coppers are feeling trigger-happy tonight.

It's Khan who climbs out. She levels a torch beam at him so he has to shield his eyes. The patrol siren shuts off, but the lights keep blinking red and blue. 'Walsh, what happened here?'

'Xavier rammed the train. He's dead in a ute over there.' Ryan gestures to the other side of the wreckage. 'He had Angie in the cab with him and Waylo on the back but they're not there now and we need to find them.'

The beam shifts. 'Holster your weapons.' The command is to the two uniformed cops with her. They're young blokes, built like brick shithouses. 'Where's the Major?'

'Here.' The Major appears from the shadows. 'You're wasting time. Help or get out of the way. The driver's clear of the loco but needs attention.'

'Where's Julianne?'

On cue they hear her call out for Angie in the dark, frantic. She's on their side of the track now, further down the line. Khan shrugs deeper into her jacket and heads after her, walking backwards long enough to send one cop to confirm Xavier's death, and the other to interview the driver. Ryan is about to jump down from the train when a movement in the scrub catches his eye. He swings the torch beam over the saltbush. Was that a hand? His chest tightens. 'Over there!'

He leaps from the radwaste cask—absorbs the impact in his knees, old and new—and keeps the beam on the patch of salt-bush as he sprints for the spot, aware others are running after him. Closer, closer and then he sees khaki pants, boots...

It's them.

He props in the dirt and for a devastated, suspended breath, all he can do is stand there with his heart hammering. Waylon's lying awkwardly in a washed-out rut, head lolled to one side. Angie's two metres away, facedown and not moving. Waylo must have been breathing a second ago to raise his hand, but seeing him bent up so badly momentarily paralyses Ryan—until he's knocked back into the moment by Khan on her way to Angie.

'*Mum!*'

Ryan catches Jules before she can get any closer, using her momentum to swing her into his arms. She squirms, pushing at his chest. 'I need to see,' she sobs.

'Give them space.'

'For fuck's sake get that light back here,' the Major barks.

Ryan angles the torch on to Angie and Waylon. Jules shudders inside her hoodie, her fingers in constant motion at her throat. Ryan forces himself to take a proper look at Angie. Her femur is broken—the bone has speared through flesh and denim—and her face and arms are grazed and bloodied. Is she breathing? Khan rests fingers against Angie's throat—

Waylo groans and Ryan's legs dissolve. *He's alive.* Waylo opens one eye and tries to focus on the Major.

'Had to shoot out the window, sir.' It's an effort for him to speak. 'Dragged Angie through...We jumped...I think I landed on her.' He tries to move and gasps. 'Ah, shit.'

French appears and kneels down in the dirt. She unrolls the first-aid kit and pulls out a green pain-relief whistle; helps Waylo hold it steady while he inhales.

'Slower, mate. That's it.'

The Major keeps pressing and probing, searching for injuries. 'Collarbone's broken,' he tells Waylo. 'And that ankle's suspect, but stay put—'

'I can't get a pulse,' Khan says, bent over Angie. 'I thought I had one, but it's gone.'

Jules stops fidgeting in Ryan's arms.

Khan rolls Angie onto her side, not caring about broken bones, and sticks fingers down her throat. 'Airway is clear.' She repositions Angie on her back—'Major, help me'—and starts chest compressions.

Khan counts them out. 'One, two, three...'

The Major crawls to Angie's side. He brushes hair from her face, picking a strand from between her lips with surprising gentleness.

'Oh God,' Jules whispers.

Khan is working hard, her small frame rising and falling with each compression.

She counts out thirty and then the Major bends down and

places his mouth on Angie's. Ryan watches her chest inflate, once, twice.

Breathe, woman.

Khan puts her fingers to Angie's throat. Shakes her head at the Major, stricken.

They go again.

Ryan twists around to check on the other flashing lights coming in from the highway. One of them has to be an ambulance but it's minutes away—maybe longer given the spread of the wreckage. Jules claws at his arm, fingernails breaking skin.

Another thirty compressions. Another two breaths.

Nothing.

The Major lifts his head. His face is bleak in the torchlight but there's no missing the intent there.

'Julianne. We need you.'

Her mother is pale. Motionless. *Quiet.*

Angie's heart, so full of fury and fire, is lifeless inside her chest.

Her mum is dead.

Just...gone.

Jules hasn't seen Angie in days, hasn't heard her voice. Why didn't she insist on making contact? She's never going to hear that voice again. What if it fades in her memory like her dad's has? The sky collapses onto her, drives her to her knees. She claws at the clay. Her fingernail tears but it doesn't hurt. She can't even feel the current, barely feels Ryan holding her upright.

'De Marchi,' the Major says. '*Julianne.*'

'She's dead...' The words fall on the unforgiving ground between them.

'Your mother's in cardiac arrest. She'll only be dead if we can't restart her heart.'

Khan snaps her fingers to get her attention. 'You can bring her back, Julianne, but you have to do it now.'

The charge flutters as she understands what they're asking of her.

'I'll show you where to put your hands. Come on.'

'You can do this,' Ryan says, guiding her forward. Jules' teeth chatter. Her mother will live or die depending on whether he's right.

Khan hikes up Angie's T-shirt and jumper to expose bare skin and the frayed bra Jules threatens to throw out every washday. The sight of the tattered fabric almost undoes her.

Jules positions her hands where Khan demonstrates, one above Angie's heart on the left, the other beneath it on the right. She's grateful for Angie's warmth: her mum *feels* alive.

'Take it easy,' Khan says. 'You only need enough charge to shock the heart into beating again. Start with two hundred volts, okay?'

Jules has no idea how to deliver a measured charge. Ryan rests his palm in the small of her back. 'Start with the smallest amount you can release.'

She closes her eyes and Ryan's touch falls away.

'Now, Julianne,' Khan urges.

Jules sends a jolt of current into her mother. Angie's legs and arms jerk with a violent spasm and Jules recoils.

'That's normal,' Khan tells her and feels for Angie's pulse. 'Go again.'

Jules takes a shallow breath and repositions trembling fingers. Nothing about this is normal. She releases another burst and this time when Angie lurches from the ground Jules smells charred flesh. She snatches back her hands, horrified.

She's burning her.

Khan leans in, searches for signs of life. Angie's chest is blackened and blistered, Jules' fingerprints seared into her flesh.

'You need to give more,' Khan says. 'Burns will heal.'

Oh God.

Jules has to find a way to do it again. The sirens are closer, but not close enough.

She shuts her eyes and pushes back the night, the horror of that bone jutting out of Angie's leg and Waylon's laboured breathing. Pushes back the reality of radwaste casks scattered around her. Ignores Khan's urgency. She knows Angie's energy and all of its moods. It's been wrapped around her all her life, threaded through bone and sinew, pushing and pulling. Driving her. Jules flattens her palms against Angie's chest and searches for a sense of it, that fire. She takes a slow, calming breath. Feels Ryan standing behind her.

There. An ember.

Jules angles her hands in that direction and releases the current. Angie's shoulders leave the ground and the ember sparks a wave that rips through her mother. Jules feels the nerve endings catch fire—and Angie's heart stutter back to life.

The Major catches Angie's head before it hits the dirt. Khan leans in. 'We've got a pulse.'

'Sweet Jesus,' Ryan says softly.

The Major puts his good ear to Angie's lips, listens, and then he pinches her nose and resumes mouth-to-mouth.

Jules looks to Ryan, confused.

'Your mum can't breathe on her own yet,' he says and draws her closer so she can rest against him.

Angie's chest inflates with the Major's breath, again and again. Her palms are upturned to the sky in supplication. Utterly helpless. The current hums, ready to go again, but there's nothing Jules can do now but watch.

'Ambos are here,' French says at last.

Heavy-soled boots pound the dirt and a paramedic orders them to move back. They stabilise Angie with a respirator bag and splint her leg, firing questions at the Major. Khan sits with Jules on the ground. They watch as paramedics ease Angie onto a stretcher, the respirator bag replacing the Major. Waylon is still sucking on the green whistle when the second crew carries him off.

Jules follows the stretchers, letting Ryan guide her steps. Twice they have to pass Angie over the busted fence to get around the overturned freight wagons. A man with silver hair and a craggy face sits inside the first ambulance, dazed and bleeding from his forehead. He sees Angie and Waylon and squeezes his eyes shut. More vehicles are coming up the track. They'll all be here soon: cops, the media, politicians.

The paramedics transfer Angie to a gurney and the Major props open the ambulance door while she's loaded onboard. Khan stands with him, her face streaky from tears and dirt.

'Bloody Paxtons,' she says. It's the first time Jules has ever heard her swear.

It seems appropriate to Jules to quote her mother in the moment: 'Money and influence make people think they're untouchable.'

The Major surveys the scene: Waylon waiting to be loaded into the ambulance, the radwaste casks scattered across the track, fire trucks racing for the scrub fire under the power lines.

'It's time they find out they're not.'

'Don't scrub.'

'I'm not.' Ryan eases up with the sponge.

'And don't use conditioner on your hair. Soap only.'

Ryan sticks his head under the shower to rinse off. He heard the first time. The army medic is pacing in front of temporary decontamination showers in the Port Augusta Hospital car park, repeating instructions as if the Q18 crew is a bunch of six-year-olds. Clean fatigues are folded on a plastic chair inside the curtain and he has to minimise movement to avoid getting them wet. His own clothes have gone with everyone else's for burning. Nobody's admitting there was a radiation leak from the train, but the fact their clothes are in an incinerator and the Q18 weapons are on the way to disposal is not a good sign.

Cold air creeps under the curtain and grabs his ankles. He turns off the water and dries himself with a towel the size of a serviette. His skin is damp and he has to wrestle to get into the shirt.

Ryan hasn't seen Jules since she left the crash site. Khan brought her into town and he assumes they're both being decontaminated inside the hospital. It's not that he wants her to be roughing it out here; he didn't expect to be apart from her again so soon. The look in her eyes when she was driven away...

Ryan rubs his eyes with grazed fingers and thinks long and hard about staying in the cubicle. Keeping the world at arm's length a while longer. He can hear it rushing by beyond the curtain: choppers, shouted commands, static-filled radios and steel-cap boots on concrete. The hospital grounds became a military facility as soon as troops arrived in Chinooks from the newly commissioned Whyalla base. The car park is crowded with staging lights to form a makeshift command centre complete with media scrum, and a triage tent for the steadily increasing number of locals worried about radiation exposure. It's coordinated chaos out there.

'You waiting for a blow wave, Walsh?'

He sighs and pulls back the curtain. One look at Frenchie and he knows her wind-up is barely half-arsed. She's as wrung out and exhausted as he is. It's been a shit of a day for all of them and he wishes he hadn't been the one to give her that swollen jaw. And the day's not over. As soon as Q18 is prepped, they're off to help with roadblocks until the quarantine zone is lifted.

Frenchie's buzz cut is already dry. 'I don't know, Walsh, you boys and your high-maintenance hairdos. You really should pull a comb through that mess—'

She cuts herself off because the Major is weaving his way towards them through patrol cars and flashing lights. Like them, he's dressed in fatigues. He's striding, not stomping, which could be a good sign.

'Sir?' Ryan says, moving to meet him.

'She's breathing on her own. They're patching her up now.'

It's like stepping into sunshine. The Major can't hide his relief either.

'And Waylo?'

'Collarbone's broken in two places and he's got a couple of bruised ribs but everything else is intact. Ankle's only sprained.'

'Good.' The tag on Ryan's new shirt itches and he tries to shrug away from it. 'Did you see Julianne?' He's got no standing to ask but he's asking anyway.

'She's with Khan. She's fine.'

362

He doubts that.

'French,' the Major says. 'You and I are taking a trip to the airport. Go sign out a vehicle.'

She disappears towards the command centre. Ryan glances at the troop carriers.

'Have I got time to check on Waylo?'

'No.'

'Sir—'

'Not if you want to see your family.'

'They're here?'

'Your old man's threatening to punch a lieutenant if you don't make an appearance.' The Major nods in the direction of a marquee at the far edge of the car park. 'You've got five minutes.'

Two steps from the Major and Ryan breaks into a jog.

The marquee is crowded with civilians watching a news update on a wall-sized flex screen. Ryan's mum and dad hang towards the back. His dad's arm is across his mum's shoulder, hers around his waist. The sight of them leaning into each other brings a lump to his throat. Tommy chugs from bottled water as he scans the room and his face relaxes when he sees Ryan.

Ryan's mum reaches him first.

'Thank God.' She squeezes Ryan like she used to when he was a kid, pinning his arms to his sides to stop him squirming away. He rests his cheek against her hair and breathes in cheap motel shampoo.

She lets go sooner than he expects and his old man is waiting. Jamie Walsh stands in front of his son, rough hands hanging at his sides as if he doesn't know what to do with them. The spikiness between them is distant and blunted. His dad's mouth quirks down and he grabs Ryan by the back of the neck and drags him into a hug. It's awkward and unpractised but the contact loosens something deep in Ryan's chest. He grabs fist-fuls of his old man's shirt and hangs on, unashamed. There's no lingering eye contact when they pull apart, and it's okay because Tommy swoops in for a hug and back thump.

'You saw it happen?' Tommy asks when they disentangle.

Ryan doesn't know what they've heard but he nods. He touches his grazed elbow, his black eye. He feels every sore spot from the brawl at the oval and his run-in with the merc in the packing house.

Tommy's tapping the half-empty water bottle against his leg. 'Is Jules all right?'

Ryan pictures Angie crumpled in the dirt; Jules' tear-streaked face as she shocked her mother back to life. 'She will be if Angie pulls through.'

The screen in the marquee is showing an aerial shot of the train spotlit by a news chopper, followed by footage of protesters queuing up for potassium iodide tablets not far from where Ryan's standing. The live coverage shifts to an ambulance turning into Hospital Road. Ryan can hear the siren now, getting closer.

'Someone got shot trying to scale the nuclear plant fence during the blackout,' Tommy says. 'Dickhead.'

One of Xavier's goons, no doubt. That mess continues to unravel.

His mum points at the words scrolling across the bottom of the news screen. 'What's ARPANSA?'

Ryan didn't know himself until twenty minutes ago but he says it like he's an expert: 'Australian Radiation Protection and Nuclear Safety Agency. They're flying in to figure out if there's any risk of exposure from the train.'

Tommy scoffs. 'Pax Fed and Happy Growers are fucked if there is.'

'Don't use that language,' Ryan's mum says, out of habit. Nobody states the obvious: their land might be too, if the breeze is blowing the wrong way.

The Major appears in the marquee entry.

'I gotta go. I'll see you when I can.'

His mum gives him another hug and then he joins the Major outside before the urge to stay with his family overwhelms him. The Major nods in the direction of the Q18 soldiers gathering around the troop carrier.

'Go,' the Major says. 'See if you can follow orders this time.'

'What about you, sir? You coming?' The world has gone sideways and he wants his hard-arsed commanding officer close by, running the show.

The Major surprises him with a grin—a shared moment that Ryan doesn't fully understand.

'I have someone to see first.'

'I think she's awake.'

Angie knows the croak in that voice. She opens sticky eyelids and her vision sharpens enough to see that she's in a hospital. Everything hurts. A pale face hovers into her line of sight and Angie's breath escapes in a choked rush.

Oh thank God.

Jules' hair is caught up in a messy ponytail and her eyes are puffy—but she's safe. 'I was trying to get to you,' Angie rasps. Her throat's raw but she needs Jules to know.

Jules stifles a sob and Angie's breath deserts her.

'Waylon? Is he—' She breaks into a hacking cough: a thousand tiny knives in a stabbing frenzy.

'He's okay, but you...Mum, you were dead.'

Those last moments with Xavier are fragmented and full of shadows, a blur of noise and pain. Angie remembers the gunshot shattering the back window, Waylon dragging her over shards of glass...the two of them jumping from the back of the ute and that awful moment, airborne, before the night filled with shrieking metal.

'Your heart stopped.' Khan steps into Angie's field of vision. The kohl around her eyes is smudged, her shirt's untucked and her sleeves pushed up past her elbows. Angie's never seen her dishevelled. 'Private Waylon landed on you and the impact caused a cardiac arrest. *Commotio cordis*, the doctor called it. You were gone there for a while.' Khan nods at Jules. 'She brought you back.'

'I burned you,' Jules whispers. 'I'm so sorry.'

Angie lifts her free hand—there's a monitor clipped to her finger and a drip in her arm—and finds bandaging on her chest with monitor leads sprouting out. Then she locates the pulse in her throat and feels the beat, slow and steady.

'You started my heart.'

Jules nods. 'I hurt you—' She falters as Angie fumbles for her hand.

'Thank you.' She squeezes her daughter's fingers. 'Are you okay?'

Jules bites her lip. Nods, not quite certain.

'Where's Voss? I'm going to have his balls for taking you to that woman.'

'You might want to thank him first,' Khan says. 'He kept you breathing until the paramedics arrived.'

Angie's not sure what to do with that.

Jules wipes her nose with a tissue balled in her free hand and sighs. There's something different about her daughter, but Angie can't quite name it. Khan touches Angie's good leg through the blanket.

'I need to get showered but I'll be back.' She heads for the door. 'I'll send in your next visitor.'

The door doesn't even click shut before it swings in again and Vee appears. Hesitates as she processes the sight of Angie so banged up. 'Oh God, Ange.'

'Settle down—'

'You *died*.'

Angie pulls a face—not because Vee's wrong, but because it's easier than dealing with the truth. She tries to muster her anger at Vee but she can't remember what it was about. Must be the drugs.

Vee drops her handbag on the chair and takes Angie's free hand, careful not to dislodge the monitor on her finger. She reaches across the bed to touch Jules on the shoulder.

'Vee, what are you doing here?'

'I was coming to get you out of that protester camp, and now by sheer timing I'm the minister's rep on the ground. I'll need to get back out there in a few minutes for the ARPANSA briefing.'

'How bad is it?'

'We don't know yet. There's no visible damage to the radwaste casks. We could get lucky.'

Angie checks Jules over, spots the band-aid inside her elbow. 'Your geneticist found Jules, then.' It's not a question.

Vee levels her gaze. 'She's in a decontamination tent as we speak. Without her data.'

'Who has it?'

'Nobody,' Jules says. 'I short-circuited the lab equipment and set fire to the samples.'

'On purpose?' Angie asks.

'Yes.'

Vee checks her phone. 'I'm trying to find out if Peta and Bradford got out before the roadblocks went up.'

'*Both* of them were here?'

Vee catches Jules' eye. 'You haven't told your mother?' She raises her eyebrows.

Jules blows out her breath, hesitant. 'I offloaded the current into Bradford.'

It's in the way Jules says it—without shame or self-loathing or regret—that Angie understands what's different about her daughter. Jules has finally come into a sense of her own power. And how to use it.

'Couldn't happen to a nicer bloke.'

'Yes, I thought you'd be proud,' Vee says, and Angie is, but not for the reasons Vee thinks. Angie lets Jules see that she understands.

Jules smiles and wipes her cheek on her shoulder, not willing to let go of Angie's hand. 'Khan says you heard about the trials in Afghanistan?'

'Yeah.' And there it is: the anger Angie's been missing.

'Peta says I'm all that's left.'

Vee presses out a crease in Angie's hospital blanket. 'That may be true from Pax Fed's perspective, but there's a paper trail in my department. Granted, it's under *several* layers of classification and it's unlikely those files have the level of detail Peta Paxton could provide, but there is something in the system.'

'It's never going to be over, is it?'

'Maybe not, but you have options now.'

'Like what?' Jules asks and Angie smiles to herself. Her daughter's taking charge. *At last.*

'Access to answers, for a start. Professor Mian knows about you, so why not have her run those tests in an environment we control?'

'What if she says no?'

'Then the problem goes away. She's not going to risk her integrity and reputation talking about your DNA if she can't support it with evidence. And if she runs the tests again it will be under an iron-clad confidentiality agreement with the department.'

Jules glances at Angie. 'That's one option. What are the others?'

Vee offers a calculating smile. 'You go public. If the Afghanistan trials come to light, there'll be compensation.'

Angie shakes her head. 'Too risky for Jules, and you know the army's not going to pay out on a class action.'

'Pax Fed might. And it would be in the Paxtons' best interests to provide compensation before it gets that far.'

'Blackmail?'

Vee shrugs. 'Up to you.'

Angie looks to Jules and feigns confusion. 'Would that be hypocritical?'

Jules gives a surprised laugh and Angie realises how long it's been since she's heard that sound.

'No, Mum. I think that's what's known as poetic justice.'

Peta Paxton sits under fluorescent lights in borrowed nurses scrubs with her hands clasped in her lap. Her platinum hair is slicked back and her make-up long gone. The Major rests his arm on the back of the chair between her and him, savouring the moment.

'I'm a victim here too, Major.'

Across the desk, Khan offers a thin smile. The three of them are in a clinical office on the ground floor of the Port Augusta Hospital.

'Define victim.'

'I'm caught up in my brother's machinations as much as everyone else here.'

'So why did Major Voss intercept you at the airport attempting to leave?'

Peta wets her lower lip. 'Because, Agent Khan, I was unaware you were in town and I didn't think the local police were equipped to handle the situation.'

'Major Voss and his unit were at the Happy Growers sun farm—'

'The Major had his hands full.'

'Yes, protecting a Paxton Federation facility from mercenaries your brother hired to kill Angela and Julianne De Marchi.'

'I don't know anything about that.'

Khan checks with the Major. He nods. *This should be good.*

'Ms Paxton, Major Voss has handed over audio files that indicate you clearly understood what your brother had planned.'

Paxton turns on him. 'You recorded me?'

'Standard operating procedure.' It's not, but she doesn't know that. She also doesn't know that if Angela De Marchi had died beside that railway line, this night would be turning out very differently for her and her brother.

'You're under contract, so any associated material belongs to me—'

'Our contract ended the minute your brother derailed a train loaded with radioactive waste.'

'I had nothing to do with that!' Her neck flushes.

'But you knew Z12 was coming for Julianne.'

'I was trying to protect her, as you well know.'

'You wanted samples from her while she was still breathing.'

Peta blanches. 'I want my lawyer.'

'Why?' Khan says. She's fresh from decontamination, dressed in borrowed fatigues. 'At this stage you're only a witness and this is a routine conversation.'

Peta reaches for her wrists and finds them bare. 'You're out of your depth, agent. Neither of you should underestimate my brother. One of your team shot him, Major, and he'll put your unit in the middle of this if you're not careful.'

The Major scoffs. 'That pencil neck wore a bullet from a weapon registered to mercenaries *he* funded, and right now he's probably in a safe house having it dug out by someone who's not a doctor. Good luck getting all that to fit into a stitch-up job.'

'This is where you help yourself,' Khan says, closing the noose.

'How?'

'You have accounting records showing Xavier was on the Paxton Federation payroll.'

'Why would I give them to you? Any connection between my company and Xavier would be devastating for our reputation and share price.'

'I think we can say that ship has sailed.'

'Not if you want to protect Julianne's secret from becoming public.'

Khan raises her eyebrows. 'That *secret* will cripple your company. There's a difference between evidence proving your brother went to extreme measures to discredit the Agitators and evidence that he hired a mercenary team to clean up the illegal activity of *your* division.'

Peta taps her thumb and middle finger on her breastbone. The Major turns in his chair and smiles at her. He's enjoying this even more than he expected.

'You're an intelligent woman, Paxton. Read the writing on the wall: one or both of you are going under the bus. You can choose who it's going to be—or I will.'

'*BALL!*'

Ryan, Tommy and their dad yell it simultaneously. This time Jules doesn't flinch. The football spills out of the pack and a player in black and white scoops it up and kicks it clear.

'I don't understand the holding the ball rule,' she says.

Ryan grunts. 'Neither does the umpire.'

They're in the Walsh lounge room watching the Adelaide Crows play Collingwood. Outside the sky is low and grey. Jules and Ryan are on the couch, close but not touching. Tommy's sprawled on the carpet and Jamie is in a battered recliner nursing a cup of tea. They run through what's turning into a pattern of game commentary:

Jamie: 'Pick 'em up.'

Tommy: 'Who's on him?'

Ryan: 'Tackle!'

Ryan and his dad rock back and groan in concert when a Crows defender handballs straight to an opposition player. Jules catches Tommy's eye and she wonders how long it's been since the three of them watched a game together like this.

The train derailment was a week ago. Jules and Angie have been at the farm for three days, since Angie was released from hospital. The quarantine zone hasn't been lifted but the Major secured clearance for them to leave with the Walshes, despite the farm being outside the blockade perimeter.

The current has barely stirred all week. Jules is trying to figure out if she's managing her emotions better or if she's actually in control of the charge—or if they're one and the same thing. The last knots in her chest have been working themselves free since Angie's discharge. Her mum's heart was given the all-clear, even if doctors couldn't explain the blistered skin. That's healing too, now.

The Crows score from a turnover and the Walsh men erupt. Ryan bumps his knee against hers, sharing the moment, and Jules is well aware of how strange it is to be with him in his home, doing something as normal as watching a game of football. He's wearing army-issue cargo shorts and a T-shirt a size too small—it could be his dad's or Tommy's—and he seems to take up even more space than usual.

Jules was awake waiting for him when he came home late last night in an army jeep, dropped off at the gate. She'd wondered if it would be awkward, not having seen or spoken to him all week. They barely knew each other, after all. She'd started second-guessing their moments together, wondering if the way she remembered things had been distorted by adrenaline and stress. And then he unlocked the shed and found her standing inside the door—his bed unmade because she'd been sleeping in it. He'd dropped his swag and caught her in a hug, and when he kissed her it was so tender that she wept. They talked for a while, and then their conversation shifted to one without words...before they talked some more.

Now Ryan is so close on the couch she can barely stand not touching him. He catches her watching him and his mouth softens, knowing. Jules is well aware they're not alone, so when she hears the back door slam she gives him a guilty smile and slips from the room.

Michelle and Angie have been on the verandah drinking tea, continuing to bond over their mutual loathing for Pax Fed.

'What's the score?' Michelle asks Jules, rinsing cups in the sink. Angie leans her crutches against the counter and eases herself onto a stool. Her leg is heavily strapped and she's wearing a moonboot. She pants a little from the effort.

'The Crows are down by three goals. It's half-time.'

'A win would be nice. Be good for the boys.' Jules can't tell if Michelle means in football or life, and suspects she'd take either.

'Oi,' Tommy calls out from the lounge. 'The news is on. There's something coming up about the Paxtons.'

Jules and Angie exchange a look and Michelle turns on the kitchen screen.

> Federal police have today released the name of the man responsible for Saturday night's train derailment near the Spencer Gulf Safe Energy Storage Facility. As speculated, it was Agitators leader James Clay Xavier, who died after driving onto the tracks and colliding with the train, sparking the ongoing emergency blockade of Port Augusta.
>
> To date, ARPANSA has detected minor radiation leakage from one of the twelve radwaste casks attached to the train. Locals, travellers and protesters caught within a fifty-kilometre radius of the crash site continue to undergo radiation testing and potassium iodide treatment as a precaution. Despite reassurances from ARPANSA, a wave of anti-nuclear protests has risen in cities around the nation.

The images that have dominated the news all week since the crash get another showing.

> Sources have now also confirmed that former Agitators leader Angela De Marchi—who we now know was in the vehicle moments before Saturday's near-catastrophic crash—was working with federal police for reasons yet to be made clear. She is not a suspect.

The footage shifts to a shot of Bradford Paxton being driven into an underground car park behind tinted windows. The skin on Jules' arm prickles.

Speculation continues to mount over the role of Paxton Federation in the radwaste train crash and the attack on its own Brisbane headquarters earlier this month, following the alleged link between Bradford Paxton and James Clay Xavier. The board has temporarily stood down Paxton from his position as acting chair, with his sister Peta replacing him in the interim. She has refused to comment on the accusations against her brother and he continues to deny all allegations. Meanwhile, Paxton Federation shares continue to plummet, compounded by the news that the Happy Growers sun farm will require rigorous and ongoing testing for up to a decade to ensure its produce is safe for human consumption...

Jamie appears in the dining-room doorway with Ryan and Tommy behind him. 'No mention of the Priority Ag Practices Bill,' he says to Michelle.

'The Senate doesn't sit for a few more weeks,' Angie says. 'It's not over yet.'

Tyres rumble across the sheep grid at the top of the driveway and the dogs race up the fence. Tommy peers out the window.

'The Major's here.'

They file out onto the verandah and Tommy calls the dogs to heel. The breeze is cool; Jules pulls down her jumper sleeves. It feels like rain. Ryan checks the sky but says nothing: he doesn't want to jinx it.

Waylon climbs out first, his left arm in a sling. Angie elbows her way through the gate and grabs him in an awkward one-armed hug. She drops a crutch and Ryan scoops forward to catch it.

Major Voss nods at Jamie and Michelle but is more interested in watching Angie and Waylon. The Major's wearing army fatigues and combat boots, and looks nothing like Jules' dad, but it brings a familiar ache all the same.

'You look better,' Waylon says to Angie when they break apart. 'Should you be on your feet?'

'I'm not an invalid, Waylon. And you still need a haircut.'

'Geez, you're a hard woman.'

Up until the army cleared him and put him to work, Waylon visited Angie every day in hospital. There was a lengthy conversation about Waylon's mother—Jules left the room to give them privacy—and they've since settled into a new rhythm of mutual nagging. Seeing them fall easily into their patter, Jules realises that motherhood might have been easier for Angie if she'd had a son.

'I saw Khan this morning,' Waylon says. 'Peta Paxton's agreed to keep paying for treatment.'

Understanding passes between them. The consequences for Xavier's sister have weighed on them both. As has Xavier's death: there's no way to know if he was always intending to stay behind the wheel, or if the events in the camp pushed him over the edge.

Tommy steps forward and introduces himself to Waylon, drawing him away from Angie. While they're chatting, the Major takes the crutch from Ryan and hands it back to Jules' mum.

'I thought I would've heard from you before now,' she says, not quite accusing.

'I've had a bit on my plate.'

'Your phone not working?'

His nostrils flare, the tiniest of reactions. 'Get on with it then.'

'With what?'

'The bollocking you've been saving up for me.'

'Is that your idea of an apology, Voss?'

Ryan and Waylon both have one ear on the conversation. Jules is a little riveted herself.

'I make decisions based on tactical need. They're not always popular.'

'Bloody hell, you could be a politician.'

He grimaces. 'Low blow.'

'No, Major, you'd feel a low blow if I gave you one.'

He kneels, trying to hide a smile while he resticks a Velcro strap on Angie's leg brace. 'De Marchi, you're not half as scary as you think you are.'

'Is that right?'

He straightens. They eye each other for a long moment before the Major lifts his hand and brushes his thumb beneath the stitches on Angie's cheek. 'That's going to scar.'

Angie doesn't pull away. She gives a small shrug, eyes not leaving his. 'Doesn't everything?'

Jules watches the exchange. This is definitely the start of something interesting.

'We fly out of Adelaide tomorrow afternoon. There's room for you and Julianne.'

Jules' mouth instantly turns to dust. 'On a Hercules?'

The Major turns around and seems surprised to find everyone still there.

'Walsh tells me you enjoyed the flight down?'

She shoots Ryan a dirty look.

'That it, then, Major?' Jamie stands on the house side of the gate, the rust-coloured kelpie leaning against his leg for a head scratch.

The Major's face settles to its usual stony contour. 'You need to get used to your boy being in danger. He's a soldier, and if he learns to follow an order he has the potential to build a career in the military.'

'A career?' Michelle says. 'You've got him for four more years, Major. Don't get greedy.'

'He might not want to come back.'

Jamie grunts. 'That'll be his choice. Not yours, and not ours.'

Jules feels the ripple in Ryan's energy. His gaze drifts to the paddock and she sees the call of the dirt, the sweat, the heartache. All of the things that make this home: the push and pull of

his parents…jamming with Tommy and Gemma and Macka…
kicking the footy on the road under gum trees.

'He'll be back,' Tommy says, but he doesn't sound confident.
Maybe he sees the conflict in Ryan or the way Ryan and Waylon
stand shoulder to shoulder, stances mirrored.

The Major hands over a fresh supply of potassium iodide—
the official reason for his visit—and Jules watches the jeep
crunch back up the driveway when he and Waylon leave.

When they're clear of the gate, Angie hobbles to the verandah
and drops awkwardly to sit at the table. She nudges a chair with
her good foot in Jamie's direction. 'I want to write about what's
happening here.'

Jamie shakes his head. 'We've copped enough shit from the
district.'

'You think silence is going to change that?' She catches
Tommy's eye. 'Do you have a notebook I could borrow?'

Tommy disappears into the house and Jamie takes the chair,
wary. Jules sits on the concrete with her back against a post,
looking out over the house paddock. It's turning colder and she
should go inside; but it's been a while since she's seen her mum
hungry for a story that's not theirs. Ryan stays in the driveway
with the dogs, his arms resting on the gate to watch from a safe
distance.

'Pax Fed will survive the scandal. You know that, right?'
Michelle says, joining them. 'It'll be business as usual in six
months if the rest of the country doesn't start to understand
what's happening to people like us.'

Jamie digs around in one ear, staring out at the paddock.
He's washed his hair and had a shave and his eyes are less bloodshot after a week off the rum. The tractor's parked up near the
shed, the alien-looking seeder unhooked. 'Nobody cares, Shell.
I'll sound like a selfish prick.'

'No, you'll sound like a farmer who understands the land and
what it takes to be sustainable for a century. *We* know there's no

going back once you contaminate your soil with modified seed. *We* know you can't undo genetic modification once you throw mutant genes into your breeding line. But do people in the city get it when they're sitting in their cafes eating their artisan bread and feeling guilty about global hunger? Do they understand the cost of this mad rush to "fix" the world?'

Her energy thrums and Jules understands how long Michelle Walsh has been waiting for this fight.

Tommy reappears with a spiral notebook, flipping through it before he hands it over. He carefully rips out a handful of used pages. 'I'm a writing a song with Gemma,' he says, unapologetic, and heads back inside.

'Why can't we lobby for export practices that support the global grain supply *and* our own agricultural industry?' Angie says. 'You'd be viable right now if you had access to drought relief and the inland water supply, correct?'

'Probably.'

'That's not a big ask: all it does is give you the same support every other farmer gets around here. It would force the banks to stop letting Pax Fed dictate who gets a loan.'

Jamie scruffs his palm on his stubbled jaw. 'What do you reckon, Ryan?'

Ryan straightens, surprised to be asked. He thinks before he answers. 'I reckon Angie knows what she's talking about. And we've got nothing to lose.'

Jamie rolls his shoulders. Exhales. Finally he pushes back his chair. 'I'm watching the rest of the footy first.' He gets up and goes inside. Angie and Michelle smile at each other, co-conspirators. They head indoors too.

A raindrop lands on Jules' nose, carried on the wind. She leans out from under the cover of the bullnose and another hits her eyebrow, runs into her eye. Thunder rumbles in the distance.

'You coming inside?' Ryan says, entering the yard.

'I want to watch the rain come in.'

He lowers himself beside her, lets his shoulder rest against hers. 'It might only be a few drops. It doesn't always pour when it gets like this.'

Lightning stutters inside the clouds massing over the paddock. The air charges with static, lifting the hairs on her arm. The charge hums. Not frenetic, not threatening. Simply there.

'I think it will today.'

Acknowledgments

Thank you, as always, to the professionals who keep believing in my work and bringing it into the world: my agent Lyn Tranter, and Mandy Brett and the rest of the incredibly supportive team at Text Publishing. Special thanks, Mandy, for your insight, patience and skill at prompting me to come at my story from new directions.

Thank you to Rebecca Cram, Michelle Reid, Vikki Wakefield, Alison Arnold and Tony Minerds. Your feedback was again invaluable and always appreciated.

Thank you to Paul Weston, who explained why and how gas explodes. Any errors occasioned by creative licence in writing about said explosions are mine alone.

Thank you again to all the readers, bloggers, booksellers, teachers and librarians who support Australian fiction—especially Australian young adult fiction. Huge shout out to the #LoveOzYA crowd.

Thank you to the most enthusiastic network of family and friends a writer could ask for—and to my former colleagues at Logan City Council for your friendship and support during one of the most challenging times of my life.

To my husband, Murray: for your unwavering belief in me, and endless capacity to make me laugh when I take myself too seriously—thank you. Again. You are my whole world.

And to you, holding this book (or device). Thank you for reading.

GUARANTEED GREAT READ— OR YOUR MONEY BACK

If you bought Paula Weston's *The Undercurrent* and didn't find it a great read, here's what to do:

Remove the front cover, write your name and address below and send the cover and this page to:

The Text Publishing Company
Swann House, 22 William Street
Melbourne VIC 3000
Australia

Name _____

Address_____

_____ Postcode_____

Daytime phone number _____

Please enclose your bookshop receipt

Please allow up to eight weeks for your refund. Refunds are only payable if this page, the cover and original proof of purchase are provided. Expires 31 December 2017. Applies to Australia and New Zealand only.